The Irontrace Saga: Malformation

T.S. Night

Content Warning:

This novel contains graphic scenes of surgery, medical peril, dystopian peril, and emotionally intense situations that may be triggering. Readers with chronic illness or medical sensitivities may not want to read this book.

READER DISCRETION IS ADVISED.

Author's Note:

While this book draws on a wide range of real-world medical knowledge, it is a work of fiction, set in a dystopian future that does not reflect current medical practices or ethical standards.

The procedures, diagnoses, and medical systems throughout this work are speculative and dramatized for storytelling purposes.

DO NOT interpret any part of this book as medical advice. If you have medical questions or concerns, consult a licensed healthcare provider.

I've done my best to balance realism and imagination. If you're a medical professional reading this, I hope you forgive the liberties I've taken in service of building a whole new world.

– T. S. Night

A love letter for KS.

The boundary means nothing to a story like ours.

Bastion Charter

We, The Bastion, vow to use The Kernel to eliminate human preju-dice. Laws will be interpreted with zero bias. Justice will be adminis-tered without human intervention. Prisons and jails will only exist in history books.

We will care for the citizens of the world by utilizing near-perfect diagnostics in seconds with the new AI healthcare system. Thanks to our tools for disease prediction, life expectancy will be increased. Re-moving human physicians from direct patient care will ensure accu-racy and objectivity.

Human intelligence will boom as AI educators constantly adminis-ter adaptive assessments to students. Children will thrive as their strengths are found in early years. Prodigies will enter a fast-tracked curriculum in their field, supported by The Bastion throughout their career.

Infrastructure will be more reliable than ever as we implement a per-fect distribution of energy and balanced personal carbon usage. The environment will have time to heal under our control.

Natural disasters will be eliminated by AI weather geoengineering models. Atrocities inflicted on the earth by World War III will be replaced by aesthetic recreational areas.

We will blend logic and compassion to heal the world.

0

The day my sister's birthmark kills her, part of me will be lost forever.

No matter how fast I sprint along the cliff of Rising Park, her screams linger in my ears. *Push.* Ignore the burn in my chest. *Faster.*

Lark won't be the only one in pain if I keep running like this.

When she was a baby with hair not much more than golden fuzz, we noticed a black spot about the size of a quarter low on the back of her neck. Her doctors call it an arteriovenous malformation, or AVM. They're wrong. They have to be.

This morning, I woke to the sound of her wails. I dashed in her room to find her curled in bed, sobbing. Her birthmark bulged out like an angry black cloud, dark tendrils creeping across her pale skin. I went into emergency care mode, pulling her hands away so she couldn't claw at it.

Mom ran in with ice packs. Lark threw them off. I put drops of steroids and blood pressure medicine under her tongue. Mom gave an injection of pain medicine into her thigh. Her shrieks of pain wouldn't stop. Defeated, I called Dad and let him know we were on our way to his hospital.

ALICE, her "doctor," met us and took over at the door. As expected, Lark's medical team decided to proceed with yet another medically induced coma.

When they finally let me back in, I took up my usual station in a chair beside her.

"You're not alone. I love you, Lark. Get better. You and Mom worked so hard yesterday on those cookies. Grandma will be proud. I made six colors of the fluffiest buttercream icing last night when I finally got home. It's my best batch ever. I don't think I put too much salt in it this time. Wake up and give it a taste test. You know I'm no good at that."

My voice gave out. That icing will spoil. Again. The cookies will get dry. Again. Might as well throw it away tomorrow.

"You deserve so much better. I'm gonna make these incompetent doctors find a way to save you."

I'm secretly gathering data on how human surgeons used to operate. We live in the most medically advanced healthcare system in history. But that comes with costs. It's all data driven. If the data isn't on your side due to a rare condition, treatment is delayed. In some cases? It's delayed too long. There's a missing key to save her. I'll stop at nothing to find it.

For now, I run.

The beauty of my Lancaster running route contrasts with the chaos I carry. Lush hills roll for miles until they touch the vast Hocking Forest. Even from here the massive white signs around the dark forest stand out: *NO ENTRY WITHOUT PERMIT.* Rumors have flown around for years about rumbles and lights in the forest, but people are too smart to ask questions.

On my right is a rocky cliff with paths to take you down to the white sand beaches of Lancaster Cove. The Bastion made a sea in central Ohio to hide miles of deep craters created by World War III. It's a beautiful, ridiculous replacement for what used to be thousands of acres of corn-fields. I've always been fascinated with how the water starts as a pale blue shimmer then deepens into the most exquisite turquoise. When I was a kid, I'd ask Mom how the water captured part of the sky. I wanted some sky too if I could find a way.

Then a blurry rocket of feathers slams into my right shoulder.

I shriek and try to gather myself into a semblance of a tuck and roll. But I'm not an athlete. I can't do cool moves like that. Instead, I go down hard, face first.

"Grosssss..." I sputter. Not only did I just get a mouthful of dirt, but I think bird talons raked into my shoulder blade, leaving a hot, wet trail of pain. "You've got. To. Be. *Kidding*!"

A quick peek skyward shows a massive hawk lifting into the air. It's still close enough to see color transitions from brown stomach to red leg feathers striped with white. A small metal bar glints in the sun from on top of its skull.

"What in the world is wrong with you? Stupid bird!" I scramble to my feet and dust my clothes off. "Did that really just happen?" I pour some water from my bottle on my face to scrub the dirt off.

Reaching my shoulder wound is difficult. I have to lean to the side and do a little dance to dribble the rest of my water on the cut. It won't kill germs, but it's better than doing nothing. I'll run home and get a shower then do proper wound care. Normally, I'd run this final stretch in a peaceful, even pace, enjoying the sunset. Not today.

I throw myself into a mad sprint, scanning the sky.

Then I see it.

Straight ahead, the hawk is streaking in a downwards arc...directly back at me.

"No! Get away!" I scream. There's nowhere to hide. I duck, but the monster bird's talons scratch my forehead. My hand flies to my hairline to swipe a small trickle of blood. I stay down on my side, holding pressure on the tiny cut and racking my brain.

"Play dead! I'll play dead. Predators can't see you if you don't move, right?" Wait. Is that only what they do in dinosaur movies to hide? I dunno. Either way, I'm not moving.

Be reasonable. It wasn't a prehistoric beast. We have all kinds of birds here in Ohio. Was it a rabid bird, though? I think rabies is a mammal thing. I'll look it up in a med school textbook when I get home. My long, red curls stick like a veil to my sweaty face, but I'm too scared to check if it's safe to get up.

Relief washes over me when I hear a vehicle slow to an idle on the road near the running path. I sit up and nearly scream for joy. I know the driver of the huge green truck.

"Richelle!" I screech. I grab my navy long-sleeved shirt that's tied around my waist and put it on over my running tank top. If she finds out about the hawk thing, I'll never hear the end of it.

"Story Ross? Girl, what are you doing?" my cousin, Richelle, calls out from her truck window.

"I...was running. And needed a break. Too much going on with Lark right now. I'm wiped out. You heading to the city?"

"Yep, want a ride?"

I nod, pretending to fix my hair. There's nothing I can do to help this mess of curls right now, but it gives me a chance to swipe a hand across my forehead and make sure it's not bleeding.

"Yes, thank you! First, tell me why your dad let you free from the farm to head to the city?" I ask.

Richelle will talk for hours about how badly she hates farm life. This will buy me time to process what just happened.

Why would a hawk come for me?

From a few houses down, we catch sight of my dad stepping out of his car in our driveway. The late evening light catches on his salt and pepper hair, and he squints behind his wire-framed glasses.

"Wow, your dad's home for once while the sun is out." Richelle laughs, pulling to the curb.

"It's a miracle. Thanks for the ride, you saved me from running the last couple of miles. Have fun shopping!" I jump out as soon as she parks.

"Bye, Richelle!" Dad yells to her as she drives away, grinning at him.

"Hey, pops!" I hop up the porch steps to our blue two-story house.

"Hello, how was your run?" he asks.

"It was great." I tuck a loose tendril over my scratch. He has enough to worry about. I'll manage this on my own. "How's Lark and Mom?"

"Lark's the same. Your mom's in hospital mode." His eyes narrow. "What happened to your face?"

Shoot. I should've known a man who's been a doctor for thirty years wouldn't miss it. "Um. A Helston's hawk clawed me when I was running.”

“You can’t be serious, honey.” He pulls me into the kitchen to get a paper towel and dabs my hairline. “Tell me exactly what happened.”

I scoff when he sneaks a picture of my face. “It just whacked into me. Maybe it was blind?”

Woosh.

He just sent that picture to someone! What has gotten into him? Why is his face so pale?

“Dad! Seriously?” This is why I’m not showing him my shoulder. He would probably call an ambulance. I reach in the painted white cabinet and pull down the red first aid kit. He tears open a pack of quick heal cream with his teeth then smears it on my head. “Gross! That’s not sterile procedure, Dr. Ross!”

“Glad you’re okay. I’ll be right back.” He sprints up the stairs two at a time.

My finger leaves a dirty print on the water filter button on the fridge. “Yuck! I’ve had enough nature for one day.” I swipe it clean with a disinfectant wipe. I need to get the road dirt and hawk ick off in a blistering shower.

Dad’s panicky whisper floats from under his bedroom door when I walk past their room, “She doesn’t know why. She said it just slammed into her. What does this mean?” *Don’t eavesdrop.* “But one came for Story! You said-” he cuts out.

Talk about an overreaction. I’m sure he’s already writing a case study for The Bastion about the effects of hawk talons on forehead skin.

When I come down from the shower in my pink flowery pajamas, Dad’s on the couch tying his shoes. “I’m going back to the hospital to sit with your mom and Lark. Didn’t think you’d mind.”

“Not at all. Let me know how she’s doing. Later, Dad.”

“Sorry to leave you. Bye, sweetheart.”

I used my allotted visiting hours before my run. The ICU won’t let me visit again until tomorrow. That means I’m on my own for the night. I know just what to do.

Lark is an avid collector of handmade bracelets. She says they're snapshots to a memory. But for me, it's a way to mark the victory of her coming back home to us. They say there's a day she won't. So I try to make every hospital discharge into a celebration. I'll make her something summery. Colors that pop and will make her smile. I lay out the beads and string and open my laptop.

"What shall I learn tonight?"

My downloads folder is cluttered with my treasured videos of human surgeons operating decades ago. I choose one labeled *AVM Removal of the Posterior Neck* and hit play.

I shiver when the video starts. It shows a twisted mass of blood vessels.

This is what it looks like inside Lark's neck.

The glossy tangle shines navy blue, a purple so dark it's almost black, and deep red. If only I lived in a time when I could be like him, using *my* hands to save this patient. Instead, my hands nimbly slide beads on strings and weave threads into colorful patterns. The plan to make Lark one bracelet turns into a stack.

My phone rings. I fumble so fast to hit pause that I throw beads across the floor. Watching videos like this is a *very* stupid idea in 2050.

"Hi!" I say in a bright voice.

"Lark's stable. Don't worry. Turn on LNN," Dad says in a rush.

"Oh, good. Okay." I flip the TV to Lancaster News Network.

A blonde reporter speaks in a hokey broadcaster voice, "Critical software patches have been deployed to fix the AI weather model malfunction. Thirteen regions report acid rain downpours. Heavy metals have leached into the soil and will keep the areas contaminated for months."

The footage shows wilted late spring flowers, murky low-lying fog, and dead aquatic life floating in oily looking bodies of water. I drop the bracelet I'm making.

The reporter continues, eyes twinkling. Her morbid enthusiasm is contagious.

"Residents are being housed in secure facilities until it's safe to return home. Initial reports state that over one thousand adults and children have burns and inhalation injuries. Victims are receiving care in secure pop-up facilities. These are gruesome injuries that may lead to fatalities, folks. The samples show little water, and extremely elevated levels of acid. Can you imagine this burning you and your loved ones as it poured from the sky?"

To say I'm stunned is an understatement. "Dad, how? Nothing has happened like this under The Bastion. Ever."

"I can't imagine. Your mom just came back in. She says hi. Do you want us to stay on the phone?"

"No. Go keep Mom company. Say hello for me."

"Stay inside please. I'm worried about you being alone. The hawk, now this news story…" Dad's voice trails off.

"I'd rather have a hawk smack into me than get acid rain on me. Love you all," I say.

"Personally? I'd rather neither happen to you. Love you, bye," he says, ending our call.

I wish Richelle was here to keep me company. Or I wish I could go stay at her farm. Her six wild brothers and tough as nails parents would make acid rain and hawks seem less scary.

Watching videos of acid rain damage won't help me fix Lark. I turn the TV off and hit play on my video. The surgeon is slowly cutting around the edges of the mass. His work transfixes me. I drop my beads and try to hold my hands just like him. *Imagining* I'm doing surgery like they used to isn't illegal.

Two days later, I sit beside Lark's hospital bed with my feet up, tapping my bright teal running shoes on the wall in front of me. I wish she would squeeze my hand back. Or her bright blue eyes would flutter. Just give me something to let me know she's in there behind the dark circles and deep hollows.

Ugh! I taste blood. We all have our coping mechanisms to get through these hospital stays. Some are healthier than others. Mine is shoving my crippling anxiety down so deep it feels like I've swallowed a boulder and gnawing on my cheek when I plaster on (fake) smiles and use my (also fake) everything-is-okay-and-the-world-isn't-falling-apart voice. Mom crumbles and turns into a snappish, fire-breathing dragony version of herself. Dad goes into Super Doctor mode, staring at Lark's vital sign monitors until his eyes water and refreshing her chart tab every few minutes.

It doesn't matter how I feel. Lark comes before me. Always.

Dad walks in from getting breakfast. His eyes flick to the screens above her bed. "She had another good night," he says. Mom hands him a coffee from the tray she's carrying. "Thanks, Amelia."

"You're welcome," Mom says, giving him a tired smile. She hands me a blueberry bagel before sitting in a squishy green chair by Dad.

"You ready to go into the forest tomorrow, Story?" he asks.

The Hocking Forest is about to lose some of its mystery. Years of academic success earned my spot on a biology expedition for the top students graduating this year from Bastion University Lancaster. I'm going as the ASTRA program's valedictorian.

"Ugh. No. But they sent another reminder letter that I can't get my doctorate if I refuse to go on this trip. I've heard myths for years about the forest. It's probably the most boring place ever." I tear off a chunk of bagel and offer it to Dad.

He rolls his eyes dramatically, taking the bagel. "It better be."

A monitor beside Lark's bed brightens until we see her ALICE's face.

Lark has the usual care team: ALICE (Advanced Learning Interface for Clinical Excellence), artificial intelligence doctors; ASTRA (Advanced Surgical Tool for Robotic Autonomy), AI surgical robots constantly in training from "surgeons" like Dad and me. Instead of operating on people, we create programs for ASTRA to do the work in our place; ORION (Operational Robotic Interface for Optimized Nursing), AI nurses who do most patient care, supplemented by human nurses.

They vary in appearance depending on their function. Some are friendly faces on monitors to deliver results or do consultations. Others for direct patient care are a variety of cabinets on wheels with arms.

ORION assessments units are my personal favorite. Standing six feet tall, they have a monitor with a smiling face attached to a human-type body on six wheels.

"Thank you for your patience, Ross family. She's done well since we began her wake up protocols. She can go home tomorrow."

"Thank you, ALICE. How did her scans compare to her last stay four months ago?" Dad asks, reaching to hold Mom's hand.

"The extended survival and wellness estimation program reports Lark's date of death has now moved to January 23, 2057. Her condition is worsening. That's 159 days less than she had on the last generated report. Again, I offer you my early condolences on your loss."

The monitor goes black. Six and a half years until she loses her battle. I taste blood again. She won't live long enough to get her driver's license. Never get a job. Graduate. Go to college. Fall in love.

Unless someone convinces them she's not a lost cause.

"I'll work to find a way to save her, even if ALICE has given up," I vow, rubbing Mom's back as it shudders with sobs.

Suck it up, Story. Don't cry. Breathe.

"ALICE! Get back here!" Dad yells, but the monitor stays off.

Lark blinks slowly. The bed rail creaks as Mom leans on it to give Lark a hug.

"Hey, kiddo!" Mom greets Lark in a voice like velvet. Her acting is flawless. Her smile is radiant. How does she do that? It's unnerving. I'd have mental whiplash if my emotions cycled that rapidly.

"Welcome back!" Dad says, wrapping Lark in a sweet hug.

Mom nudges my shoulder and whispers, "Remember your surprise for Lark?"

The bracelets! I rush across the room to get them from my purse. "I went a little overboard in the craft room."

Lark's face lights up as I untangle the messy pile.

"More for my collection," she says, admiring her nine new woven and beaded treasures. "Thanks, sis!"

"You're very welcome." I hug her. *Please don't die in six years, baby sis.* We spent the day with Lark in her room, watching TV, coloring pictures, and eating a never-ending stream of snacks.

Before I can go home and pack, she makes me put on one of her rainbow bracelets. She said that way I can "take a piece of her on my trip into the nightmare forest of doom."

1

"You are going to learn so many things that will help you in your medical career. A basic awareness of zoonotic disease is crucial. Learning about survival and how the body reacts to different stresses like dehydration, hunger, hyperthermia, and hypothermia will prepare you for emergency situations."

Dad is in full professor mode. He could go on and on for hours telling me how learning most things in life will help me as a surgeon. He comes alive when he talks about it, so I listen attentively, hiding a smile.

"Wow, I didn't know I signed up for a trip where I'll be hungry, dehydrated, and hypothermic. Any chance we can head back home now?" I ask.

"Oh, no, you're in this for the full experience. I paid extra for that," he says in a serious voice that gives way to laughter as he parks. My parents didn't pay a cent. I earned my spot.

His message notification dings. "Hang on, your mom sent me a news link she said we should read." He taps his phone a couple of times, and his mouth drops open. "Unbelievable. Listen."

The first sentence takes my breath.

"BREAKING NEWS: Epidemic in New York City!

Hospitals overloaded, patients turned away. Citywide looting outbreak. Bodies stashed on morgue barges in the harbor.

Hospitalized patients: 1,940

Deceased patients: 424

Multiple infected patients rode the subway late last week, spreading the ChAse-417 Virus throughout the city. Entry and exit are not permitted due to a full lockdown. State officials will be holding update meetings daily at noon. AJA has identified anyone involved in looting or those dis-obeying lockdown. If you have made any attempts to engage in criminal activity, the police will be coming to visit you."

We swipe through the photos. It looks like scenes from before the war. People stand or lay in lines outside of hospitals. Roads are closed, guarded by armed police. Subway tunnels have large barriers erected so no one can enter. Ports are closed. Businesses have broken windows and arson damage. Massive barges in the bay are full of stacked, white shipping containers being used as floating morgues.

My voice shakes. "The ChAse Virus is back? That was one of the first viruses eradicated by The Bastion. How is it killing people so fast?"

"No. No more news for the day. You're safe from the virus here. New York is hundreds of miles away." He locks his phone and tucks it in his door pocket.

"Two awful things in just a few days. First the acid rain, now this. I already didn't want to go on this ridiculous trip. Did the ALICE doctors miss it and cause this?"

His face goes white. "Story! Don't blame the AI systems. I taught you better than that!" he whisper hisses.

"But still, *come on, Dad,* how could this happen?"

He turns suddenly. "Stop it! Listen. This is important." He pauses until I meet his eyes. "Pay attention to your surroundings. Watch out for anything unusual."

What a strange little rant. I laugh from the awkward tension. He keeps staring. His mouth snaps in a tight line. He's not moving on until I agree.

"I will, Dad. They said we can't bring our phones. Call me on the teacher's satellite phone if you need me. Love you!"

"Will do. Love you. Get going, forest explorer."

The group is waiting for me to take pictures for the university newsletter.

"Story Ross! You actually came to a school event." Seth grins, clapping slowly.

He's the top WARN meteorology program graduate. He'll work to train weather AI models. We've been in a friendly competition over grades for years in any shared classes. Admittedly, I may qualify academically for all the clubs, trips, and competitions that come with being a top student, but I've skipped most of them. Afterschool activities are always an immediate no from me. He won't let me forget it.

"Someone has to come make sure you don't eat the specimens! Did you see the news about the virus?" I ask the group, hoisting my banana yellow backpack into the van.

"That's quite the color choice! Won't lose you," Isla says, not trying to hide her distaste. She's a brilliant young star in the field of anthropology.

"Yeah, my parents were freaking out about the news. Old people, am I right?" Seth grumbles.

"Ooof," is all I can manage as a response.

I frown and turn away. An extinct virus coming back is not something to brush off. This is exactly why I don't try to talk to my peers anymore. I find them generally disappointing. For being a book smart guy, he's missing the point. The ChAse virus was a biological weapon released in the earliest attacks of World War III. People are still dealing with the fallout of alterations it made to their DNA.

If it's back? There has to be a reason.

On the drive out of Lancaster, I ride silently. The chatter of my classmates is nothing but background noise. Sunshine coming through the window of the transportation van is hot on my left arm and the side of my face. It's too early in the day to be this hot. The trees should shade us from the sun so we don't swelter on our hike. I hope.

We stop outside a gate that must reach at least thirty feet high, guarding the entrance to the forest. Several armed men in green uniforms walk towards our van from a brick warden station. The ChAse virus news already had me tasting bile. Seeing their huge guns and stoic faces? I'm considering how to commandeer the van and speed back to Lancaster.

Professor Milner, a middle-aged man with a pleasant face from the biology department, stands and says, "Congrats again for qualifying to go on this trip, you have worked extremely hard. You're no longer students; you're now peers in the science community. Welcome!" He claps enthusiastically.

Okay. So this trip is a *bit* exciting.

"I'll go show them our permit. Get out and stretch your legs." He grins and hops out of the van.

We've had multiple meetings about the route we are taking. As I stand and look at the wall of trees, I see why. At Lancaster Cove, I can see the horizon. Here, at the juncture of the parking lot and the forest, the sky is blocked by a dark wall of trees.

This looks like a place you'd go to get murdered.

Callie, an assistant staff member from the university, has come too. "Let's take a peek."

She leads us to a large metal sign listing species of plants and animals that can be found in the forest. Callie can barely contain her excitement about the mammals, birds, reptiles, and amphibians. Then she launches into the fauna portion of the sign, bouncing to point at the pictures of giant tulip trees, elegant hemlocks, white oaks, red maples, and beech trees.

I desperately try to bring my attention back to Callie, but my eyes drift to the towering gate we'll pass through. It has such a familiar pattern. My mind traces the panels to figure out where I have seen it.

The Bastion! Sunlight filters through the leaves onto the top panels to reveal a subtle shimmer—the logo of The Bastion. I would recognize this unsettling image anywhere. It has a globe with robotic, not quite human hands reaching out from a computer screen. I never can tell if the hands are reaching out to help us or trying to pull us in.

A loud alarm squawks through the forest, followed by a metallic clank. The gate swings open and Professor Milner motions for us to follow him through.

"Thanks for your patience," he says. "Take a minute to soak this in. The wardens at the gate informed me that since we're in a reforestation zone, the government only allows forty people per year to enter. Yes, this trip is exciting. However, we must all feel a sense of gravity to be entrusted with this responsibility. Get out your checklists, and let's proceed."

This isn't my first time seeing a forest. But I've never been in one like this. As soon as we enter, the temperature drops several degrees. Thin beams of light peer through the swaying canopy. Birdsong drifts around us. The humid air is heavy with the scent of greenery. A soft, constant breeze blows my thick red curls away from my face and dances on my skin. The forest is cradling me, pulling me in.

A prickly feeling washes over me. I'm being watched, I know it. I look intently into the trees around us, but I don't see anything. What am I even looking for?

Shake it off, Story!

Callie jumps back to teaching us about the small flowers dotting the shaded forest floor around us. When there are breaks from Callie pointing out flowers for our checklists, Seth, Isla, and I chat.

"Have any of us camped before...ever?" Isla asks. Both of her parents work with finance models in Columbus. She has been cocooned in condominiums and high rises for most of her life.

"I have never camped, but I've spent a lot of time at my cousin's farm," I say, swatting at a swarm of gnats for the twentieth time in five minutes.

"Oh, I've roughed it for sure. We have a cabin by the lake about ten miles north of the city. It only has *two* bedrooms and *two* bathrooms," Seth says with a laugh. "I guess that's two more bedrooms and bathrooms than we'll have out here!"

A hawk swoops between us. I scream, throwing my hands on my head.

Seth laughs until he almost falls over.

"It's just a bird," Isla chokes out between laughs.

"It...it really surprised me. That's all." I can't bring myself to tell them that a hawk hit me the other day. If it wasn't for the seven inches of possibly infected talon injuries on my back I've been tending to, I wouldn't believe it myself.

"Incredible! A Helston's hawk!" Professor Milner is fairly bursting with excitement. "Here it comes again, look!"

It glides over us, surveying our group. There's something weird on its head too. This bird can't be wearing the same tiny metal hat as the one that hit me in Rising Park. Right? The chances of that are too much to figure out right now. And I'm a math nerd.

"Hey, what's on its head?" I ask.

"Maybe one of its feathers was sticking up?" Professor Milner suggests. His enthusiasm grows as the hawk does a few more passes over us. Then it bursts out of view through the canopy.

Feathers don't turn into metal just because they're out of place.

We continue our hike up and down hills until my thighs and calves burn. Callie has us mark what we see on our checklists. So far, I've got wild violets, trilliums in shades of pink, wild geraniums, and eleven trees.

About seven miles in, we reach the small clearing where we're setting up camp. The "cleared" ground is covered with flowers, sticks, and wild roses.

I pull out my checklist and mark off *rosa carolina*.

This is going to be fun to sleep on. I thought they'd have prepared a mini campground or campsite of some sort. Instead, we're getting an authentic camping in the wild experience.

I slide my bag off my shoulders, thankful for my bright color choices. Isla can scoff at them all she wants, but I'll be able to see (and panic) about any bugs that crawl onto my light backpack. I unzip it and pull out my book to reach my tent. Most people wouldn't have wanted the small amount of extra weight from a book, but to me, books are my escape. I had to bring a favorite.

"We're setting up camp right next to each other, right?" Isla asks, gathering sticks.

"Yeah, for sure," I say, helping her pick them up.

The rest of our day was peaceful. We lit campfires, put down tarps, assembled tents, made dinner, reviewed checklists, and went over the plan for tomorrow.

After sunset, everyone lazes sleepily in fold-up chairs around a camp-fire. Small patches of starry sky peek through the treetops.

"I'm going to get ready for bed. Night!" I announce to the group.

Everyone says good night. No one follows. Cool, cool, cool. I'll just journey through the inky black forest by myself to the tents. I'm on high alert for the walk, but I make it to the tent without being chased by a murderer.

Safe! I bend to unzip my tent. A branch cracks directly behind me. A horse makes a huffing sound. I freeze.

"H...hi?" I call to the darkness. "Horse? Ax murderer? You there?"

You idiot! A horse can't answer. I stare into the darkness, waiting for my eyes to adjust. I gasp when I see the faint silhouette of a rider on a horse between trees. *I need a flashlight!*

I snatch one from my tent.

"Who is there?" Of course I can't get the flashlight on. Did I even put batteries in this?

"Come on, come on!" I fumble with the power button until it turns on and aim the beam of light where I had seen the horse and rider. The moonlight filtering through the trees must be playing tricks on me. "Nothing's there. I need to go to bed."

I dive into my tent.

"Okay, I *will* make it through a few nights of this. Then I'll be a real doctor and I can help Lark. I got this. I can do this." I sit on my camping mat, wiping my sweaty palms on my pajama shorts. There's no way I'm leaving my tent until sunrise. But ugh, it's humid in here.

My book will help calm me. After several minutes of reading, a hand trails along my tent. Should I scream? Sit quietly? Before I make up my mind, the hand pulls on the zipper, opening it in small sections. I cower behind my book. Real useful, Story.

Isla sticks her head in then frowns. "Oops, wrong tent. Bye!"

Did she do that just to scare me? This forest is too much. I collapse backwards on my mat as she zips my tent door shut. She almost gave me a panic attack for nothing.

Every noise puts me back on high alert. I curl on my side and open my book. The bookmarked chapter is about a family's world falling apart.

Everything changes. They can't go back.

2

Waking up in a tent feels like the continuation of a dream. Light filters through in shadowy patterns. An intricate weave of tiny noises creates a living background hum. A breeze ripples the tent fabric, making a soft flutter.

I scramble into a sitting position then crawl out.

"Ow, oh." Taking my first few steps makes me realize my sleeping mat does not have enough padding to keep me from being skewered in my sleep from sticks under the tent.

"Morning, Callie! Did my parents call or text?" I ask.

"Your dad sent you a message. Lark's doing well. She wants you to bring her back a few pressed flowers," she replies, continuing to stoke her fire.

"Will do, thanks!" The opening and closing pages of my book will be the perfect spot to keep her flowers safe. I fish it out of my tent and throw it into my small day pack.

We gather around the fire for a camp style breakfast until Professor Milner breaks it up with an announcement. "Today is our northwards expedition toward sector N21. Grab your checklists and let's go!"

He's treating these checklists like a life or death matter. He has to prepare a presentation to show what we found to the wardens and university.

Navigating up the root-laced, mossy terrain of the small forest hills makes our trek feel as risky as mountain climbing. Instead of focusing on finding checklist plants, my gaze drifts to the thick tree canopy for hawks.

After three miles we hit a carpeted patch of wildflowers. Honestly, this place isn't so bad. The cheery flowers, the green nature-y trees, the calming aesthetic of the brown and gray rocks. It all blends like a vision board goal of where to escape city life.

"Perfect spot for a rest break!" Professor Milner calls out. "Halt. Drink water, have a snack if you need, then work on your checklists."

I wander south, sipping my water. Clumps of large blue, leafy plants catch my eye. I can make it over the hills to them and back in twenty minutes. That's plenty of time to fumble through my identification charts.

"Hey, Callie," I say to her while she sits and drinks. "I'm going to run down past that small gorge and look at those blue flowers? I don't see them anywhere else."

"Don't be long. Good initiative!"

"Be right back." I take off in a fast run. Maintaining this pace without falling in a mature forest is immediately harder than I thought. I guess I'll take this at a light jog.

The downhill slope forces me to slow to a walk. I'm not going to make it back in twenty minutes. Oh well. It's not like they're gonna leave me.

"Oh...shootshootshoot!" I catch myself on roots when moss sheared off the rocks and nearly sent me tumbling down the hill. That would have made my errand faster, but at the cost of rolling an ankle or snapping my neck.

Finally, I make it to the small ravine with a few inches of water moving through it. Almost there. Just follow the water for a bit and the stump should be right above me. I trace my fingers along a ten-foot-high rock wall on my right.

Tiny fossils have left delicate imprints in the rock. Ferns grow from paper thin cracks. Water seeps through, staining the ravine wall a rainbow of orange, red, and purple. The sandstone has eroded and my boots squish through wet sand instead of mud. It feels like I'm walking on a tan cloud in a fairytale forest.

"Success!" I take my final steps up out of the ravine. Clumps of flowers are growing around a massive stump. The blue plant leaves are huge and covered with purple flowers as small as my pinky nail. Lark will love these!

I pick a few, take my book out from my daypack and smooth them out, pressing them between the back cover and the last page. The stump they grow around is at least as high as my waist. I climb up on it and sit to fan through my identification guide. What are these? I haven't seen them anywhere else. They're not on our checklists.

Did I stumble across some new plant species? If I did, Lark gets to name it.

Branches snap like small cracks of thunder on my left. I whip at the leaves shaking on the bushes. *There's no wind.* This is something different, intentional. I freeze, thinking of the entry sign at the gate that pictured the animals in the forest. Is it a coyote? A wolf? Black bear?

Yell at it! Get big, sound scary. I take a deep breath and open my mouth to let out a ferocious *I will tear you up* predatory roar, but...

I can't even squeak.

My legs are still working. They're ready to sprint me back to Lancaster. I'll use my stump as a mini lookout tower to see what I need to run away from. More branches snap. The creature is moving away from me. What is it? Get taller! I stand on my tiptoes.

"Story! Come here! Follow me. Now!"

My heart nearly stops. Not a whisper. That was a yell. I think I know that voice. Adrenaline has my heart thumping so loud I can't quite place the man's voice. It's so...familiar? But not Mr. M. or any of the boys.

I stay frozen. "Story! You're in danger! Run, now!" The voice is farther away but crying out in a way that screams *"run, girl, you're about to die."*

There they are! A person's back is retreating into the dense trees, fast. The graying hair peeking out from under the black hat and the way their shoulders are set stirs recognition. They sneak a quick look behind them. I'm dumbstruck.

It's my dad! *Catch him. Run.*

"Dad! What are you doing?" He's close enough to hear me, I know it. I half-fall, half-climb down from the stump and tear after him.

"Dad!" I yell. He keeps going.

The trees thin out. He picks up his pace. I do too. I'm running so fast I slip off sharp rocks and fall into a goopy mud pit. *Great!* I pull my muddy self up and keep running. Something is off with my left knee. Each stride sends searing pain through it.

Is he spying on my trip? Does he have a permit to be here? He doesn't stop. The more I yell, the faster he runs. The trees get thicker, connected with thorny vines.

"Dad!"

I've lost sight of him. My face, arms, and legs are scratched. Blood drips from my knee to my brown hiking boot. A long scrape has taken most of the skin off my shin.

He saw me. He heard me. He left me.

Why?

When I was about Lark's age, Mom and I were swimming out in the water of Lancaster Cove. Dad was on the beach napping. Something like a rip current sucked Mom and I out. To this day, I still remember being shocked by how fast and relentlessly the roaring waves came.

With our breath being taken away, we could only choke out occasional calls of help. When Dad heard us, he rushed straight into the deadly current. He helped us swim parallel to the shore until we could make our way out of the waves safely.

Dad is a man who has lived his life showing how much he loves us. If we need him, he'll be there, even if it means rushing into danger. It doesn't make sense that he would lure me out here and leave me.

Gah! Should've paid attention. What direction did I run? It's humid, but I can't stop shivering. To my right and in front of me, the trees and vines twine closer together until there's no room to go in either direction. I need to go back out the way I came.

The bracelet Lark loaned me has several tiny twigs hanging from it. I pull them off and toss them down. *Lark.* Get home. Learn how to fix Lark.

I can't leave without trying one more time. I cup my hands around my mouth and yell, "Dad! I'm hurt! Over here!"

What parent could resist that?

Apparently my dad can. The only response is the ebbs and flows of forest sounds. I stand, testing to see how my knee feels. What if I'm asleep and this is all a dream? That would explain it. I pinch my arm, but instead of waking, I scream.

A black flash crashed into the thicket, resting at my feet.

Another hawk!

"How many birds are in this miserable forest?" I shout into the green void of the thicket.

The Helston's hawk tilts its head at me. There is nothing metallic or out of place on this bird.

"What do you want, bird?" It hops close to my foot and makes soft sounds before flying to low branches.

Walking out of here is going to be rough. Sharp twinges of pain hit when I do some test bends of my hugely swollen knee. I can't stay here. There are sturdy maple branches around the trunk of a huge tree about fifteen feet away. I can make it to them. I'll make one of them into a walking—well, limping—stick. Up and at em, I guess.

"I wish I had my daypack," I mutter. It's got my first aid kit, book, and Lark's flowers in it. I could really use a drink, but my water is clipped to it. "This is fine, I'll just limp twelve miles to the ranger's station. If nothing eats me on my way."

I lean against a tree. Nothing looks familiar. I can't see the hill where I left my group, or the stump with the blue flowers. I'm totally lost.

The hawk sits on a branch about five feet away from me. We stare at each other until a sharp whistle pierces the air. The hawk darts off into the sky, as if an unseen master had called it.

That bird was oddly comforting. Might as well go the direction it flew. I've never realized it before, but man, listening is *work*. My life depends on my ability to pick out sounds from Dad or my class. I keep hearing faint notes of whistling, but it's probably another bird.

I stop every few feet to strain my ears.

Whistling.

It's getting louder. It's a cheerful tune, unmistakably human. Something moves in the brush, rustling closer to me with the melody. I hunker beneath low pine branches and try not to make any noise.

This forest does have horses!

A massive black draft horse moves gracefully through the forest landscape. Each step is executed smoothly, like it has lived here for its whole life. On its back sits a rider, dressed in black head-to-toe, happily whistling, moving their free hand like they're conducting an orchestra. The saddle horn is much larger than those at Richelle's. It has a hawk perched on it.

I hide behind the branches the best I can, but the hawk flies straight towards me. It lands a few feet above me and lets out a quiet trill. The horse looks at the bird, and the rider moves the reins to guide it in my direction. *No, scary forest man, shoo!*

"Whoa," the rider says, pulling the horse to a stop. He slips off the horse with practiced ease, stops to pat its neck, then walks towards me.

He pauses and holds out a tan, thickly muscled arm. His lips purse to make several kissy sounds. *What is he doing?*

Oh. He was calling his hawk. It lands on his wide leather cuff. He feeds it a treat, and it dips in a happy bird dance. The two of them have a quiet conversation as he walks to the horse. He smooths the hawk's feathers then feeds it another treat. It hops from his arm to the saddle perch.

He adjusts his stirrups and checks his girth. I think he's leaving.

Follow him!

Maybe he can help. Maybe he's a murderer. Maybe he's one of the forest wardens and he'll arrest me.

The Bastion utilizes algorithms to predict people who are most likely to commit crimes. Future criminals are removed from society. We don't have prisons. I've never put much thought into where people end up after they're taken by AJA. If murderers are still a thing in 2050, they'd be locked in by gates and guards.

Here's what I know about mystery man. He has a horse. I like horses. Also, the bird is his friend. Scary men probably don't coax hawks to ride on their arms with cutesy little kissing noises, right? Hopefully, he's not a murderer. But those arms of his could totally snap me in half if he wanted.

Before I've made my mind up about asking for help, he makes a bee-line for my hiding spot. When he crouches eye level with me, I take in his black hair, olive skin, and almost onyx eyes, brimming with mischief. The man in all black lurking in the forest is a broad-shouldered giant, a few years older than me.

He parts the branches and gives me a huge grin. "As far as hiding spots go, this is truly abysmal. Who taught you to play hide and seek?"

I don't answer.

He extends a hand to help me up.

No thanks, dude.

I put a hand on the tree and slowly stand. A wave of pain tears through my knee that almost drops me. I will myself to stay composed even though I'd rather scream and punch the tree.

I tip my head down fast to see if the bone is sticking out. My bloody, muddy leg is plastered with pine needles. I wince. Blood doesn't bother me. But I'm a doctor. I don't like seeing injuries caked in dirt with no way to clean them.

"Ouch, how did this happen?" He drops to one knee to examine my leg. My mouth stays frozen shut.

"Are you hurt badly?" he asks, frowning at my knee's sticky mess of leaves, pine needles, and blood. Like a rider checks their horse for injuries, he grips my leg, feeling the area above and below my knee. He pauses and pulls off the large leaves stuck to me and then *BLOWS* on my open wound to knock smaller bits off.

Who is this man?! But at least now I can see there's no chunks of bone jutting out. So, thanks?

"It's not the worst I've seen, but it needs cleaned. I'll take you to the station and get you fixed up. Come on, let's go for a ride." He smiles and holds out his arm to guide me to the horse.

I look from his arm to him and then limp my way over to the horse without accepting help. Panic strikes. I don't want to ride a horse with a stranger.

"Do you need help climbing up?" He moves close and offers a stirrup.

Please don't touch me! I stay silent.

He smirks. "Are you physically able to respond to my questions?"

I'm tempted not to. But this guy may be my ticket out of here. "Are you sure he can hold two people?" I ask.

"He sure can. But for this one, how about you ride? I'll walk." He bows the tiniest bit and tries to hold back a smile. "By the way, I'm Ivan." He raises his eyebrows, prompting my name.

"Story. Nice to meet you." No idea what proper etiquette is in a forest, so I do a stiff, sad bow back at him. Why did his bow look so cool?

"Nice to meet you, Story." He presses his lips together firmly, but the corners are trying to sneak into a smile. "Here, I'll make a step with my hands. Use your good leg to jump in the saddle. This is Obsidian. He's *mostly* reliable. He's only fallen on me five or six times."

I blink at him.

"I'm joking! He's as sure-footed and reliable as could be. We've never fallen." He laughs. "You've ridden a horse before, right?"

I nod.

"Come on, then, Silent Story."

How am I going to jump in the saddle? I can't even walk.

Hands the size of baseball mitts grip my hips and settle me into the saddle so fast I don't even have the chance to protest.

"Sorry. I'd hate for you to have to ask me for help. That would involve talking to me." He winks and pulls Obsidian to a walk, keeping the reins in his hand like a lead rope.

It's difficult to balance with no reins and a bad knee. And a hawk between my thighs staring up at me like a friendly feathered dog that

I'm too scared to pet. This bird is at least the size of a toddler. I put my hands under my legs, giving it a wide berth.

Also, if I hide my hands, Ivan won't see them shaking.

"That's Helga, don't worry about her. She makes life in the forest much more fun. And she does some important jobs."

"Like finding people that are avoiding you?"

He snorts. "Yeah, that's one of her many talents. Nothing missed by those sharp eyes. So. Tell me. Whatcha doin' here in the forest?"

If he wants me to talk, I'll talk.

"I'm on a camping trip with my university. We were on our way to sector N21 but then I went to look at some flowers across a little ravine. I thought I saw my dad in the forest, which doesn't make sense. I chased him. Then got lost. Helga found me." I pause to glare at him. "You *better* not kidnap me. Someone will notice. I'm not scared of you. I'll fight you."

A loud, rich wave of laughs from him surprises me. "That's not what this is. You're a full-grown woman. I'd call that abduction, or maybe unlawful imprisonment. I was wondering how you got in here without getting shot." He looks around. "You made it deeper than anyone else has in here."

What sort of new world is in this forest where being shot is a possibility? That's not a normal reaction to finding someone out on a walk. If it was, I'd have been killed years ago while on one of my daily runs.

"Do people normally get shot in here?" Lark has always told me that animals are great judges of character and if they think someone is a good person, believe the animals. I am really hoping she's right on this one. He seems relaxed and normal.

"People? Not on a regular basis. Did you say you saw your dad?"

"My bag!" My lost daypack and water bottle are a few feet apart on the ground. *This is the stump!* With the flowers. "Yes. This must be where I saw him and then got lost."

He leads Obsidian over to the bag and hands me my things.

"Do you know why your dad would be in here?" he asks.

Oh no, this man must be some sort of forest law enforcement. What if he works for AJA, The Kernel's Automated Justice Administrator? Did I get Dad in trouble?

"I only think I saw him. Must not have been him though. He wouldn't have left me. My dad is the best...and super law-abiding."

He turns thoughtful. It's a few minutes before he speaks again. "I need to show you something. Please don't freak out," he says.

I *think* we're back where I left Callie. But this can't be where I was just a few hours ago...

"Ivan, what happened?"

He rubs the back of his neck, then says, "There was a sudden storm. From what I can tell, everyone from your trip is gone."

3

A storm? No. We don't have storms anymore. The Bastion schedules our weather events, and they only happen through the AI weather models. No catastrophic weather events have happened in this country for my whole life.

Powerlessness hits like a wave. I can't jump off Obsidian. "Stop. Please. Let me down."

"Do you promise not to run away?" he asks, pulling to the side to slow Obsidian. "I can help you, but you have to absolutely trust me."

Absolutely trust him? I don't "absolutely trust" most people I know. I trust Richelle, though she has a history of pranking me. Normally I'd say I absolutely trust my family, but safe to say Dad is dropping off that list after today. I can't deal with that right now.

"I won't run."

He hesitantly helps me down.

I've only seen videos and pictures of storm damage. But this would have been a severe storm. It was serene here this morning. Now the forest looks like a deluge has come through. Branches are cracked and thrown; trees are displaced. Random possessions are strewn around.

"Isla! Seth!" I scream their names as loud as I can, letting them settle in the air.

"Stop! Stop that!" Ivan steps towards me with his hands out in a calming, non-threatening, way. "Please stop screaming. I'll help you look for them on the way to the station, but you can't scream anymore."

"How long is it to the station?"

"Another hour if we keep at this pace. The wardens are already looking for you. They might find us on the way," he says, looking around.

"Okay, I need a minute, please." I can't fix what happened here with a storm, but I can do something for my leg.

Years of training take over. I open a few packs of sterile gauze squares and leave them on their wrappers on the rock beside me. Picking one up, I pour some water from my bottle on it, then let the rest of the water trickle down my cut. I press the damp gauze to my wound, cleaning from the center outward. The routine comforts me. I grab some medicated swabs and clean it again before putting a bandage on it. Several times, I glance up.

He's watching me closely. "Looks like it's not the first time you've done that."

"My dad is a surgeon. He's made me fix up every cut and scrape since I was a toddler the *right way*. I've dreamed of doing his job my whole life. I worked my butt off, graduated early, and wrapped up my degree a couple of weeks ago. This trip is a big deal, a reward for our academic careers, they said. If I can get out of this stupid forest, next week I'll be looking for my first job with ASTRA."

Stop talking, Story.

"Impressive. It's a real shame The Bastion is too stupid to see their AI models are garbage without people like you."

I've never heard a person say something like that. There are hushed rumors that people who speak against The Kernel or Bastion have terrible things happen to them, but I've never seen anything proven. The Bastion has done so much for people, society, even the entire world that I can't feel any resentment towards it.

"What do you-" I start to ask him what he means when Helga screams. Ivan's eyes go wide.

Another Helston's hawk slices through the forest.

"Helga! Take it down!" Ivan yells, wrapping me in some kind of bear hug.

He throws me to the ground, shielding me beside the rock pile. My heart pounds as I struggle against his chest to get free, but he won't let me out from under him.

This maddening wall of a man is going to crush me. "Get off! Get up!" I grunt.

Helga takes off like a rocket from Obsidian's saddle in pursuit. Just as fast as he threw me down, Ivan springs back up into a standing position, pulling me with him.

"Sorry about that. Those things are dangerous," he huffs, pushing my hair back from my face and smoothing it down.

"What is wrong with you?" I slap his hand away. He raises his hands and gives an innocent smile. I glare at him, but the earnest look in his eyes disarms me.

"Sid, come!" he orders. Obsidian trots over. "We can't stay here anymore, it's not safe. Please, come with me, we need to go. I'll explain everything. Get up in the saddle then scoot back behind it."

I don't want to be alone in the forest. He's clearly not staying. I'm barely able to hold back a scream from my knee's twisting motion to get in the saddle. He jumps up in the saddle, and my breath catches at our sudden closeness. When I wrap my arms around his waist, he locks them in place with his free hand.

"Go!" He urges Obsidian to a fast lope.

After several minutes, we slow to a trot, stopping by Helga. She's perched on a rock, beaming with pride at her kill.

If Ivan didn't have a death grip on me I might have fallen off Obsidian. The Helston's hawk she ripped open is not actually a bird. It has feathers and correct markings. Yet instead of its shredded chest spilling blood and organs, it's strewn with broken mechanical components.

I wiggle my arms free and slide backwards off Obsidian. I grab the dangling drone hawk's head and flip it up. Sure enough, it has the odd metallic piece.

"I've seen this hawk. It's been following us. I know this sounds crazy, but one of these hit me in the head the other day when I was out for a run."

His jaw clenches. "The storm that hit your friends was not an accident. Let's go."

We get back on Obsidian, and he spurs him on. Helga wheels in wide arcs, seeming to survey the area.

A small green building appears from seemingly nowhere in the forest. Ivan pulls Obsidian to a stop about forty feet away from it. He dismounts, then helps me down.

"Is your knee okay?" He doesn't look at me as he speaks, instead his eyes busily search the trees. The joking Ivan is gone.

"Yes, thanks." *No. It's miserable.*

Helga flutters down from the canopy onto her saddle horn perch. Ivan reaches out to smooth her feathers then in a fluid motion he pulls me close with the crook of his arm.

"Story, listen. Please. Please believe I'm going to help you. Do not tell anyone in this station about your dad. No matter what happens. You didn't see him."

He leans in closer and pulls a leaf from my hair. "Please, Story. Don't tell them," he whispers.

What is happening? Why are his eyes so clouded with worry?

"I won't," I say. He gives me a clipped nod and skims his hand down my arm for me to follow.

We walk to the entrance of the small building, and a man opens the door before Ivan can knock.

"Warden, I've got a trespasser," Ivan says in a serious tone.

I nearly choke. That's news to me.

The man's badge says Warden Donegal. He looks me up and down, eyes narrowing as he takes in my knee bandages, scratched face, arms, and hands. No doubt he thinks I look the part of a trespasser lost in the forest. He jerks his chin, signaling for us to enter.

Ivan holds my elbow and leads me through a series of closed doors which open as we approach.

"So far, so good," Ivan whispers. "Give short answers. I'll be watching."

A door on our right swings open. He squeezes my arm reassuringly as we enter a small room with walls painted black. He guides me into a chair in front of four large monitors and gives me a tight smile. Without a word or another look, he leaves me alone in the interrogation room.

In school, we were shown videos about The Bastion's AJA models. You are evaluated while being interviewed, and they flag any responses that deviate from your baseline.

The monitors flick on. I'm on three of them, being filmed from different angles. The fourth monitor has a Bastion logo bouncing corner to corner.

Hidden speakers broadcast a voice that's an unnatural mix of human and robot. "Please wait for your interrogation to begin. Thank you for your patience."

As if I have a choice. Any fear I had of Ivan initially was nothing compared to this. He was kind to his animals. Kind to me. I need to make it through this, then I can go home.

The fourth monitor flickers on, and a shadowy AJA figure looks at me. "Hello. I am here to talk to you today about your trip to the forest. Please state your name."

"Story Ross," I say. Stay calm. It's just a computer.

"Please tell me what you had for breakfast," the officer says.

That one throws me for a loop. "Um, a protein bar and berries."

"What day of the week is it?"

"Tuesday."

"Why are you here today?"

"A biology trip to the forest with a group from Bastion University Lancaster. I got separated from them and brought here by Ivan."

"Who is Ivan?"

"Not sure. He found me in the woods when I...fell." Ivan cautioned me not to say anything about my dad. I wince and point to my bulky knee bandage.

The AJA's voice stays even. "Can you walk me through everything you did today?"

"Woke up with my classmates and teachers. Made breakfast and packed our daypacks to hike to N21. On our way to N21 we stopped for a break. I saw some flowers on a distant hill and went to look at them for my reforestation checklist. And I picked some for my sister. She loves flowers and wants me to bring some home to her. Is that illegal? Is that why I'm here? But then I got lost. I panicked and ran to find my hiking group. Then Ivan found me and brought me here."

Uh oh. Long answer.

"How exactly did you get separated from the others on your trip?"

"I heard a noise in the bushes. I thought it was an animal and ran away."

"Your class is back in Lancaster. Why aren't you?"

That's a relief. "Because you're holding me here. Can I go now please?"

"A witness in the woods reported you were yelling for your dad."

Ivan didn't want me screaming for my lost classmates. Who is in there listening?

"I was confused." New tactic. If this is a confrontational computer, I'll play scared young girl and maybe it'll back off. "I had no idea what to do. City girl here. I've never been in a forest like this. I would really like to go home to my family now please."

The tears that spring to my eyes are real. I'm homesick, exhausted, thirsty, and I want to see my family.

"Soon. You said you were on your way to N21. Why?"

"We have a list of sectors we'll travel to each day. The forest permit from the wardens told us where to go. We document the flora and fauna we see on the way."

"What kinds of plants have you seen so far for this list?"

I name off the list of things Callie had pointed out to us. Her wonder at each flower type we found made them easy to remember.

"What types of animals have you seen in the forest?"

"My teacher has spotted a couple of Helston's hawks."

I know I messed that up. My voice sounded off. It wasn't a hawk. It was a drone. That's their eyewitness in the forest.

"What were the hawks doing when you saw them?"

"Flying around like hawks do? We don't have them on our checklist. I wasn't paying much attention."

"Did you speak with anyone today aside from your teachers, classmates, and a person named Ivan?"

"No."

"Thank you for participating in this interview. I see you need medical attention. Someone will be along to escort you to the clinic." The monitors go dark.

I sit and replay the questions and my answers for what feels like an hour. I turn, expecting Ivan when the door opens, but it's Warden Donegal. I hide my disappointment with a quick smile.

"Follow me." He walks fast out of the room, down the green hallway. I limp behind him, trying to keep up.

At each set of doors, we stop. He scans his face on a wall panel before they open. Hmm, the doors opened automatically for Ivan.

"I want to make a phone call. Have you contacted my parents?" I ask.

"Trespassers in custody must wait to make phone calls until their interview has been submitted for review."

That's a gut punch. *Ivan, where did you go?*

He leads me to a bed at the far end of a clinic. No robots or human staff bustle around. No patients in the other beds. No alarms softly beep. *No one will hear me scream.*

Donegal pulls the curtain around my bed halfway shut. "Shut the curtain the rest of the way. Change into the hospital gown."

That doesn't seem like something I want to do. How will I get out of here if I look like a patient? I don't need to be admitted to this or any other hospital. I shut the curtain and sit on my bed to think.

"Hello?" a voice calls from outside my curtain. "Are you ready?"

"I guess," I say, sitting on the bed, fully dressed.

The curtain pulls back automatically, and I'm face-to-face with a spindly tower on wheels. It has a computer monitor instead of a head. Shoot. I was hoping for a human to ask for help. This place is abandoned. I don't want to be in here with robots and crabby Donegal.

"Hello. Ms. Ross?" the ORION asks.

"Yes. Can I call my parents please?"

"I don't have any information for you on that. I am here to assess your injuries. Please change into the gown. I'll be back." The curtain closes again. I don't hear the ORION wheel away.

I don't move.

"Ms. Ross. Are you ready?"

"Yes."

The curtain opens. "Please change into the gown. I'll be back," the ORION says.

"No. After I make a phone call."

"Change into the gown." Wheels stay parked under the edge of the curtain, whether to haunt, annoy, or intimidate me, I'm not sure. Maybe it's a mixture of all three.

My refusals aren't getting me anywhere. I grumble about how badly I hate robots and throw the gown on like a cape. There's no way I'm taking my clothes off just because a robot said to.

"Ms. Ross, are you ready?"

"Yes."

The curtain opens. "I see you have only partially complied. I made a note in your record." I don't like the sound of that. The ORION launches into a detailed explanation of wound exams it wants to do on me.

The curtain across from me wiggles then slides open. The vital sign monitor above the empty bed lights up. Words scroll across it in huge font.

Nice cape, you little rebel! -I

Ivan is here! Can he hear me?

"ORION," I say to pause the video. "When will my interview be reviewed so I can call my dad?"

"I do not have that information. Please continue watching this wound assessment video."

Most of my attention focuses on my peripheral vision to see if Ivan will answer.

Soon! Don't worry. -I

Okay, he can hear me. Good to know. Someone is here on my side. I smile. Lark's right. If animals trust a person, we can too.

Stop smiling.

You're injured, act like it. -I

"ORION. My knee pain is getting worse."

Nice job, faker! -I

"Ms. Ross, your condition requires a full assessment. Change into the gown." The curtain closes. It's tempting to throw a pillow at the ORION. If it tips over, I can make a break for it.

But Ivan's here.

If he's really helping me, and I run, then I'm totally on my own. Looks like I'll be wearing the gown after all. I watch my vital sign monitor when changing to make sure it doesn't flicker on.

"Ms. Ross, are you ready?" the ORION asks.

"Yes." The curtain slides open.

The curtains across from my bed are shut too. Ivan is gone.

4

The ORION unit begins an assessment of my scratches, bruises, and injured knee. Then an ALICE monitor turns on. I have to go through most of the process again with it.

"Your knee shows a fluid buildup. I put you on the schedule for a procedure early tomorrow with the orthopedics ASTRA team to drain the fluid," the ALICE says.

"I don't agree with your assessment. I don't need surgery."

"Ms. Ross, you do not have any medical authority here. You *will* be having surgery."

The ALICE continues to explain my diagnosis. It clearly doesn't care that I've known the difference between an abrasion and a laceration since before kindergarten. The curtain behind my doctor's monitor does a little wiggle.

Words scroll again.

Tired?

Tell the doctor you need a nap.

Listen to them for now. I'm here with you.

See you soon. -I

The curtain slides shut.

"Thank you for watching that joint effusion video. Do you have any questions?" ALICE asks.

"No. Can I get some rest now?" Whatever Ivan has in mind has to be an improvement over this.

"Yes. Do you have any questions?" it prompts.

"Can I call my parents? You can't keep me trapped here."

"I don't have any information for you on that. This concludes your assessment review and pre-op instructions. A nurse will come in soon to start your IV."

I wave the ORION away. Since Ivan says I'm tired, I lay back and wait to see what will happen next.

Do something. Wow me, forest man.

An ORION injection unit rolls up. It looks like a cabinet on wheels with a clear tunnel. "Ms. Ross, please place your arm in the automated IV insertion system," it says, rolling close.

Well, this was a letdown, Ivan...

"Why? I don't need any medicine."

"Ms. Ross, we need to prepare you for surgery. Place your left arm in the automated IV insertion system."

I lay my arm in the clear, bright tunnel. Blood vessels appear like a delicate web. A small robotic extension tool hovers over my forearm and in a flash, it inserts the IV painlessly. After applying a sticky bandage, the machine flushes my IV and leaves it capped off.

"Ms. Ross, thank you for your compliance. One of my human counterparts will be in soon." The ORION unit turns and wheels away.

I peek to see if any curtains move or monitors light up. *Ivan, come back.* There's no movement, but footsteps are coming towards me. Please be Ivan.

"Good evening, I am here to get your IV fluids running," says a dour looking lady, pushing an IV pole with a clear bag hanging from it. "Gimme your arm."

Cripes. Not Ivan.

"Can I call someone now? I feel like I am being held hostage," I say, resting my arm on the cold bed rail.

"I don't have any information for you." She attaches the tubing and sets the IV drip rate.

"Can I have something to drink please?" I ask.

"You rest. I'll go see what I can find." She hands me a call light and steps out.

This empty clinic is as cold as a morgue. I wrap the pile of blankets tight around me, leaving my IV line trailing out. Leaning back against my pillow stack, it's actually a pretty comfortable spot to watch the bed across from me. Ivan will be back. He wouldn't have made such a big deal about trusting him just to abandon me.

The nurse comes back. "These are pre-surgery antibiotics to prevent infection." She flips the cap off a huge syringe in her left hand.

LIAR!

I saw the med name on the label: *morpentanyl.* That's not an antibiotic. It's an incredibly strong pain medicine that is immediately fatal in large doses. I'm about to get a syringe full. I do quick math and estimate it's about twenty times the maximum safe dose. They're giving me an overdose. I've got to stop her.

"I don't need those, I'm not having surgery tomorrow," I say.

"ALICE's orders. Good news. I'll be right back with a phone for you."

"Those aren't antibiotics. That's morpentanyl! Too much morpentanyl!"

"Aww, you poor confused thing."

"No, stopstopstop, read it! Check the dose you're giving me. I'm a doctor. That's too much!" I bark, wrestling to make sure my hands are hidden.

She looks at the label on the syringe as she attaches it to my IV port.

Nurse! You didn't even clean that port. She didn't clean it because she's going to kill me.

"This is exactly what the doctor ordered." She jabs the plunger, pushing the med in one fast motion.

The clinic goes black. I hear running, a thud, scuffling. That dose of sodium morpentanyl would have killed me by now. I lay with my eyes closed in case the nurse expects me to be dead.

A hand drops heavily on my head, stroking my hair. "Story! No!" Ivan snarls. My bed rocks like a boulder smashed into it when he kicks the frame. "Where's the reversal drug? I'll bring you back." Cabinet doors slam into the wall behind me and he throws several things to the floor.

My eyes fly open. "Ivan? It's dark."

A light turns on. Ivan's face is etched with fury. My breath catches in a squeak when he pulls me into a crushing hug.

"Story! You're okay?!" His hands curl around my ribs, pulling me tighter to his chest. "I almost had a heart attack!" He breathes into my hair.

I don't try to pull back. The stress of the day must have temporarily rewired my brain. I always pull away from people. If he lets go, I'm sure I'll fall apart.

Please hold me together for just a minute.

I press my cheek against his warm neck. Was I really almost killed? Over his shoulder, the nurse is still. That could've been me. She hasn't tried to get up. Her shoulders rise and fall in a regular pattern. I should get up and check on her, but there's no way my legs will work right now. My shivers progress to full body shakes.

"Shh, Story. I've got you. It's really okay."

He holds me tighter, tucking his chin against the side of my face. The clinic and nurse are blocked from view. All I see is the hollow of his tan neck where it meets his chest and his black t-shirt collar. And for now, I'm okay with my world being no bigger than this while I catch my breath.

Today was supposed to be a leisurely hike in the forest. Instead, it's been full of disasters, secrets, and apparently, I wasn't supposed to make it out of here. Ivan settles a hand on the back of my head and strokes my hair with a soothing, smooth motion.

He grounds me. Ignore the world. Forget your weird day. Focus on Ivan. After a few more breaths, my shakes ease to occasional shivers.

Yes. Someone tried to kill me.

Why?

Ivan finally tilts me back a few inches but keeps one arm behind my shoulders to support me. His dark eyes study my face. "How are you alive?"

"She said she was giving me an antibiotic. I saw the name on the label. I ripped out my IV." I show him my bloody hand.

"You genius woman! Very clever." He rips a gauze pack open and presses it onto my IV site, grinning as he tapes it on. "We need to go. Come on. Change back into your clothes."

"Thanks for not leaving me." I shut the curtain after he steps out.

"Not a chance, Doc."

My stomach lurches at the sight of the nurse's motionless legs while I change. "Did you check to see if the nurse is okay?"

When I step out, he's swiping a small screen on his wrist cuff with typing motions. After a few seconds, he folds a leather flap over the screen.

"No. She fell. I'll call someone to help her. She's also not a real nurse. You'll love this. We have to sneak out. No talking, chatterbox." He takes off with long strides.

Don't leave! I jog/limp to grab his hand. He whips to look at me; black eyebrows raised in surprise.

"Sorry. I'm slow...but I can't get separated from you again." Heat creeps from my neck into my cheeks.

A sly grin touches his mouth. "Smart. How's this?"

He loops an arm around my waist and pauses. I nod. That's all the permission he needs to secure me to his side and take off. In minutes, we burst out of the warden station into the forest where Obsidian is waiting.

"We'll go somewhere much safer. Sorry. I had to bring you here first. The wardens were looking for you."

"Thank you. Glad we're out of there."

"One sec." Ivan busies himself typing on his wrist computer.

I tuck under Sid's neck and throw my arms around him. He does a happy nicker. I give him lazy scratches on his neck. He bobs his head onto my back like he's returning the favor. Most people would think this is a waste of time, but horses and dogs have a special power to make bad days manageable. I need some fuzzy mammal time today.

"Hey, Sid! What a good boy. Thanks for waiting." He huffs a breath in my ear, blowing curls in a tiny frenzy. "Oooh, you're a hairstylist. Needed that today. I almost died. Your dad saved me. Is he your dad? Or are you more like bros?" I whisper, patting his wide neck. "I wanna go home. I miss my family. My little sister would love you. Can you get us out of here, bud?"

The whole thing took less than a minute. But between Ivan and Sid's hugs, I'm feeling worlds better. I turn. Ivan is watching us.

Scratch that. He's not looking at Sid. He's full-on staring at me, dark eyes glowing like coals. His mouth is open like he was going to say something but couldn't get the words out.

I'm such a dummy! I shouldn't touch people's stuff. This might be why I don't have friends aside from Richelle. I see their pet and get excited then make a total fool of myself.

"Sorry. I love horses. Probably more than I like most people." He stays frozen. Great. I crossed some unspoken boundary and freaked him out. "Ivan, I'm really sorry. Do you not like when people touch him?"

I wish I knew him well enough to read what this face is. He's just wordlessly gawking at me.

"I-I..." He scrubs a hand through his hair. "Nothing. It's...I'm glad you like him. Touch my horse *an-y-time*."

He gives a fast, tight smile. *Forest man is flustered.* That's what this is.

"I think...Obsidian just, uh, fell in love with you. Come here. Time to go." He puts me behind Obsidian's saddle again and climbs up in front of me. We take off deeper into the forest, cantering with Helga soaring above.

She shoots down, screeching.

"I hear you, Helga." Ivan sweeps his gaze across the forest. "Something's wrong. I need to figure out what she's telling me." He looks at his wrist cuff. "Okay, we'll go this way."

We veer down a steep slope covered with pine needles. At the bottom, we enter a small hollow. I feel like we're nestled deep in the bones of the forest. The air is hushed except for birdsong echoing around us.

"Stay here for a minute with Obsidian. I'll be right back." He drops from the saddle in a fluid motion.

"No. It's creepy. And you said we should stick together. Don't leave me alone."

He looks shocked I would say that about the forest. "You aren't alone, you have Obsidian," he says, walking backwards. "Please, wait here. Just for a few minutes." He disappears up a sunken path at a sprint.

I scoot into the seat of the saddle. Sid stands rock steady. His ears flick at the occasional sound. We wait for several moments. I try to calm myself by reaching down to pet his neck.

"Good boy. Stand," I say.

Helga shrieks in the direction Ivan ran. Obsidian tosses his head and snorts, shifting his weight. He twists his ears and dances restlessly. Helga does another screech. Obsidian lets out a loud challenge of a whinny. What if Ivan needs help and Obsidian can help him? Trusting animals and Ivan have kept me alive so far.

"Fine. I miss him too. Go." I tap his sides with my heels.

He thunders forward. Branches claw at us, but he's guided by a mission to get to his master. When we get up to where Helga had been diving, the forest is quiet.

A faint trail of broken branches and disturbed earth lead my eyes through the undergrowth to a figure in black. Ivan. He stands watching, waiting. Helga sits on a log by his knee. Obsidian barrels straight for him.

On the forest floor around him are fallen pieces of a dozen Helston's hawk drones. He has a gun clutched firmly in each hand.

"Why did you let him come up here?" Ivan huffs through ragged breaths as I pull Obsidian to a stop.

"Obsidian was worried about you."

He laughs, clearly not buying it. "Sid was worried, I see."

"Where did you get guns? No one uses guns anymore. I don't even think it's legal to own one."

"These are not guns. They're used to take down drones when they won't stop chasing ladies I'm protecting." He spins a not-gun on each palm with dangerous grace. Looking pleased with himself, he tucks them away in thigh pocket holsters I hadn't noticed. "You sure attract a lot of drones, Story Ross. Good thing you're with me."

"Do you save many ladies in the forest?" I kick free of the stirrups and scoot behind the saddle.

"You're my one and only." He wiggles his eyebrows then hops up.

I snort and tuck my arms around his waist. After about thirty minutes the forest changes. It feels heavy and secluded. The temperature has dropped and the terrain slopes upward. The tree canopy is much thicker, making the late spring evening darker than it should be.

Helga darts towards us screeching. Ivan mutters and pulls Obsidian to a stop. He flips back the leather cover on his wrist cuff and swipes around on the small screen.

"Unbelievable. This is getting old." He holds the screen over his left shoulder for me to see. It's some sort of thermal imaging of the area around us. On the screen there are several human outlines blinking towards us. When I look up, they're concealed behind the brush, unable to be seen with the naked eye.

"Who are they?" I ask.

"The foolish forest wardens again. I can fix it, hang on." He swipes around on his wrist cuff.

I try to peek around his arm to see what he's doing, but it makes me slip to the side. I catch myself by latching tight around his ribs. Without missing a beat, he clamps his elbows down on my arms to catch me.

"It's killing you, not knowing what's going on, isn't it?" he asks, laughing.

"Absolutely dying back here." I grab a handful of his shirt to lean out and see his wrist. He's too tall and his shoulders are too wide to see what he's doing.

A fast-moving band of fog rolls in on the ground. The green forest undergrowth disappears under pale gray swirls. I suck in a deep breath as the world is lost to the cool vapor, pooling in a fast-rising wall.

"They won't be able to see us soon," Ivan says.

Thick streamers of fog curl down from the treetops until they meet the tall gray waves surrounding us. The air changes from damp forest scents to that sharp smell that fills the air before a scheduled thundershower. A solid wall of clouds obscures the forest. Ivan, Obsidian, and I are in a clear pocket. We're untouched, protected. Eerie pulses of lightning outside our fog dome flash near constantly in shattered streaks. Outlines of trees blink into view through the fog and then vanish.

"Go, Sid." Ivan rocks his hips forward. Obsidian takes off at a slow walk. The fog ripples in a shifting veil with us.

"What is this?"

"I edited the time of some planned forest weather events to get the wardens away from us. I turned up the lightning a few notches to make sure they go home for the day."

That's nonsense to my tired brain. "Oh. How?"

"It's part of what I do for work," he says, as if that explains creating a wall of clouds out of thin air is some sort of normal job. "We only have about thirty minutes to go. We'll be there soon. Sit back and enjoy the ride."

It's been a long day. Riding a horse in a fog and lightning shield through the forest, wrapped around the tank of a man who made it for me is *not* how I envisioned my evening going, yet here I am.

Ivan has proved he will keep me safe. Might as well give myself a few minutes to breathe. I lean forward, resting my cheek and shoulders on his back. He tenses, then rests his free hand on my arms. He's given me permission to relax and soak in the show he created for us.

"Thank you. This is amazing."

"The fog and lightning? Or this?" he teases, giving my arms a squeeze that's a preview of his raw strength.

Richelle will scream for days when she hears about this.

Oh, be careful, Story Ross. It's too easy to just melt into him as we ride along. Even though we just met, he doesn't feel like a stranger. There's an echo of him being someone I've always known, always carried with me, and it's making me nervous in a way I can't pinpoint.

Stop being weird. Talk. You're a woman of science. "Can you tell me how you made the fog and lightning? I'd like to learn about it."

"Happy to." His deep voice with a hint of a southern accent launches into an explanation of things I've never heard of. Something about computer code, scheduling, event timers, system services, and how to use AI models to manipulate atmospheric conditions. While he speaks, his fingers trace small patterns on my forearms. He uses the movements to punctuate what he's teaching me. I'm glad he can't see my face right now.

My mind feels quiet. When was the last time the noise and stress went silent in my brain? Five years ago? A decade? I don't know, but him and that voice just shut it all out. I press my cheek on his spine to hide another smile.

The rumble of a waterfall was background noise, but it's growing into a roar. Rocky, uneven ground turns to a smooth path. Ivan's fog fades away, revealing a massive sandstone ledge with a rushing waterfall.

The area at the top of the falls has huge trees sprawling out over the edges of the falls, roots wrapped around boulders, braided together, disappearing into seams in the stone.

The sandstone ledge turns into a towering horseshoe-shaped cliff that must be ninety feet high and several hundred feet wide. Cool air blasts an icy mist on my back and neck as we ride to the far end of the falls.

"I've never seen anything like this." I shiver closer to Ivan.

He rubs my arms. "I'll get you warmed up soon."

The curtain of water ends, leaving a dry gap of about thirty feet to pass through. Ivan stops Obsidian, dropping lightly to his feet.

"Scoot up in the saddle. Welcome to my home sweet home." This time, he lets me keep the reins.

"Charming. You're a...cave man?"

His dark eyes sparkle with laughs. "It's much better inside. I promise. It used to be called Ash Cave. Hikers loved it here. The Bastion rerouted water to create Baltimore Sea. What used to be a trickle is now this raging fall that hides The Helm."

"The what?"

"I forgot The Bastion keeps you all clueless. We have so much to talk about."

Behind the falls opens to a wide cavern with many smaller openings used as horse stalls. The farther we walk into the cave, Ivan's whole demeanor changes. He squares his broad shoulders and projects confident authority.

A young boy runs over to us and grabs Obsidian's reins. "Welcome back, Sir! I've been waiting for you."

5

Sir? Why did that boy call Ivan Sir?

"*Merci*. Sorry. We ran into some delays," Ivan says to the boy. "Francois, this is Story. Story, Francois."

"Nice to meet you," I say.

He looks like he's a couple of years older than Lark. "Are you...?" Francois starts, but Ivan gently interrupts.

"*Je suis désolé, Francois.* Her injuries need to be taken care of." Ivan speaks French? "Can we catch up with you another time?" Ivan doesn't wait for Francois to answer. He motions for me to follow him.

"*Oui, monsieur. Au revoir!* Bye, Story!" Francois calls after us. I smile and wave goodbye. We walk past at least a dozen stalls.

Ivan pulls me to a stop with an arm around my waist. "Can you walk, or do you need me to carry you?"

I laugh nervously. He drops his arm. "Walk. For sure."

"Just checking."

We continue along quietly, his shoulder touching mine. I catch him sneaking glances at me as we pass beneath a rocky arch. There are decorative stones arranged in a beautiful pattern overhead. We enter a long, gray hallway. Above, a speaker system plays the sounds of the falls. After a couple hundred feet, the left side of the hallway opens to a large clinic.

"Ooooh, cool!" I stop to peek in the bustling mini hospital. Charcoal walls have a soft, clinical glow from LED lighting. Monitors faintly beep. I see several human staff members. This is definitely better than the forest clinic. Top-tier ALICE and ORION units roll over polished black floors around a large central station. "I've never seen doctor and nurse units like those."

"We've got the good stuff. I'll take you in there sometime," he says.

"I'd like that, thanks."

We turn into an inviting blue apartment hallway. Doors with numbers and peepholes line the left side. The right wall is plated metal.

"You were right, it's better in here," I admit.

We walk to the last door on the left, apartment two.

"After you. Yeah, it's not too bad in here. I need to go to work. You're safe. Eat, relax, nap in the bed, shower. Whatever you want. Don't open the door if anyone knocks. How are you doing?"

"I'm good. Thanks for your hospitality. Can I call someone?"

"Oh gosh, of course. Here." He hands me a phone from his back pocket.

I don't know who to call. Dad left me. Mom's home with Lark. Richelle would come. I stare at the phone for a few seconds before calling Dad. Maybe he's still in the forest.

Before it could get through one full ring he answers, and he's mad. "Ivan! I've been waiting!"

What? This has to be a joke. Did I hit my head off a rock and I'm hallucinating?

"Dad! You know Ivan? How?" I cut him off. Add that to today's list of mysteries.

"I'm so happy to hear your voice. Ivan's a...colleague. Are you okay?"

"Yes. Can you come get me?"

"I'll be there in the morning. Can I talk to Ivan please? I love you so much!" That's the dad I am used to.

"See you tomorrow. Love you, Dad." I shoot Ivan a look full of accusations.

"We'll talk later, I promise. Okay?" Ivan whispers and gives me a sweet, lopsided grin. I can't explain why I'm willing to trust him when he's been withholding information, but I nod. He takes his phone from me and squeezes my arm. "Hey, Alan."

Interesting. He's on a first name basis with my dad. "You got it. I'll take Story to meet him, and he'll bring her to you. Bye." He tucks his phone in his pocket. "Okay, feeling better now that you know you're going home tomorrow?"

"Much."

"Good. See you in a few hours. Don't go out of here please. Well. Wait. You're not a prisoner and I didn't abduct you. Go out if you want. If anyone finds you, tell them you're with me. Later!"

"Bye, Ivan." His efforts to reassure me are sweet.

I have no idea who could be lurking out there, aside from Francois, and I'm not going to find out. His apartment is a refuge. It's not huge, but it's a nice, open concept space. The kitchen has a square granite island with two stools. The cabinet wood is stained a dark charcoal color. The appliances are full-size, stainless steel. The whole place is hospital-level clean. There's a wooden dining table with chairs for four between the kitchen and living room area.

The living room and kitchen have blackout curtains from ceiling to floor over five windows. There are two recliners and a brown leather sectional couch for six. Leather is worn smooth on the chaise lounge seat of the sectional. The rest of the couch has factory crisp cushions and armrests.

A doorway directly across from the couch leads to a master bedroom. It has a king size bed with no decorative pillows and a neutral (mostly black) color palette. Each side of the bed has a nightstand and lamp, but only the one closest to the door has a charger, a textbook, and a tidy stack of notebooks topped with a sprawl of pens.

Overall, it's a basic bachelor pad apartment. It reminds me of a large hotel suite that you'd stay in while passing through.

My stomach growls, pulling me from my tour. He did say I could eat. I grab a handful of wheat crackers, a bag of dried fruit, and some cheese slices from the fridge. I've got to try the favorite seat on the couch. I plop onto it and the surprisingly plush cushion sinks under me. It's got the perfect amount of give. I tuck my legs up and settle under a thick black blanket.

I like it here. This is way better than the clinic. My daypack sits on the middle couch cushion. I unzip it and check my book for Lark's flowers. They're safe. I'm safe too, thanks to Ivan.

He was so gentle with me in the clinic. There's no way to fake that level of concern. Why didn't I pull back from Ivan? Was it because I almost died today? Does Mom know my dad went into the forest today? Did Lark do okay at school? My bizarre day replays in my head until I drift to sleep.

I wake to the sound of a door shutting. The clock hanging in the kitchen shows it's 3:10. Way too early to wake up, but I'm too jittery to close my eyes again. A stack of black clothes is on a table beside me with a note.

Get cleaned up if you want. I'll be back soon. -I

My reflection in the bathroom mirror makes me gasp. Scratches cover my face, arms, and hands. I turn to check the back of my shoulder where the hawk clawed me. Great. The meds I'm putting on it are apparently useless against drone talon bacteria. Redness spreads around the deep scratch. It's hard to clean and bandage by myself. But if I tell Dad about it now, he'll have a meltdown I didn't tell him right away. I'll make an appointment with an ALICE when I get home. Maybe they'll treat my knee too. It's got a rainbow of bruises and is puffy with swelling. I also have a lovely abrasion that stretches several inches down my shin.

Sir Ivan has me acutely aware that right now I'm not looking so good.

The shower was divine once I figured out how to work the seemingly unlimited settings. The five shower jets at different heights initially pressure-washed me with ice water. I bit back most of a shriek and counted it a win I didn't slip and break my neck trying to escape their spray.

After some shivery fiddling, I adjusted the temperature and it was perfection. The hot jets worked in unison to unravel knots of tension I didn't know I was carrying in my shoulders and back. After standing under the hot water for a long time, I drug myself out and put a new bandage on my leg. The soft, black, pajama-like shorts Ivan left for me have a drawstring that I cinch tight. His shirt sleeves are too long and need to be rolled up a few times.

Lark's soggy bracelet hangs on my wrist. So far, it's made it through the nightmare forest of doom with me. Speaking of nightmares, what am I going to do about my hair? I can't find a hairbrush. His perfect black swoop of hair probably takes two seconds of combing with his fingers to look like that. I give up the search and twist my red curls into a wet knot on top of my head. That'll have to do.

I walk into the living room and Ivan's sitting on the couch. He's throwing nuts in the air and catching them in his mouth.

"Sounds like you had fun in there figuring out the temperature," he says with a laugh. "Left is cold-"

"Right is hot. Got it." I sit beside him, wrapping back up in the soft blanket. "So, this is how you spend your days? Working as some kind of forest weather creator, killing nurses, shooting drones, and doing tricks with your food?"

"Close. But I didn't kill the nurse." He touches my bracelet. "Looks great with the Irontrace pajamas."

"It's my sister's. Thanks for the clothes. The food. The shower. And, you know, saving me today. I don't know if thank you is adequate."

"Anytime." He leans his head back and rubs his eyes.

"Have you gotten any sleep?"

"Sleep is overrated. I'd like to talk to you to clear up some questions. I really need some coffee first though. Do you want some?"

"Sure."

He leans forward. "Tell me, how much do you know about The Kernel and The Bastion?"

6

I recite facts taught in school about the Third World War. "A team of engineers came together to form a council called The Bastion. Their goal was to use artificial intelligence under an operating system called The Kernel to bring peace, security, and stability to the world. They fixed the world's biggest problems. I've seen videos of how mad people were at first, but they started loving The Bastion when they saw how great we live now under the AI models."

He looks at me with something resembling pity.

"Dad is a rarity. He was a surgeon back when humans still did surgeries. Since The Bastion took control of healthcare and kicked humans out of the operating room, he has worked for ASTRA," I say. "Most little girls want to play with dolls. Not me. I hung on his words for hours as he talked his way through writing surgical training programs. He made it like a game, teaching me medical concepts using fun things in our craft room. He would take me to his lab and let me use his surgical robots to do origami, pretend to operate on several types of human tissues, and do sutures."

"What a cool way to grow up." He pours two cups of coffee.

"I memorized anatomy charts, medications, and learned disease processes. He helped me find labs and mentors to teach me everything I needed. We can't even hope to work for ASTRA without at least a few years of work under experienced trainers like him. He and my mentors let me do simple surgeries by myself on simulators. That makes writing training programs for them easier. I know what the robots need to do. Sorry, I think most of what I told you is about my dad, not The Bastion. But he's the reason I flew through medical school and surgical training."

"Well, he helped you, but he didn't take the exams and pass the skills tests. You're extraordinary. You can work for ASTRA I'd guess, what, ten years before your peers?"

I give a noncommittal shrug. I'd hate to seem braggy. Forcing myself to fly through school is the only way to get closer to saving Lark.

He hands me a cup of black coffee and sits by me. "I always drink it like this, hope that's okay."

"This is great, thank you. Love it. Was Dad expecting you to call him?"

"Yes. He's been panicking most of the day, waiting to hear how you were. I know that means you have even more questions. Let's take it back to the beginning. Want to know some more Bastion facts? I know, they stopped the third world war and made life better in some ways."

That's the understatement of the century. "*Some* ways?"

"You heard me. I've asked you to trust me a couple of times. Can I trust you to keep a secret?"

I nod silently.

"The Bastion experimented with raising humans using AI parenting models."

Before I can stop myself, my face shows what a horrible idea that is. A grin tugs at his lips.

He continues, "The Bastion is always hunting for kids who excel at something from the time they're in diapers. You're a healthcare prodigy, I assume?" I nod. "Good for you. They pick some technology prodigy kids to hand over to AI parents. The Bastion gives the parents a hefty sum of money in place of their dear child." He shakes his head slowly.

My mouth drops open. "You've got to be joking."

"They're raised to be part of a special black ops team, called the Irontrace Squadron. Their whole life becomes maintaining the computer code for The Kernel and protecting it, here at The Helm. There are forty-one Helms spread out worldwide."

He's talking about himself! "Were you one of the kids sold to this secret Irontrace Squadron?"

"Sure was. I've got a special role on the team that came in handy today. The warden's verdict for you was 'criminal trespasser guilty of perjury to a judiciary.' That's yet another crime punishable by immediate execution. Hence the pint or so of morpentanyl with your name on it. Aren't you full of warm, fuzzy feelings towards The Bastion?"

That explains why crime has been wiped out. I wonder how many innocent people are taken in for interviews and fail because humans get nervous. How many are convicted and executed without anyone hearing of it? If I hadn't lived through these events today, I wouldn't believe him.

"Were you lonely?" I ask quietly.

A look of confusion crosses his face. "Meh, no. Not really. There's lots of us here."

"You can be surrounded by people and still be lonely."

"The AI parents aren't too bad, really. They didn't sell me, so they're doing better than my birth parents."

"I'm so sorry."

"Don't be. It's all been worth it to save you today." He shoots a grin my way and waves a hand like it was nothing.

"Are they still looking for me?"

"You're safe. I have a special clearance to override and overwrite any of its data or decisions, because at the end of the day, The Kernel is just a stupid computer. To anyone who would care, you passed their interview with flying colors. I tried to throw out your results right away when I saw your response swerved off your baseline twice. That lovely fake nurse booked it into your room before I could stop the execution order. I'd have been faster, but I had to take care of our friend Donegal with a manual override."

"I don't know how you do a manual override but thank you."

"Eh, let's just say it's a creative slap on the wrist. How severe is left to the judgement of the slapper." He winks.

My eyes drop to his hands. They don't have any fight wounds on them. I'm hoping that was a metaphor. "How do you know my dad?"

"I've known him for most of my life. I see you have a particular deep scratch there on your forehead. He called me about it a few days ago." He almost touches my face but stops a few inches short.

No way! He's the one Dad called? *And the one Dad sent that awful picture to...*

"Yeah, from a hawk. It gave me this, too." I drop the neck of his shirt I'm wearing to the side and show him the red talon scratches I can't reach. "Dad doesn't know about these. Please don't tell him."

"I won't. It doesn't look good though. Can I feel it?"

Odd question. Does he think the drone implanted something in me? I'm scared to ask. I lean closer so he can reach.

He lays the back of his hand on the cuts. "It's hot and swollen. I'm pretty sure it's infected. Trust me. Hawk talons are gross, even drone hawks."

"I'll put more antibacterial cream on it when I get home."

He gives me a sure-ya-will face. "I've been working an investigation related to bizarre hawk activity. Someone has been manufacturing fake Helston's hawk drones. Looks like they sent one for you."

"Why?"

"I'll find out and let you know."

"Why are you telling me all of this?"

"The Bastion is full of evil. Yet they masquerade as good." He smiles, leaning forward to put his coffee cup on the table in front of us. "Those milk chocolate eyes of yours have more intelligence in one glance than most people muster in their entire lives. You deserve to know every secret the world holds so you can let its truths collide with your brilliance."

Whoa.

"Oh. Intense. But thanks." My entire body lights up in a crimson wave. I gather our coffee cups and jump up. He looks thoroughly amused by the storm his words caused. "Do you want some more coffee?"

"I'd love to sit here and drink coffee with you all day. Honestly, it feels like the first meaningful conversation I've ever had. But we need to get ready to meet your dad, sorry."

"Oh, I thought you told my dad someone else is bringing me to meet him?"

"I'd rather do it myself. You're a drone magnet and I never miss. Do you want to see the clinic? I'd like to get something for you."

"Sure."

The clinic lights are dimmed, and the closed patient curtains make it seem like we should whisper. In an arc around the station, several ORION units are parked, blue charging lights blinking softly. A couple of volunteers stop their quiet conversation when they see Ivan and I.

"Morning, Sir," one says, tipping her coffee cup at him.

"Hey, grabbing some first aid supplies." Ivan gives them a quick wave.

The other one calls out, "Ivan! Where were you yesterday?"

He'd been letting my limp set our slow pace. He wraps an arm around my waist and half-carries me past them in a rush. This is different than the gentle way he helped me in the forest clinic. His arm and chest muscles are tense. He ignores their question and speaks just to me, "They're used to me treating this like my own personal medicine cabinet."

"They seem...friendly," I say.

He snorts. "That's one word for it."

Got it. He's using me as a human shield.

We stop at a door marked *Central Supply*. It slides open automatically. There are about twenty aisles with racks of supplies from floor to ceiling. It's a medical wonderland.

Ivan follows several feet behind me as I greedily snatch things I've never seen off the shelves. Stick-on discs to stabilize and monitor brain activity after trauma. Mini injectable cartridges to deploy anti-bleeding gel deep in wounds. Single-use face masks to clear airways of respiratory contaminants and administer breathing treatments. An array of nano-bots you can deploy to rebuild many types of tissues. Palm sized scanners for mobile CT scans and x-rays. Tons of orthopedic devices to rebuild bones, ligaments, and tendons.

"This is so far beyond what's medically possible," I say.

"Not here."

I limp to the pharmacy wall. I've never heard of many of the meds. A whole floor to ceiling section is for bleeding control. Antivenoms. Anti-toxins. Ointments with skin regenerating factors to speed healing. Creams to treat laser and thermal burns.

"Where do you get supplies like this? It's incredible!"

"We build it." He shrugs. Hmm, when he's wearing this proud smile, he gets a dimple on the right. That's...not what I'm here to focus on.

I turn away. "Oh, just like that?"

"Yup. Look, here's what I wanted to get for you." He hands me a package of what looks like a sock with the label *CombiCradle*. I open it and a lightweight, clear polymer sleeve unfolds. "It's a brace that will fix your leg fast. Try it on."

I slip off my hiking boot and remove my bandage.

"Here, I'll take that." He crumples my bandage in his hand. I balance on my right foot to put it on, but wobble. His hands immediately catch me. "Gotcha."

I pull the CombiCradle up. It compresses from my mid-thigh to shin. It's delivering a pleasant, cool buzzing sensation.

For the first time since my fall, my knee feels completely stable, unrestricted from swelling. "Wow. That's much better already." I do a little wiggly dance to prove he fixed me.

"I'm glad. It emits low-frequency pulses to stimulate blood flow and force your tissues to repair themselves faster. Here's a few extra to take home."

"Thanks. Are you some kind of doctor for the Irontrace?"

"Definitely not! I'm just incredibly accident prone." A hesitant look takes over his face. "Can I fix the talon scratch on your shoulder too, please?"

I can barely reach it. "Okay."

"After you." He guides me to a supply rack full of bandages, grabbing a package and tearing it open. "I need to clean it first."

I pull my arm out of the bottom of the shirt. He slides it up in the back, careful to only move it just enough to access my shoulder blade area and tucks it under my arm to hold it there. This is awkward enough, at least he's trying to let me keep a semblance of modesty.

"This is how we destroy infections." He shows me what looks like a black camera. "Specialized UV lights kill any bacteria, even if a severe infection has already taken hold. It takes before and after views of active bacteria cells in the wound for patient records."

The dim supply room flashes with bright rays of light from behind me a few times. He comes around to face me. "Look. Here's the before. Notice the gross colonies of bacteria." The small screen on the UV device shows a layered view of my skin and scapula. There are two lines from the talons overlaid with splotchy red spots. "And after." He swipes it and the same area shows no red dots.

I grin. "Thank you! I was bracing for a painful wound cleaning session."

"No. We don't have time for that. Fast, effective fixes only. Next step, healing mesh. Here. Read the package insert while I put it on you. You look like a person who likes to read."

I jerk to look at him.

"Steady there, sweets. That was a compliment." He smooths a clear, sticky bandage on my shoulder with his palm. "Why didn't you tell your dad about this? You know it needed treatment days ago."

"My little sister has some health problems. Whatever happens to me pales in comparison to what she deals with. Anything that pops up, I figure it out and fix it by myself."

"Ah, not the best plan. Dying of an infection would surely take the focus off your sister. At least for a day or two."

I plaster on one of my fake smiles. "So, you're telling me this will prevent swelling, release anti-infection agents, and tissue scaffolding proteins?"

His lips twitch into a frown. "Yes, they're great. I'm glad you told me about your shoulder. Keep talking to me about things." He nods for me to follow him out of the supply room. "You don't need to handle every problem yourself. If you're looking for help, someone to vent to, or bored and want to chat, I'm your man. Whatever you say will stay between us."

A friend? I made a real friend. "That's kind. Same for you. I'm not your man though. I'm your woman. Oh goodness. Not *your* woman! I should...I'm going to shut up."

"Please keep talking. I think that's the fourth time you've turned that shade of rosy pink in the last twelve hours?"

I cringe and tilt my face away from him. He cracks up with contagious laughs. The heat drains from my face. Yesterday was one of the most stressful days of my life. How am I laughing (and actually having a good time) in this secret clinic hallway in a cave with him? His laughs settle into a huge grin. Turns out if you really make Ivan light up, he has dimples on *both* sides.

More volunteers have gathered at the central station. The group waves to him, calling a chorus of cheerful greetings.

He groans softly and picks up the pace. "Meet Dr. Story Ross!" We're nearly in a jog by the time we get to the station.

"Story Ross! Come hang with us!" a young woman says.

He sucks in a sharp breath. "Do you wanna stop?" he whispers from the corner of his mouth.

"Do you?" I ask.

He twists his lips to the side and looks from me to the crowd, then back to me. That's good enough of an answer.

"Sorry! I've got to get off this bad knee." To back up my words, I crumple against Ivan's side and hip. The girl's eyes narrow with a quizzical look. He shoots his hands around my ribs to keep me on my feet. I turn away from the group to smile up at him. His dimples make their second appearance.

"Now's not a good time, Voss," Ivan says without breaking our eye contact.

We both ignore the questions they hurl at our backs as he ushers me out of the clinic.

He arches an eyebrow. "Hmm, the CombiCradle's not working?"

"It's working just fine. You didn't seem like you wanted to stick around with the crowd."

"I didn't."

"Why?"

In the hallway, he switches to helping me with one arm. "Life is short. I'm very...particular about how I spend my time."

"Sorry. I'm taking up so much of it."

He clears his throat. "Honestly? I wish I had more time for you."

More time? We're both lost in our thoughts for the rest of our walk.

Back in his apartment, he types into his wrist cuff, then says, "Feel free to do whatever you want in here while I get things ready. I'll be back in about half an hour to take you home."

"Okay, thanks." I pour more coffee and wrap up in a blanket on the couch after he shuts the door. Ivan hates The Bastion. I would too. And is the world really run by him and these Irontrace? That's news to me. My mind drifts back over our conversation, trying to imprint his words in my mind.

When his door opens, he's accompanied by several people carrying matte black helmets with face shields.

"They're doing perimeter security evaluations with the horses and hawks today. You ready to go on a patrol mission with the Irontrace?" he asks, handing me a helmet.

"I am," I say. Riding a horse today on this sprained knee will really test the functionality of the CombiCradle. He hands me a black bag. I open it, my yellow daypack is tucked inside.

"We don't do bright colors here." He laughs, ushering me into the middle of the group. "This is Story, everybody."

As we make our way to the stables in the cave, they take turns introducing themselves.

The little boy from last night runs at a full sprint towards us when we enter the cavern. "Sir! *Ça va?* I got Hero and Storm ready for your friend."

"*Bien merci, Francois!* What will you be doing today?" Ivan asks, smiling at the boy.

"Using a convolutional neural network to identify common skin conditions affecting animals based on images. I can't wait to show you the progress I have made with image recognition and processing when I am done!" Francois says, handing us the reins for Obsidian and Hero.

From the way Francois is acting, the real goals of his project are approval and recognition from Ivan.

"Looking forward to it. You are going to help so many animals. See you in a few hours," Ivan says, giving Francois a high five before continuing our walk to the break in the falls.

"Well, that was adorable, Sir. Am I supposed to call you that too?" I ask.

"If you play your cards right? Someday." He bumps his shoulder into mine.

What a goofball. There's no way I'll ever be an Irontrace. I'm the opposite of a tech prodigy. "So, you speak French?"

He shrugs. "Only well enough to know I'm bad at it. I do speak Spanish and Russian." *Of course you speak four languages.* "Can you get on a horse with that knee?"

I walk to Hero's left side and climb in the saddle, flashing him a smile. "I'm good. What now?"

"Patrol helmet on."

He jumps on Obsidian and leads the way out of the cave. The rest of us follow. We walk our horses for a few minutes, then break into a canter. When we come upon a small clearing, Ivan pulls Obsidian to a stop. He turns to the group of Irontrace, lifting his face mask.

"My friends, you have done a great service today by helping Dr. Ross. It will allow the other Dr. Ross to continue working on Project

Agora."

They stand in their stirrups and cheer.

"Thank you!" I say to them.

They call out various versions of "you're welcome." This whole crew seems as friendly as Ivan. I wonder if I'll see any of them again.

"Keep this sector clear from wardens so we can head to the east exit." He lowers his face mask. They do the same. "Story, let's go."

Ivan and I trot through the clearing then slow to a walk as the trees thicken. Even though the fog on this gray morning is dreary, we're content to chat on our ride.

Ivan pulls Obsidian back beside Hero and removes his helmet. "You can take off your helmet. They'll keep us safe."

I shake out my hair. "What's Project Agora?"

"A special project to help the Irontrace Squadron. Part of the agreement with our families to let us come here is this." He turns in his saddle and swipes up his thick black hair from the base of his neck. "They call it an Agora."

Lark's birthmark!

"No way! My sister, Lark, has one of those!"

"And she's out there, alive?"

"Yes. But she has bad days and is in the hospital a lot."

He pets Helga. "Agoras were made to keep the Irontrace in line. It's a neural chip they implant when we arrive at The Helm. It creates a fatal tangle of arteries and veins, a type of arteriovenous malformation, or AVM in our necks. The Agoras allow us to access secure areas inside the Helm and a boundary around it. Go outside the boundary? You're dead."

No wonder he hates The Bastion.

"That's horrific. Lark has an AVM at the base of her neck. It sucks. I swear the doctors are wrong about her diagnosis. She's the sweetest kid. All she wants to do is play outside and talk your ear off. She'd die of happiness to ride horses. I've studied it for years. It looks exactly like yours."

"Hers must be different if she was born with it though. These are surgically implanted. What's her estimated death date?"

"January 23, 2057. It always shifts closer, never farther away."

He slows Obsidian and hops down before the huge horse fully stops. He lays his hand on my knee. "Don't worry. There will be a way to save her by then."

I shouldn't ask this. But I'm going to. "Do you have one? An estimated death date?"

"Never checked. No one will care anyways when I die, so I've never run a report to see it. When it's my time, they'll cremate me and throw me in some unceremonious heap of Irontrace ashes in the woods. I've always hoped I'll keel over when I'm in the middle of something super important. You know, really screw with The Bastion that way."

He winks at me.

He wants more time. Hot tears prick my eyes. *Just talk to him.*

I grab his shoulder in a desperate grasp. "Please don't joke like that."

"Hmm. Laugh and joke? Or be devastated about something I have no control over? I'll laugh while I can."

"Ivan, I'll care if you randomly keel over. I'd care a lot. Stay alive. Someone has to stick around and keep drones and Donegal away from me." I squeeze his shoulder even harder for that last sentence.

He laughs. "That's honestly the best reason I've stumbled across yet to stay alive."

I wish he'd stop smiling so much when he talks about the fine line he walks between life and death. "Let's talk about more depressing things. Where's your family?"

"Ha! You're a ray of sunshine, aren't you? I haven't heard from my parents since I came here on my ninth birthday. My teachers identified me as an asset early. I heard my dad tried to keep me around, but my mom saw too big of a paycheck coming."

"Do you have any brothers or sisters?" I ask, picturing his whole happy family out there, living on the money they earned from selling him off.

"I had a little sister. She died."

"I'm so sorry."

"It was a long time ago. The thing that makes me furious? I love my job. I get to help keep the world running. But I'd like to see the ocean and not die on the trip there."

"You need a vacation."

"I do. Badly."

The trees thin as we approach the edge of the forest, and a faint shimmer of The Bastion logo is painted on many of them. It seems grossly out of place in such a beautiful area.

When Ivan looks up at me, it's different. He's getting pale. Even though his mouth smiles, his eyes don't.

"What's wrong?" I pull Hero to a stop.

"Don't get down, your knee hurts. I'm fine."

He tries to urge Hero to keep walking, but I pull the reins back and climb down, putting my arm around his waist. "Let me help you," I say. His face is ashen.

"Ivan! What are you doing out here?" Dad's voice echoes.

"I had to make sure she got to you without any more drones coming for her," Ivan says. "I'll see you later, Story. I need to head back now. It was nice to meet you." He turns to Obsidian and puts his hand on the saddle horn, standing for a second with his back to us.

My blood turns to ice. For years, I've seen this crisis strike Lark's neck. Maligna Neohemangio Proliferoma. MNP.

MNP originates from the AVM. It creates thin, crimson red arterial tributaries. They fan out in merciless spirals from his Agora. Growing parallel to them, navy blue jagged lines of veins bulge outwards. Tentative at first, these vascular threads meet and thicken, turning deep purple, then pitch black. They pulse with sinister insistence across his neck and into the back of his shirt. He must be in agony.

"We're going to walk with you until you're better," Dad says. He grabs Ivan's wrist to check his pulse. "Pain, numbness, tingling?"

"I feel like a champ," Ivan mumbles. Each pulse must be sending a torrent of pain into his neck and shoulders. He's still holding onto the saddle, not moving to climb in it. His free hand touches Helga, then makes a circular motion. She shoots into the air, back the way we came.

"Ivan, I saw that distress call." I didn't know my dad knew how to ride horses, but he gets in Hero's saddle like an experienced rider. "Story, get on his horse. Ivan, get behind her and hold on. We need to get him back over the boundary right now."

"She's injured, I don't want to hurt her if I go down," Ivan says. His speech is slightly slurred.

"Come on, Ivan." I jump on Obsidian and tug Ivan's shirt to join me. He moves like he's stuck in mud as he hoists himself up behind me.

"I really am fine," Ivan says against my neck. "Mmmm. Smells like flowers in your hair."

"Hold me tight," I say. He leans heavily like a human cage over my shoulders. I cluck to Obsidian. We take off at a fast trot into the woods.

Helga soars back with another hawk. Then a third hawk, and a fourth hawk. Three Irontrace Squadron riders appear. We stop our horses, and they encircle us.

"He went outside the boundary," Dad tells them.

A rider grabs something from their saddle bag and races over. Ivan's grip feels a bit floppy, so I pull his arms around me like I'm wrapping up in a blanket.

"Don't fall. Grab onto me, I'm not made of glass." He adjusts his arms, but not enough to help me keep ahold of him. "Ivan, for real. Harder," I say, clinging to him. He locks his arms around my ribs. "There you go. We got it now, you won't fall. You're okay."

The Irontrace rider pops the cap off a syringe in his hand and injects something into Ivan's thigh through his pants.

"Thanks, Evans," Ivan says. He leans forward, resting his chin on my shoulder. "You're a really good rider. I mean it, come play with Sid and me anytime."

I'm unsure if he's in a fog of pain and won't remember telling me that, but I'd love to.

"Thanks. How are you?" I whisper, rubbing his forearm. I can only see part of his face, but his breaths come evenly against my neck. He lays his stubbly cheek against mine and sighs.

"Back in prison, so my Agora feels better," he mutters.

Dad hops off Hero and narrows his eyes at the Ivan cape I'm wearing. "Wrist, please?" Dad orders. Ivan sticks out his right arm. This is clearly not the first time they've been in this situation. "Your pulse has come down. Your color is better. Stop squeezing Story to death."

"Yessir," Ivan says, scooting backwards off Obsidian's rump.

"He's sir, too?" I ask Ivan quietly.

He reaches his right arm up and sweeps me down from Obsidian. "Only if I'm in a good mood."

"Are you really okay?"

"I am really okay. Thank you." He sounds better, but his dark, bright eyes I've become accustomed to are glassy now.

"What was in that shot?"

"A type of rapid acting systemic sclerotherapy injection. It identifies and kills off the new vessels grown by the MNP. A potent mix of ethanol, steroids, cytotoxic agents, and a touch of blood thinner to help it not clot so painfully when the MNP dies. We call it a neovascular repair med. I wonder if it will work on Lark."

"I'll ask Dad, thanks." It's very kind of him to think of helping Lark when he's miserable.

"If we hustle back over the boundary and use the neovascular repair med within a minute or two of crossing, look what it does." He turns slightly and swipes his hair up. Impressively, the MNP is already receding. In place of the tendrils is now a swollen, bruised area. "I'm pretty wiped out. I better go."

"Thank you for keeping me safe. Please go lay down and get some rest. So. Goodbye, I guess?"

"*Not* goodbye. See ya later, Doc." He gives a lingering smile, walking backwards to Obsidian. "I'll have Helga and Storm watch you for a couple of miles to make sure no drones come."

"It was an honor to help your daughter!" Evans calls to Dad.

"Thank you for doing this. I don't have all the details yet. I trust you'll get them to me as soon as possible from your debriefing," Dad says, looking at Ivan. Who knew my dad could order a debriefing from anyone, let alone a 'Sir' on a black ops team.

"I'll have it to you this evening," Ivan replies.

"Rest, first, Ivan. I know you were busy last night with work and Story. Again, thank you for saving her. We won't take up anymore of your time," Dad says, waving to them.

"Thank you," I say, waving goodbye.

The last twenty-four hours have changed my life. I have so many questions for Ivan. Maybe he can help me figure out how to fix Lark's AVM.

I look back over my shoulder. Ivan is watching. He and Obsidian look like a dark statue placed to intimidate trespassers. He raises one hand to wave at me and grins. I wave and smile.

As we emerge from the last few trees, Helga soars over the open area where Dad parked. I look back into the tree line. Ivan has been swallowed up by the forest.

7

We don't even make it to the car before Dad launches into a classic dad lecture. "Pause. Any questions you have, ask them now where it's safe to talk. Ivan said you're injured. Where? And *why in the world* are you in Ivan's pajamas? They have clothes there. Lots of them!"

Ivan's pajamas. What did the Irontrace I met think of my outfit? "My clothes had blood and pine sap on them. I sprained my knee. It's swollen but doing well. He gave me a few CombiCradles."

"Ah, I see he still has no respect for my inventory system." He sighs. "He got news that something was possibly going to happen while you were in the forest, but no specifics. We had to get you out of there. I felt awful leaving you, but I sent Ivan to get you. He's unstoppable."

"I was worried you'd be arrested. Does Lark have an Agora? What happened to Ivan?"

"Years ago, The Bastion made the decision to protect The Kernel at all costs. They hunt for children with the highest IQs and photographic memories. They teach them expert-level engineering of all types and make them learn to fight for their lives in tactical simulations. But at the end of the day, they're human. They realize their whole lives have been taken away. No family. No future. Just The Kernel."

This aligns with what Ivan said. "They're prisoners. Spectators looking into life, forbidden from having one."

"Some left their Helms. The Bastion was furious to lose time, energy, and millions of dollars invested into building them into 'perfect' guardians."

"What happened when he crossed the boundary?"

"The neural chip activates and clamps around their vertebral arteries. If they don't get back in the safe zone, the tendrils of the chip can sever it. Ivan was feeling the start of the squeeze. The farther outside the boundary they go, the faster they die."

"Can't they take out the Agora?" I ask.

"No. It's engineered to thrive once implanted."

"Ivan showed me his Agora. It looks like Lark's birthmark. Does she have an Agora?"

"Please don't be mad I didn't tell you." His voice is both full of anger and choking with heartbreak. "If a baby's parents both die while it's young, it becomes a ward of The Bastion. That's a death sentence. A handful of such unfortunate babies through the years have been used as test subjects for Agoras at the forest warden station. Lark was one of them. When her parents died right after she was born, she was designated to be used for medical testing. Her Agora is a failure since the boundary detection doesn't work. I took her in and out of the forest many times when she was a baby and never had an issue."

My world tilts a bit. I don't remember any ultrasound pictures on the fridge. No baby shower with a hugely pregnant Mom surrounded by friends and family. To my busy pre-teen brain, Lark was *there* one day, and I didn't question it.

Was I so wrapped up in school, Richelle's horses, and staying eyeballs deep in medical facts with Dad that I accepted a whole new person in my life with no clue how she got there?

Come to think of it, for a kid wrapped up in all things medical, if Mom had been pregnant, I'd have followed the weekly steps of fetal development with boundless excitement. I love babies and can't wait to have my own *someday*. How did I miss this? It's like being hit with a dump truck of my own stupidity.

"Her data points generated by the AI healthcare models at the Helm clinic deemed her incompatible with extended life. She was to be eliminated as a test subject at three weeks old. I convened an emergency meeting with The Bastion when I heard. Some video leaks happened around this time, not by me, to show the wardens doing medical testing on orphaned babies at that clinic in the forest. They shut that program down lightning fast."

"Ivan seemed shocked when I told him my sister has something that looks identical to his Agora."

"He doesn't know about her. The Bastion handed me care of Irontrace here fifteen years ago. The horrible wardens in the forest clinic have an ASTRA to implant Agoras."

Ivan's incredulous face makes sense now. Francois. Taken from his family to that sad, green building.

"I persuaded them to let me adopt and monitor her. I hope you can forgive me for not telling you."

"Lark is my sister. Nothing will ever change that." The Bastion is okay with science experiments on helpless babies? What else are they doing?

He grabs me in a hug. "She is."

I've learned so much but still need to know more. "What happened to Ivan's sister?"

"Some people refuse to stay in the boundary. Ivan was horrified when his sister was sent to The Helm too. He tried to help her make friends and adjust. She couldn't. She ran away after a few years when Ivan was seventeen. He found her outside the boundary and rushed her to the clinic, but the injuries to her brain were too extensive. After leaving the boundary, he had a stroke."

My brain is on overload.

"That's why I was so upset to see Ivan outside the boundary. Agoras have not been kind to Irontrace. Not sure if you noticed, but Ivan is one of their highest ranked, most experienced commanders. He's getting old at twenty-five. The Agoras keep rupturing. Not one of the Irontrace Squadron has reached thirty. They pulled me into Project Agora to try to keep them alive longer. Agoras are just too brutal, too deadly."

I can't imagine the pain Ivan has been through, both physical and mental. He still rides Obsidian, whistling in the forest.

"What is Ivan's estimated death date?" Hopefully, Dad's answer to my question won't ruin my day.

"April 30, 2051." He gives me a sideways glance. "I keep track of it since he's coming up on it. Don't get friendly with him. Making it to April is pretty optimistic for the way he treats himself."

Day ruined. Week ruined. Month ruined. He has a few days over eleven months left. I have to find a way to fix Lark and him.

"How do we get into the forest?" I ask.

He turns so fast it startles me. "*We* do not get into the forest. *I* do, on coordinated meeting times with the Irontrace. You are not going into the forest. No matter what. Promise me."

"I promise."

8

"Story!" Lark screeches, grabbing me after she flings my car door open. "You look awful! How did you get those cuts?"

"Missed you, baby sis." Knowing more about Lark's life as a person with an Agora makes me love her even more if that's possible. "I brought you some flowers! Let's go look at them."

"Welcome home. I made you a big breakfast. Let's get you comfy and you can tell us about it," Mom says, wrapping an arm on my shoulders to guide me inside.

"Look, Lark. Here's your flowers," I say, opening my book. A small note falls out. It has an email address on it written in small block letters.

I hope you're home and safe when you find this. In case of an emergency, here's a way to contact me. Our phone use is limited. -I

Ivan had taken such good care of me while I was with him, I'm not surprised he'd keep a line of contact open. I tuck it in the pocket of his shirt I'm still wearing until I can put it in my room later.

"Thanks! They're so pretty. Let's put them in wax paper," Lark says, tearing open a kitchen cabinet. "Tell us the whole story of what happened."

It's not a lie to say I was lost and ended up with the wardens. I can work with that to spin Lark a tale she'll love. I focus on Callie's details of flora and fauna, telling her about the animals on the sign at the forest gates. I leave Ivan out and Dad tells the part about coming to get me.

We talked, we laughed, Mom cooked great food, and the day flew past until we all went to our rooms for the night.

I got a quick shower and threw on some pink pajama shorts. Ivan's shirt hangs on my bathroom door. It's something of his, a connection to him. I pull it back on over a white tank top and lay in bed. The weight of the last two days settles on me. Lark and Ivan's Agoras have become so intertwined and tangled up with important internal structures that it may kill them, and soon.

"Gah, I can't sleep." My mind won't stop buzzing with Agora questions. I get up and walk through our short hallway to the craft room. It's a large sunroom, full of relics of projects worked on by my family throughout the years. Some are closer to being done than others, but it makes a timeline of our life, frozen in snapshots of unfinished works.

Mom has quilts she has stopped and started for friends and family members, an almost finished delicate white summer dress for me on a form, and intricate beaded jewelry with her flair for the colors of nature. Dad has decades of scientific models he's built, drawn, or painted in a variety of mediums.

I flip on the light by Dad's desk and open his anatomical charts. The massive pages easily fold over the back until I find the one for the circulatory system. Tracing the routes of blood vessels and their names consumes me.

"Odd night to study," Mom says from behind me.

"I can't shut my mind off." I lower the chart pages.

"Studying the circulatory system this time of night?" Dad asks.

"I've been thinking about Lark's birthmark. I need to choose a specialty. I'm going to be a vascular surgeon ASTRA trainer. I won't stop until I find a way to fix Lark."

Dad sits on his desk, listening. "Through the years she has seen ALICE models that are neurosurgeons, interventional radiologists, and hematologists. ASTRA hasn't been able to come up with a surgical robotic plan that can manage dissecting the blood vessels and nerves without leading to her death. Dedicate yourself. You may be the person who trains ASTRA to do it."

"I will. She's my baby sister and deserves a full, long life."

Mom wipes tears from her eyes and smiles. "We believe in you."

Dad walks over to his desk and unlocks a drawer. He pulls out a 3D model with blue blood vessels to show veins, red vessels to show arteries, and black to show Agora. The black is interwoven with silver pieces that I assume are the neural interface tendrils Ivan told me about.

"This is what Lark is dealing with," he says, handing it to me. "If you are going to take this on, then this is yours."

He's inviting me to join Project Agora. "Yes. I'm in."

9

The next morning, Dad called Mom and I on our way home from dropping Lark off at school. He told us to come to the hospital and meet some of his colleagues. He's never invited us to do something like that, but it's been a weird few days and not much surprises me now.

Mom and I can't function without a caffeine kickstart, so we stop at Hocking Hills Coffee Emporium. The cute gray café used to be near the Hocking Forest, but like a lot of other businesses in that area, The Bastion forced it to re-locate when they shut forest access down. Now it's on the edge of Lancaster.

It's still as perfectly charming as it used to be with multi-level porches and comfy outdoor furniture. I browse the gift shop items lining the area where we wait to order. The smell of the coffee wafting around makes the long line worth it. Mom and I quickly become absorbed in planning what to do this weekend, when a low shout distracts us.

"Mom! It's the lady from the TV!" The little girl in front of us points back and forth between the screen and I, yanking on her mom's arm for attention.

The large screen to our right has a reporter side-by-side with my picture from the med school class register. My jaw drops when I read the headline: *Freak storm hits university trip; 3 fatalities, 4 injured, 1 found by wardens.*

"Let's get to the hospital." Mom pulls me to the porch.

"What happened to everyone else when I got lost?" I barely croak out. I pictured the destroyed area Ivan had taken me back to. "Who died? I don't want any of them to have died, but I hope Isla, Seth, and Callie are okay."

Tears are streaming down my face by the time we get in the car. Mom grabs tissues from the middle console and throws them in my lap, steering with her other hand.

"Did you see or hear a storm?"

Thanks to Ivan, I did see some unusual weather. "I saw lightning. And strange clouds. I had gone up a hill and through a little ravine by myself, then got lost." I won't reveal Dad and Ivan's secrets, even to Mom. It's unbelievable that I was safe with Ivan while people were dying. The news app only has stories about the storm, not the names of the deceased.

When we pull into the hospital parking lot, several news crews are camped out by the main entrance, blocking the way. Dad's tall, slight figure stands by the entrance to the staff lot, waving.

He rushes to meet us, and his words tumble out abruptly. "Story, Amelia, come with me. A freak EF3 tornado hit the trail Story's class was on. It was a limited, *targeted* area."

"Dad, who died?"

"Professor Milner had taken the boys to the side of the trail to shelter, and a tree fell on them. They were crushed. Seth, Pete, and Mr. Milner died."

I can't hold back my sobs. They were so excited for this trip.

Dad continues, "I'm sorry, Story. It's good you weren't there. Isla is injured, but okay. She's been asking about you."

"I would have tried to save them."

"No one could have saved them. It was too fast," Dad says.

"How did a storm happen? We don't have natural disasters anymore." Mom's words rush out in disbelief.

"There was a software update, and it caused The Kernel to malfunction in the area for about a minute. That's been fixed," he says, sadly. "This is proof of how fortunate we are to have The Bastion. They work so hard to constantly keep us safe."

I jerk to glare at him. His eyes meet mine, then flick back and up to his left. A blinking security camera hangs from the ceiling. They're watching.

Before entering Isla's hospital room, I press my forehead on the door to take a few deep breaths. The guilt from surviving will haunt me forever. I knock on her door and hear a quiet "Come in."

"Story!" Her face lights up. She grabs me by the shoulders when I lean to hug her. "Where were you?"

I tell the same story from last night. I need to keep it consistent. As we talk, the monitor at the foot of her bed lights up and her ORION appears.

"Ms. Varshovski, do you need something?" it asks.

"No, I'm with a visitor. Goodbye."

The monitor flicks off. Her leg in a thin pink cast rests on top of the blanket. The right side of her face has bruises and scratches, so do both of her arms.

"Tell me what happened to you and the others. How are you? I was so worried for you!" I cross my arms to hide my shaking hands.

"I heard you say you were going to go up the hill to look at something. Then the sky got all dark and grayish green. Thunder boomed so hard, it rattled my teeth." She keeps stopping to catch her breath. "Seth, the meteorology nerd, was freaking out. Yelling to get low, hide. Lightning was hitting trees, cracking branches and splinters off."

I grab a box of tissues and put it in her lap. "How did you survive?"

"Callie heard a roaring sound and grabbed me. We ducked in a little ravine and held on to roots. The wind was whipping all around us. My leg was sticking out. A branch fell and broke it. I was sure we would die. Then the storm stopped. I lost my voice from screaming for you."

I shouldn't have left them. "I'm so sorry I wasn't there."

"You couldn't have known. Callie had a rescue whistle in her pack. The forest wardens came right away to save us. They said they had seen the storm pop up on the radar and they loaded up to find our group."

Sobs punctuate every couple of words. "We pulled Matt and Greg out. They're okay. Seth was smashed. Completelyyyyyyyyyyy!" She holds a pillow in front of her and screams into it. "I'll never, ever forget seeing that…”

The monitor flicks on again. “Ms. Varshovski, your vital signs show you’re in distress. Visiting time is over. Get some rest. I’ll check on you again soon,” the ORION says. The monitor remains on, with the outline of the nurse leering at us.

“Isla. I’m so sorry. Thank goodness the forest wardens got to you right away.” The vaguely shadowy figure on the monitor gives me a pit in my stomach. “I’ll leave. Be back later.” I give her a quick hug and get up to leave.

She looks towards the window, giving way to a fresh round of sobbing. The monitor shuts off as I step away.

Callie is in the room next door. On some level, it feels like I deserve to be punished for making it out safely. Part of that is listening to their stories and seeing exactly how stupid I am for leaving them. After a knock, I enter her room, ready to give myself another well-earned mental beating. She has a broken arm and a few bruises but gets to go home soon. A few more tears, and we part ways with a shaky hug.

Dad’s waiting for me in the hallway. My face is still red from crying with Isla and leftover sniffles occasionally shake my shoulders.

“How are they?” he asks.

“I shouldn’t have left them. I could’ve tried to save them.” I press the heels of my hands to my eyes, leaning against the wall. “Why did you and him leave them?”

He grimaces and covers his mouth, making a shushing noise. “Stop it! You don’t know what would have happened if you stayed,” he hisses from behind his hand. “Listen, I have some papers for you to go over about a job with a colleague. I need you to look at them right now. Focus. Turn to the job description on page three.”

Dad reaches out and pulls my right hand from my eyes. He shoves a stack of papers in it. The front paper says: *Lancaster Medical Hub Vascular Surgery Department* in an elegant font. He makes a circle in the air with his fingers to tell me to hurry.

I flip to page three, titled *Story’s Statement*. It’s a series of events with time estimates to account for my time with Ivan.

Went to document a new type of flower on a hill 0930

Got lost, scared, and ran 1030

Continued running in the wrong way since compass was lost and is a 'city girl'

Injured knee tripping in a hole while running, couldn't keep going 1100

Found an area with thick pine needles and stayed there

Warden Donegal found her 1400

Happy family reunion 05/25 0915

-Finalized by Commander IR

I drop my voice. "I.R.?"

Dad tilts his head to whisper, "You know who that is. They're everywhere."

He adds in a normal volume, "I pulled a few strings this morning. You have a video interview with Dr. Benedict, a legendary surgeon, in one hour. You'll be doing essential work, filling a gap for ASTRA." Dad motions for me to follow him. "Do what you need to do to present yourself as a peer, not a student. I brought something that may help." He reaches into his pocket and pulls out the model of Lark's birthmark.

I grasp it in my hand. "Thanks."

He weaves out through silently gliding ORION units. "Story, this is your shot to fix the things we talked about. Take it seriously. I'll meet you in my office in thirty minutes to help you get set up."

It's overwhelming, but I can handle this. Last night I spent about five hours studying and reviewing every anatomical structure from Agora images he gave me. Dad assures me that they're structured mostly the same. Find a solution for one, it will apply to all.

My phone rings with a call from Mom. "Hi, honey! The news wants to know if you can speak with them about your trip?"

The hits keep on coming today. "Yikes, no. I really don't want to do that."

"Oh, do it," she pleads.

"Did Dad tell you I have a job interview in an hour? I'll be mentally drained after that." I have no idea who knows my story or what they know, but if I stick with the statement from Ivan, at least it will match the official record.

"That's great, I'll call him to get the details. Wishing the best to you!" Mom's voice brims with hope. I don't know if anyone has ever given my parents real hope to fix Lark.

"Thanks, Mom. Bye."

I head to Dad's office early to compose myself. The best way for me to prepare for something like this is to focus on the end goal, not what's happening right now.

My mind drifts to what Lark's Agora-free life could be like. She can run, get mad, get sad, and not end up in the hospital. The tired hollows around her ice blue eyes will be filled in. When her light blonde hair swings in a ponytail as she plays, the Agora won't peek out. She can grow up into a beautiful young woman and work as...well, whatever she wants, she'll have options.

She can get her driver's license!

Lark, completely carefree, driving to the beach. She's always wanted independence. It seemed unbelievable to imagine her like this a few days ago.

Dad pops in and hands me a coffee, pulling me back to the rather depressing present where Lark and Ivan are on countdowns to their death. "Mom said you ran out of the coffee shop when a girl saw a news story about you. Figured you could use this."

"Thanks." I take the lid off and blow on it. It's full of cream and sugar, just the way I like it. I would happily drink black coffee with Ivan for the next eleven months if I could get back to The Helm.

"You'll get this job, don't worry." He picks up some papers from his desk and turns to sit in a little lounge connected to his office.

I pick up Lark's Agora model and name the vascular structures on it under my breath. My stack of scans and notes is available to review beside me if I panic and my mind goes blank.

Dad's computer screen flashes. I lean in, expecting to see Dr. Benedict. Instead, there's a message on the screen.

You lied to me, Story Ross. -I

I gasp. He's here too! But *what*? I didn't lie to him about anything…I stare at the computer, trying to figure out what he's talking about.

That cup of coffee in your hands is nearly white with cream. You told me black coffee was "great" and you loved it. All this time, I thought we were black coffee buddies. -I

I smile. But now I'm a bit paranoid. Are the Irontrace in every electronic device watching? Listening?

Is that an Agora? -I

I don't want to be midsentence if the doctor joins the meeting link, so I shake my head yes.

Lark's? -I

I shake my head again, nearly imperceptibly.

You were right yesterday. She has an Agora. Your dad tells me you're joining Project Agora. I'd like to help you if you want. I know you're already smart enough to figure it all out on your own. -I

I grin at the computer. I'm scared to move or talk and be distracted when Dr. B joins.

I know you are busy. I wanted to let you know I am rooting for you. I was disappointed you didn't email me. Waited all night for a notification to pop up. -I

I gasp. "You said…" A video pops up of a smiling Dr. Benedict. My loud protest at Ivan dies in an exaggerated choke.

Ahhhh! Ivan! Instead of making a solid first impression, I was caught with my mouth open, yelling at someone. Infuriating. I try to hide it with a cough.

"Dr. Ross, hello! I'm Dr. Warner Benedict." I estimate he's several years older than my dad. He looks like a person who has spent most of their life deep in books.

"Hello, nice to meet you Dr. Benedict." The next time I talk to Ivan, he'll get an earful about this.

"I hear you've been through a traumatic event recently. Sorry," he says, narrowing his eyes at the computer. I have almost gotten used to the scratches crisscrossing my face. They're probably shocking to see initially.

We go through the typical interview pleasantries, our backgrounds, why I want this job, and the ways my ideas for approaching fixing Lark are different than what has been tried. To avoid any questions about the black and silver areas in the Agora, I explain those represent particularly problematic areas.

"Dr. Ross, I'm impressed with your early career talents. If you will accept me as your grumpy old mentor, I would love to help you accelerate your career and figure out a way for ASTRA to fix your sister."

"Thank you. When can we get to work?"

Confetti pops up across the computer screen. It falls in rainbow bits, bouncing from corner to corner. The confetti is not from Dr. Benedict. Ivan has been here the whole time. My careful, composed smile curves into a grin. It's impossible to stay annoyed at him.

10

After we wrap up the interview, Dad bounces in. "You did it! Now the real work begins. Let's find Mom and tell her. Also, guess what? You, Callie, and Isla are going to be on the news. Your mom set the whole thing up."

"Dad, no, I look like I lost a battle with thirty feral cats." I hate being the center of attention. A one-on-one interaction like an interview is fine. The news? No way. My mom should know better.

"Come on, you got this! Plus, everyone loves a hero, it'll be good to get your story out there." He grabs my shoulders and shuffles me out. I look back at his screen. It has gone dark. I don't think I'll ever look at a computer the same again.

Callie, Isla, and I are taken into a long, narrow conference room with a table. Three chairs are arranged side by side, across from a single empty one. Small cameras and lights are set up along the table.

We sat for a few minutes, making small talk about the storm. Then a tall, blonde woman in a business suit rushes in, followed by several assistants who hurl themselves in chairs and stare at their phones.

"Hello! I am Julianna Deveraux from LNN. Don't be nervous." She smiles at each of us and shakes our hands. Her bored expression gives the impression she's only interested in the views this will generate.

Julianna begins the interview by speaking with Isla, who clearly looks the worst out of all of us. Isla was overcome with emotion a few times and had to sit and hold my hand to recover. I didn't get many questions aside from what the forest wardens were like. Being lost and found is not as exciting as a software malfunction nearly killing you with a tornado.

Towards what I hoped was the end of the interview, they announced that there will be a triple funeral for the victims on Saturday accompanied by a city-wide moment of silence. That's news to me, but I'm glad they are being honored in some way since they were effectively murdered.

"Ladies, I'm glad you survived the horrific glitch that killed your dear friends. Do you think the engineers behind it should be held responsible?" Julianna leans forward in her chair, a glint in her eye. It's not concern. It's anticipation that we'll say something out of line.

Callie speaks up right away. "We need people out there protecting us from things like this. Too many terrible events related to AI have happened lately. Why was no one from The Bastion there to stop it? I want answers, Bastion."

Julianna's face lights up. A person is placing blame on live television. "Wow, you obviously feel strongly about this. Do you think The Bastion owes the public an apology?"

It's a trap, Callie!

Julianna is perfectly composed. Every hair is in place, makeup meticulous, but something in her cold eyes reminds me of a shark. She's caught her favorite scent in the water. Controversy.

I think back to my time with Ivan and what he had taught me about The Bastion. This sounds like a dangerous conversation. Someone needs to speak up for Irontrace. How can I do so without betraying Ivan's confidence?

I clear my throat. "Sorry to interrupt, can I say something?"

"Yes! I'd love to hear your thoughts on recent AI malfunctions, *Dr. Ross.*" Down, girl. Julianna is really leaning on the detail that I'm a doctor.

There's no room for error. I sit tall, spine straight, hands folded in my lap, projecting the calm that I wish I felt. Fake it 'til you make it, right? Don't think about millions of people who may be watching. This isn't for them. I want to talk to Ivan. The fact that this may be the only thank you he ever gets in front of the world makes the words taste sweet.

"Acid rain, storms, disease breakouts are unheard of in our times. If those would have been allowed to continue to spiral out of control, even for moments longer, think how many more people would have been injured or killed. The number of lost lives would have continued piling up. I would like to say thank you to whoever implemented a swift, incredibly skilled response to those critical situations." Callie, Isla, and Julianna radiate fury so hot it makes my skin prickle. "More personally, I'd like to thank my rescuer. I was lost and you found me. You made sure I was warm, safe, and taken care of. The world appreciates you being our calm in chaos. I'll never forget you. From the bottom of my heart, thank you, Sir."

Not my brightest move, calling him out like that. He's dangerous to my good judgement. Julianna frowns. I'm not earning her any views by expressing gratitude.

"I don't agree, The Bastion owes all of us an apology. And! They should compensate the families affected by their faulty software," Callie spits out.

Oh, Callie. She usually exudes happiness.

Julianna keeps inciting Callie to expound on her points of how The Bastion has failed. Time blurs. One commercial break, then another, questions keep coming.

I don't say anything else. I won't even look at the camera, lest I betray how I feel. I hope Ivan and Dad won't be mad at me.

"Thank you for your time, ladies. Hope you feel better soon," Julianna says, finally releasing us after almost half an hour.

The second the camera shuts off I leap from my chair. A run would burn off my nervous energy, but that's not an option with my knee brace. I wonder if I can go to Richelle's later and get some fresh air.

When I get back to Dad's office, he and Mom are having a nice little chat over coffee.

"Mom, are you ready to get Lark for the day? I'd like to see if she wants to go to Richelle's," I say.

"I am. I heard you got a job!" Mom wraps me in a hug.

"I'm officially a surgeon here," I say. "The next four days will drag."

"We watched your interview. You did a wonderful job. I'm sure whoever rescued you was *riveted*," Dad says, eyebrows pulled down in a wrinkly line. "Callie sure talked a lot."

"Felt like it would never end," I say, rolling my eyes.

"Let's get Lark. She'll be happy to do something fun with you," Mom says, putting her purse over her shoulder and giving Dad a quick kiss.

"I'll walk you out. It's a circus in the parking lot with the press," Dad says, leading her into the hallway.

"I'll be right there. Let me grab something." I get the Agora model from Dad's desk drawer. My printed off reports and scans are out of order from discussing them with Dr. Benedict. While I stack them in their folders, Dad's monitor flashes on.

Your scratches didn't look bad on TV. You looked tough, and to be quite honest, incredibly beautiful. From the bottom of my heart, you're very welcome. -Sir

Ivan!!! Guess he was paying attention. Didn't expect him to pull out a card like calling me beautiful though.

"Are you always there?" I speak quietly, hiding a smile behind my hand. "Creeeeeepppp."

She speaks to me at last! I'm not following you. Your dad stays in contact with us off and on throughout the day for one reason or another. I work all day, most days. It's easy. I get bored. I bug your dad for fun. -I

"Bug me too, please."

I will. Sorry to hear about your friends. How are you holding up? -I

I shake my head and shrug. "It's been a long few days."

I bet. You need to get some rest. -I

"You didn't have to take me over the boundary. Are you feeling better?"

I am, thanks. The neovascular repair meds won't work on Lark. Sorry. I checked with your dad and then did my own research. No offense to him, ha! -I

"Thank you. That means a lot. Your note said your email was for emergencies." I glance beside me to make sure my parents aren't coming back in. "I would think that running The Kernel would be a job that required brain power and focus, not a boring, routine job you'd want to chitchat your way through."

You letting me know you got home safe is an <u>emergency.</u> I didn't sleep a wink last night waiting to hear from you.

Working on The Kernel isn't hard. Just tedious. -I

He may be miles away, but he makes things feel lighter. "Now you're the faker. Get some sleep tonight." I wave bye to him and jog out.

I wouldn't last a week in the Irontrace Squadron. It's a cage hidden behind the façade of honor. No wonder they cling to conversations outside the boundary. I'm sure it's a way to remember there's an entire world outside, full of life and people.

~~~

Lark is pale but smiling when we pick her up from school. She chatters about her day for the whole drive to Richelle's family farm. Their breathtaking property stretches out until it touches the forest behind it. There's a view of sparkling Lancaster Cove on the opposite side.

Richelle sprints over to greet us by the barn's parking area. Her long blond hair swirls behind her until she crashes into me. "You made it out of the storm! How are you?" She pulls back to stare at me; green eyes clouded with worry.

"Hey! We're good. I sprained my knee, but it's getting better," I say, looking around in the large barn.

"So glad you weren't killed! Okay, you and the busted knee should take Mom's horse. She's eighteen years old and her fastest pace is a slow walk." She leads me to a stall with a beautiful chestnut horse. I take the sweet old mare out and fall into the familiar routine of grooming. Stress fades away with each pass of the brush.

"Lark, come here. Mikey, my old pony, is gonna pull your cart today. He's such a good boy. He'll keep you safe," Richelle says, leading Lark to a little black and white pony. "Any pain today, Lark?"

"Nope," Lark replies, and I smile.
~~~

Mikey is like other animals with Lark. After a minute of her entering his stall, you can tell they are friends for life. Little birds in the barn have landed around Lark, and she tosses them scrap grain pieces from Mikey's food bucket.

"How long do you usually have between pain episodes now?" Richelle asks Lark.

"I don't know. Story?" Lark looks at me to answer. I'm not sure how much Lark talks about it to people outside of home and her teachers.

"Maybe every few months." Today is supposed to be fun. I make a silly face at Lark, prompting a laugh from her, and change the subject. "Richelle, how many horses do you have in here?"

"It varies. We rent them out to people. Our maximum is thirty-six. Right now, we have nineteen."

"This barn seems much bigger than I remember. You must have hours of work when there's thirty-six."

"I want out of here so bad. I can't wait to move. Dad keeps trying these crazy new business schemes, so we won't have to sell any more land. He's looking into rehabilitating animals or something now." She points with the brush to some stalls that are under construction.

"Wow, you'll see some cool stuff with a rehab."

Richelle and I finish tacking our horses and get Mikey hooked up to Lark's little cart. She would love to ride, but it's too dangerous for her.

Riding in the north field, I realize how close we are to the Hocking Forest. The horse barn is only a couple of miles from the edge of the tree line. Dad goes into the forest from the other side. He must want to keep Richelle's family entirely unaware of his work there.

Lark keeps us laughing with silly tales from school today.

"My day wasn't as entertaining as Lark's, but I was on TV," I tell them.

"Amazing! A job in the city and on TV? Tell me everything. I'm so jealous!" Richelle gushes. That's one thing I've always loved about her. She never conceals how she feels about anything. "I live right by Hocking Forest, and I have never gone in. Dad's always like 'you go in there, those guards will make sure you don't come out.' What's it like?"

"Peaceful, but loud. It seems alive. The terrain is always changing. You'll come on groups of trees in thickets you can't squeeze through. That's how I got all of these." I point to my arms and face.

"Why were you trying to squeeze through a thicket?"

"I was desperate, scared, worried I'd be in trouble because I got lost."

"Glad you didn't get in trouble," Lark says, twisting her lips into a mock evil grin. "You'd be a criminal now!"

"Me too! There were streams and several waterfalls." I stay silent about my favorite waterfall that houses The Helm.

"A big bird!" Lark squeals, pointing up.

"I hope the horses don't get spooked," I say in a tight voice, clenching the reins so hard my knuckles turn white. Aside from Helga and Storm, my shoulders tense now when I see birds.

The hawk swoops down, close to us. I hold my breath. A flash of metal near the top of its head catches the sun as it flies back up.

Not again.

Mikey plods along as Lark dances in her cart seat and makes bird calls. Normally animals love her, but the hawk stays out of sight. That doesn't make me feel better. I don't know if fake bird drones come to kid's bird call antics.

"Sorry, girly, it hasn't even been half an hour, and I need to rest my knee. Can we head back in?" I ask, turning my horse.

"Sure," Richelle says, turning her horse to follow. "I don't want your knee to get worse."

I message Mom that we're riding back so she can wrap up her coffee time with my Aunt Anna.

We almost made it to the barn when two hawks fly over us at a blistering pace.

"It's back!" Lark yells.

They crash in a tangle and flail to the ground. I think of Helga and Storm. How far outside the boundary do they go?

"Oh, that's so sad. That will draw predators. I'll have Dad go pick that up later," Richelle says.

11

The whole drive home, Mom grips the wheel like she's hanging on for dear life, barely speaking to Lark and I. Once we pull into the driveway she says, "Lark, Dad's waiting for you in the backyard to play."

"Yes! Dad's home!" Lark throws her car door open and runs to the house.

Dad's home?

Mom turns towards me, putting her hand on my arm. "I have sad news. Callie was on her way home from the hospital and got in a car crash. She was killed after colliding with a truck."

The Bastion! Ivan was right. A chill goes down my spine. I want to talk to Ivan about it, but I can't leave Mom here crying.

Sometimes, when I am stressed, I can't cry. My brain goes into emergency mode, and I feel, well, nothing. I hug Mom for a minute, hoping this will compensate for my dry eyes. "Mom. It's...I'm shocked. I need some time alone."

"You've been through so much this week. Go. Rest. Talk to a friend. That could help you process it all." She wipes her tears and takes deep breaths.

I hop out and jog into the house, rushing upstairs. Last night I put Ivan's note with his email address in my closet in a box of treasures. I fish it out and type.

Hey! I have questions.

Is this secure?

Are you actually waiting for my email notifications?

Callie died.

-Story

I hit send and get up to grab stuff for my shower. Not even thirty seconds later, the laptop screen flashes and a chat pops up.

Number one. Yes, I built this messaging system.

Number two. Absolutely.

Number three. I heard, I'm so sorry. -Your humble servant, I

"Can you hear me? Can you talk to me? There's no way to reply to your messages."

I can see you on my screen and hear you in my earbuds. No way to talk out loud to answer you at this moment. Sorry. -I

I imagine him sitting in some dark room, surrounded by a sea of computers. "I know it's you. You don't have to sign every message," I say, unable to stop smiling.

Just for that, I'll never stop. Ever. -I

"Was Callie killed by The Bastion?"

You can't say things like that outside The Helm! That's a dangerous question. You were wise in the way you spoke during the interview. I am proud of you. -I

What could be listening? Ivan wouldn't allow The Bastion to monitor our conversations. My phone! I hold it up to him. I hope he can see me if I don't say anything. I silently mouth, "This?"

Yes, those things get people in a lot of trouble. -I

I hold up a finger, asking him to wait. Running downstairs, I put my phone on the kitchen counter then run back up to my room. His chat is still there.

"Can I talk now? My phone is downstairs."

Sure. I set up a security bubble on your house for us to talk for a little while. You're safe to say what you need. -I

Even though he said it's safe, I speak in a hushed tone. "Something happened, and I don't know if it's an emergency. I went horseback riding between my cousin's farm and the forest today. A Helston's hawk swooped down near us. I'm sure it was a drone. I told Lark to make bird sounds at it, but it didn't come back when she did. Animals usually love her. When we were almost back to the barn, we saw two hawks in the sky close to the forest. One attacked the other hawk. Richelle said her dad is going to pick up the dead hawk later, so it won't draw predators. Is he going to get a drone instead of a hawk and flip out?"

Gah, that was way too much information. Maybe he doesn't care. "Sorry. That was a lot."

Thanks for letting me know. Can you please give me a few minutes? I just got out of tactical training, and I need to get situated. -I

"Of course. I actually need to do something, but I'm not leaving you. Can I come back in like twenty minutes?" Mom will come check on me soon if I don't get my shower and go help her make dinner.

Yep. -I

I leave my desk to lock my door, so Lark and Mom can't come in and see my laptop. I hurry into my bathroom for a shower then change into pajamas.

I plop in the chair, waiting to hear from him. I prop my knee on the desk in front of me to apply more antibiotic ointment and put a new CombiCradle on. Sitting at my desk, I go through my hair routine of brushing it, adding oil to tame my curls, and braiding it. Still no new messages from Ivan.

"Are you there?" It's disorienting not being able to see or hear him.

I am. Nice shirt! -I

I laugh, looking at his shirt I'm wearing with my pajama shorts and say, "Oh, I'm hoping to keep this as an Ivan souvenir. Sorry. I can send it back with Dad this weekend if you want."

No! It's yours now. Enjoy. I'll have more information for you on the hawk soon. Please, do not ride or go over there until you talk to me again. The drone you saw was taken out by an Irontrace hawk out on perimeter patrol. I'll let you know when I've made sure you are not in any danger.

This is the type of info that can keep you and others safe. Your knee looks a bit better.

Can I see your shoulder since I'm the happy guardian of your secret injuries? -I

I snort and turn, pulling up the back of my shirt to show him the clear bandage is still there.

Looks great. Rest up. You've got a lot of work to do Monday. -I

"I will. Don't do anything dangerous. Please."

Later! -I

Well, that's not encouraging. How many times has he shrugged off the rules of the boundary? "Ivan...I don't know your last name, I was serious. Stay safe."

It's Rhys. I know you were. -I

"Talk to you later, Ivan Rhys." I smile and shut my laptop.

Dad got called back to the hospital. Mom, Lark, and I had an uneventful dinner. After cleaning up, we headed to the craft room. I need to work on my Agora studies, but I want to have family time before my job starts. I choose white, blue, red, black, and silver embroidery threads and weave them together intricately.

It's remarkable how well human hands can manipulate things. That's the biggest limitation in robotic surgical approaches for the deadly AVMs that lurk within Agoras.

Human hands have unique touch receptors built in. We can make decisions based on what we see and feel at that exact second. The robotic tools are so rigid they can damage delicate structures. The silver neural interface parts of the Agora require gentle force to remove, but all the other structures require controlled pressure, at risk of death for your patients.

"Story? You have woven and unwoven that bracelet like a hundred times. You ever finishing it?" Lark asks, snatching it.

"I'm thinking about how happy I am right now to be here with you and Mom. Next week, I'll be a lot busier." Is this my last peaceful evening to linger in the messy, cozy craft room with her and Mom?

A devastatingly sad thought strikes me. My family and I use these evening chats to help us unwind and process events of the day. I can't imagine not having someone to make sure I am okay, to let me know that it matters to them if I had a good day, and help me cope with the rough spots. I should check in on Ivan more often.

"Hey, girls! I am going to heat my dinner, and I'll eat up in there," Dad yells from downstairs.

Mom looks at me, several dress pins in her mouth and points to the stairs. Lark has a hot glue gun, attaching seashells around the edges of a picture frame and doesn't see Mom.

I jump up. "I'll go help him."

I make my way down the stairs, glancing back up to make sure Lark didn't follow. While Dad fills me in on his day, I grab a notebook from the kitchen junk drawer and write what happened at Richelle's in a fast scribble. I hesitate before adding I had let Ivan know.

He cuts out a sharp breath. *You should _not_ be talking to Ivan!*

Really? Me talking to Ivan is what he's mad about. I grab the pen from him to jot my reply. *I'll email him, or I'll find my way in the forest to talk to him. I'm twenty-two years old. I'm NOT going to stop talking to Ivan.*

He circles *email* then taps it several times before tossing the pen down and turning in a huff.

"You need to focus entirely on studying for Monday. I am heading up to sit with your mom and Lark."

"See you tomorrow." I grab my water and ice pack and rush upstairs.

My room is such a mess. I never let it get like this. Several small stacks of items are accumulating. I put my hands on my hips and kick at a small pile of laundry by my bed before throwing it in the hamper. I haven't gotten much sleep since before the trip and I'm on edge.

"Forget cleaning tonight." I collapse onto my bed. Something pokes me from under my pillow. I reach under it and pull out my favorite book. I'll read for a bit before I message Ivan. The familiar pages slowly pull me into their world until I drift to sleep.

12

I wake to the early morning light streaming in my window. Before my eyes fully open, a pang of guilt hits. *I didn't message Ivan!*

What can I say that won't seem creepy? I'll keep it simple. Friendly.

Good morning, Ivan Rhys! I meant to send you a message last night. But I took your wise advice and got some rest instead. Just wanted to say hello and that I hope you're doing well. Talk to you later! -Story

He'll probably think I'm a weirdo. Oh well, it's sent now. I snap my laptop shut and jump up to get ready for the day. Dad has been pushing me to study a lot to prepare for my new job, so I'll spend my day in the craft room with his charts and models.

Mom and I got Lark ready for school and dropped her off.

As we drive out of the school lot, Mom asks, "I know you're busy prepping for your big job, but can we go to Lancaster Cove for a bit of mother-daughter time? We won't walk far."

"That would be great, let's do it."

It's a beautiful morning. The sun shines over the water, casting sparkles like diamonds. Mom and I wander down the shortest path. Sandpiper birds dart into the receding wave line, gulls fly over the sandy shore, pelicans soar low across the water. The sights and sounds transport me to hundreds of other perfect mornings like this. Filling my pockets with shells that washed up in the high tide line overnight breathes peace into me that's been missing all week.

"Look!" Mom points to a venomous mass of tentacles from a calico-moon jellyfish wrapped around a small sandpiper. "Can we save it?"

The young bird lacks adult feathers. It lies tangled in the long, thin tentacles of a jellyfish washed up on shore. It's got wild eyes and is making awful squeaking noises. *Poor baby.* When a calico-moon jelly touches prey, it causes debilitating pain until the animal gives up and drowns.

"We gotta help it, Mom." I grab a couple pencil-sized pieces of driftwood and use them to untangle the bird. It stops making any noise but keeps its wide eyes trained on me like *I'm* the problem. "I didn't do this, bird!"

The driftwood isn't going to cut it. I use a large clam shell from my pocket to scoop up the bird and run to the water. When a wave hits my hands, the water swirls the tentacles, slowly untangling the bird. "It's working, finally!"

Mom runs out to me and before I can stop her, picks up the bird, pulling the last strands of tentacles from it. "Mom, no! Your hands!" I gasp, using my stick and shell to keep the loose tentacles from swishing back on to her.

"We did it!" She holds the little wet bird, smiling triumphantly. I would not be grinning like that if my hands were crisscrossed with welts like hers.

"Let's get you cleaned up. Hold your hands underwater for a minute, I'll be right back." I run to lay the bird in a lush grass hiding spot.

"Can you drive us home?" Mom calls from the water.

"Are you sure you don't need to go to the hospital?"

"I'll be okay, we've got sting cream at home."

I rush Mom to the car. A Helston's hawk swoops down at us.

I do not have time for this! I jump in the driver's seat, slam my door, and speed out of the parking lot. I refuse to keep looking for the hawk. Maybe it was a fluke. *Maybe it wasn't.*

"Honey, my hands are fine. Please don't drive like this. It's scary."

"Sorry Mom, my knee still hurts, makes me drive funny I guess." My heart hammers against my ribs as I merge onto the road to get to the city. I'm safe, we'll be home soon.

"I'm glad we saved that bird. I hope it lives," she says, inspecting the welts on her hands.

We are one of the only cars on the road. It's hard not to crash between scanning the sky for birds and keeping an eye on Mom. Forget trying to find a bird. Out my window a hawk flies parallel to us. I stare at it, wondering if the sun will catch any flashes of metal on its head. The tires make a terrible vibration when I hit the rumble strip then overcorrect the wheel.

"Honey!" Mom yells.

"Sorry, there's a Helston's hawk over there. Can you see it?" I ask her, sneaking peeks at it.

"Oh wow, that's pretty. Haven't seen one of those in years." She glances at the hawk, then back to her hands.

The irony of her not seeing a hawk for years and me feeling stalked by them lately makes me snort with panicked laughter. I look one more time, squinting to see if it's a real hawk. The flash of metal on its head hits the sun. It's a drone too.

"Do you need me to drive?"

"No, I'm okay." One mile left until the city. We're the only car on the road. I wish there was some traffic around. I look for the hawk, but all I see is blue sky with stacked white clouds.

Two black trucks appear on the opposite side of the road. Thank goodness, we're not alone. Right after they pass us, they do a U-turn and follow us. I speed up. So do they. The leading truck is too close, and I can't see its license plate in my rearview mirror.

This seems worse! I'd rather be alone again.

"Why is everyone driving like maniacs today?" Mom asks, whipping her head to look at them. "Do you see those trucks?"

"Yes. I have been looking at your hands. You need to go to the hospital. Dad will be happy to help you." There's no way I'm leading the trucks straight to our house.

The truck rides my back bumper into the city. I switch lanes with no blinker and speed up. It stays with me. "Call Dad," I say to my phone.

He answers after several rings. "Story, how is studying?"

"Don't be mad. Mom and I went to the beach for a few minutes. Her hands got stung by a jellyfish saving a baby shore bird. We'll be at the hospital in a few minutes."

"No! You were supposed to focus today," he snaps.

"It gets worse. There are trucks behind us driving weird. It's freaking me out. I don't want to go home. Can you meet us at the entrance and help Mom?"

He groans. "I'm not there right now. I had to go to another clinic for the day." He speaks fast, in a clipped tone. "I'm putting you on speakerphone. Repeat what you told me, slowly."

I do. Shuffling breaks out before Dad replies, "What kind of bird did Mom save?"

"A sandpiper?"

"Did you see any other birds today?" Dad asks.

"Yes! There's a Helston's hawk with a weird head stalking me right now." Trucks are getting closer. "Also." My voice is way too squeaky, I gotta dial that in. "Big trucks were coming at us, southbound. We're going northbound. They did a U-turn. The leading truck got on my bumper and is driving way too close. I'm not going home."

More voices and commotion on his end.

"Drop your mom off at the entrance to the hospital. I called my assistant, Benjamin. He'll meet her at the door. Make sure she goes with him. Stay on the phone."

"Okay," I say, weaving through the city traffic. Only about a minute and a half to the hospital. The trucks are still following us, but not as closely. I turn onto the road leading to the hospital and see there are four trucks now.

"Honey, how's your day? These trucks are bizarre," Mom tells Dad.

"It's good. What happened at the beach? Story should have been home today to study," he says sharply.

Mom ignores his grumpiness. "We found a little bird tangled in jelly tentacles. Story's much smarter than me. She wouldn't touch it with her hands. She tried driftwood pieces and shells to help it, but I got impatient and grabbed it."

"I hope your hands aren't too bad."

"No, they look worse than they feel. I see Benjamin waiting. See you later, honey!" Mom says as I pull to the curb. I stare at the trucks as they go off into a different part of the parking lot. "Bye, Story. I'll wait for you in Dad's office."

"I'll be up soon." I hug her so hard she gasps before Benjamin helps her out of the car.

"Head out of the hospital lot please," Dad says.

I drive out from under the hospital car port to the parking lot exit. The trucks stay parked. Had I made a mistake, and they were heading the same way I was? Was Mom some sort of target?

"Story, are you okay?" Ivan asks.

Ivan! Of course, Dad's there with them in the forest. I immediately feel a lot better about my situation.

"Hey, Ivan. Yes, I'm good. Where do you guys want me to go?" I turn on to the main road.

"Head back to the beach," Ivan answers. Angry grumbles alert me that a disagreement has started on Dad's side of the phone. "One sec."

They go silent but stay connected. In my mirrors, I see the trucks making their way through the other traffic.

I have to decide on the route to take. "The trucks are following me again. Hello?"

They unmute. Harsh voices are still murmuring around Ivan.

"We're here. Watching you on satellite imagery. You're *not* in danger," Ivan responds.

I keep glancing in my mirror. Why am I being followed? Is someone mad at me? As I make the curve for the highway entrance ramp, the line of sleek black trucks follows me. Their windows are so darkly tinted that I can't see who is driving.

"Why did you and Mom go to the beach? You need to rest your knee and study," Dad says.

"She asked for mother-daughter time. It was nice until the jellyfish."

"Take the next exit please," Ivan tells me. He's enunciating weird.

"I feel safer with people and other cars around. That way to the beach is desolate. Don't they say safety in numbers or something?"

"Safety in numbers doesn't apply when you're working with us. You're safe," Ivan says. "Don't miss your turn."

They're all hanging out in the forest while I'm by myself, an open target. I hesitate, waiting until the last second to turn. I'm not even sure if I'll do it. "Might as well," I whisper, taking the exit towards the lower beach road. I look in my mirror and the trucks follow.

"Wait until the road is straight and then floor it," Ivan mumbles.

The beach access road curves south. This takes me back to where we had been this morning. In about three miles, this road will sweep back up to connect with the main beach road.

"Go faster," Dad says.

Down on the straight road, I'm totally alone. This is fun. Now no one will see me crushed to death by these trucks except for Dad and The Irontrace. The first truck is on the straight stretch now too and accelerating to catch up to me. I wonder if this is how Callie spent the last few minutes of her life.

In my mirror, I see the fourth truck on the last curve before the flat, straight road I'm on. The massive truck disappears into a fireball. Black shrapnel blows meters into the sky. The remaining trucks fan out in my rear-view mirror, swerving to avoid debris.

"Was that supposed to happen?" I gasp.

"Keep going, Story. I did that," Ivan says. If he can pinpoint and blow up a truck that's chasing me from miles away in a forest, he can do anything.

Another explosion. The third truck goes up in a ball of fire. Then the second. There is only one truck left, and it's not far behind me.

"If that last one blows, is it going to take me with it?"

"Nah, you're safe," Ivan says. His voice is so rough it distracts me from the murder truck still chasing me. The final truck slams to a stop, putting some distance between us. Then it blows up too. I'm far enough away that no shrapnel comes near my car. "Drive back to the main road.

Stay on the phone. Get your mom. Go home. I'll be watching."

"What if there's another hawk up there?" I picture myself going through this process again, and it makes me grip the wheel, desperate for control.

"There won't be," Ivan says.

"Were there people in those trucks?" I fear his answer. If he says yes, no matter who they are, I have to go check on them.

"No. I confirmed they were unmanned vehicles," Ivan says. Phew! "I'm going to mute for now."

I catch myself checking my mirrors. Why? That's futile, he's watching out for me. He'll notice long before I would if there's a new problem.

I wonder how often Dad goes to the forest. As a kid on school breaks, it felt like we would go for days without seeing him during daylight hours. Sometimes, he'd sneak into my room and wake me up to say, "I needed to tell you good night, and I love you." He'd look like the weight of the world was on his shoulders.

"Story, stay on the phone with us." Ivan snaps me out of my thoughts as I pull into the hospital lot.

"Okay." I tuck my phone in the front pocket of my purse.

Mom sits in a cushy chair in the room connected to Dad's office, watching something on her phone. "Hey! Look, Benjamin fixed me up. Parking took you a long time. I found a recipe we should try for dinner. It's a new pasta dish."

"I'll make whatever you want. Sorry that took so long." I watch closely to see if my voice betrays I had been on a terrifying adventure. She's focused on her phone and doesn't even look at me. "My knee hurts from our walk today. I'm sure your hands hurt. Are you cool if we head home?"

"Of course, let's go."

Dad's computer monitor flicks on.

Message me tonight, please. Also, you cook? -I

I give him a tight smile.

You're safe. I swear. -I

I mouth "Thanks." His message disappears.

The drive home was uneventful. I've never seen the roads so empty. I helped Mom inside then told her I needed to go back to the car to get our purses and seashells.

"Hey, Dad. We're home," I say.

"He's busy," Ivan replies. "It's just me and you. Your good morning message was the highlight of my day. Thank you." His speech is thick.

He's injured. "Why aren't you moving your mouth correctly?"

"We put satellite camouflage around your house and cars. No one can listen to you now in those areas."

"Ivan. Please tell me what's wrong."

"Stay home, please. Your dad will bring Lark home from school."

"You're freaking me out!" I blurt, then feel bad. *He doesn't owe me any explanations.* "Your voice sounds weird. Is it your Agora?"

"I promise my Agora's fine." He blows a deep sigh. "I need to go. Don't play with anymore jellyfish today."

"Can't promise that. Thanks for saving me again. I'll message you."

"Looking forward to it. Bye."

Jellyfish tentacles are a disaster to unravel. Agoras are a knotted mess. Maybe I do need to play with jellyfish to solve the mystery of Agoras.

13

"Your dad will be sad if you don't study," Mom says from the couch while I make lunch.

"I will. The beach was surprisingly helpful. That bird reminded me of Lark's healthy blood vessels and nerves. They're like the fragile bird. The tentacles of her birthmark are wrapped around it in a tangled, difficult web that robots can't fix yet. It was a great visual seeing my problem in a different context."

"Driftwood sticks and surgery robots aren't your answer then. Move on."

"What do you mean?"

"Before The Bastion took control of healthcare, human surgeons did amazing things in operating rooms. They'd operate on blood vessels and nerves all throughout the body, even microscopic ones. Surgeries were done on tiny babies still in their mother's wombs. Organs were transplanted. The list goes on and on. Yes, human surgeons would make mistakes sometimes. But they were innovative. They could adapt."

Is my mom suggesting humans do surgeries again? That hasn't been done in decades. If Ivan hadn't put some sort of camouflage on our house, I'd be scared for her to speak like this.

"Your dad says it all the time. The ASTRA models do what you surgeons train them to do. But they aren't human. You can't program a robot to have the ability to reason that we do. They don't have our senses to be able to manage surgical complications. It's why they've given up on Lark. The sticks today got you so far with untangling the bird. Some good old-fashioned human touch was the trick." She holds up her bandaged hands.

"Mom, are you saying humans should work with robots in surgery again?" How would that even work?

"No. I'm suggesting you figure out a way to do the surgery yourself. If you use a robot to help you, a robot can help *you*. But it shouldn't be the primary surgeon."

According to Ivan, that will lead me straight to execution. But can I save Lark? Can I add fifty years to Ivan's life? It's at least worth discussing.

"So, you're unwilling to even hypothesize a way to save Lark?" Her eyes have a cold glint. The love of a mother knows no bounds, I guess.

"I...well, I just mean there must be a way to save her that won't cause trouble. Plus, I haven't operated as primary on a human." I imagine myself being the one to wield a scalpel over the back of Lark's neck. What would it be like to dissect Ivan's blood vessels?

Never. No way. I joined this project as a researcher. A trainer. Not the person to slice through human tissue myself. What if I slip? What if I freeze? What if I kill someone?

"Oh, please. You've done surgeries in labs for years on simulators as a student to figure out what the robots need to do. See yourself doing a much more intricate version. Start thinking about it right now. Do you want to sit and practice untangling things this afternoon while we are laid up? Get some fishing lines and thread from the craft room. Grab some ASTRA suture kits from your dad's desk, and my lighted magnifier I sew with."

For hours, Mom sat with her bandaged hands and coached me through entangling threads in the tight fishing line. Then she worked with me on staying calm, following one thread at a time so I didn't get overwhelmed.

It was a wonderful afternoon. The kind that burns into your memory, slightly blurry at the edges, but bright and clear where it matters.

Today I learned my mom is wicked smart. I never realized that before. It's the kind of smart that gives me the impression she's been actively hiding it for my entire life. She's thinking up ways to get this done that would've never occurred to me. Maybe she's put years of thinking into this and is thrilled to have a buddy to chat about it with?

"Lark has wanted to have a house full of her own babies since she was tiny. Do you remember her carrying at least one baby doll everywhere we went?" A smile bends the edges of her lips. "Story, this could make her dreams possible. I know her medical condition is rare, but someone, somewhere else in the world will benefit from this too. Don't you want to save them all?"

She blinks, waiting on my response. I know people who could benefit from this. What if they trust me and die? "I do want to save them."

"Then this is the only way. Be brave. Work smart. Keep your mouth shut about it. Become a real surgeon."

Pretty sure it's not going to be as simple as she thinks. I agree that it's at least worth a try. I've known for years I'd do anything to save Lark. Actions speak louder than words. I guess it's time to show how far I'm willing to go for her.

"Appreciate your help today, Mom. Thanks for helping me think about a new approach. I'm out of tangles. Gotta get this cleaned up."

Dad and Lark breezed in a few minutes later. He made tea to sit with Mom. Lark and I made Mom's requested pasta dish for dinner while we talked. I avoided the details of Ivan blowing trucks up for me this morning but told her the dramatic story from the beach. We made Mom a *Get Well Soon* card with some of the flowers from my trip.

The burnt broccoli alfredo pasta bake was eaten, the beautiful flowery card was given to an appreciative Mom, and the house is settled in for the night. The conversation with Mom today sparked new plans. I sat for a long time making sketches and notes while they were fresh in my mind.

Time to message Ivan! He's seen me scratched, muddy, sweaty, and terrified. I need to show him I'm not always a mess. I took a few minutes to do my hair and makeup. What should I say? I stare at my unopened laptop, thinking. Maybe lead with something witty about jellyfish? I don't have any jellyfish jokes. I don't know anything remotely witty about jellyfish.

He's funny. I'll just say 'hi' and follow his lead.

Someone knocks on my door. I jump up to answer it, complaining, "Ah, no! It's Ivan time. He gets all my spare minutes while he's alive."

My dad waves when I open my door. "Hey, your mom told me you had a good afternoon."

"Come in. She and I had a good time. Her hands seem okay."

"Sorry the morning spoiled your study plans. What did you do this afternoon?" he asks, sitting on my bed.

"I'm working on diagrams of what we talked about today. I know the general idea of what surgical plans they've tried to come up with for Lark. I'd like to see surgical simulations in action. Then learn how I can improve on the tools they use. Or see how they could assist me while I operate as the primary surgeon."

He puffs out a dry laugh. "You? Primary surgeon? No. The Bastion will never relinquish control. We train ASTRA. They do the work. Honestly, it has improved survival rates and surgical outcomes."

"I agree, but on a case-by-case basis. You've spoken to The Bastion to appeal things you disagree with. You swayed them in the past. I'm going to make them let me fix Lark. How?"

"Research." He sighs and shrugs. "You must have case studies to present. Make it seem profitable. How could your approach either save them money, or make them money? It's horrifying. But honestly, it comes down to that."

I snap, "You'd think saving lives, or even one life would be more important than money."

"Well, it's not. Also, consider the ethical concerns from this. That alone may keep you tied up with the AJA models for years. If you operate on a minor with experimental surgery, that'll get you in hot water. Especially a kid you're related to."

"True. However, if I prove it's possible, I can train another surgeon or team to do it once it's approved by The Bastion."

"Now that's how a surgeon thinks. Good job, honey. Study. Plan. Prove it works. Train a team. But really it starts with research and simulation surgeries."

The Helm is the perfect place to become an expert in Agoras. "Ivan showed me the clinic. Equipment there is decades ahead. Can I do my research at The Helm?"

"No. That's more of an emergency clinic for traumas like today." His cheek twitches like he made a mistake.

My breath catches. "Did something bad happen? Is Ivan okay?"

"He's...no worse than normal."

"Dad, you have to take me to the forest, or I'll go by myself."

"We can't tonight. It's not safe."

"If I get arrested, Ivan will save me. You know he will." My backpack sits on my floor, already stocked with my hospital gear. I jump up and throw it on. "It's dark, we can make it to the east entrance and meet them."

"Story, they need their rest. Especially him."

"You help me get there, or I'm calling Ivan."

He sighs. "Let me talk to your mom. We'll leave in fifteen minutes."

14

Dad's not fighting me on my decision to go to The Helm. That scares me more than if he had outright forbidden it. He told Mom he's taking me on a call at a clinic and it's a good learning experience for Monday.

"Okay, we're here. Listen. The next person in the chain of command after Ivan is a Commander named Moriah. She's sending out some Irontrace for us," Dad says as he parks the car. "I'm the chief surgeon. The Bastion knows I go in and out of here whenever needed, day and night. Somedays, I'm here more than at the Lancaster Medical Hub. Also, Ivan's not happy you insisted on coming."

"He'll survive. If the clinic is only for trauma care, why do you work there so much?"

"The Helm is frequently targeted by terrorist attacks. Criminals want control of The Kernel's unlimited power. That's why Irontrace are trained to be tactical experts. If they can't fight, and fight well, they'll be killed. They were attacked at five this morning."

Impossible! No. We don't live like that anymore.

"There's no such thing as terrorists in 2050. The Bastion wouldn't allow that," I say confidently. He's wrong. I grab my bag off the backseat and hop out. We meet at the trunk. He looks at me, wearing the same sad look of pity Ivan gave me a few nights ago. He's serious. Too many seconds pass.

His jaw twitches. My world view fractures. If *Irontrace* aren't safe, no one is. Anywhere. It's all been a lie. I've spent years blissfully drinking iced coffees, studying, and coordinating my running shoes of the day to my athletic wear while they're attacked. Killed. In secret. It's disgusting. If I wasn't so focused on getting to Ivan right now, I'd be sick.

I clear my throat. "Was anyone killed?"

He tips his chin, relieved I'm caught up to the reality he and Ivan live in.

"Three. Ivan is...more or less fine. Their top commander died. Ivan got a promotion. Two young ones were killed. There are some serious and critical injuries too. We're not on a social trip. I had to come back tonight anyway. If you're going to take on Agoras and help the Irontrace, you cannot shy away from the emergency medical care they require. The constant threat they live under is another reason they don't have families, get married, or have *ANY* semblance of life outside The Helm." He shoots a loaded glance at me.

"I'm here to work, Dad."

Francois is waiting on the other side with horses for us.

"Welcome, my friends!" he calls out. I assume we cross the boundary about fifty feet in, because he runs up to us, smiling and hands us the reins for Hero and a stunning white horse named Cloud.

"How are you, Francois?" I ask. Dad said two younger ones had died. Oops. I didn't think to ask if he was okay.

"I'm good, I'm happy you are back so soon! It's an honor to be sent to get you. Come. Get back quick." He scrambles up onto his horse and waves for us to follow.

Tonight, the cave feels surprisingly cheery. Bright fires crackle. Rope lights strung along the ceiling cast a warm glow. The last time I came here, I was someone in need of help. I return as someone who belongs.

"I'll take your horses. *Adieu!*" Francois says, jumping down. He handles the three huge horses like he's walking a group of Chihuahuas.

"Thank you, see you later," Dad says, waving to him. "This way, come on."

The clinic is busier than I expected this late. ORION and ALICE units roll from bed to bed, making a near constant rustle of curtains against the metal frames. Murmurs of conversation blend with the beeping of machines, creating an urgent symphony.

"Where do you need me?" I ask.

"Have a seat. I'll assign your patients. Read their charts, get familiar with them. I'll check in with Moriah and we'll go from there." Dad wheels a chair to a laptop station, signs in, and opens six patient files. "Start with these. They're some of the surgical cases."

I scan my patient list. *Rhys, Ivan* is patient number six. I can't open that yet. It feels like an invasion of privacy.

Reading the clinical notes on patients one through five paints a chilling picture of this morning's chaos. Crush injuries from collapses. Close quarters combat injuries. Burns from explosions.

I need a minute to process. This is why Dad doesn't want me here.

A message pops up on my screen.

So...you came back? -I

My shoulders drop with relief. He's at least well enough to type. "Nothing could've kept me away. Hope you're not mad. Where are you?"

Mad? To see you? Never. You aren't going to read my chart? -I

"What bed are you in? I want to see you."

I'm not in the clinic, I'm good. -I

"Faker. Not even a halfway decent faker. I'm going to read your whole chart now. I *knew* something was wrong. For real, where are you? I wanna see you now."

There's a long pause with no answer. I chew a nail. That was too much. I shouldn't push him that hard.

Don't chew your fingernails. You're gonna get sick. Go see some patients. Yell at robots. I'll have someone find you and bring you to me when you're done. I can't leave work right now, sorry. -I

Talk about bossy. I smile and drop my hand. "I was joking, I won't read your chart until we talk."

Are you sure you're a real surgeon with that attitude? -I

"Aren't you supposed to be working?" I remind him.

"Story, come with me," Dad says, ripping my attention from the screen.

"See you soon, 'k?" I whisper. Ivan sends a thumbs up.

Dad hands me a badge with a picture of me on it that says *Dr. Story Ross, Attending Vascular Surgeon.*

"An attending? You must be pranking me."

He smiles. "You're a healthcare prodigy, sweetheart. You get the royal treatment per The Bastion's orders. Welcome to The Helm. Senior Commander Delac pushed the paperwork through already. Did you get to read all your patient's charts?"

"All except one."

"Good. So, you know what they went through. I hoped you wouldn't be upset by Ivan's."

"No. You said he's okay. I trust you."

He stops, eyebrows raised. "*HIS* is the one you didn't read?"

"I didn't have time. It was the last chart tab."

"Compared to a lot of others he's okay. I'm fairly confident he'll make a full recovery."

A prickly unease creeps in. *Fairly confident?!?!*

Dad hurries ahead, guiding me to a hallway marked *Alderman Center for Surgical Excellence.*

"Surgical robots do great work, but we have to get our eyes and hands on every patient to check their work," he says. "Go see the five down here. Then we'll find Ivan. He refuses to stay in bed yet again. He's one of the only engineers in the control room."

My first patient had been caught beneath debris when the initial barrage of bombs hit. His right leg had to be amputated above the knee. His left leg is a mangle of shattered bones and crushed tissue. Once he's more stable, he'll have a series of extensive surgeries.

The second patient suffered an abdominal crush injury from flying debris during the second wave of bombs. She had emergency surgery to repair torn muscles and a pelvic fracture.

The other victims were injured in hand-to-hand combat with autonomous units. They have a variety of wounds on their hands, faces, and upper chest.

Given what they've been through, they're stable and in good spirits. No signs of infection. Lungs and hearts sound good.

Ivan is my only patient left. I can't find Dad or any volunteers to take me to the control room. Wandering the halls alone does not seem like a wise option. I go back to my computer and try something.

"Ivan? Are you there?" Ah, that was so awkward. Please hear me in the void.

Yes. What's up? -I

Phew, he caught me from that weird electronic trust fall. "I've seen all my other patients. How can I find you?"

I'll come to you. -I

The station is disorganized tonight. I throw away trash from snacks and supplies for a few minutes. I debate opening Ivan's chart but won't have time to read it all now. Two volunteers sit at the station for a break. A rowdy, laughing group joins and suddenly there's too many people.

I'm not here to make new friends; I just want to see Ivan. I'll go hide in the supply room while I wait for him. I fetch a fresh stack of common items for the post-ASTRA assessments: sterile gloves, gauze pads, antiseptic wipes, surgical tape.

I exit the supply room and the world stops. Everything slips from my hands. Seeing Ivan knocks the breath from my lungs.

Ivan stands next to the nurse's station, scanning the clinic. The staff at the desk go silent.

His left side is a mess. A massive line with dozens of stitches trail from his hairline, down his forehead, eyebrow, cheek, and neck into his shirt. His left eye is mostly swollen shut. Bruises blotch his face and neck. A sling holds his left arm. He shifts his weight to one leg, standing off-center.

"Aren't you supposed to keep things like that off the floor?" he asks, speaking from the right side of his mouth. "Sterile technique or something?"

I run to him so fast that my stethoscope almost gives me a black eye. He holds out his right hand like he's trying to calm a startled animal.

"I should have read your chart!" I swat his hand out of the way and wrap both of my arms over his shoulders. *How's his Agora?* My fingers fly to the back of his neck to feel it. There's no stitches or wounds on it. Thank the stars. Despite the bad shape he's in, at least his Agora is okay.

How could he have survived whatever caused these injuries?

"This is why you shouldn't be here. It's not the worst thing that's ever happened to me." He tips his head towards the beds and quietly adds, "It lowers their morale to see their commander looking like this."

Whispers swarm among the staff. They're all staring at us with looks ranging from concern to curiosity. I drop my arms from his neck. I'm making an awful impression on my new coworkers.

"Commander Rhys! Are you okay?" someone yells.

"Yep. Been in the control room working." He waves at them, not taking his eyes off mine. He closes the few inches between us, lowering his voice even more. "Plus, if my people have to listen to me being yelled at by the young Dr. Ross, it could make them question if I'm really the one in charge."

I stand on my tiptoes and whisper in my most demanding doctor's voice. "Ivan Rhys, I'll declare you unfit for duty if you don't get in bed or agree to have a full exam."

He snorts. "You pick, Doc. Bed or exam? Not here."

"You need both."

He wraps an arm on my shoulders. "Come home with me."

It takes real effort to ignore the eyes boring into our backs. Part of me wants to cry for him on our slow walk out of the clinic. Another part of me wants to yell at him for insisting he was good earlier. And yet another wants to find him a wheelchair instead of using me to help his giant frame limp along. None of those options seem right.

The idea that my protector, no, the whole world's protector, was so brutally attacked is impossible to comprehend.

I sneak several furtive glances up at him. Dried blood cakes his hairline. The outline of a surgical monitoring sticker and the edges of a large bandage peek out of his sweatshirt. It looks like someone started taking care of him and left halfway through the job.

"We have to stop meeting like this, where one of us has some scratches and a limp," he jokes as we enter his apartment.

"How long is your break?"

"I'm not scheduled to work tonight. Things have settled down."

"Let's get you cleaned up." I drag a chair by the kitchen sink for him with my free hand. "Sit, please. What shape were you in this morning when you helped me?"

"Can't remember. Head injury." An attempt at a smile ends in a grimace when his stitches pull tight. His voice is muffled. The left side of his mouth barely moves.

"I'm going to read your full chart and find the time stamps." *He won't make it eleven months,* rings in my head.

I use a warm rag to clean up the blood around his hairline.

"Hmm, it's coming back to me now. On my way to surgery, I saw your name on your dad's phone and made him answer."

"You didn't have to do that." I frown, recalling how off his voice sounded this morning. The cuts on his cheek look the deepest. Before his stitches were in, this area would have been a wide-open gash. My heart is hammering so hard that I'm sure he can hear it. If my hands would stop being so shaky, I'd seem much more like a professional.

"I wanted to. Your dad knows I'm the best. He was okay with the delay so I could watch over you."

He lays a hand on my back and gently rubs it, anchoring me from the storm raging in my chest. His sweet smile hurts my heart. He was almost killed, and he's comforting *me*. I muster a smile at him. *How did he do that? My hands aren't shaking.*

Duty snaps me into action. I turn to the sink.

"Listen, Story. I really am fine. Is your shoulder better?"

"Yes. Thanks." I scrub the rag on my hands under warm water until it finally runs clear of his blood. "You know even more than I do, injuries to the head and neck aren't good for these." I gently clean the area around his Agora. I hate these things as bad as he hates The Bastion. *Just*

116

say it. "I want to find a way to remove these someday."

He shakes his head slowly. "Even if you find a way to take it out, I'd want to stay in the Irontrace. You should save Lark though. Give her a chance. The rest of us are ticking time bombs. I'm a calamity magnet." His voice has the worn calm of a person who made peace with their countdown long ago.

His only option can't be death at an early age from an Agora. I wipe the last of the blood from his hairline then stand in front of him. He tips his face up to look at me. Damp strands of his black hair have fallen out of place from my work to clean him up. Droplets trail onto his forehead. I brush it back with my fingers, careful around his stitches.

"You have a concussion, so you may not remember this conversation. Being in your Irontrace Squadron sounds awful. You are trapped here, in this boundary, helping people who are effectively holding you prisoner." He doesn't respond, just watches me intently. "If I can find a way to get Agoras out, that's fine, stay in Irontrace if that's your choice. Keep working and show The Bastion you want to be here willingly. But go on vacation, go to a restaurant, you should see Lancaster, it's huge now. I'll take you on a tour of all my favorite places. Or don't leave, work here until you're old then retire because your Agora didn't kill you at twenty-six years old." I have to shut up. He doesn't know his death date. Hopefully head injury Ivan will forget I said that. "I want to find a way for you to have a life where you can make choices."

He sits unusually still while I speak, holding my gaze. I need to keep his assessment moving. "Do you have injuries anywhere else?"

He leans back and unzips his sweatshirt. His left shoulder and part of his chest are covered with a large post-op bandage. It's clean and dry, so I leave it for now. His bare chest has a web of scars from healed wounds that should've killed him.

"They cut off my shirt. I can't get my arm up to put a new one on."

If he can't even dress himself, he shouldn't be working. He should be in the clinic with staff to take care of him.

"*Ivan,*" I breathe his name in a sigh. "Tell me what happened. You have serious, possibly critical injuries depending on what's under this bandage. I'd rather hear it from you than read it from a chart."

"Alarms went off to let us know there was something in the airspace above the Helm. We had a couple minutes of nonstop rumbling from drones deploying infiltration units on top of the falls."

I lean behind him to pull his sweatshirt onto his shoulders then crouch in front of him to zip it up halfway.

"Thanks. We took out the drones. But the units they launched got in the elevator shaft to the control room. One with a scythe arm cracked me in the face and left this beauty." He points to his stitches. My lip quivers. I frown to hide that I'm about to lose it. "Got hit pretty bad in the shoulder a couple of times. Went down backwards. I don't know what happened to my leg. I had x-rays. Nothing's broken."

My efforts to stay objective fail. Hot tears fall. "Did you hit your Agora?" He needs me to focus on being a surgeon right now. It doesn't matter how I feel.

"I did. But your dad made me get a scan of it. It's okay."

Thank goodness.

I reach behind him and lay my fingers on the pillowy surface of his Agora. It's warmer than the rest of his skin, but not hot. There's a chaotic, buzzing rhythm to it, like a second pulse that doesn't belong. Knotted roots extend outward, disappearing into the flesh of his heavily muscled shoulders.

It looked okay when I was cleaning him up. To the touch, it feels normal for an Agora exam. If he says his shoulder was hit "pretty bad" I can't imagine what's under that bandage. As soon as I'm done with him, I'm going to read his chart. ALICE, ORION, and ASTRA will have the medical details to fill in the blanks on what really happened. Dad was right, he's not going to survive until April.

Annnddddd I've been lost in thought, staring down at him, twisting the thick, soft hair on the back of his head between my fingers.

He looks ridiculously pleased to have distracted me.

Dr. Rhys! Hands off. I shove both hands in my scrub shirt pockets.

"Do you care if I look at the results of the Agora scan in your chart?"

My tears keep rolling. I take a deep breath. *No crying. I'd have failed medical school if I acted like this with patients.*

"Go for it. To you, Story Ross, I'm an open book."

"Sorry." My voice catches. Where are tissues?

He leans forward, wincing. His right thumb gently wipes the stream of tears from each of my cheeks. "Since I have a head injury, I can say whatever pops into my banged-up brain. I'm gonna marry you, Story Ross."

I shake my head. "This head injury is really getting to you. Dad said Irontrace don't get married."

He snorts. "Let me get this straight. You and I met. Then *Alan Ross* just randomly felt compelled to educate you on the Irontrace marriage policy? I wish I'd heard that conversation."

"Keep talking like that and you're getting another CT scan." I loop his sling around his neck and put his arm in.

"So, that's a maybe to the marriage thing," he says.

My eyes go wide. *Don't joke like this with patients.* He genuinely laughs for the first time since I have been here. Will his left dimple come back? Or is it lost forever to the scar from today?

"Do you ever take life seriously?" I ask.

"Rarely. None of us make it out alive."

"Go get ready for bed. You need ice packs and sleep."

I make myself busy in the kitchen prepping sandwiches and drinks. When he walks back out in pajama pants, he grins. "Wow, a surgeon who cooks for me." He points to his left ring finger and wiggles it. He may be outrageous, but he sure is entertaining.

"We've been here for a couple of hours. I haven't seen you drink. You're in recovery, you need lots of fluids." I tuck under his arm like a crutch and walk him to the couch.

"Thank you."

"Here." I lay ice packs along his shoulder and chest injuries. "Put your feet up." I scoot the coffee table close to the couch and throw a pillow on it for his legs. I put two more cold packs on his left ankle and calf. "Are they in the right spots?"

"Yes. Feels great, thanks. I want to hear more about this pasta dish you made the other night," he says. "Cooking is one of my favorite activities."

I collect our little couch picnic and carry it to the living room. My nose wrinkles, remembering how badly I burnt the sauce. "Bad news for you, my friend. It did not turn out well. Cooking is not my strong suit."

He smells his sandwich before taking a small bite. "Well, this is the best peanut butter sandwich I've had by far."

I laugh. "I can't believe a couple of days ago, we were sitting and talking when you saved me. Today you saved more people. You save everyone."

His eyes flick down. He's suddenly miles away, somewhere I can't follow. "I can't save them all. Three people died." His deep voice has a sharp edge to it. "I keep seeing their faces. Trying to think of what I should've done differently. One of them was our top commander. He was...Titus didn't deserve that." He stops. I lay my hand on his arm. "Now I'm one step closer to Senior Commander. That's not a role I want, ever."

His words hang in the air before I respond. "Sorry. I wanted you to know you're a hero to a lot of people. To me, for sure."

That brings him back. He cocks his head slightly. "It would be nice if life would be boring sometimes. Less heroism required, more boredom occasionally. How often is life boring out there?"

Out there. *Ouch.*

"Depends on your personality. There are boring times, but my mom always tells us being bored is your brain's way of saying it needs to create something. My parents taught us to turn boredom into productivity at my house." I smile, swallowing the bitter taste of rage burning in my throat. "Someday, I'll make sure you have the most boring day ever."

"Looking forward to it."

"To bed with you. Come on." I tuck myself under his right arm again. "My dad will be coming to tear your door off to find me soon. Can you please tell me how to get back to the clinic?"

He gives me directions to the clinic while I reposition the pillows and ice around him. Even though he's managed his Agora by himself for years, my right hand forms a protective shield over it while he gets situated. I keep my hand on him until he's in the perfect spot to keep it supported but not compressed. When he notices what I'm doing, the right side of his face perks into a smile.

"Get some rest." I tuck the last cold pack in his sling and pull the blankets higher on his chest.

"Thanks for this. All of it."

"Anytime," I reply, ducking out his door.

I walk around his apartment for a quiet minute, stopping at his bookshelves and desk. I'm not snooping, just looking. He doesn't have any pictures. No decorations. Textbooks and manuals fill every shelf.

People need something to remind them of what's important in life. I pull out my little notebook and pen. Though I'm by no means an artist, I draw a simple sketch of us with Obsidian's head. Along the bottom I write, *You needed some art in here! -Story R.*

It's basic, but not bad. I snag a piece of bandage tape from my pocket and stick it to his fridge. I'll probably be long gone back in Lancaster when he finds it.

A knock on the door startles me. I open the door and hold a finger on my lips for my dad to be quiet. "Just got him laid down," I whisper.

"He really should be on monitors, but he always refuses. I think you should stay here with him and make sure his stubborn self makes it through the night with those wounds. They were *so* close, Story. Too close this time. The other patients are doing well. I have work to do. I'll get you in the morning and we can head home."

Dad's words make my throat feel tight. I barely know Ivan, but losing him to some random, stupid attack would devastate me. "Can someone bring me a clinic tablet so I can see his Agora scans from today? He needs pain meds too."

"Sure, I'll have someone run them to you."

"Thanks. Later, Dad." I shut the door.

This is unexpected. I hope Ivan isn't annoyed to have me as a surprise house guest. Speaking of annoying Ivan…I'm going to need to snag another one of his shirts for pajamas. My plan to spend the night working in scrubs has gone off the rails.

I peek in his room. He's sleeping. Sneaking across the tile in my socks won't be hard. I tiptoe to his dresser, snag my prize, and inch the top drawer shut.

"Stealing more of my shirts? I could arrest you for that." He sounds more amused than like law enforcement.

"Sorry! I thought you were asleep."

"Nah. Can't turn my brain off."

"Can I borrow this, just for tonight? I promise I'll return it."

"I was kidding. Take whatever you need. Keep it."

"Guess what?" I walk to his side, clutching the shirt I'm risking a felony for. "Dad said I can stay with you tonight since you won't go to the clinic."

"Finally. Medical care I won't turn down." I hear the smile in his words.

"I'm going to get a shower. I'll be back when your medicine is here. That should knock you out for the night," I say, shutting the master bathroom door.

After taking a quick shower to get the clinic germs off, I tuck my hair into a loose bun. Maybe he's asleep out there. I don't want to blast him with light if he is. I shut it off before opening the bathroom door. He doesn't say anything when I scurry past his bed to the living room. I'm just in time to hear someone knock softly on his apartment door.

It's a young clinic volunteer. The young girl is not much older than Francois. She grins, juggling her stack of things to hand me his medicine and chart.

"Here. Ivan said to bring these for you." She hands me a small cooler bag. "Bye!" She runs away before I can respond.

I smile when I see what's inside. A plethora of small bottles of coffee creamer. Coconut caramel, Italian sweet cream, vanilla, peppermint mocha, hazelnut, raspberry mocha, cinnamon dolce.

This is a far cry from his favorite black coffee. A glance around when I put them away confirms these are the only coffee add-ins taking up fridge space. I hope I'm here long enough to sample at least a few. Maybe he's hoping that too?

I sneak back in his room. "Ivan? Medicine time."

"Hello again." He sits up to take his pills. "Thanks."

"Will you please stay in the clinic when I go home?"

"I know it's annoying, but I'm never sure what day will be my last. I refuse to spend any more time in the clinic than I have to already," he says, rubbing his Agora.

While he's got me here, he doesn't have to be alone. Leaving his cup on the stand, I walk to the other side of the bed and turn on the small lamp. If I'm going to watch over him, I'm going to do it right. I shuffle out of his room, getting myself a glass of water and turning off all the lights. When I pop back into his doorway with my tablet and water, he looks at me with a flicker of confusion.

"Can I read in here while you sleep?" I ask before entering.

"Goodness. *YES!* Please." He flips back the blankets on the opposite side of the bed.

"Nope. You go to sleep. Over there." I smooth the blankets back down and tuck them under the mattress in a clear *I'm not joining you under there.* "I'm not sleeping. I'm reading. I'll be here if you need anything." I sit cross-legged on the opposite side.

He tries, and fails, to hold back a smile, then scoots away in a *message received* gesture. We've got a respectable distance of most of his king-sized bed between us. I add a few small pillows in a wall along his hip just to be extra safe. Plus, with the pain med cocktail he just took? He'll be knocked out in less than a minute.

"There. Totally separated."

"You just wanna see if your future husband snores."

Do not encourage him! "I am here as your *doctor*. Go to sleep."

"Mmhmm, Doc." He tucks his right hand over my left hand. "I'm not trying to be a creep or anything. I just...I can't believe you're really here. Is this okay?"

I prefer to be prickly and keep a safe distance from everyone. But when I hazard a glance at our intertwined hands, his huge, rough tan hand encompassing my freckled ivory hand looks suspiciously perfect. "Yes."

He threads his fingers between mine. It's not a soft, sweet grip. He's speaking to me without using words. He's grateful I'm here. He needs me to stay. I remember feeling the same desperation towards him in the forest warden clinic after the morpentanyl drama. His hug kept me from falling apart that day. If simply holding my hand can return that favor? I'll read like this for as long as he needs.

"Thanks for the creamer."

"I'm hoping to lure you into staying with assorted flavored things." His words come slow. The pain meds are kicking in.

If he knew how easy luring me would be, he'd bust his stitches from smiling. "Sweet dreams, Ivan." I squeeze his hand.

His patient record has sixteen years of Agora scans. Watching its incremental growth between images is like a horror movie. The deadly tendrils creep closer to vital structures with each year.

Within seconds, he's asleep. I cling to his hand, unsure how he's survived the beast in his neck.

15

Until the early hours of morning, I had leaned back in a nest of pillows against the headboard, careful not to disturb Ivan. The only time I let go of his hand was when I got up to get a sweatshirt, long pajama pants, and socks from his dresser. Once I was warm and snuggly in his clothes, fatigue took me out. And sleeping Story had no respect for the pillow wall. When I woke, not only is his hand still in mine, but now I'm cuddling his arm, anchored to his side. He doesn't stir, so I lay, enjoying this unexpected moment of...contentment? *Is this what that feels like?*

The line of stitches on his tan face looks brutal at rest. He's completely relaxed for once. Not trying to think up his next joke or figure out what threat to guard me from.

His strong jawline is still well-defined on the right. On the left it's swollen and bruised, striking a drastic contrast. There's a quiet warmth in his sleeping expression, almost like he's amused with life, even in his dreams. I gently set his hand beside him then stand to stretch, suddenly cold without his touch.

My future husband.

Don't be foolish. I'm just tired. And freezing. But if he wasn't my patient, I'd be appreciating how handsome he is, even when he's got stitches holding him together. Honestly, even if he wasn't...all the things that make him Ivan, he'd be as close as I could get to describing the person I'd like to sleep next to for the rest of my life.

Nope! That's unprofessional. Get out of here.

It's coffee time. That'll get me thinking clearly. I trudge to the kitchen instead of getting back in the warm bed and sleeping all day. My hand bangs on a cabinet door, slamming it shut. I freeze.

"Morning," he says through a yawn.

"Good morning. Sorry for waking you," I call from the kitchen.

"Don't be. I need to get up." From my spot by the sink, he's out of view, but his voice sounds rough.

"I was hoping to ask you something. I'm trying to find a way to remove Agoras. Can you build a robot to assist me with that?" I walk into his room carrying his medicine and pause to see his reaction.

"*You'll* do the surgery, and the robot is your assistant?" His face is shocked but not displeased.

"Yes. AVMs used to be removed by human surgeons. It was risky, but they made it happen when they could. From scans I've reviewed, Agoras are not too deep. Not in the brain tissue. Most don't even reach near the skull, and I want to-" A soft knock on the door interrupts me. "I bet it's my dad. Be right back."

"Morning!" Dad says cheerily as I swing the door open. "Ready?"

"Hi! Actually, we were just talking about my research. He doesn't want to go to the clinic. He really can't be alone yet."

"I assume this means you want to stay here?" Dad asks in a low voice. "You need to come home tomorrow. Lark wants to spend time with you before you start work." He leans into Ivan's room. "Rhys. Will you just go to the clinic and make my life easier for once?"

"Nope!" Ivan chirps.

Dad grumbles. "Story, come with me. Round on your other patients. You can get him more meds and bandages, then come back if you want."

"Okay. I need a minute first," I tell Dad. I'm jostling a stack of ice packs on one arm while carrying cups of coffee and water with my other hand.

I step in Ivan's room. He greets me with a crooked, sleep-rumpled smile. A swell of warmth spreads through my chest. *Stop that, Ivan.*

"Did you sleep good?" he whispers. I nod and smile. He takes the water and meds from me.

I arrange cooling gel packs on his shoulder and chest. The dressing is clean and intact. His skin around it isn't red or warm.

"I slept much better once you finally dropped the tablet and laid your head on my arm," he says softly.

My shoulders hitch up. "Sorry! I woke up like that. I don't remember falling asleep."

"I'll never forget it. Last night, I learned my future wife does not snore. Although I wouldn't care if you do. Snore. Drool. Talk in your sleep. Nothing is going to scare me away."

"Ivan! Shh!" I laugh, nodding towards the kitchen where my dad stands. Someone is going to report me for being the worst doctor ever. He's really not kidding about getting married. The idea *is* growing on me...

Ivan smiles and leans back on the headboard. He watches me lay ice packs along his leg. We swap his water cup for the coffee I brought him. Our movements are like a dance. What is my life right now? I don't need to get used to this. To being here with Ivan. Life is natural with him. Easy.

Easy? In a cave. That just had a terrorist attack. Also...he's dying.

Nothing is easy in Ivan's life.

"I have to go. To the clinic. To the people...the other patients." My feet get tangled in rapid retreat. I stumble, catching myself on his doorway. I turn back and give a composed smile. I am the picture of grace right now. "I'll be back. Do you need anything else?"

He's wearing a wicked one-sided grin. He gestures to all of me. "I *need* you to be careful. Don't break any of that. I'm good. Thank you."

"See you soon." I pull the bedroom door shut and smash my forehead on it. *Real cool, Story.*

Dad waves for me to follow him. We step into the hallway and I pause mid-step. I've never seen anything so beautiful.

The metal wall from last night is raised, revealing a floor to ceiling row of windows. It's a stunning panorama of the back of the waterfall. I reach out to touch the window to make sure there's really glass there. Yep. The glass is cool and has a faint vibration from the power of the falls.

They've planted a rainbow of giant tropical flowers on a ledge between the windows and water. I press my shoes where the windows meet the floor. It looks like I'm standing in a nest of flowers, water, and sky. The ambient speaker volume is turned up today. I can't hear birds or forest sounds. The waterfall thunders in a constant rush. Occasional crashes of water hit the rock ledge by the flowers in sharp slaps.

I'm in paradise.

Paradise that was built on brutality against its guardians.

"I'm still shocked by the view every time. They have these flowers out there from March through December. Never had time to ask why or how. It looks more like Hawaii than Ohio," Dad says. "They keep an impenetrable, secure barrier down on it during the night. Is this the first time you've seen it during the day?"

"Yes. I haven't seen this yet." I fight to keep my voice neutral. Dad won't be pleased that everything in The Helm is growing on me by the minute.

The clinic is a lot less chaotic this morning. Dad already discharged some of our patients. I made rounds and then a volunteer took me on a more thorough tour of the clinic. We parted ways so I could get meds and wound care supplies for Ivan. I was digging through a bin of dressings bioengineered with healing agents to speed his recovery when my phone vibrated.

Dr. Story Ross,

This is an automated message from The Bastion. To ensure your region is not overpopulated, we introduced a new AI model to calculate the usefulness of residents.

You scored 100/100. Go enjoy a celebratory dinner with your new friend, Commander Rhys.

Please stand by for next steps.

-The Bastion

Is this a prank from Ivan? Dad walks up, so I lock my phone and slide it in my pocket.

"The surgical patients are doing well," I say. "Fresh, sparkly notes in their charts. I'm heading back to Ivan's. Sorry he won't come here."

"Ivan hates praise. I'm not surprised he's in hiding." Dad lifts a shoulder.

"What does praise have to do with his injuries?"

He chuckles. "I see he didn't tell you the full story of the attack. The top two commanders, Titus and David, were activating emergency Helm protocols. Ivan was left to find a solution by himself. He disabled the air attack units above the falls. That's a monumental task."

Ivan's level of nonchalance about what he did is remarkable.

Dad continues, "Titus, the most senior in command, saw a different type of AI unit coming out of the elevator shaft outside the control room. Titus went out to stop them and was immediately overwhelmed. Ivan ran out with no cover. He drug Titus into the control room but they couldn't revive him."

That's how the Senior Commander died.

"Ivan saw the elevator door open and a few young Irontrace come out. Of course he ran out again by himself to get them. He was hit, bad. He fell, but before he lost consciousness, he used his wrist cuff to detonate the last few AI units by the elevator. They're planning another ceremony honoring him."

Ivan will hate that. "Don't call him a hero to his face. It's a sore subject."

"Noted. I'm going to take off."

"Tell Mom and Lark hi from me please."

"Good job here. I'll be back for you in the morning." He gives me a quick hug and leaves.

I'm done in the clinic for now, time to go home. *No! Not home.* Ivan's. Hmm...Ivan's apartment gives me the same feeling of going home for the day. That's an interesting development I didn't foresee.

Ivan is up and ready for the day, standing in his kitchen when I open his apartment door.

"You can move!" I scoot a stack of notebooks over to arrange my clinic haul on the counter.

"Sure can. I made breakfast. I wasn't sure if you had eaten." He points to a plate of breakfast tacos.

"No, I didn't eat without you. How did you do that?" I hurry over to help him walk to the fridge.

"Watch, I'm fine." He does a wobbly little dance that doesn't inspire confidence in his range of motion. "So. This is perfect. Is the R for Ross? Or is this your way of saying you'll be Story Rhys when I-?" He taps the picture I taped to his fridge.

"Glad you like it," I cut him off. He gives a mock exasperated sigh. I pull a kitchen chair close to mine. "Here, sit. You're the talk of the clinic. You didn't tell me the full story of what happened. Dad said they're going to do some kind of hero's ceremony for you."

"No clue why."

I hide a smile behind my coffee cup. If he won't take a compliment on his hero status, maybe he will on his cooking. I pick up one of the tacos and glance at him before poking around in it with a fork. Steam rises from the flour tortillas packed with egg, crispy bacon, avocado, tomato salsa, and jalapenos topped with a little bit of cheese. He watches me take a bite. My eyebrows shoot up when the flavors hit.

I'd never eat something creative like this. But it's *so* good. "This is a 12 out of 10, Chef Rhys. Beats peanut butter sandwiches by far."

"It was just stuff I had in the fridge. Glad you're a fan."

"When do you go back to work?"

"I swapped shifts with Moriah. You're leaving tomorrow, so I'm staying holed up in here with you until then." He reaches to the counter, grabbing a notebook and pencil. "Check it out, I worked on a couple of things for you this morning."

He pulls out a few printed sheets and lays them in front of me. They're ALICE data on Lark. How did he get this? My eyes race over the percentages and dates splayed along the line graphs.

"I ran some numbers. If Lark's Agora is removed, look at how her health evens out on the blue line. The yellow line shows her estimated hospital stays become nonexistent." He runs his fingers along the chart.

"This red line shows her new estimated date of death will be May 18, 2121. She could live to be eighty! Let's do it. We'll get this thing out of her."

The look on the uninjured side of his face lights me up.

He's your patient. He's your patient. He's your patient.

I lay a hand on my chest to settle the fireworks bursting in there. "Thank you. Ivan, I mean it. Thank you for helping me with this."

"Thank you for letting me." He flips open a notebook to a green tab that marks a page. He's made several sketches of surgical robotic arms and tools. "Are these anything like what you need built? These are basic. Throw better ideas at me."

"The plan affects a surgery you may have someday. Are you sure you want to hear it, especially at breakfast?"

How can I have this conversation without sounding like a butcher?

"I'm not getting any younger here. Fix me up, Doc." He taps his pencil, ready to draw.

Six hours and two pots of coffee disappear in a blur of ideas and laughs. We move from the table to the couch, continuing to pass his notebook and pencil between us while I keep him on a rotating schedule of ice packs.

I sketch the anatomy and incisions we'll need based on Agora scans, explaining each layer and risk. He draws more refined ideas as we go.

"The biggest risk is massive bleeding. I can use artificial volume expanders if a hemorrhage happens. I'm sure you know giving blood transfusions creates fatal alterations in DNA since the ChAse virus. I won't try a save for you that will kill you from Sanguitoxicosis. That's a horrific death."

"Appreciated. I'd rather bleed out in surgery under your hands than deal with that," he says, matter-of-factly.

I can't kill Ivan. Or Lark. Or anyone. Don't cry. I carry our cups to the sink to breathe.

He continues, "Saving every drop of blood is goal number one. But if we start to hemorrhage or something ruptures, you need a way to save us?"

"Yes."

"Glad I'm not totally lost. Robot priorities: work with the angiogram to make you a map of the good and bad blood vessels, steady your hands, lighted magnification for deep, tiny blood vessels, and the smallest robotic arms ever made," Ivan says in review.

"Yes, that's the gist of it. There's another thing worrying me. You want to stay in the Irontrace, right?"

Before I can finish asking the question he's already nodding. "Absolutely."

"If I remove it, will they let you?"

"Let me worry about that. In the meantime, these will be ready for you to try in a couple of weeks." He looks down at his sketches.

"You sure about that? You're still recovering."

"My countdown clock started years ago. Plus, I get super bored at work." He tries to flash me a cocky smile. His stitches keep it to half a grin and a squint. He winces. I laugh.

"Can I show you something weird?" I pull out my phone.

"Always."

I snort and shake my head. "I got a message I don't understand when I was in the clinic. Look."

He reads it a couple of times before moving to his desk and opening his laptop.

"What do you think it means?" I stand beside his chair as he types in a login prompt. "At first, I thought it was a prank from you. Maybe, like...asking me to dinner in a weird way. Or something. Not a date, obviously! You're my patient. So that will never happen. I'm a professional. But. Well. I don't know, sorry, I'm tired. This has been a long week."

Shut. Up. Story. I walk to his living room window and stare out.

"Technically. I'm your boss. So, the power imbalance lies in my favor. But...you're fired from being my doctor. If you want to stay in my apartment here with me, stay as a highly-skilled friend or whatever you want to be called? Just take the whole doctor-patient thing out of the scenario. Hope that helps."

Helps?! No. No, it doesn't.

Thank goodness his back is to me. He can't see the crimson wave hit my face and neck. Maybe we can move on and forget this.

"Story," he says. I turn. He picks up his right hand, beckoning me to him.

I sit on the arm of his office chair. Long, silent seconds pass.

Why is he staring at me with *that* face? He looks...completely happy. Not just happy though. There's more to it. He's unguarded. Tender? It's like he's forgotten that we've known each other for a few days instead of years.

My breath catches.

I think Ivan loves me.

How? He doesn't know what size of shoes I wear. Or my favorite flavor of ice cream.

He's dying.

If you're dying, but also falling in love, does that mean you get to skip the whole will-they-or-won't-they nonsense and just dive right in? Because right now? *I will.*

I wish his left eye was open so I could read him better. It's stupid to let myself fall for someone who has less than a year left. That's a path to misery. Stay distant like Dad said to. Distant? What distance?

I grin and give a one-sided *I give up* shrug. He smiles.

I might already love him back.

That's impossible. Right? I've never really dated anyone. I've certainly never been in love. What would he think if he knew I'm secretly calling him future husband? Don't say that. You're going to lose all credibility as a surgeon here in the first twenty-four hours. Is this what love feels like? Absolute pandemonium.

Wait.

...Not pandemonium.

Hmm, take a second. Assess yourself, Dr. Ross. Dr. Rhys. Ha! I'm happy. I'm sure. Look at that face. He knows what he's done. Smug man. He knows he owns me after five days. I don't need to guess. *He loves me.* I don't know how. Or why. This genius, kind, funny, intense, protective man chose me.

A palpable understanding passes. To anyone else in the world, I'd be mortified to be completely exposed, seemingly to my very core as he drinks me in. But with Ivan? I don't want any walls. No defenses.

He sweeps my hair to the side.

"Story. My apologies if I've left you wondering how I feel about you. I despise ambiguity almost as much as I despise The Bastion. I want the rest of your life. Not just a dinner with you." *Oh my! Ivan doesn't play games.* I look away, adjusting his sling strap. He raises his shoulder, pinning my hand between his stubbly cheek and shoulder. "Let's see what's going on with your mystery message first. I can't have this conversation until I know who sent that to you."

He turns his video on, launching us into a conference call. "Hey, it's Rhys."

"Geez! Commander Rhys. You look half dead. Scratch that, closer to three-quarters," a woman says.

No he doesn't! He looks like a survivor.

"Thanks, Moriah. What's up with usefulness scores?" he asks.

"Weird ask from someone who should be in the hospital." She laughs. "Ohhhhh, I forgot, you have a doctor in there with you. It's nice they're making house calls now." *Yikes!* "People around the world got usefulness scores. It seems to imply they'll be eliminated if they receive a low score."

I stand and try to slink away. He mouths behind his hand, "You're fine! Look." He shows me a message on his laptop screen.

Michael Mullins,

This is an automated message from The Bastion. To ensure your region is not overpopulated, we introduced a new AI model to calculate the usefulness of residents.

You scored 13/100. Make sure you have a difficult conversation with your family tonight about the score you received. Your time left is reduced.

Please stand by for the next steps.

-The Bastion

Ivan laughs. "Gracious. Who did Michael Mullins tick off? What's been done so far?"

"Nothing yet," Moriah says. "Our initial troubleshooting didn't find anything. We're down several people and you're out of office playing."

"It's mine now," he says, ignoring her snarky tone.

"Thanks. Let us know when you're done."

"Will do." He mutes his mic. "I need a few minutes, sorry. You can keep watching, but it's very boring."

I sit on the couch, out of the view of his camera. "I'll lurk from here. Sorry if I got you in trouble."

He turns his chair to me. "I can't be in trouble with my inferiors, but she better not have embarrassed you. Moriah has never really adjusted to being here."

"No, I love being in here with you," I blurt. *Overshare!* I press my lips shut.

A grin plays at the right side of his mouth. Wordlessly, he spins back around to work.

He types silently for about twenty minutes. I jump when he yells, "Got it!" He unmutes his mic. "I've identified how they sent the messages. They originated from IP addresses hosted in a cloud environment. I blocked them and threw together a program to look for message patterns that seem spammy. It feeds into our existing firewall rules and dynamically updates a block list for us. Let's review it, improve it, and extend the functionality."

"Great work. Thanks, Rhys. Go to bed," a man says from off camera.

"I will. First. I want everyone's attention. Now. Get in view." Several Irontrace crowd in front of the webcam. "We all need to be on the same page about Dr. Story Ross, our new physician. Dr. Alan Ross asked her to stay with me since I refused to accept an in-patient bed in the clinic. She is a consummate professional and has been reporting to him about my condition. There has been no impropriety on her part."

Thank you, Ivan!

"If there is any chatter within the control room or elsewhere on her presence in my apartment, shut it down immediately. If I hear of it happening? There *will* be disciplinary action. Thanks to her excellent medical care, I was able to step in and fill this gap in the on-shift engineer's skills to resolve this hack." He looks pointedly at the screen.

Oooh, Ivan is gonna make some people mad...

"Got it, boss," Moriah says. Several others nod.

"Rhys. Go rest. That's an order," a blonde man says.

"Wait! Senior Commander Delac, I sent a message to everyone who got the usefulness score to assure them it did not come from The Bastion."

Sure enough, my phone has a message:

Friends,

The Bastion views every life as having immeasurable worth. The fake usefulness score was sent through a complicated hack, which has been fixed.

We know this was a frightening time for you. Please know your safety is our highest priority. You are all essential, cared for, and never just a number to us.

-The Bastion

"Excellent. Rest. Now," Delac says.

"Yes, Sir." Ivan snaps his laptop shut.

I walk to Ivan's room to get his bed ready. He should sleep while I work. I hurry to get under his right arm when he appears in the doorway, but he doesn't lean on me. Instead, he walks towards the bed, leaving his arm draped on my shoulders. We sit on the edge.

"No one has ever taken care of me or fussed over me. You don't need to do this."

"That's not how your life is going to go anymore now that I'm in it.

I'm going to fuss over you until you're sick of me."

He squeezes my shoulders. "Impossible."

"I've got other patients that need my attention. Get some sleep while I'm gone."

He hesitates before softly pressing a kiss to my forehead. His beard is softer than I'd expected, and his stitches are rough against my skin, but I don't care. It was perfect.

My mouth drops in silent surprise.

He lifts my chin gently with his finger, meeting my eyes for a wordless check-in. I should be flustered. Embarrassed. I'm not. If that was a glimpse of my future?

I am *all* in.

"Don't do that. You'll hurt your stitches." I smile and bump my shoulder into his chest. "I'm sorry. I have to go."

"Come back soon, Story R."

Come back soon? He makes it hard to leave in the first place...

"I will."

In the hallway, the windows draw me like a moth to a flame. I can't go to work yet. My chest is buzzing. The sun is what, ninety-three million miles away? But I swear I'm glowing with pure sunshine and adrenaline and hope and something that makes me feel alive, awake...I can't put my finger on it.

I blame Ivan.

Breathe. Focus on the view. It's stunning. The forest pulses with such life and color it's easy to forget I'm in a place built on brutality against its guardians.

The post-op patients in the clinic are doing well.

"Doctor Story! How are you?" Francois asks in a chipper voice.

"I'm great, thanks. How are you?"

"Super busy. The horses and hawks have been bored. I'm trying to keep them happy. But I had to come see my friend." He nods towards the young man resting in a clinic bed.

"I bet they love having you take care of them. Keep up the good work!" I give him a thumbs up.

He turns back to his friend. They both speak rapid French. Ivan said they chose the brightest kids from all over the world. Was Francois scared to make the journey to a new country, with a new language? Did Ivan learn other languages to help new Irontrace feel like they have a friend?

"Do you need anything, Dr. Ross?" a clinic volunteer asks. "I'm Mai, by the way. I'm an engineer. I work with our ORION units."

"Nice to meet you, Mai. I don't need anything in the clinic, thanks. But is there somewhere to buy food and drinks?"

"Yes, keep walking down this clinic hallway. You'll run into Atlas Cavern. They'll give you whatever you need. The food is good, and they're always open. Plus, there's lots of people there to hang with."

"Good to know, thank you." People? I've never shown up some-where seeking conversations with random strangers. That sounds drain-ing. Just the thought of it makes me want to flee to Ivan.

"You're welcome. Can I ask you something?" she asks, her cheek twitching.

"Of course."

"Some of us...well, we're wondering. Is Commander Rhys okay? He looked awful the other day. Then you took him away and no one has seen him."

Physically, Ivan has a lot to recover from. Mentally? He seems to be in good spirits. He's definitely got me in good spirits. She doesn't need to know that though.

I settle for saying, "He's cracking jokes and cooking."

"Phew, good to know. I was one of the people he saved the other day. He's saved all of us many times. Take good care of him. He's kind of a legend. Can I tell the others he's okay?"

I like Mai. She's proof other people see how awesome he is. Ivan would want his people to have a morale boost. Telling Mai might be as good as making a control room announcement about his condition.

"Yes. It was lovely to meet you."

"Bye!" She practically skips away.

Atlas Cavern is more of a world market than the small café I expected. Several restaurants with cuisines from around the world line the walls on the right. The middle is a large seating area with tables, booths, and cozy chairs. Shops extend along the left wall.

I stumble on a cute little restaurant with a downhome menu of classics. I'm not sure what Ivan likes. I choose some comfort food and hope it'll be okay. After placing our order for chicken and noodles with salads, I stand, waiting, with money in hand.

"Do you need something else?" the young man asks.

"The total please."

His face hardens. He leans across the counter towards me so fast I recoil. "*A total?* You don't need money here. Wait, who are you? Everyone knows that."

"I'm the new surgeon in the clinic." I hold up my badge.

He blinks for a long second then smiles. "You can have a seat. I'll bring your stuff to you."

"Thanks."

There's a low stone wall a few feet away surrounding a Mediterranean restaurant with low palms. Taking a seat between sweet smelling planters of large red and magenta flowers, I watch groups of Irontrace make their way through Atlas Cavern. The artificial sunlight and open atmosphere create an almost convincing city in the cave. A city with no financial system. Didn't see that coming.

The boy brings our stuff out about ten minutes later. "Thanks for stopping by, enjoy."

"Have a great day!" I take the bags from him and leave for Ivan's.

In his apartment, I peek in his bedroom. He's resting with his eyes closed. There's no need to disturb him. I put our food in the fridge and walk to his desk. His office chair is the biggest I've ever seen. I plop onto the smooth-worn black leather seat and settle in. My feet don't fully touch the ground.

How many times has he saved the world from this very chair? It's the perfect spot to study the sketches he drew this morning. They're incredible. Each has explanations of the prototype and how it would relate to my proposed surgical procedure.

I get lost reviewing Agora scans my dad has done over the years. He's right. Across patients, they seem to be the same. The only variance is the anatomy of each Irontrace. Mapping out the blood vessels and neural chip tendrils will make up for the differences between individuals.

"You're back," Ivan says from his bedroom doorway.

"Hi. I'm doing more research from scans."

"Finding anything you'd like to add to my sketches?" He walks slowly to the kitchen.

"Nope. I'm glad you got up. The dressing on your shoulder and chest needs changed. I'm also going to do a full assessment to add to your chart."

He pours drinks and carries them to the couch, balancing them on his right hand. "We need to talk about some things first. Honestly, they may scare you."

16

The last several days have been so full of action. Ivan's apartment is my refuge. What could he have to say that would scare me?

He lays the pain pills on the table in front of us.

"I'll take that in a bit. It makes me tired. I need a clear head for this." He pauses to feel the track of stitches on his face. "Helston's hawk drones. Those are run by a paramilitary group of merciless AI judiciaries. Thankfully, I can keep you safe from them. They wreak terrible havoc and spy on people. But these drones don't show up in people's lives for no reason."

Uh oh. In a few days, I saw drones multiple times. Then really bad things started happening around me.

"Am I in trouble with someone?"

"At first, I hoped it was counterfeit drones following you. Some random crazy person would be easy for me to handle. I checked the serial numbers from the ones that have shown up in the same areas as you. It's not good." He takes my hand. "The Bastion is coming for you."

"Why?" I gasp.

"I'll find out. It's not just this, though. The acid rain and other storms. The ChAse-417 outbreak. We have safeguards in place to stop events like that from happening. I believe someone is sabotaging The Kernel."

"Who and why?"

"Not sure yet. You must be so careful out there. I want you to have something if you are willing to wear it." He holds up a small white box and shakes it. Several items rattle. "These are trackers. Anywhere you go, I'll be able to keep an eye on you. If you need help, they have a panic button built in that you can activate. The whole Irontrace Squadron will have eyes on you. We'll be able to help you from here. Your dad has had one for years, but he's never needed to use it."

"I'm a surgeon here now, so it makes sense for me to have one," I say, reaching for the box.

He pulls the box away. "I need to finish setting it up. Necklace, brace-let, or ring? It needs to be something you'll wear twenty-four hours a day."

I think of the jokes he's made about marrying me. He sits, injured, refusing his pain medicine so he can find a way to keep me safe. I've never been more sure of anything in my life.

"Ring."

He smiles. "I've been trying to figure out why someone would be watching you. It may be related to your surgery research. Have you talked to anyone about your idea?"

Mom! But not until after they came for me. It can't have been her. She'd never betray me. Not even gonna mention her. I rack my brain. I may have hinted to Richelle about it. But she loves Lark. She wouldn't betray us.

"If anyone has heard you want to do surgery as the primary, im-portant people could get very mad. Have you said anything negative re-garding ASTRA? Made comments while Lark was in the hospital? The hospitals and most public places are under constant video and audio surveillance."

He pauses, tracing circles on my hand with his thumb. It's *very* dis-tracting.

"Story, you could lawfully be killed. Of course, they keep that in the small print of the charter. Absurd, right?"

My shoulders sink. "I called the ASTRA models incompetent. I have mentioned to my cousin, Richelle, that I'll find a way to fix Lark someday. But she's my best friend. She wants that too."

"When did you call them incompetent? I'll fix it." He jumps up but takes a jolting step and stops, muttering. After a beat, he walks to his desk and removes a padded bag from a drawer.

"A week ago. Lark was in the hospital in Lancaster. I also had to write a research paper for school on neurosurgery. There are a bunch of drafts of it on my computer that explain why and how humans would have done several brain surgeries better than ASTRA can." His mouth drops open. I hope he's not on the verge of having me arrested. "It made me realize how much better humans could do a lot of other medical practices too. So...I wrote steps for humans to do surgeries on each major body system without robots like we used to."

He dissolves into laughs. I continue, "This sounds *bad,* but I downloaded a hundred or so videos of surgeries being done by humans decades ago that I watch in all my free time."

"My, oh my, Doc. You're a menace to the healthcare system." He lays the bag on my lap and unzips it to reveal a shiny black laptop. "This is like the one I built for your dad. Completely secure. Make new accounts for everything. New passwords. I'm going to have your dad bring your old laptop to me. I'll put your precious surgery videos on the new one, but I'll do it safely. Is that alright with you?"

"Do whatever you need."

He walks into his room and makes a brief call. "Okay, he's bringing it tomorrow."

"Is this going to be okay?" It's mind-blowing to me that insulting a robot can cause all this trouble.

"Yes. Part of my job is to review information and decide if The Kernel correctly identified threats. My Senior Commander and I do not designate you as a threat. He even hired you as a high-ranking staff member. Congrats, by the way. Welcome to The Helm, Dr. Ross. Officially time for you to start calling me Sir."

He playfully elbows my ribs. "I can edit your data with AJA. This is nothing illegal for me as a Commander. Computers don't make good choices sometimes. But you must never, *ever,* tell anyone you want to fix something with robot-assisted surgery. The robot is primary. You're its assistant. Don't tell Dr. Benedict. Don't talk to Richelle about it."

"I promise. Thank you. Enough about me." I press his pills in his hand and reach for his water.

The food from the café made a nice late lunch for us. I told him about meeting Mai. We talked about Atlas Cavern versus the real world while waiting for his medicine to kick in.

No one has ever taken a real interest in me. Most of my classmates never knew my name. Instead of chasing friend groups that never made space for me, I bookmarked pages in my favorite academic journals to read during lunch and school breaks. It was easier to be a silent fortress, walled off from people than live through their silent undercurrent of rejection.

Ivan is unburying the deep parts of me no one has ever bothered to care about. When he asks me questions, he really listens, continuing to draw me out, smiling like each new story is a gift.

"Dressing change time," I announce after cleaning up from lunch. "You ready?"

"Sure."

"Let's start with your face." We're quiet while I clean the line of stitches and add more tissue-repair antibiotic ointment.

"Okay. Can I see what's under the bandage?"

"Only if you're not squeamish." He looks almost apologetic.

"Not at all."

I sit on the coffee table in front of him to take off his sling then unzip his sweatshirt. He winces as I work my fingers under the sticky edges of his large shoulder and chest bandage.

"Sorry, you Irontrace need to invent an adhesive that doesn't hurt to pull off."

He laughs. "Science hasn't come that far yet."

I ease the bandage off the rest of the way, and my heart explodes into palpitations.

Years of physical training and horsemanship have built his chest into something solid. Powerful. I knew from his chart the attack was a mix of severe blunt-force impacts and sharp-force injuries. But reading what happened and seeing how badly he's torn up are two very different things.

Move. Help him. Muscle memory takes over.

A few eight-inch sections of skin were stripped away in uneven swaths across his upper left chest and shoulder. The ASTRAs took hours to reconstruct it with flaps and artificial skin grafts. He has stitches. Staples. Surgical adhesives in shiny lines on the shallower injuries.

"I'll clean it, assessing as I work. Tell me if you need me stop for a break."

"I'll be fine."

"Ivan, I'm really sorry. I can't believe this happened to you."

"Wounds look good. Yes, to stiffness and pain. No fever or signs of infection," he says. "This is not my first rodeo."

"Excellent assessment. I'll add that to your chart. Time to put on a new dressing."

I prep and apply the IT-51 ASTRA dressing. It's a novelty to me. We don't have anything like these bioactive dressings outside The Helm. They're embedded with sensors to promote cell repair by using low-intensity lasers to deliver targeted light therapy.

It gets them back to work as soon as possible. I'm sure if they took time to recover from nearly dying like a normal human, The Bastion would find another way to punish them.

He watches me with a soft smile while I listen to his heartrate and lungs with my black stethoscope.

"Tell me if this feels the same on both sides." I trace my fingers along his neck, collarbones, arms, and down to his hands.

"It does."

"Squeeze, please." He grips my hands with a firm, equal grasp. "Pulse checks." His brachial pulse beats steadily. Sliding my hands down, I confirm the radial pulse on his wrist is good.

My mind can't comprehend who could hurt him. He deserves so much better than a life where this is normal. *How many times will this happen to future husband in the next eleven months?* Tears fall before I can stop them.

"You cannot cry every time you see your patients. It's not very surgeon-y." He lays his palm on my cheek to wipe my tears.

My face melts against his hand. "You're the only one that makes me cry. I can't leave until you're better." I slide his sweatshirt onto his shoulders and zip it.

"I really appreciate this. You're truly the only person-" Someone pounds on his apartment door so loud it rattles. Ivan shoots a furious look at the door. "Who on earth is that?" He growls.

They keep beating on the door. He strides over to look out the peephole while putting his sling on. "Story, go in my room for a minute."

"No! I'm not leaving you." Is another attack coming? I'll stay to fight with him.

"Please. Let me handle this," he says in a commanding whisper, trying to shuffle me away from the door.

"No. Come with me." I run behind him and put my hands on his lower back, pushing him towards the bedroom. Try as I might, I can't budge him.

"Ivan! We know you're in there!" a laughing voice yells.

I dodge around him then cut to look out the peephole.

"Listen to your commander, woman!" Ivan's trying to be serious, but he can't stop laughing.

He swoops me up with his right arm, swinging me away from the door, but not before I see a group of Irontrace standing outside with a sign that says, *Get Well Soon, Ivan!*

"Put me down! You'll hurt yourself!" *Oh my word.* His grip is like iron. Wiggling and fighting don't help. I'm stuck. I hang, slumped over his arm. "Let me go!"

He might take me seriously if I wasn't hysterically laughing in helpless defeat.

"You're a shockingly terrible fighter! The worst I've ever seen. Francois is eleven and fights better than you." His voice shakes with laughter. He squeezes me tight against him one more time before putting me down.

"Goodness!" I take an exaggerated deep breath and wrestle my shirt back into place. Wagging a finger, I pretend to scold him.

His laughs fade. We were having a blast, but now the air around us feels softer. Serious. He smooths back my messy hair, and his hand trails a long coil of curls as it falls behind me.

A thought hits in a quiet storm. I need to be here every day, laughing and playing with him for the rest of his life. Don't think about that! It'll ruin the fun. I give him a dazzling smile then lunge forward, opening the door.

"Hello there!" I greet the group brightly.

"That's our boss!" Ivan scrubs a hand through his beard.

The crowd stares at me like they've come to the wrong place until Ivan pops into view.

"Sounds like you guys already started a party from that ruckus behind the door!" a tall blonde man bellows. Laugh spread to the crowd.

"Hey, David. Everybody. Come in. Story, this is Senior Commander David Delac." Ivan motions for them to enter.

What a wonderful night. We talked. We laughed. They told stories about growing up with Ivan. They're like a family. Around midnight, a few left to get a stack of pizzas and drinks from Atlas Cavern.

They came to tell Ivan he's their hero. He looked miserable hearing their praise. I memorized every word.

He's extraordinary.

17

Morning came painfully fast. All too soon, Dad knocked on the door, and any leftover Irontrace asleep throughout Ivan's apartment told us goodbye and left.

"You're due for medicine," I tell Ivan. I don't want to leave yet. I've got to find ways to delay.

"No more pain meds for me. I need to work," Ivan says, taking my laptop from Dad.

"You're not going to ride Obsidian, are you?" I ask.

"Not yet. I need to get back into the control room though. I've never had this many hours off work in my life. Alan, she agreed to wear a tracker. Let me get it ready."

"Look at what we did yesterday." I hand Ivan's sketches to Dad.

"When I got here with the party crowd passed out around you two like you're the King and Queen of the Irontrace, I was sure you'd forgotten this was a work trip." Dad arches an eyebrow while he scans the pages.

"Those will be ready in a few weeks for her. We cannot tell anyone what she's doing. Including Dr. Benedict," Ivan says.

Dad's face tightens. "That's wise."

"Story, my leg hurts. Can you please come here to get your tracker?" Ivan asks from his desk chair.

My ears perk up at this very un-Ivan request. I hurry to stand in front of him. He peers around my hip to see how far away Dad is, then speaks quietly, holding a thin gold band pinched firmly between two fingers.

"Trackers are usually one-way. You need the Irontrace? Squeeze it like this. We'll access audio and video surveillance around you. You'll be safe. I fixed this one up just for you. If you feel it buzzing, that's me. Get to a screen somewhere, anywhere. I'll have a message for you."

Displaying impressive dexterity, he flips the ring over his finger to reveal a massive pear-shaped diamond. It's obnoxiously perfect. My whole face lights up.

"Your ring, *my lady*," he purrs in a voice just above a whisper, sliding in onto my left ring finger.

My heart thumps so hard I cough. He's not joking. Looking thoroughly pleased with himself; he holds my hand for a few extra seconds before letting out a soft laugh.

I lean down. My long hair falls to make a small curtain of privacy. "I'm really going to miss you. It feels like home here with you."

"Come back home to me anytime, Story R." He spins his office chair to bump his knee into mine.

I take a deep breath. I'm supposed to just...leave him? How? I have to do more for him while I can. "If you won't take medicine, you need to use ice for a bit."

While he talks to Dad about our plans for the next several minutes, I bring him coffee and a granola bar, then tuck cold packs in his sling.

"Ready, Story?" Dad asks from the couch.

"Yeah, let me grab my stuff." I walk around, gathering my new laptop and backpack then stop at his desk to tell him goodbye. I whisper, "Stay alive. For me. Please."

"Thank you for taking care of me. Bye, Alan. Francois will get you guys out of here, but I'll be watching." He looks between my dad and I, eyes making quiet calculations. When he reaches his right arm out to me, I bend down and wrap him in a hug.

The one-armed embrace he gives me is so fierce it catches me off guard, making my breath squeak out into his neck. He laughs softly and keeps me pinned to his chest for several seconds. Two can play this game. I carefully dig my nails in, sliding down his spine to his waist, melting closer with the movement.

He gives a happy grumble.

We whisper at the same time. "I want to stay." "Stay with me."

For five glorious seconds, I imagine saying yes. Then my grip tightens with a silent goodbye.

"Because of Lark?" he whispers.

I press my cheek against his and nod.

"Well then, I'll be right here waiting for you."

I give a pained sigh and one last frantic squeeze before dropping my arms. He's much slower to let me go. The uninjured side of his face smirks when I give him a *what was that* look.

"Goodbye, Rhys," Dad says with edge to his voice.

Leaving hurts like mad.

Francois has horses waiting for us. I'm riding the same graceful white horse named Cloud. Sunlight casts a soft hue through the trees. Cool air carries fresh forest scents to us. A constant chorus of birdsong echoes through the canopy.

It's truly the picture-perfect morning to be on a ride.

I'm a mess. My mind is on a tilt-a-whirl. Will I ever be able to fix Lark and Ivan? The thought of another attack on The Helm makes my hands shake and my stomach churn. Ivan should be in the clinic. I play through scenarios that could tempt him to leave the boundary. That loops me back to needing to find a way to remove them as soon as I can.

"*Au revoir,* my friends! Please come back soon. It makes us all so happy to see people from outside," Francois says, taking the reins for our horses.

I loop my new laptop bag over my shoulder.

"We'll be back, Francois, *au revoir*!" I tell him as we walk out of the trees. "How's Lark and Mom?"

"Good. Mom's hands are better. They're both confused about where you went. I told them you have been observing a rare case. The funeral yesterday for Professor Milner and the boys from your trip was all over TV."

I fidget with my ring. "I can't believe I missed it."

"I'm sure it's online somewhere. I got notifications every time you visited a patient and updated their notes. You were in the clinic working during the funeral, not goofing off with Rhys. Excellent job."

"Thanks?"

He gives me a piercing glance as he starts the car. "How is Ivan really doing? We are friendly, but clearly not as close as you two."

"He's excited about my plans. In more pain from the attack than he lets on." A smile tugs at my lips when the sunlight catches my ring. It casts tiny glints of rainbow on the car's ceiling. Even if it's only a tracker to Ivan, I love it. It's something to tie me to him wherever I go. "He doesn't want to be a top commander. But he loves his job. Loves being an Irontrace."

For the rest of the drive home, he fills me in on what they have been up to. When we turn onto our street, Mom and Lark are out front making a colorful scene with sidewalk chalk.

"Story! We missed you! How was the...whatever you've been doing?" Lark asks, running to hug me.

"Amazing. I learned a lot. How are you?"

Mom snatches up my hand. "Where did you get THIS?" When she twists it, the sun dances through the facets of the diamond.

"Did you get married while you were gone and didn't tell us, sis? How much did that cost? I bet it was a whole fortune to buy a diamond that big," Lark sings, grabbing my hand.

"It was a new job gift from my friend," I say.

Dad is by the trunk, unloading new summer toys Mom bought for Lark. His face looks like he bit into a lemon.

Mom continues squinting at it for a few seconds. "It's gorgeous," she says. She must really like diamonds. I've never seen her smile like this about jewelry.

A feeling of purpose and hope settles over me. Ivan is going to help find a way to fix Lark. Tomorrow my new life as a surgeon begins.

"Can we go to the beach? I'll keep Mom away from jellyfish, I promise," Lark whispers.

"Sure! I can't wait to spend my day with you. Go get changed," I reply. She dances up the steps.

The day passes by in a blur of sunshine, swimming, collecting shells, and snacks on the beach. Lark deserves every happy moment, every wonderful day. I focus on enjoying this day together, scared to let my mind drift to her countdown clock.

How many more days like this will I have with her? Will I get any more days with Ivan?

Before I know it, we're driving home to grill dinner. It was a perfectly boring day. No heroism required.

Ivan would've loved it.

18

Focus on the robot as the primary. Write the training program for Lark's AVM removal and see what the robots can do. It's such a mindset shift from discussions with Ivan. He's finding a path for me to make the cuts myself. With ASTRA models, once the surgical plan is written, I relinquish control. I sit at my desk, reviewing plans for tomorrow until my eyes refuse to stay open.

Lark fell asleep reading in my bed hours ago. When I finally curl up on the opposite edge, my anxious thoughts are overpowered by exhaustion.

My eyes fly open. What is that? I feel it again. My ring buzzes repeatedly.

Ivan!

I don't want to disturb Lark with a computer light. I'll answer him from the craft room. I turn on my new laptop and navigate to create a fresh email account. I stop when a message pops up on the screen.

Hope I didn't wake you! -I

"Well, we sleep at night out here. But I'm really happy to hear from you." I catch my reflection in a mirror on the craft room wall and duck out of Ivan's view. If you fall asleep with wet, curly hair, you look like you've been in a tornado when you wake up. I try combing it with my fingers but give up and twist it all to the side.

Sorry! I have good news. And I wanted to see you. Where are you? -I

"The craft room. Lark's asleep in my bed. Please, buzz me anytime. How are you? Are you okay? Are you using ice? Resting? Drinking? Did you eat lunch and dinner? Will you go to the clinic for your next bandage change?"

Whoa. Hey. You seem to be spiraling a tad. I'm good.

I found the problem recording from Lark's hospital room. I got rid of it. Also cleared your search history data from anything related to humans doing surgeries.

David put your house under constant comms shielding. He codified it since you and your dad are both senior Helm staff.

We're generating old, normal activity from your house. That way it doesn't appear as a quiet spot. This gives you freedom to talk to your dad about your findings. Remember, do NOT speak about it outside your house!

You should be completely off the radar now if this is why they have been targeting you. -I

"That's great, thanks. How's work? I'll never believe you when you say you're fine. I have to see for myself."

I'll make it happen. Sadly, messaging you is the best I can do right now from the control room. Work is fine. Boring. -I

Mom's voice from the doorway nearly makes me leap from my chair. "Story, are you talking to someone?"

"Hey, Mom. Sorry."

"You need rest, honey. I don't want you to get run down."

Tell your mom I say hi. Ha! -I

I struggle to hide a laugh. "Yeah, things have been busy lately. I'll head to bed in a few minutes. See you in the morning."

"Night, sweetie," she mumbles, turning towards her room.

I watch her walk away to see when it's safe to talk again.

"Sorry, she worries about me."

Ah, so that's where the worrying comes from. She's a good mom. Again, sorry I woke you up. -I

"Don't apologize. Buzz me anytime."

Despite saying I needed to go every few minutes, I sat, whisper-chatting with him for the next three hours. He wasn't exaggerating. He *really* is bored when he's working on The Kernel.

Hate to say it, but you need to go to bed so you're not falling asleep tomorrow at orientation. -I

I frown. Not ready to leave him yet. I hold up my hand with my tracker ring. "Oh, is this waterproof?"

Yes. What if you get attacked by ninjas in the shower? Get a cramp while swimming? Or what if you unwisely choose not to listen to me and get wrapped up in calico jellyfish?

We're a full-service rescue team. -I

"Glad to hear it."

No more delaying. To bed with you. -I

"Stay safe, Sir." I give him a slow smile.

Gah. No! You're too far away to call me that. Sweet dreams. Wish you were here. -I

He's right. I wish I was there too. "I'll come back to you soon. Good night."

I shut my laptop and head back to my room. I wonder how his wounds really look. Is his eye open? Who will change his bandage? Will he let them do assessments of his grip strength? His motor skills? Is he still wearing his sling? Keeping ointment on his stitches?

So much for sleep. I attempt a cleansing breath and tiptoe to get ready for the day.

Working in the surgery department at the hospital means fresh scrubs are available in the locker room for me. The rest of the time, we'll dress in business casual clothes. Today is my first in-person meeting with Dr. Benedict and I want to make a good impression. I chose a navy-blue pencil skirt, a white silky tank top, and a lacey pink cardigan. With the height dad passed to me, I'm already tall for a girl at five feet nine inches. My summery wedge heels put me a touch over six feet tall. Ivan would still tower over me in these shoes...

One final mirror check, and I gotta admit, I'm pleased with the way my dark reddish brown curls contrast with my outfit. *You're ready for this, Dr. Ross.*

"Hey, everybody!" I greet my family in a bright and cheery voice.

"Morning," Dad says. "We need to drive separately today. I have to leave Lancaster around noon to visit another area clinic."

"That's fine. Drive safe." *If only he could take me too*, I lament into my coffee.

"It's the first day of your real adult life. We need pictures!" Mom lines us up, taking a series of pictures with me in my white coat until I can escape to my car.

Traffic isn't bad. What a relief. I'm starting my day with heavy eyes, jittery hands from too much coffee, and racing thoughts of how to solve the Agora puzzle. I stop at a red light to exit the highway, wondering if I should've messaged Ivan this morning. The huge electronic billboard advertising local sports and events flashes to show flowers and huge words.

Knock em dead today, Story R! -I

Apparently, I'm never alone now. Can he see me? I roll my window down and wave to the billboard, grinning like an absolute fool. The electric screen switches back to school athletic announcements.

The grin stays plastered to my face for the rest of my drive. Traces of it lingered through a boring meeting with an elderly gentleman from Human Resources. He walked me through screen after screen of onboarding documents. It felt like hours passed of signing PDFs until the words were a blur.

He finally said the words I'd been anxious to hear. "Have a good first day, Dr. Ross. Your lab is on the nineteenth floor, suite 1974. Scan your badge to access it."

"Thanks. Have a great day!" I gathered my bag and nearly sprinted from his office. If I stay another second, I'm sure he'll find some random form to pull me back in.

When the elevator doors open on the nineteenth floor, the glittering urban sprawl takes my breath. I've never been high enough to see the view of this perfectly engineered city. It's unreal. Sleek silver and glass skyscrapers rise in clean rows. They divide the business district with checkerboard precision. Pockets of lush greenery punctuate the symmetry for 'coworker recreation.'

Large apartments and condominium complexes are topped with

roof gardens. I don't understand how the flowers are blooming in eerie unison, tumbling over every structure in May, but the effect is breathtaking. Each residential building has oversized patios, and the vertical gardens climbing the exterior walls make the structures look more like a paradise blooming in perfection than part of a towering metropolis.

For an industrial hub, the natural beauty is surreal. Lark would love this. I'll record a video for her. "Look, Lark! This is unbelievable. I'll bring you up here if they let me. You've gotta see this." I pan slowly across the skyline.

"Dr. Ross! Welcome to the nineteenth floor."

Shoot! It's Dr. B. and I'm fiddling with my phone. He barrels at me and pulls me into suite 1974.

Yikes. He's got a death grip on my hand. I twist, but he only tightens his grip. *Let go...*

I plant my feet and yank my hand free.

Please—just be a nice, grandpa type of person. That feeling of him forcing me through the door like a wet rag left a sour taste in my mouth.

"My lab is next door to yours. Suite 1972. Let's meet your robots. Can I call you Story?"

"Uh, sure."

The lab door clicks shut, sounding more like a gunshot than a door closing.

Did that door just lock? Oh, I am NOT liking this.

Maybe the triple shot of iced espresso I chugged from the coffee cart outside HR is what's giving me this fight or flight response? He's highly respected around the world. He was nice. Seemed normal in my interview. Keep an open mind and learn from him.

"I was watching you out there," he says.

I don't answer. I'm working to appear engrossed with the emergency cleanup station by the door.

"What do you think of Lancaster? Seems like it's your first time up here." He turns a chair backwards and sits.

Great. He's settling in for a chat. I'm twitching to explore every nook and cranny of my lab. But I'd like to get off on the right foot. Just focus on work talk and be a good employee.

"It's a stunning view from up here. You're right, I've never seen the city from this high." I walk to one of the lab tables and put my bag down. "My dad's office is on the first floor by the surgical hallway. Much more in the thick of it."

"Yes, he prefers to be down *there*."

"Can I have a few minutes to get familiar with where things are in here?" I ask.

"Take your time, then we'll chat."

The lab is a long, rectangular room. White walls and stainless steel everything screams that this is a sterile area. Along the right wall hang huge monitors.

"Those allow spectators like me to keep an eye on what you and the robots are doing. We can also tie in other facilities with video conferencing to present your work."

Great. I'm working under a microscope. I'll have to be careful to keep my Agora research absent from this lab.

The back wall has a series of refrigerators with glass doors. They hold several types of tissue samples to simulate operations. Bones. Brains. Nerves. Blood vessels. Organs. Skin segments.

The left wall has three patient beds, each with a different ASTRA model. These are better than any I worked with at school.

"Congrats on your proposal being accepted by the hospital board. After your interview, I knew they would be interested in throwing a lot of funding your way," he says.

"Sorry, what proposal was that?" I smile to project calm.

"You came so well-prepared for the interview, I took your ideas, put them in a proposal, and sent it off to the board. They said anyone your age and skill level with such new, innovative ideas should be supported and rewarded. They sent it straight to The Bastion to get their eyes on you. This is The Bastion's gift to make that happen."

"Oh, extraordinary," I choke out.

The Bastion? Really? Ivan just got them to leave me alone. Now they've built me a lab as a gift. This is a loaded, strings-attached gift. I fan through a heavy manual entitled *Surgical Approaches for Dissecting Human Tissues*. Of course it's all robotic surgery approaches. This book won't help me with Agoras. I snap it shut.

"What should I start with today?" The espresso is hitting me harder than normal. My nerves feel like blaring alarms, flashing red.

"Here's the first ASTRA you'll train. An orthopedics cutting and sawing station. Learn this for any vertebrae incisions." He waves me closer.

I'll learn about this station as a requirement of my job here. But to remove Agoras, no vertebrae need cut. The model number is displayed in large silver letters along the rotating arm. ASTRA-4921. I didn't work with this model at Lancaster University. The robots there were all about ten years behind this one and twenty years behind The Helm.

Dr. Benedict pushes me closer to the table with his hand low on my back. I jerk away like his hand is on fire. He does not need to touch me. For any reason. Ever.

"Look at how the robotic arms end in precise surgical instruments for delicate bone cuts. Deep enough to not damage the underlying tissue you'll be training the models to work on," he says in a smooth, unapologetic voice.

He places his hand on my back *again*.

I jerk away *again*.

That settles it. I do not like this man.

"How do I change the tools on the arms?" I move to a supply area to make sure I'm beyond his clammy reach. A cabinet between the wall and the bed has a plethora of instrument options. I haven't done much with these types of ASTRAs. I have a lot to learn at this station.

What are my available tools? Good grief, the font on the labels is so tiny I might need reading glasses. I lean forward and squint to read what size of saw blades to use with each arm.

Hairs on the back of my neck stand. I can feel it. He's there. I brace myself and turn. The supply cabinet is behind me. The robot is on my left; wheels locked by a lever out of my reach. The patient simulator table is on my right. My only path of escape is straight ahead. But Benedict is blocking me in.

He's not merely in my path. He's in my space. Far too close.

Get out of here. "Excuse me. I'm done looking at this station, can I get out?"

He steps even closer, reaching his arm out. "Dr. Ross, I must say, you're just lovely."

Plastic crinkles as I tear open an orthopedic bone saw arm. It has a serrated blade about eight inches long. Since he refuses to back up and I'm much taller than him, it's only a few inches from his nose. "Back up, please. I would hate to cut you accidentally."

He pushes my hand away. "That's sharp, be careful." It works. He steps just enough to the side for me to flee.

My lab door had better lock. It's not the espresso setting me on high alert. It's him. I don't want to seem like a friendly, good employee anymore. I just want him to leave.

"The robot here works on surgeries for blood vessels," he speaks, staying several feet away from me, eyeing the bone saw I'm fidgeting with.

Duh. It's a vascular control ASTRA. What else would it do?

Electrocautery tips in a range of sizes with smoke evacuation filters are lined up on a wheeled cart. Special tools to allow for knot-tying and guided suturing eliminate unsteady movements that would lead to errors.

"Wait. These ASTRA are all separate?" I ask. That can't work well in emergencies.

"Correct. We wheel them in and out as needed through stages of the surgery. It's cumbersome, but that's one reason you're here. Find a way to fix it for your vascular specialty," he says, tone sharp.

Is this my punishment for not wanting his hands on me? Being suddenly accountable for figuring out why twenty-five years of surgeons haven't fixed this puzzle for ASTRA?

I don't respond. I focus on the items at the station. Suction tips to remove fluids. An arm to irrigate the surgical field. Balloon catheters to dilate blood vessels and temporarily block them off. Vascular clips for closing tiny blood vessels.

This robot and I will be best buddies. Much of what lies before me can help me at The Helm.

A hand on my shoulder makes me stiffen. "What do you think of it so far, Dr. Ross?"

"The lab is great. I have a concern though. I'm very introverted. I don't like being touched. Do not touch me again." How can I be any more clear?

"Oh, I'm only being friendly, come on," he says. Then he winks.

Ew.

"I disagree. Being friendly does not require you to touch me." Plus, touching a person when they've made it clear they don't want you to (by words *or* actions) is creepy, disrespectful, and intrusive.

"I see your wedding or engagement ring. We are a couple of colleagues, working closely together, both in committed relationships." He holds up his hand to show me his wedding ring.

My ring.

If I squeeze this beauty right now, Ivan would call me. He'd ask what I need. I'd say, *"Hey Sir, hate to bug you. But can you please blow up Suite 1972 to scare my touchy new boss?"*

I'm sure he'd respond with something that would make my heart skip a beat like, *"I'd absolutely love to, beautiful!"*

Surely that would put some fear into Dr. B. I spin on my heel to hide a smile.

"Ready to show me the last station? You need to get out of here and get back to your own work, Dr. Benedict."

The imaging ASTRA provides and interprets high-definition views. Tiny ultrasound probes will identify blood flow in near microscopic vessels. Extending over the bed is a C-shaped angiogram machine to keep track of progress as the robot works.

To come up with a plan for a human to be the primary surgeon, I need to spend time reverse engineering the way surgeries work now. How helpful are surgical robots, really? Why haven't they been able to fix a problem like Lark's?

"Dr. Ross. What do you think of the lab?" Dr. Benedict tosses an arm around my waist. He does it so fast it tips me off-balance, making me stumble towards him to keep my feet.

Surely my dad doesn't know this guy is such a freak. He'll flip out when he hears about this. I try to step away. He holds on, digging his fingers into my side. I've had enough of this.

I smile down at his disgusting, charm-laced smirk. Then smash my wedge heel down hard on his foot. He makes an annoyed grunt. I step away.

I'm so done with him.

"The lab is great. I would like to know our typical workflow. Will you work much in here with me?"

I'll hand in my resignation right now if he says yes.

"I'll pop in and out. You're not the only young surgeon under my mentorship. I require your sample work videos and research papers to be submitted on Thursday afternoons. We'll review them on Fridays in a one-on-one meeting. Otherwise, the lab is yours for now."

He holds the keys out to me.

I don't move. After several seconds, he walks over and presses them into my hand. The look in his eyes is a warning that I'll probably be fired soon.

Oh well. Delac hired me at The Helm. Dr. Benedict is disgusting, but he's out of my lab. Finally. Time to get to work. I jog over and lock the door from the inside, twisting the handle several times to check.

Problem number one strikes me as the easiest to fix. Why are the stations separate? One full surgical suite would make a smoother workflow between cutting, imaging, and vascular control. That's an Ivan problem to figure out.

The orthopedic ASTRA is fun to play with, making cuts into the skull sample based on the simple training program I throw together:

IF (target = occipital) AND (bone.length = TRUE)

   THEN INITIATE oscillating saw

ELSE

   NOTIFY: "Cut complete."

After generating enough NOTIFY messages to cut the skull sample into something resembling white confetti, I'm bored. This doesn't seem incredibly relevant to Agora surgery.

Time to work with my vascular ASTRA. I walk along the fridge wall, reading their contents. *Vascular simulation tissues.* Bingo. I dig through the shelves until I find a bin of AVM samples to work with. I have to see why the robots miserably fail on these.

Someone knocks loudly on my lab door.

I slam the fridge. Please don't be Dr. B! My lab door is heavily frosted. I can only see the outline of a person.

"One second, my hands are busy," I call from about ten feet away.

"No rush. Open up whenever," Dad says.

Thank goodness! I fumble with the keys to unlock it.

"Dad! Hello, come in." I lock back up before turning to him.

"Hello. I wanted to see your lab. Are you scared to be alone in here?" He twists the doorknob to see if it's really locked.

"Mmm...Kinda?" There is no freedom of speech here. Benedict could be watching. "Want to see what I have been working on?"

"Sure, then we can head home for dinner."

What? There's no way it's that late. My eyes jump to the clock behind dad. It's almost eight pm. "I lost track of time."

The lab goes dark.

19

The ceiling lights cut out. The vascular ASTRA console powered off. All other lab monitors shut down. Faint sunlight spills in from the high, small windows.

"The generators will kick on if there's a problem. Give it a minute," Dad says.

Shadows cast on the metal robots make them look ominous instead of familiar. I'd rather go in the hallway and risk facing Dr. B. than stay here with the dark metal machines. Plus, Dad is with me now. Surely Dr. B. will behave if we run into him.

"Hmm, grab your bags. Let's go see what's wrong." Dad flips the light switch a few times.

I unlock my lab door. The far end of the hallway is in complete darkness. This end has some light from the windows by the elevator.

"Does the hospital ever lose power?" I ask.

"Never," Dad replies.

My tracker ring softly buzzes on my finger.

Ivan. I wish he was here. There are no screens in the hallway to check what he wants. I look out the windows over the city. Maybe he'll have a message out there for me. Power is out everywhere. People are milling on sidewalks, looking around. Stoplights aren't working. Cars are stopped in the streets. Electronic billboards have gone dark.

"The elevators won't work. Stairs it is. The generators really should have been on by now," Dad says.

I stare out the window, ring buzzing on my finger.

Dad's phone rings. "Hello. Yes, we're good." He pauses. "Okay. She's right here." His jaw clenches when he hands his phone to me.

"Hello," I say.

"Hi. Can't talk long. I needed to hear your voice to make sure you're okay," Ivan blurts.

"I am. You?"

"Yes. Do me a favor? Squeeze your ring occasionally to let me know you're okay. I'll buzz you off and on so you know I'm there."

"I will. Did The Helm lose power too?"

"No."

"Good. Is this something you can fix?"

"Of course. I'll go work on it. Call you back as soon as I can." The call ends.

"Ready to go?" I hand Dad his phone.

"Let me call your mom real quick." He leaves her a voicemail message to text him while I stare at the scene unfolding below. People dart out of buildings are look up.

"I can't believe the generators aren't on yet," Dad says, pushing open the door for the stairs. "We'll peek into each floor to see if anyone needs help."

When I chose my outfit for the day, I didn't foresee a nineteen-floor descent in wedge heels, but here we go. Small emergency lights outline the edge of each stair to guide our steps. Dad turns on his phone flashlight.

We're the only two people exiting the nineteenth floor. Once we get to the eighteenth floor, a few people join us in the stairwell.

"Dr. Ross, where's the generators?" an older man asks.

"I'm not sure. Does anyone need help on that floor?" Dad asks.

"No. Just a few old researchers. They'll be the last to leave the ship."

More join as we descend. We're all bumping into each other now. I have to be careful. One misstep and I'll go down for sure. And since the crush is now elbow-to-elbow, I'd take at least a few people with me.

The stale air is stifling. I take off my cardigan and tuck it in my bag. After another flight of stairs, my hair is a hot, frizzy trail down my back.

I pause to pull it up and am met by nasty looks for holding the line still.

"Sorry," I mutter.

My ring softly buzzes. I give it a couple squeezes and keep walking behind Dad. He turns to check on me on the fourteenth floor.

"You okay? Give me your bag."

"Thanks." I trudge along behind him.

On the landing of the twelfth floor, he opens the door and calls into the sunlit hallway, "Hello! Does anyone need help?"

A hugely pregnant woman stands with a wailing twin toddler holding each of her hands. "I can't get ahold of my husband. He went to get our car. Can you help me find him?"

"Of course, come with us. I'm Dr. Alan Ross." Dad holds the door for her.

She tries to pull her kids in. They catch sight of strangers moving in the dark and make a break back onto the main floor. Showing impressive sprint skills for a lady who's ready to give birth, she catches up with them.

"Come on, Ben. Kira, let's go meet Daddy," she pleads. "I'm sorry, I can't carry them down all those stairs." Tears spill from her eyes.

"It's okay, this is my daughter, Dr. Story Ross. Can we carry them for you?" Dad asks.

She nods and smiles. "I'm Kelsey."

Dad tries to make it sound like an adventure. "Nice to mee you, Kelsey. Hey, Ben and Kira. Let's find your daddy. Do you like big sugar cookies? With icing and sprinkles of course." The kids nod. "The cafeteria has those. My kids love them."

The little girl steps towards her mom. Kelsey scoops brown-haired Kira up and hands her to me.

"Let's get some cookies," I say settling her on my hip. She's little. I'd guess maybe two years old? "My name is Story. I'm a doctor. What's your name?"

Kira doesn't answer. Her huge brown eyes are bright with tears. She reaches over my shoulder for her mom.

Fair enough, kid. I'm not a fan of strangers either. Dad picks up the sniffling little Ben. He's much better with kids than I am. Ben listens attentively to Dad's car salesman-like spiel about cookies and sprinkle colors. Even if I tried, I couldn't make them sound interesting like he does.

Two doctors in lab coats make a gap for us to fall back into the crowd. I'm carrying Kira with my left hand, clinging to the rail with my right. It was already hot here, now every face drips with rivers of sweat. It's getting too hot, too fast. If the power is out, the furnace can't be on. But it *really* feels like the furnace is on.

We're still up on the floors with medical suites for appointments, labs, and offices. You'd think there would be less people here on a Monday evening. More people—too many people—funnel into the stairs. The crowd has stalled. Voices have been quiet, but now people are getting anxious. And loud.

"Move!"

"Keep walking!"

"It's so hot. I'm going to pass out."

An elbow jabs me in the back, nearly throwing me off the step I've been stuck on for two minutes. A young woman's face peeks around my shoulder.

"Ah! So sorry, miss. Thought there was a spider."

"It's fine. Be careful." I readjust Kira on my hip. *I would die if a spider crawled across me right now.*

My ring buzzes. There's no way I'm letting go of the rail to squeeze it.

"Dr. Richardson, can you please check in at each floor and see if anyone needs help? That's how I found this little guy," Dad says to a person I don't recognize.

"Yes, Dr. Ross." She exits onto the floor.

It sends a woosh of less hot air my way when she shuts the door. I'm tempted to run after her. Why are we even on the stairs? There might not be an actual emergency. We could be sitting in an empty office, stretched out on comfy furniture, not stuck in this vertical oven with people touching me on every side. I would kill for some air conditioning right about now. Well, not kill, but I'd consider doing some sketchy things.

Ivan must be worried. My ring buzzes constantly.

"Where are the generators?" I ask Dad.

He glances over his shoulder and shrugs.

"Tell me more about your dog," he says to Ben.

Ben takes off in a nervous kid jabber about a "black dawg, small as a po-day-to" named Taco.

"Is Taco your dog too?" I ask Kira. She glowers at me. I pat her back. "It's okay. You're going to be a big sister soon. I'm a big sister. It's so much fun."

I hope Lark and Mom are okay. It's almost Lark's bedtime. If the power isn't back on when she's supposed to go to bed, she'll be so scared. But maybe our house has power? The Helm does. This might have only hit Lancaster's city center. It could be an early summer brownout.

Alarms shriek and acrid smoke trails down from the vents. I tuck Kira's head under my chin and bounce her from side-to-side. Smoke rolls heavy around us.

People are trying to get a better look with phone flashlights and it's giving the smoke a sickening strobe effect.

Kelsey shines her phone to check on Kira and me.

My tank top has streaks of residue clinging to it. I swipe it with my forearm. It smears a dark trail down my chest. My fingers are left with a powdery soot I can't get off. This has to be coming from the smoke. I was clean when I left my lab.

That's it.

It's roasting hot in here. Thick black smoke. The hospital is on fire somewhere. We're dying in here today.

I'm glad Lark is home, safe. Maybe Ivan can run with my research and help someone fix her. They can fix him too.

If he was here, he'd have some crazy fix to save us.

"There's no fire. Do not be alarmed!" a man in a maintenance uniform yells. "WALK SLOWLY DOWN THE STEPS!"

How does he know that?

"Keep moving down the stairs!" Dad yells. "Get the crowd moving."

People echo his calls, straining their voices over the alarms. Ben and Kira sob.

Kelsey holds her stomach with one hand and pats Kira with her other hand. My eyes drop to her huge baby bump.

Please do not go into labor right now.

"It's okay, babies. I'm sure Daddy is waiting at the bottom, keep moving," Kelsey says, oozing fake confidence. Her voice gives way to coughing. She stretches her shirt up over her mouth.

"Let's make masks from our shirts too." I briefly let go of the rail to pull my shirt over my nose.

Kira tries but is crying too hard. Her little chubby toddler hands can't do it. I take a risk letting go of the rail again to help her.

My ring is nagging me, adding to my other irritations and anxieties.

The alarms.

Crying Kira.

Yelling people.

I'm lightheaded from heat.

Smoke hurts my throat.

Despite telling everyone to move, the crowd is frozen. I can't pass out while holding a kid. If I put her down, the crowd won't see her. She might get crushed.

I turn to the spider lady behind me that elbowed me earlier. "Don't step on me," I choke in a harsh bark.

Spider lady nods, wide-eyed.

I crouch to sit on the step behind Dad. Talking to Kira might calm me. I open my mouth to speak, but smoke fills my mouth. I cough into my elbow and try again. My voice won't work. *Forget it.* I pull my shirt back up on my face and rock Kira, staring at the solid, unmoving wall of legs around us. I'm awful. I can't even talk to comfort this poor kid.

I heave in a deep breath but still feel starved for air.

Slow down. Breathe.

My ring buzzes. Ivan is fine.

Imagine him pushing some button to check on me from his office chair. Focus on that. Picture his hand. I *know* that hand. I studied it while he slept.

The buzzes come in fast bursts, six at a time. I breathe in during a burst of vibrations. Breathe out for two bursts.

The storm inside me is relenting. Ivan is saving me again. I can't bring myself to push the button yet and tell him I'm okay.

I'm not okay, Ivan.

The tightness in my chest and throat is replaced by hot, smoke-filled air. I hoist myself back up. Kira leaves her head on my shoulder. I pat her back gently and bounce in place on our step.

I find my voice to talk to Kira. "I've never had a dog. I want one someday. Do you like horses?" She nods on my shoulder. "I *LOVE* horses. Want me to tell you about my favorite horse?" She nods again and sniffles. I sway gently, telling her about Obsidian.

Several minutes into my "made-up" tale of riding Obsidian through a forest to find his owner (a handsome, black-haired prince, of course) the power flicks on. Kira jerks her head up.

The smoke coming out of the vents cuts to a trickle.

Deafening applause and cheers tear through the staircase.

Kira covers her ears and breaks down. "I go see daddy! Now!" she wails.

Dad's phone rings in his back pocket. *Ivan.* I grab it.

"Hello?"

"Why didn't you squeeze your ring?!" Ivan nearly yells.

Dad looks at me. I mouth "Ivan."

"Who's crying? Tell me you're okay?" Ivan blurts.

"Mmhmm."

"Words please," he says. *Words?* I can't right now. If I talk, especially to *him*, I'll sob. "Please, Story. Give me something. How are you?"

"I'm okay."

"Doesn't sound like it. Leave the stairwell. Take the elevator down. There's no fire. No danger. This was a trap to cause panic."

"It worked."

"Get out of there and get some fresh air. I'll make sure you get home safe. I promise. Call you later." Dad's phone goes dark.

Why did I leave The Helm so easily?

20

Dad and I met up in the craft room after Mom and Lark fell asleep. They had spent the power outage in the yard playing and barely noticed anything was amiss.

"The story from the hospital board is that there was a fire in the electrical room that led to emergency protocols being activated. The generators failed because of a missed maintenance cycle. I don't buy it," Dad says.

I don't want to talk about the nightmare in the staircase. It took a loofah and half a container of lilac sugar scrub to get the smoke residue off my skin. The smell still clings to my hair. "Let's go over my notes from today."

Dad thinks my idea to combine surgical robots will be a huge help.

"It's such a flaw," I say. "Why does ASTRA do one surgical function per bot? An orthopedics robot does skull or neck surgery. A vascular surgeon robot works on arteries and veins. General surgeon robot removes a foreign object like a neural chip. It's never been addressed?"

"They've tried. Haven't yet found a permanent solution. It's a stupid setup. Even our most advanced robotic models only work on one body system. Ivan will be able to build whatever you need for Agoras. I'm sure he didn't let you leave without a way to contact him?" Dad asks.

I nod.

"Go. Talk to him. My decades of fumbling with ASTRA haven't helped." He runs a hand through his hair. "He'll figure it out. Love you. Night, sweetie."

I grab his hand. "You haven't spent all those decades fumbling with ASTRA. You're Helm's chief of surgery. That's more important. You know it. Night, love you, Dad." He looks exhausted. I'll talk to him about creepy Dr. Benedict another time.

I peek in on Lark. She sleeps peacefully, softly illuminated by the glow of her horse nightlight.

Today was a harsh reality check. I'm planning what tools will help someone cut into her fragile neck someday. But actually seeing those tools in action, thinking of them slicing deep into Lark makes my chest ache. She's so sweet and has been treated monstrously.

"Why is it so cold in here tonight?" I mutter, grabbing a thick down blanket from the hallway linen closet. I wrap up like a mummy and shuffle to my bedroom. Lesson learned. I'll never complain about the AC again. I'll just add layers. I throw myself into the recliner and open my new laptop.

I'm ready to send today's notes to Ivan. Sharing the burden makes the whole project seem more manageable. Seconds after my laptop opens, a message scrolls across the screen.

Hello! Cold? -I

"It's freezing in here tonight. Get ready, I'm sending you a bunch of notes. How was your day?"

Wait. I have a surprise. -I

My screen flashes. A video feed takes over most of it, with about an inch gap around it.

"Hey, stranger," Ivan says, grinning until his stitches pull taught.

"It's you!" Panicking in the stairwell left me exhausted. Dr. Benedict freaked me out and filled me with rage. The thought of anyone I love needing Agora surgery makes me feel helpless.

Seeing Ivan causes an actual pain in my chest. His left eye is open most of the way. Bruises have darkened black on his face and neck. There's no t-shirt collar peeking out of his sweatshirt. He still can't raise his arm to get dressed.

I'd give almost anything to be there with him. It's too much. I put my laptop on the floor out of the camera view.

"Did you drop your laptop? Where did you go?"

I bury a loud sob in my lap pillow.

"Are you crying at your favorite patient again? I told you that you can't keep doing that." Ivan's voice is threaded with worry. I need to get myself together. I grab tissues from the stand beside my chair.

"Story, where are you? Please come back," he pleads. "I'm kidding. Come cry at me. Cry at me anytime, I don't mind."

One more shuddery breath. I can't leave him hanging. I pick up my laptop.

"Where's your sling?"

"I'm, I...I didn't know my sling was that important." He reaches behind his laptop and loops his sling on. "Look! All slinged up. Better now?"

"Much." He may not be here with me but laughing at his efforts to be a good patient takes some of the weight off my chest. "Sorry. Seeing you made me so happy. I couldn't hold back my weird stress from today anymore."

"Tell me about your weird stress. I'm an expert at fixing your problems."

"Okay. But first hold up your right hand and promise me you won't blow anything up. No cars, no labs, no people."

He tries to frown. "Under no circumstances can I ever make a promise like that."

I snort. "I'm serious."

"How about we make a deal? For you, Story R, I swear that blowing something up will be my last resort."

"Deal. Can you teach me how to fight?"

"Robots? People? Did the robots hit you today? Who we going after?" He makes a tough face and holds his right hand up in a fist.

"Ivan!" I laugh. "People! You said I'm bad at it."

He peers into the camera, scrutinizing me. "Okay. All jokes aside. Today was the first day of your exciting new job. Why do you think I'm going to be so upset by it that I'll want to blow something up? And *why* is your next question for me to teach you how to fight?"

I walk through my experience with Dr. Benedict. The more I speak, the icier his silence becomes.

"So, he touched you, multiple times, and blowing something up is off-limits?"

"Correct. You cannot blow him or anything adjacent to him up."

He looks down. I hear him peck at the keyboard with his right hand.

"Hey, Rhys, quit typing. Hands off those keys."

"You don't trust me?" He holds his hand up with mock indignance.

"I'm still figuring you out. I do know you like to blow things up."

"Got it. Earning trust. I'm being trustworthy." He smiles before continuing to type. "Done. Tomorrow is a fresh, new day."

"What did you do? You didn't hurt him, right?"

He puffs out an amused breath. "You need to understand something about me. I do not hurt or kill people. Robots? That's a different story. But a person?" He shakes his head. "Never. However. I'm *very* creative, baby. A couple quick clicks and I just turned his life upside down."

Baby? I bite my lip to hold back a grin. "Happy to hear it. I wouldn't have really hurt him with the bone saw I waved in his face."

His booming laugh might have just woken Lark, my parents, and half the neighborhood. I love it.

"Bone saw, huh? Good girl. Are you okay?"

"Yeah. Just mad."

"Same. How are your knee and shoulder?"

"Better, thanks. How's your pain? Why don't I see a bandage peeking out of there?"

"What bandage?" He shows me a few small band aids on his chest. They don't cover his injuries.

"Did the clinic okay that when you went for a checkup?"

"That question sounds like a trap. Can I see your shoulder injury to make sure it's better?"

"No! No more shoulder for you until I see some clinic notes proving you're taking care of yourself."

I tilt my head at him in disapproval. He gives a smoldering half smile.

He's off the hook for now.

"Well played. You need to get some rest. Let's go over your notes," he says.

While I speak, he busily sketches. He occasionally interrupts to ask engineering questions.

"I'll have these ready in a few weeks. Can you come try them out then?"

Weeks? If I don't go back to him for a few weeks, that means he'll only have ten months left.

"Sure," my voice squeaks out.

He drops his pencil, whipping to look at me. "Hey. I really miss you, Story."

There's no hint of hesitation in his voice. It seems like a perfectly natural thing to say. I admire the way he always leads with honesty, not attempting to hide how he feels.

Speaking of being honest...time to admit a few things myself. He's incredibly handsome despite his injuries. A couple locks of black hair dangle in the middle of his forehead. And those nearly onyx eyes? They're magnetic. I couldn't look away if I tried. But I'm not trying.

"I miss you too. Are you busy tonight? I'd be much happier if I had more Ivan time in my life."

He rubs the back of his neck before giving me a bold smile that almost melts me into a puddle. "More Ivan time? You got it."

We climb into bed and talk for hours before falling asleep, illuminated by the soft glow of our screens.

The next morning when my alarm goes off, my laptop is still connected to Ivan's. His camera is aimed at his now-empty bed from his dresser. He's nowhere in sight.

Might as well get ready for the day. I stand, braiding my hair, staring into my closet to choose an outfit when I hear him.

"Good morning, Story." He's dressed and ready, holding his coffee.

"Morning! You're ready for the day. I'm in my pajamas, trying to tame this unruly hair."

"You look beautiful, slacker."

Look at his sparkly-eyed smile. It matches mine.

"What are you up to today?"

"Work." He aims his screen at his shoulder. "Look, the sling is on."

"That's why you're my favorite patient. Can we do this again to-night?"

And every other night.

"Absolutely."

"Stay alive for me, please."

"I'll try!" He waves then disappears.

I don't love that response, but Mom and Lark are clamoring for me to come down for breakfast. I'll message him later to tell him I meant it.

21

When the elevators open on the nineteenth floor, a large desk is positioned by the window. A man in a security officer's uniform sits facing the elevator. None of this was here yesterday.

"Dr. Ross. Good morning, I'm Officer Schrader," he says. "I'll be here daily for your check-in and check-outs."

That's odd...

"Good morning, Officer."

He points to what looks like a small scale. "Please place your bag on the scanner."

"Okay." I force a smile.

"New security protocols. Bastion's orders," he says. A shiver traces my spine. "Have a good day, Doctor Ross."

I smile brightly and walk away. Dad was gone this morning before I woke up. Hopefully, he's at The Helm and he'll let me talk to Ivan. I lock my lab door, glance around to make sure I'm alone, and call Dad.

"Morning, honey," Dad says after it rang once.

"Can you do me a favor? Please?"

"Mmhmm?"

My lab is under surveillance. *Act normal!* "Can you please give me the phone number for our family dentist's office?"

"You need this right now, at seven in the morning?"

"Yes, Dad. I do."

"Did you hurt a tooth?"

"No. This was stupid of me, right? Forget it, I'll look it up. What are you doing today?"

"Workkkkingggg. Do you have something else to tell me?"

"No. I want to hear all about your day so far. Where are you working? Lancaster Medical Hub?"

"What are you-? You know I love you, but I do not have time for this. You don't either."

"If you have any friends there who can give me a dentist recommendation, tell them to call me."

"Story. What is going on? Is something wrong?"

"Not at all! If you won't tell me about your day, I'll tell you about mine. This is super cool. The Bastion has a security guard posted outside my lab now. Watching them scan my stuff made me feel like I'm famous!"

He sighs. "Wow. That is an interesting new security measure. I'm glad my daughter is safe."

"I knew you would love it. Have a good day, Dad."

"You too. Bye."

Come on, Ivan. Take the bait.

Today I'm focusing on the vascular control station. I want to see how my ASTRA dissects blood vessels. I spend an hour writing my plan for the day before I check my phone.

I have a message from a number I don't know. It's an Irontrace logo and a softly flashing gray link.

"Well, phish me, it's an Irontrace." If this is a scam, they win; they can have my money and social security number. I tap the logo.

A small black terminal opens on my phone with a message: *Hi! David approved a secure phone channel for you and me. Your dad called me. Said he had a worrisome conversation with you? Are you okay? Don't worry about Schrader. I've got an eye on him. -I*

He's here now too!

I send a quick reply. *Thank you. Yes, I am great. Can't wait to see you tonight! -<3*

Work flies by. Before I know it, I'm at our kitchen table coloring with

Lark while Mom makes dinner. I can't shut my brain off. As Lark and I work on coloring a vase of flowers, I'm mentally reviewing diagrams from today. Everything I do with robots in Lancaster; I need to replicate with my own hands at The Helm. I have to commit it all to memory to discuss with Ivan as soon as possible.

What if I fix him and he can come color with Lark and me? She'd be impressed by his drawing and shading skills.

Lark shivers, digging a bony elbow into my ribs. "Brr! I'm freezing, Story. Aren't you?"

Her arms are covered in goosebumps. Man, I must've been totally checked out. I'm all goosebumpy too.

"You sick?" I check her for a fever with the back of my hand. *Am I sick?*

"Nope. It's just super cold in here. Let's go outside and play to warm up," Lark says.

"You're right, baby girl, it's freezing!" Mom says, walking to the thermostat. "Fifty-five?! Brrrbrrrbrrr!" Mom repeatedly jabs the button. "Uh. Shoot. I'm making it worse! It's thirty-nine now. I'll call the electric infrastructure company. Maybe they need to reset something."

"Lark, let's go play." I open the glass doors to the deck. The Ohio humidity will warm us up.

"Soccer time!" Lark yells, kicking a ball to me.

We sprint and play until I'm dragging.

"Goal!" I cheer when Lark kicks the ball onto the porch.

I peek inside to check on Mom. Where is she? A pot is boiling over on the stove. The oven door is open. I push up on my tiptoes. She lays in a tangled heap below the thermostat.

"Mom!" I scream, running inside. Her pulse is steady. She's breathing. *Wake up! Blink!* I shake her shoulder. "Mom! Are you okay? Lark! Get my phone!"

"What happened?" Lark cries, throwing herself down by me.

"Lark, grab a couch blanket. We have to roll her on her left side."

Mom is stable. I just need to support her until help gets here. I can do this.

"I think she got shocked, Lark. She'll be okay. Use her phone and call Dad. I'll call 911." I turn on my phone flashlight and do a quick pupil check on Mom. That annoys her. She jerks awake.

"Girls," Mom groans.

Lark hugs her and talks ninety miles an hour about how scary that was while I answer questions for emergency services.

"Mom! Dad wants to talk to you!" Lark shoves Mom's phone in her face.

"Amelia! What happened?" Dad yells through the speaker.

Mom looks at me for help. I answer him.

"Something's wrong with the air conditioner. Mom called the power company. I think they were trying to get her to reset something. The thermostat shocked her. I'm on my phone with 911. She was unconscious briefly. Her pulse and breathing were good. Pupils even and responsive. She has a burn on her right hand."

"I'll be waiting for her in the ER. Can you stay home with Lark?" he asks.

"Of course. We hear sirens. Keep talking to Mom," I tell him. "Lark, go open the front door. They're almost here."

Watching them wheel Mom out is surreal. Was this another attack? Is anyone safe in 2050?

"I'm still cold." Lark stares at the ambulance as it drives away.

Poor little girl. I give her a quick hug. "Let's have some fun. You get the soccer ball. I gotta call a friend."

Ivan answers immediately. "What's up, my lovely Story R?"

"Mom got shocked. The ambulance took her. Lark's cold. And scared. How did this happen?"

"No! What can I do from here? Anything. Name it."

"I have no idea. I'm not sure why I called you, sorry."

"Are you kidding? *Always* call me." His rapid typing clicks away in the background. "Are you staying home, or going to the hospital?"

"Dad said keep Lark home. But...are we going to get shocked too?"

"No. No one else is getting shocked. Tell me Lark's favorite dinner."

"Cheese pizza and salad."

More lightning-fast typing from his end. How do his fingers move like that?

"'K. A night of warmth and fun. Coming right up. Give me just a few minutes. Tell me about your day."

I try. My thoughts are too scattered to focus on what I did in the Lancaster lab. "Dad messaged me. Mom's doing good. Her heart is in a normal rhythm. They're keeping her for a few hours."

"That's great. I fixed your HVAC system. Dinner will be there in thirty minutes. A party company is on its way to set up some fun for Lark."

"Thank you. Wish you could be here."

He sighs. "Me too. Call me when you can. Bye for now."

"I will."

The kitchen is a wreck. I just finished cleaning the worst of it when someone knocked on the front door. A crew from a party supply company had me open the gates to our backyard. Lark and I watched them turn our yard into a wonderland.

First, they set up an inflatable bounce house with slides. Then they strung up enough tropical flowery lights to cast a neon glow on our whole block. One man made a roaring fire and placed chairs and a table by it. Lark jumped for joy when they covered the table with smores supplies. Near the deck, they made a painting station with regular and glow in the dark acrylic paints. Lark clapped when she saw the variety of blank canvases and mini ceramic statues to paint. Then they set up a slushy machine and a pina colada mixer.

Another man wanders in with three huge bouquets. A dozen red roses with a card that says, *Feel better, Amelia.* A bouquet of wildflowers with a card that says, *Happy summer break, Lark!* And a third bouquet with a mixture of roses and tropical flowers with a card that has a heart drawn on it next to *Still being patient. -I.*

"Anything else, Miss?" A man hands me an invoice marked *Paid by IR.* Along the bottom it says: *Enjoy, beautiful. Drink a pina colada for me. Come home soon. -I.*

Home! He is my home. Love at first sight? Insta-love? Those seemed impossible. Made up. A trick only the inexperienced would fall prey to. Until Ivan.

He's fully consumed me. I may not know him very well, but at the same time, I *know* him. He won't get bored. Won't move on and just abandon me. No. Ivan is the kind of fire that sweeps through a forest—cleaning, purifying. Leaving hope, beauty, and a fresh start in its wake. He's changed me at my very core.

This is not some simple infatuation. Not some trauma bond caused by both of us nearly dying and relying on each other to get through. And even if this was some weird trauma thing? What's the worst that could happen—I'll spend the next year safer with him watching over me, much happier because...he's IVAN for goodness sakes, and then I'll deal with my heart being shredded when he dies. That's worth the risk to spend the next year with him. I'm in. It's simple. He *has* to be a part of my life from now on. Anything less is unacceptable.

"Miss?" The flower man snaps his fingers. "Do you need anything else?"

I settle the bouquet from Ivan against my chest. "Oh. No. Thanks."

Lark launches into a barrage of questions as soon as the gate shuts. "What is all this stuff, Story? Can I go play? Can you go on the slides too? How many slushies can I have? Two? Three? Five?"

Ivan should be a part of this. "I need to get something, be right back."

I race to get my laptop. The doorbell rings. Geez, what now? I sprint down the stairs, trying not to trip and break my neck. That's the last thing we need tonight.

A young delivery driver from a local pizza place smiles at me anxiously when I rip the door open. "Have a great night, Miss. Hope we got the pizzas right."

"I'm sure they're great. Thanks!" I balance the pizza box and bag of salad on my hip. "Lark, open the back door please. Hurry, I'm about to drop this."

She opens the door then runs back to the bounce house.

I open my laptop and whisper, "Ivan. You there?"

You okay? -I

"Yes. Will it distract you if I leave my video on so you can be here with us?"

I'd like that. -I

"Me too. It's stupid how much I miss you." I turn my laptop webcam, giving him a full view of the yard.

Lark dances off the slide and hops up the porch steps. "Story! Did you look at the pizzas? I've never seen heart shaped pizza!"

She takes a piece and runs back into the yard.

I raise my eyebrows at Ivan.

Can't a guy be whimsical? -I

"I love this side of you. But how did you pay for all this? I thought Irontrace don't do money?"

Atlas Caverns doesn't do money. Us Irontrace? We are...(trying to be humble-ish here but you're the one I'm leaving my Merit Fund to when my Agora blows)...LOADED. Perk of the job, I guess? -I

"I don't want money! I just want you to stay alive for years—for decades."

Decades with you? -I

Yes! I press my hands to my heart and nod, fast and certain. *Please give us a whole life.* I silently wish.

Lark launches out of the bounce house slide and tears through the yard, pulling my attention from him. "Thank you! Thank you! Thank you! Best night ever. What's your favorite animal? I'll paint you one. I love you, best sister in the world!"

"Thank you," I mouth to Ivan. "I didn't do this by myself," I tell Lark. "A friend helped. Can you paint him something too?"

"Yes! What's his favorite animal?" She jumps up and down, hugging me.

I beam at the laptop behind her, waiting for his answer.

Obsidian, of course. We'll find a way to save her, <3. -I

I grin.

"Let's eat, then play." Lark hands me a piece of pizza. "I want a blue slushie. You have the white kind," she whispers, "The machine says the white ones are for adults."

"Can you paint my friend a black horse? On a beach. No forest or trees anywhere near his horse."

"Yes!"

We bounced. We painted. We made smores by the fire. Then did it all again until we could barely crawl inside for showers and pajamas.

By the time Lark brushed her teeth and fell asleep, Ivan was done at work for the day. His usually deep voice is lower, rougher than normal. The weight of attacks on The Kernel is wearing him down. Today, someone breached the electrical infrastructure models. They made it too hot or cold in homes worldwide.

"When people messed with the thermostats, they shorted out and shocked people," he says. "I'm really worried about this one. It was a test for something much worse."

"Who did it?"

He shakes his head. "We'll find them. But I want to be out there with you so badly it's tearing me up. I was fairly happy here in my prison before I met you. I knew what to expect. Work maybe another couple years, then die." He rubs his Agora so hard I'm scared he'll try to tear it out. "How can we live like this? Separate. Yet together in every way that matters. It's impossible, Story. Today it's really getting to me."

It *is* impossible. He's trapped in there while everyone else reaps the benefits of his work on The Kernel. He's always there for me. Time to return the favor and help him through this.

"Go to your big living room window. Find the spot where you can see out through the falls."

"Right now?" He's wrapped in a sheet, lazing in bed.

"Yes, go. Take your laptop. Don't leave me behind. Look." I hold my laptop up. My face is visible with the bright, full moon above me. "Can you see the sky and the moon too?"

He fiddles with his laptop, holding it at different angles before I can see the side of his face and most of the moon. "Pretty much."

"It's you. Me. And the moon. I promise it won't always be like this. I'm going to fix you. You're not dying from that Agora. Not on my watch. I'm not giving you up, Ivan Rhys." The worry lines crossing his forehead relax. "On days like today, when it feels impossible to be apart, look up. We're under the same Ohio sky."

"Smile." He gives a one-sided grin, taking a picture of our split screen videos with the moon in our backgrounds. "Thank you for keeping me sane."

What will I do when he's gone? I take a minute to push that down.

"I want to hear how those heart-shaped pizzas tasted."

"They were great. Thank you so much. But tell me, Chef Rhys, what kind of pizzas would *you* have made for us today?"

We had a wonderful night talking until we fell asleep. In the morning, we worked through our routines. He helped me choose my outfit. Then he talked his way through making coffee and breakfast while I did my makeup and hair. We're miles apart, but I've never felt this close to anyone.

~~~

"What happened to the yard?" Dad barks as soon as I'm down the stairs.

Ivan threw an epic party last night to keep your daughters happy. It worked...

My dad may have a stroke if I say that.

"Lark was stressed out. We threw a little party to cheer her up." I hug Mom. "How are you feeling?"

"I'm okay, honey. I'll have follow-up appointments, but I feel good." She points to the porch. "How did you get this stuff in the yard?"
~~~

"Your mom found this invoice on the deck from Ganahl Party Supply." Dad points to Ivan's message on it with a thundercloud face.

I fail to hold back a grin as I pour my coffee. "I need to head out for the day. Love you both!"

When I get to my office, Schrader greets me and goes through the security routine. He's not intimidating since I know Ivan is watching him.

Today I'm using the cutting station to dissect a series of increasingly smaller blood vessels. Someone taps on the lab door. "Not Dr. Benedict, please," I mutter.

It's Schrader. His eyes dart over my shoulder into the lab.

"Dr. Ross, are you okay in here?"

"Uh...yeah. You okay out there?"

He pushes a shoulder through the doorway and sprints in a circle around the lab, looking for something. "You got any plants in here, Ross?"

"No?" I'm really bad with plants.

"Come." He grabs my elbow and pulls me into the hallway.

Shoot! Is The Bastion arresting me? He drags me to the windows by the elevator.

"Look!"

The view outside is apocalyptic.

A plant killing wave is actively spreading across the ground. Jewel green patches of grass are turning pale yellow, leaving what looks like a sea of dry straw.

It's not just affecting the ground. The lush vertical gardens on the buildings are curling into brittle, lifeless brown patches before our eyes. Dead vines tear away from the walls, spinning in tangled clumps towards the sidewalk. The rainbow of flowers has lost their color, turning into brown and gray papery shells.

People are gathered, staring up. The pavement shimmers with odd waves in a distorted heat mirage. I touch the window. It's not hot. I don't think this is a heat thing.

What if the shimmers aren't heat? They could be gas. Or a toxin.

I bang on the window. "Go inside!"

That was foolish. They can't hear me. AJA units roll from the Justice Building across the street. They'll get the people to safety.

"You ever seen anything like this?" Schrader's voice is shaky.

"No!" It has to be another attack.

I run to my office and grab my phone to make a video for Ivan. The tallest buildings have a touch of greenery left on their upper floors. I zoom in on a huge bank just in time to catch the color and life being stripped away from the last of the lush, broad-leafed plants.

"Are you okay? Is the forest dying too?" I whisper. "How? The flowers were so bright and happy! Now they're all gray and shriveled." I pan to the ground. "I don't think my phone is picking it up. See the squiggly lines. Could this be a poison?"

I add a quick message to my video.

IMPORTANT!!!!!! Help?!

Then send the video of Lancaster dying to Ivan.

"Dr. Ross? Nothing's left out there." Schrader presses his face against the glass.

"I know." I step beside him.

The city felt gentle when it was wrapped in vivid green. Now bright sunlight reflects off hard edges, making a sharp glare on the sea of buildings.

My phone dings.

Are you somewhere safe? Stay inside. Tell your mom and Lark too. Find your dad. GET AWAY FROM THE WINDOWS! -I

Dad! I slap the button to call the elevator.

Schrader is on the phone talking in a soothing voice to someone. They're wailing for him to come home.

"Get away from the windows. Tell them too."

Ivan. He's in a forest. If this is a toxic plant gas thing, can it get in

The Helm?

I don't care if he's busy. I'm calling him.

"Hey," he answers immediately in a quiet voice.

"Are you okay?"

"Yes. You?"

"Yes. Did the forest die too?"

"No." He draws it out like he's embarrassed that The Helm is unaffected.

I sigh with relief. "Thank goodness. I was so worried if all the plants are dying, and you're surrounded by them…" My voice cuts out.

"Nah. I'm good. Story, don't be scared. We'll get this figured out. Just stay inside to be extra safe."

Are these disasters going to keep hitting until none of us are left to survive them? "Okay."

"We're dividing into teams now to work on it," he says. "I'm keeping my phone right by me. Call or text if you need anything."

If I was at The Helm doing Agora research, my work wouldn't have been interrupted like this. "Thank you. I'll have my phone too. Go work."

"Call you later."

"Bye."

The chaos is overwhelming on the first floor. People dash through the halls (something I don't recommend doing in hospitals!), ALICE and ASTRA units whir past, panicked voices call back and forth, and the news blares from patient TV's and staff offices.

I call Mom as I jog to Dad's office.

She answers in a panic. "Honey, I can't get ahold of your dad. Is there something wrong with nature? As crazy as that sounds, I swear it is. Our bouquets from last night died! Lark and I are coming to the hospital."

"No! Stay inside. You don't know if there's another acid event. Toxic gas or something? Or the sun? The sun could be doing it."

"That makes sense. We'll have a cookie baking day. Give me some ideas of what to make," she replies in a perky 'Lark is by me' voice.

Cookies? My brain is mush.

I can't think of a single type of cookie right now. "Surprise me? I need to find Dad. I'll text you. Love you."

"Bye!"

"Story!" Dad yells from behind me.

"Dad! What happened?"

He shrugs. "Don't know."

"Mom and Lark are safe. I called them. Do you want to go to my office and look over the city?"

"No, we stay low. We don't want to get stuck up there again. Let's go to my office and see what the news is saying."

As if I care about the news. They'll just lie. I want to know what The Irontrace has to say about the plants.

Dad and I spent our day alternating between staying holed up in his office and offering help. Patients have overwhelmed the emergency room ALICE units. Some were hit by chunks of plant matter falling from buildings. Others are there for anxiety. Many show up reporting breathing or skin issues.

It's a day of hands-on patient care. If it wasn't an emergency, we wouldn't be allowed to see them without ALICE and ORION units tagging along. But seeing the look on my patient's faces when they get to have a human physician?

Priceless.

One elderly woman hugged me for at least three minutes after I helped her with a breathing treatment. She said she misses the days of "real, not nincompoop computer doctors with their tinny voices and hot electric wands for hands."

Being called a "not nincompoop" is the highlight of my medical career so far. It's tied with the days I spent taking care of Ivan. But he *did* fire me from being his doctor. So...I guess those days don't count as real doctor days.

I'm in the hallway, documenting the post-treatment assessment of my last patient when a message pops up.

There you are. Been looking for you. -I

"It's so crazy here."

I bet. You doing okay? -I

"I am. It's been busy but good. How are you?"

Much better now that I see you. We fixed it. You and your family are good to go wherever. -I

I lean in to whisper even quieter. "Can I come home to you now?"

The relative safety of living under The Bastion is rapidly evaporating. Even if things were going great, I'd still be counting the minutes to get back to him.

You shouldn't have left. -I

He's right.

I se by that face you agree. -I

"See you tonight."

Can't wait! -I

I go back to working on my patient notes. Dad assigned nine more easy patients from the ER board to me. My poor research lab has been completely neglected today. But I got to touch real patients. I'm calling that a win. I grab a coffee for the road and head out just before the midnight shift change.

Lifeless brown remnants of plants in my headlights make for an unnerving trip home. I listen to the news while I drive. They report that a sudden blight hit from an unexpected meteorite storm.

What outlandish excuse will they come up with next? No one is going to believe that nonsense.

Ivan is on edge in our bedtime video call. "Major cities all over the world were hit by the attacks on their AI models that control atmospheric conditions. High frequency signals were released that wipe out critical cellular structures in plants. Oxygen and chlorophyll were sucked out of them. It caused widespread panic. Which led to people making lots of problems for emergency services."

"Well. Yeah...it was terrifying. We didn't know if there was something like gas or acid killing things. This week has really been wearing us down."

"Sorry. You messaged me when the monitoring systems started screaming in the control room that an attack was happening in Lancaster. Hearing from you breathed life back into me so I could focus. I knew you were okay."

"I thought you were going to say I distracted you."

"No, you kept me going, thank you."

Tonight he has on a t-shirt with his pajama shorts. His left shoulder is improving if he can get a shirt over his head. He's leaning against a cozy-looking stack of pillows in his big bed. It looks warm and perfect.

But it's missing something. I picture myself in a Story-shaped spot beside him. I'm sure he'd hold my hand again like the last time I was there.

What if the next time I visit, he doesn't only make jokes about marrying me, and we just...get married? Then it would be *our* room. *Our* comfy pillow nest.

"Story? What's with the face? I gotta know what gave you that smile."

Nope. I need to keep the inside thoughts in my head. "How many days left until my robot is done?" The countdown on my phone says sixteen days. But I don't want to stay away for that long.

"Robot progress would go a lot faster if these blasted attacks would give us a break. Unless you want me to go work on it right now." He leaps up out of bed and jogs out of view.

"No!" I burst out laughing. "Come back!"

We settle into our happy routine of stories and smiles.

Thursday passes with no emergencies. I submit my research for Dr. Benedict to review then head out a bit early.

A large black package sits on the porch when I pull in the driveway. It's addressed to Lark.

Who sends a nine-year-old a massive box with no return address? *Creepy.*

"Lark! You got a delivery."

"What? Mail for me?" She sprints to the door and pulls it inside. "Look at this, Mom! It's huge!"

I'm a bit freaked out we don't know who it's from with everything that's been happening lately. "Let me help, I have scissors in my work bag."

"I wonder what it is," Mom says, leaning close as we pull the box open.

It's a hot pink riding helmet connected to a vest that looks like it's made of inflatable egg carton material. A small tag on the side has a barely visible Irontrace logo.

A note stuck to the vest says:

Congratulations, Lark Ross!

You are an AVM warrior. A true inspiration to the people around you. We selected you to try the new line of rider safety gear from a local vascular malformation clinic.

The helmet is padded and unbreakable. The vest clips onto your saddle horn. If you fall off, it will inflate to keep your AVM safe. Happy trails!

Lark squeals with delight and snatches her new gear.

"HORSES!" Lark yells. "I get to ride horses! No more cart!"

"Aww! Your dad asked me the other day if she could try riding with safety gear made by his colleague. This is amazing!" Mom gushes. "We'll have to go try it out."

"Let me get a picture of you and Mom." They get close and smile. I send the picture to Dad. "You look great, Lark! I'll talk to Richelle and see when we can go."

I send Ivan a message. *Hmm, Lark got something in the mail. - <3*

"Thanks, Story!" She exclaims, admiring her vest.

Looks like Lark can safely ride horses now. -I

"Come on, honey, let's get cooking. I promised Lark we'd make her a special dinner to kick off summer break," Mom says.

We turn up the music and have a cooking dance party. My tracker ring buzzes as I put the garlic bread in the oven.

"I'll be right back," I say, darting for the stairs.

"Lark and I will work on setting the table," Mom calls.

Have you seen the news lately? -I

"No. One sec." The Lancaster News Network site shows big black font on a white screen.

500 internal server error.

"Do I need to reload this page or something?" Clicking the refresh icon does nothing.

You can do that as many times as you want. Won't help. -I

"Yeah. Have you-," A soft knock on my door interrupts me. "One minute, please." I open the door, surprised to see my dad. "Hey! Come in, look at this."

Hey, Alan. I needed to show Story something. -I

"Watch this." I switch to a national news site. It shows the same error screen. "Ivan are any of the news channels working?"

No. Media servers have been taken down worldwide. -I

"Is someone trying to scare people?" Dad asks.

Honestly? I think it's a symptom of something bigger. -I

"That's been happening a lot lately," I say.

Exactly. We'll get it fixed. Stay home to be extra safe. Gotta keep working. I'll call you later. -I

"Thanks for letting us know about this. Stay safe." I wish he didn't have to go. It must be bad if he buzzed me instead of calling or texting.

"Bye, Rhys," Dad says. "This is bad. Usually, they fix things like this immediately."

"He's been working like eighteen hours a day this week between the control room and tactical trainings. It's kicking his butt." I don't mention that talking to me most of the night all week has also been keeping him up.

Dad clicks his tongue. "Hmm, I see you two must be chatty."

"We talk." I smile and lift my shoulder.

"Let's go eat. Your mom and Lark made some kind of 'super summer spaghetti spectacular.' Their words, not mine."

I laugh and follow him. "I figured."

He pauses at the top of the steps. "Honey?"

"Yeah?"

"You and Rhys?"

I nod. "Me and Rhys."

Dad's face drops.

I rush to explain. "His life has been so-"

"I know, I know. I've had a front seat to the disaster of his life since he was nine." He lays a hand on my arm. "He's a good man. Maybe the best I've ever known. It's *not* going to end well. You can't build a future with someone who will be buried by this time next year."

The steps spin in front of me.

"I love you, Story. He won't mean to hurt you. But he will."

"Come on, Dad. It's time for Lark's dinner party."

I smiled at all the right times during dinner. I laughed when my family laughed. Dad's warning had me so twisted up inside I couldn't eat more than a couple bites. It was a relief when Mom took Lark to the next-door neighbor's house for a summer movie night.

While I loaded the dishwasher, Dad turned on the living room TV. The news stations are back. He paused on LNN. They're reporting strong solar storms knocked out broadcasting stations this afternoon.

Liars.

That night, Ivan was too busy to answer my call.

22

Death is imminent. I'm walking to the firing squad. My hands are shaking. I can't get a deep breath.

At least that's how it feels. I'm really on my way to my first one-on-one with Dr. Benedict. I'm happy to report that I haven't seen him all week. When I asked Ivan how he fixed it, he laughed and said, "not with real explosives." No clue what he meant by that, and I didn't ask him to elaborate.

One more deep breath.

Knock.

Get this over with.

"Come in," Dr. Benedict orders.

"Hello, Dr. Benedict."

Relief washes over me when I enter his office. He's fine! No burn marks or visible injuries on his person. His office is neat and orderly, not charred from an explosion. I trust that Ivan's not a killer. But he's made it abundantly clear that keeping me safe and happy is his number one priority.

"Dr. Ross. Your research is exceptional. The board loves what you are doing. The Bastion does too. I have positive feedback from several council members for you to add to your records. Do you have any questions?"

The stack of papers on his desk must be interesting. His eyes stayed trained on them while he spoke. He's still not looking up.

"No. I do not. Thank you. Do you have any feedback for me?"

"Not currently. You may go. Shut the door."

Thank you, Ivan!

The next couple of weeks pass much the same. Work from sunrise to sunset, spending all night on calls with Ivan. During the days I miss him so badly it's turned into an ache. He fills me with peace I've never felt.

I'm his. He's mine.

Until he dies.

Every plan I make for us ends the same. "Until he dies." That phrase taunts me day and night. I mentioned it twice and Ivan shut that conversation down immediately. He said he refuses to let his impending death darken a moment of our time together. For now, I'm clinging to the tiniest shred of hope I can save him someday.

The artificial intelligence models seem stable now. No more worldwide emergencies have happened.

At work, each surgical robot is becoming like an extra hand. The specific tasks I'm training them for mimic the movements they'll do as my assistants. I keep angiogram scans running while I'm working in surgery sims. I'm becoming a pro at reading them.

I'm keeping Dr. Benedict and the board happy. Teaching my vascular ASTRA to make microscopic adjustments on blood vessels went well this week. Previously, it had failed microvessel surgery at the base of the skull. With a new training program I built, it breezes through work on the delicate vessels.

After another Friday check-in with Dr. B, Ivan okayed my plan to take Lark for a quick horseback ride at Richelle's. I just have to make it through this ride, then it's *finally* time to go back to The Helm.

The sun is shining on this perfect late spring evening. Lark and I sang and joked on the curvy drive to Richelle's. Tonight, I get to see the robot that will help fix her.

All because of Ivan. There is hope for her to have a real life, a future. In a few years, she'll be the one driving me around.

Four black trucks I've never seen are parked by Richelle's house. *That's weird.*

A group of several men wave to us as I wind my car past. That's even weirder. Her family is pretty private, and this property is gated. I don't wave back. Lark grins and princess waves at them. They eagerly grin back at her. It sets me on edge. She's such a friendly kid, I've got to work with her on stranger danger. But for right now, I just want her to have fun riding. And we're right by the Hocking Forest. One call to Ivan, and an Irontrace can meet us at the boundary.

Richelle waits by the barn with tacked and ready horses.

"I haven't seen you in WEEKS! You abandoned me for your big city job," Richelle yells, running to us. "You owe me some girl time!"

"Richelle! How are you?" I grab her in a fierce hug. Unexpected tears sting my eyes. "When did we last go weeks without seeing each other?"

"Never, *ever* in our whole lives!"

"You guys have some guests here?" I nod toward the black trucks.

"Oh. Yes. Dad has some weirdos here he works with off and on. Ignore them." She gasps loudly. "Story! What are you not telling me?"

I'm not telling you a lot! My blank stare and silence are not the response Richelle wants. She grabs my left hand and holds it up. My diamond tracker ring sparkles.

I smile. "That's something I, uh. I picked it up on a work trip." *Kinda...*

She squeals, jumping and clapping her hands excitedly. "This is a rock! You cannot afford this. Are you engaged?"

"No, I don't have time for that."

"I think it's from her secret man she talks to every night." Lark yells from by the horses.

Cripes. *Lark!*

"Tell me more! I need details on the secret man. Does he have any friends or brothers who can give me one of these?" Richelle asks, holding my ring close to her eyes. Her mouth forms a silent *wow*. She won't drop this. She gives it a tug to see if it will come off, but it doesn't budge.

"I work all day then do video calls with a colleague at night to go over what I learned."

Had Lark snuck in sometime and seen Ivan and I talking? Knowing

Ivan, he's got motion detectors activated on our calls to watch us while we sleep. He'd know if someone had been in my room.

Richelle rolls her eyes. "Keep your secret stories about this secret man, I guess. How's Lark been doing?"

"Happier than ever. Some engineering genius made her that special riding outfit. Mom takes her to lessons at a stable by our house."

She leans in and whispers, "One time you told me you wanted to fix her. Do you think you can?"

"Oh, for sure, with my robots. There must be a way to help her." I change the subject. "You ready to ride? Lark has been dying to."

"Do you still have Mikey?" Lark asks. "He's my buddy."

Richelle waves for us to follow her into the barn. "Yeah. He's in here."

We walk halfway down the barn aisle to Mikey's stall. Lark busies herself petting him. The last time we were here, Richelle and her dad, Otto, had been working on building pens to rehabilitate wildlife.

"Oooh cool. What's in here, Richelle?" I peek in the stalls that had their wooden fronts replaced with thick metal wire.

My heart drops. There are at least twenty huge birds in the pen. They're familiar to me from my nightmares.

Lark appears beside me. In horrific unison, their heads turn, focusing black and yellow eyes on her. A few puff their feathers convincingly like Helga. I put my arm across Lark's shoulders like a shield. *I'm the shield?* I'd have no chance against these drones.

Do I call Ivan with my panic button? That seems like an overreaction. He may be able to answer a quick message and let me know what to do. I grab my phone with my free hand.

Hey! At Richelle's. Question about all the drones in her barn. - <3

"Richelle, where did these come from?"

"Some client of Dad's sends them. They hang out until they're ready to leave."

"Why do they need rehab?" I pull Lark by the arm to the barn door.

She starts to protest, but I shake my head no.

"Beats me. Dad's in charge of them. He said it's bringing a lot of extra money to the farm. Mom's making a big deal about how we'll be able to buy back some of her family's land we had to sell."

"I bet that's a relief," I say. It would be a real relief if I could get out of here and skip this ride! "I have a thirty-six-hour shift at the hospital this weekend. Let's get riding."

Richelle and her family have been farmers for my whole life. Surely they can tell those are not real animals.

Who is Otto working with? Richelle can't be in on it. She's far too sweet and opinionated. And she hates this farm. I don't think she'd care if they sold the whole thing.

Richelle makes a sour face then grabs Lark and I by the hands. "Ugh, your job is the worst. I swear a shift that long can't be legal."

Surely Ivan won't want me to stay. I don't know how to leave without hurting Richelle's feelings. I type a fast message.

Forget it, handsome. Can't wait to see you tonight!!!!!! - <3

Ivan hasn't answered, so we mount up and ride out. The trail she takes us on skirts the forest. It's breathtaking, but my mind is too busy to enjoy it.

Every few minutes, the gray Thoroughbred mare I'm on spooks, and I have to stay focused to keep my seat. When she darts off, almost throwing me for the fourth time, I scan the sky. There are no drones chasing us that could scare her. Maybe she's picking up on my jumpiness. Next time she takes off, I should let her take me to the barn.

Thunder rumbles, making the hair on my arms stand. I suppose she might have sensed bad weather coming. Did an attack hit the weather models?

"A storm!" Lark yells.

"There's no rain scheduled for us today, Lark," Richelle says. "Look around, it's all blue skies."

"What about *that* scary cloud?" Lark points. Richelle turns her horse to look, and Lark taps her horse with her heels. "Go! Race you to the barn, Richelle!"

"You can't beat me on that tiny ranch pony!" Richelle spurs her Quarter Horse after Lark.

I twist in my saddle. Sure enough, there's one black cloud low over the trees. No rain falls, but the dark cloud gives a chilling effect. A silent, bright flash of lightning strikes over the tops of the trees. My mouth drops open when I see the lightning sprawls gleaming golden letters:

Check your phone, woman! -I

I burst out laughing. Ivan! I swear, that man can do anything. I knew he could harness lightning as a shield for us, but he can spell with it too?

I pull out my phone and wave. Rocking forward and clucking at my horse, she takes off into a fast trot.

Sorry gorgeous, I was in an aquatic tactical training sim and couldn't have my phone in there. What's up? -I

'All the drones in her barn??' -I

Story Rossssss, where are youuuu? -I

I need you to answer me. Please. -I

Not to be a stalker, but I'm tracking your phone. -I

You ever going to reply so I can breathe? -I

I can't help but laugh. My poor Ivan.

Sorry! Hope you had fun in training. Lightning. Really? –Story Rosssssssssss

I urge my horse into a gallop.

She explodes forward. Her black hooves cut into the field, sending dirt clods flying as she settles into her rhythm. I'll ask Richelle about this mare's race record, but before she retired, I'm sure she would've been a formidable opponent. We're going to beat Richelle and Lark at this pace. I guide her in a long arc around the edge of the meadow so we don't steal Lark's thunder.

"I won!" Lark yells as I trot to the grooming area. "Cinnamon is the best pony ever."

I hop down and give my horse some neck scratches. "Good girl," I whisper to her cheek. "I'll ask if I can bring you to The Helm someday." I kiss between her eyes and hand the reins to Richelle.

"I'll take care of the horses. I know you need to leave," Richelle says with a fake pout.

"This was so fun, thanks!" I throw my arms around Richelle.

She rocks me back and forth in a bear hug. "Sorry your schedule is awful and you can't have fun anymore."

If only my secrets could spill out to her. She'd be thrilled. I swallow my words. "We'll catch up sometime, see ya! Come on, Lark."

My phone dings as we walk to the car.

You just aged me fifteen years. -I

I'll be there soon to fix that... -<3

The men by Richelle's house wave to catch my attention. They're all staring. One man is holding his phone up in landscape mode aimed at us.

Why? I gas it and speed past. Are they the reason for the barn drones? I grip the wheel until my knuckles turn white.

"Lark, you wanna play a game while I drive?"

"Yes!"

"Whichever one of us can find the most animals on the way home gets to pick an ice cream flavor. We'll send Dad to the store for it."

"I'm in. You have to keep your eyes on the road. I'll beat you for sure."

I don't even get ten seconds of peace before Lark yells, "A bird!"

So much for a few minutes to spiral in silence.

"What kind? A little lark for Lark?" Why bother asking, I know it's going to be another stinkin' Helston's hawk.

"No. A big one. Maybe one of Richelle's hawks?"

It's parallel to my window now. I switch lanes to get away. The hawk goes over the car to Lark's side. It hovers beside her window, peering in. I brake hard to see if it will leave, but it slows with me. Its eyes stay laser-focused on her face.

"Story, it's my new best friend. I'll call it Speedy since it can keep up with the car." My heart drops when I hear her window roll down. "Come here, big birdy!"

"Lark, NOOOO! Window up!" I yell, jabbing the window lock button with my finger.

Irontrace time. I squeeze my tracker ring a few times. We are only a couple of miles from the city, but on a Friday near the beach road, it's busy.

"I didn't do that, maybe it was Speedy!" She giggles.

Even though I locked the window, it rolls down again. Then all the car windows roll down. I choke back a scream.

Don't scare Lark! Ivan will help us. I hold my fingers on the buttons to roll them up, but they're stuck down. Tendrils of my curls whip loose from my clip, swirling around me.

"Get your hand in the car, Lark! Traffic's crazy," I snap.

The stupid drone is right by Lark. Eyes level with hers. My phone rings and Lark grabs it.

"Hello!...Yes...I'll put her on speaker."

"This is Moriah Voss. Story Ross, do you need help?"

"Yes. My little sister and I are heading home from my cousin Richelle's house. We're playing a game where we spot animals. Turns out, one of her hawks is following me home. Richelle also has houseguests I've never seen. They must have confused us with someone else because they were taking pictures of Lark and me. And to top it off, my car windows won't stay up. Probably unrelated. But it's super annoying. My hair's whipping everywhere and I don't have a hair tie and I'm about two seconds from being blinded by it."

"Hold for one minute," Moriah says.

I don't want to talk to Moriah. I want Ivan. "Moriah, is?" How to phrase this without Lark learning about Ivan. "Is Commander, uh...sir there?"

"Uh. Yes, I'm looking at *your sir.*" From her voice, he's never gonna hear the end of this.

The hawk dips, then soars over the car. It's on my side and climbing fast into the sky away from the road.

"Oh no, Speedy the hawk is gone," Lark says. Then she whispers, "Why does this lady care about our game? Do I know your sir man?"

I glance to my left after the hawk. It's far out over an open field when it disappears into a fiery explosion. Speedy really is gone. Good thing Lark didn't see that.

"She's in our game too. I bet she's looking for some animals right now," I whisper.

Lark nods. "Let's keep watching for animals, so I don't have to eat Moriah's flavor of ice cream."

"Hey, I heard that, Lark!" Moriah says, laughing. "Story, we need you and Lark to come to the clinic."

"At Lancaster Medical Hub?" There is no way I'm taking Lark to The Helm. I glance at her. She's looking out her window, scanning from the sky to the ground, then back up.

"No. The other clinic where you work with your dad," Moriah replies.

"I have Lark with me. I'm *not* doing that."

Moriah doesn't reply. Background conversation breaks out in the control room.

Ivan's deep voice chimes in. "Hello ladies. Head home and pack your bags. Then-"

"Your man!" Lark squeals, delighted. "That's the one I hear in your room all night, every night!"

I take one hand off the wheel and smush it onto her lips gently.

"Lark, no!" I hiss, shooting daggers with my eyes. Waves of laughter roll from the control room.

"Can you hear us?" Moriah sputters.

I don't answer. Complications Lark could have if the boundary control in her Agora activates surge through my brain. I'm trying to sort this out.

"Story. Go home. Pack. And come here." Ivan's quiet, steady voice carries more weight than if he screamed at me.

"Okay," I say.

"Lark, can you help me decide what ice cream to get?" Moriah asks, switching to the 'stay on the phone in case you need help' routine.

A message pops up on my phone.

Hurry. -I

23

My countdown to go to The Helm pays off. Last night I packed my work notes, makeup, and clothes. The dress Mom made for me is finished, on a hanger on my closet door. I roll it up and tuck it on top of everything else in my backpack.

The drive out of Lancaster is bizarre. Traffic isn't just light, it's nonexistent. There are no people on the road to witness The Bastion blast us with some black murder trucks. Or for them to sweep us up in a tornado. Or pour acid rain on our car.

Sorry to bother you again. Where are all the cars and people from Lancaster? - <3

My phone buzzes.

Diverted away from The Helm's chief of surgery and his only attending surgeon, (AKA, my darling Story). -I

Of course it's him.

Thanks for keeping me safe for the thousandth time. - <3

I'll never stop. -I

"You're aware patient confidentiality is vital for Story and me as surgeons. We are asking both of you to keep this trip a secret too." Dad gives Lark an intense look in the rearview mirror. "Lark, you'll love where we are going. If you don't tell anyone about it, you may get to go back."

"I won't tell anybody," she replies in a solemn voice.

There's about a twelve percent chance a nine-year-old will keep The Helm a secret. But it's adorable seeing her taking this seriously.

When we get to the entrance, two real Helston's hawks are sitting low in the trees. Lark and Mom look around like we're in a dream as we walk into the forest.

"Where in the world are we going?" Mom asks.

"You'll see." Dad twirls her closer to him by her left hand.

Ivan, Moriah, and a few Irontrace I don't recognize are seated on their horses inside the boundary.

Ivan leans forward comfortably in his saddle, elbows resting on Helga's perch. His gaze sweeps me up and down. It's like he's relearning what the *real* Story looks like. He gives me a one-handed wave and then leaves his hand up in the air. I can tell he's feeling very proud of himself.

What does he have?

There's a small black circle between two fingers.

A hair tie.

I stop beside Obsidian and sweep my hair up in a ponytail then lean towards Ivan's knee. "Wanna help me out?"

"I'd love to."

His brow furrows like he's not quite sure where to start. Then he gently brushes my neck to gather the rest of my hair. Yeah...I could get used to the soft twists of Ivan's hands in my hair.

"Got it," he announces with a final tug.

My ponytail wobbles, then collapses, laying low on the side of my neck.

So much for that.

We both laugh. "Sorry. I've never done that before."

This is the first chance to check out Ivan's stitch-free face in person. The newly formed scar leaves a dark, harsh trail from his forehead down into his shirt. *His left dimple survived!* Barely, but it's there on the edge of his scar. I thought it was lost for sure from what I could see on our video calls. People may be intimidated to approach him.

I only see the mischievous, kind man I've come to know.

"You look good. The scar makes you look tough. Well, tough-err. I love it."

He grins and reaches a hand down to me. I lace my fingers in his. A spark jumps between us. His eyes flash—he felt it too. Whatever we've been dancing around these last few weeks just changed.

"You came back," he says under his breath.

"I always will." I hold his hand to my lips and kiss it.

The cool forest evening suddenly feels a lot warmer. A hawk calls from the canopy. *Hawks!*

That's why I'm here with my whole family. "Is something bad going to happen?"

"Probably. I was desperate to make sure you got here." Ivan holds my hand for a few more seconds before shifting in his saddle. He looks above my head at the group behind me and lets out a small laugh.

When I turn, Mom's mouth is agape. Dad doesn't look surprised, maybe the slightest bit perturbed. Lark is typical, happy Lark, looking at Obsidian like he's a fairytale horse. The Irontrace give each other I-told-you-so faces and make jokes, but this is clearly old news.

"I see why you said to bring three horses for four extra people, Commander Rhys!" one of them bellows.

"That's real helpful, Evans." Ivan shakes his head, laughing.

Lark runs between the horses before unleashing a stream of questions to Ivan.

"What happened to your face? That's a giant scar! What is this place? Do you love my sister? I hear you two talking *all the time*. Are you doctors? Are these birds your pets? My cousin has hawks too, but hers aren't nice."

"We're not doctors. We're friends of your family. The hawks help us with our work." Ivan snaps his fingers quietly, then points up. Helga and Storm take flight in a swooping pattern. "How could I not love Story? She's the best."

He's gonna need to repeat that...

He winks at me then hoists me up behind him on Obsidian. Good thing he's strong because he just turned my legs to jelly.

I wrap my arms around his waist and squeeze him like he's the only thing holding me on earth. He lays his arm across mine, fingertips tracing slowly along my forearm. I go completely still under his touch.

We lead the way, following the hawks through the forest. Everyone falls into a line behind us, distracted by their horses and conversations.

"Are you okay to ride? Any pain?" I ask him while we briskly trot.

"Your cousin's barn is full of Helston's hawk drones, The Kernel keeps being attacked, and you're wondering if I can ride horses?"

I nod onto his back.

"You're here, so I'm great. How was your ride with Richelle?"

"Fun. Lark told Richelle my ring is from my secret man."

"It is. Except I'm not a secret anymore."

"About time. What's going on out there?"

"The AI models are under near constant attack. More intelligent attacks than we normally see. Do you remember when I showed you the news servers were shut down?"

"Yes."

He peeks over his shoulder to see where the others are. "That was to hide a devastating multi-region attack on the electrical infrastructure that was going to, well, it would have been bad, Story. But we stopped it. The Senior Commanders had enough and called a worldwide Helm online summit. The security measures we've built are holding things together."

"Who's doing this?"

"The source IP addresses of the attackers change or stay hidden. I checked the serial numbers on the drones in Richelle's barn. They're counterfeit, but there's a hundred or so of them on Otto's property. I sent out a security alert to monitor Lancaster for the next seventy-two hours."

"Why do they have counterfeit drones?"

"None of my investigation into Otto is good news. I wish it was for your sake. Those men that were there? I accessed their phones and sure enough, you were right, stupid creep had made a video of you and Lark. He'd zoomed in and taken pictures of your faces. Don't worry, I got rid of them."

"Thank you. How are you holding up with this stress? Is your Agora okay?" I wiggle an arm free, laying my hand on the back of his neck. His Agora is flat, and I don't feel any sharp clots in the veins around it.

"It's behaving. I'm staying in the boundary. That's enough to kill me in its own way." He slides my left hand up to kiss it then holds it on his chest pressed tight over his heart.

That's it. I'm never leaving.

"Lark, what do you think of the waterfall?" I ask as we approach The Helm's entrance.

"This is the coolest place in the world!" she cries, bouncing in her stirrups. "Can I have a hawk to ride on my horse?"

Ivan's short whistle summons Helga to her perch on Obsidian. We turn, walking to Lark. He moves Helga to the perch on Lark's saddle.

"It's so beautiful! What's its name?" Lark asks.

"Helga. She does all sorts of cool tricks," he says, smoothing out her feathers. "You can pet her like this."

Lark smiles and holds her reins with her right hand, petting Helga with her left.

Once we enter the cavern behind the falls, Ivan slides down and helps me to the ground, moving in a rush once we reach Sid's stall.

"Please hold him for a minute," Ivan says, handing me the reins. He scoots a grooming cart between us and smiles, handing me a brush with a sword-like flourish. He whispers, "You're gonna want to help me get this done, as fast as we can."

A comfortable silence settles between us as we get Obsidian ready for the night. I use the soft brush on the huge draft horse until his sleek coat is gleaming.

Ivan is up to antics while cleaning Sid's hooves and removing tangles from his mane and tail. Every time our eyes meet, he has a new face for me—silly grins, dramatic eyebrow raises, puffed cheeks, scrunching his nose.

I can't stop laughing. "You're in quite a mood tonight," I whisper.

"I've got my reasons," he says, bumping his shoulder into mine.

"Is one of them that you don't have stitches anymore?" I ask.

His eyebrows shoot up. "Ohhh. It's time to leave. Right now."

My heart takes off in a gallop.

He grabs the brush from my hands and throws it in the general direction of the grooming cart without taking his eyes off mine. It misses and clatters to the floor.

"Francois, can you please feed and water Sid?" Ivan blurts.

"*Oui, monsieur,*" Francois says.

"I need five minutes to show Story something. Then I'll take you all to her new lab. Meet us at my apartment when you're done here," Ivan says, looking between my mom and dad.

"Sure, see you in a few," Dad says, trying to sound chill. The subtle twitch of his right eye makes me shift behind Ivan.

This is going to be a happy weekend. I don't want anyone's opinions shadowing my time here.

He pulls me to his side to jog across the cavern through the stables. About twenty feet before the hallway, he takes off in a near run, pulling me with him.

"What are we doing?" I laugh at the pure fun of the moment. Is this what a life with Ivan will be like?

"I didn't know your family was coming. I have a surprise. I need to show you while it's just us."

Good thing I run most days. His easy jog is nearly my sprint.

Outside his apartment door, he turns to me with jittery energy. "Close your eyes."

His hands go over my shoulders and cover my eyes, guiding me in several steps. "Surprise."

He drops his hands. On the kitchen table is a large paper sign that reads, *Welcome Home, Story!* It lies in front of a four-foot-wide heart made entirely of flowers. The colors blend like paint on a canvas, spilling across the tabletop, and a few stray flowery vines trail off the edges. Their ripe, sweet scent fills the kitchen.

"You said this place felt like home."

"Ivan!" I grab a handful of shirt by his waist, steadying myself and pulling him closer. "Not the apartment. You. *You* feel like my home."

Words race out of him about flower species and why they grow such a large variety at The Helm. I lean to smell them while he chatters on. His voice is bright, a little breathless.

My life has become a before and after snapshot of Ivan. He's my best friend. I'm safe from anything the world can throw at me. He showed me how he feels. Now he's watching me, jabbering nonstop about flowers to gauge how I'll respond.

"They're beautiful, but stop talking about flowers," I say. He laughs and steps to my side. I rest my hand on his chin and trace the scar on his cheek with careful kisses. A soft smile spreads across his lips. I knew it. He needed to see how I feel about his gesture of welcoming me home. To his home. To be with him.

"I love you, Ivan Rhys."

He lights up.

"I love you. From the first glimpse I had of you behind the pine branches with that wild red halo framing your beautiful face. I had to hold onto Obsidian to remember how to breathe." He stops. "Marry me."

YESSSSSSSSSSSSSSSSSSS!

It's not a question. He already knows I will. But I'm gonna make him do this right. I lay my tracker ring on the counter.

His eyes are brimming with honesty. And hope. He's not using me as a prop to rebel against The Bastion. He wants something normal. His whole life has been about what other people can get from him. The price of his intellect. What he can do and who he can save.

I broke Ivan in the best way possible. I woke up the part of him that wants to choose. To use his free will and stake a claim on his future.

I'm his future.

He talks fast again. "It doesn't make sense. I'm a logical person. You are too. Irontrace don't get married. We don't get happily ever afters.

Don't have real homes. I could die any second and leave you as a heartbroken widow. I know that. It's a jerk move of me to even want this. To want you."

He holds my face between his hands, thumbs tracing my chin. Finally. These are the things we've waited to say face-to-face.

"There's a voice *screaming* inside me. I can't make it stop. I was made to walk through life with you by my side. I *know* you were made for me too." He pauses.

I tap my ring.

He smiles broadly in his oh-so-charming Ivan way and snatches it. Excitement takes over and he flings himself down on his right knee, hitting the floor with a bang. He grimaces and struggles to hold back laughter.

"Story…Wait. How have we not talked about this? What's your middle name?"

"Caroline. What's yours?"

"Oh, that's pretty, I love it. Sorry, I don't have one. Well, maybe I do, but I don't know what it is. I should investigate that." We both laugh.

"Story Caroline Ross. I will love you until my last breath. You're tough, and strong. But you don't need to do everything yourself. I want to be your helper. Your partner in life. You know I'll keep you safe. I want to hold your hand every night while we fall asleep. Spend every day making you laugh. Your laugh—ah, it kills me. I'll do anything to hear it. Keep stealing my shirts, they're all yours now. I'll build a robot for anything your genius brain dreams up."

I'm already nodding. He leans down and brushes his lips across my cheeks softly.

"I'll wear a sling when I need one. Cry at me every day if you want, I'll make you feel better. Loving you comes as natural as breathing. I think it's the only thing I'm actually meant to do with my life. I had no idea I wanted this until you showed up and hit me like a hurricane. Now I want a life. The whole marriage thing and all. Everything. With *you*. Will you do the kindest thing anyone has ever done for me, and be my wife?"

"You know I will."

He slides my tracker ring back on then scoops me up in his arms, kissing me, pulling me into a world where only we exist.

Until my mom screams.

214

24

"A proposal? If that wasn't the sweetest thing I've ever seen, I'd be furious you didn't tell me about him!" Mom quickly adds, "The door was open. We saw the whole thing."

Peeking through a haze of unfallen tears, I see my family, Francois, and Moriah frozen in the doorway as Ivan lowers me to the ground.

"Congrats, guys. You looked maddeningly content when she stayed last time," Dad says.

Mom shoots him a death look. He'll be explaining that later.

"I sneaked and sat outside your door! I *knew* you had a man!" Lark smiles and claps.

"Congrats, best wishes for you both," Moriah says, looking a little green around the gills.

"Congrats, my sweet friends!" Francois exclaims, grinning from ear-to-ear.

"Thank you," Ivan says, looking down at me and squeezing my shoulders. "Do you want to go to the lab?"

"Yes!" Francois yells before I can reply.

"Okay, is that cool with the rest of you?" Ivan asks. His left arm is wrapped around my shoulders. A tiny wince clouds his face for a second. I lean forward, inspecting the flowers, then walk to his right side, snuggling up tight under that arm.

"Sure, let's go," Dad says.

"Story, I need to hear details sometime!" Mom says, as we walk along the nighttime security wall.

"I promise you will, Mom," I tell her from Ivan's side. There's no way I'm letting go of him right now.

My lab is located a couple of doorways down from the clinic. When we open the door, I rush in, pulling Ivan along.

"How did you find time to get this done?" I spin in a slow circle. It's at least four times the size of my Lancaster lab.

"Anything you want, I'll make it happen," he says, smiling.

Instead of individual stations, there's a platform built in the middle of the room with one massive, rotating, robotics system on it. In the center is a surgical table with attachments branching out like a tree. It has dozens of arms and tools. There's a fully equipped angiography machine built around it. A semicircle of cabinets behind where I'll be working house more supplies in glass-front cabinets.

Ivan and I walk onto the platform. "Consider this an engagement gift, my love. It's far better than ASTRA. Meet INES, Ivan's Nifty Excision-bot-for Story. I'm terrible at acronyms, sorry. Change the name if you want."

"INES is perfect!" I reply. He can barely keep up as I drag him around the platform. This is everything I dreamed of and more.

"I can't wait to see the origami you make with this thing. Watch, I've waited, not so patiently to show you this for weeks. INES, Dr. Story Ross is here."

The robot's console screen lights up. Arms whir to life, gently humming overhead.

"Hey, Doc, we've been waiting for you," INES says in a perfectly human-sounding voice.

ASTRA doesn't talk to me.

"Hello, INES. Ivan, thank you so much!"

"You're welcome." He tips me back over his arm, settling me against his chest. His dark eyes fix on mine, almost pulling me in again.

I sneak a nervous glance at the five people watching us.

"Did you think this move was to kiss you like that again?" His lips twitch in amusement.

"Mmhmm," I mumble.

He lets out a mock gasp. "My bride, there are two kids down there. And I am a gentleman—save that for after the wedding."

Bride. I swallow; suddenly very aware this is actually happening. By the look on his face? He thinks this is hilarious.

"Hey. I'm doing a thing. Relax. Lay back." He laughs softly and draws me in tighter. I melt back over his arm, trusting he's steady beneath me.

I've imagined our reunion a thousand ways over the last three weeks. So far? This is *nothing* like I imagined. It's way better.

"Look up. That's where your tools are stored. There's an autoclave system in the ceiling to clean and prep them. Keeps the clutter down here minimal."

Over his shoulder, INES cutting arms hang, poised for action. The glinting metal taunts me. Someday I'll be guiding them, slicing deep into his neck. The reason he'll bleed.

That sobers the moment. I stand and step away. How can I do this brutal surgery on the man who has become my world? And will someone really use these on my sweet little Lark?

Maybe this was a mistake. Humans gave surgery to ASTRA for a reason. I'm twenty-two. How dumb was I to think I could take this on? Those aren't sim cutting tools. It's not a game. People I love will be cut open.

I lean my back against Ivan's chest so he can't see my rising panic. "Show me the rest of it, please."

He's draped over my shoulders like a blanket, staggering with me on a tour. He explains the purpose of each wall as we move in a slow circle. The wall by the door has a long row of specimen fridges and freezers containing a variety of surgical simulation models for me to practice on.

The theater wall has several monitors, a couch, and chairs.

The third wall has an office setup with a desk, lots of office supplies, a coffee maker, fridge, and whiteboard. Above the desk is a framed version of the sketch I made for Ivan.

The fourth wall is storage and desks below windows.

"Ivan and David made a sign-up sheet for any available engineers to work on this round the clock. Everybody went overboard and turned it into a three-week work party. I don't know what you're going to do in here. It must be important," Moriah says.

"It's going to be great. Thank you!" I tell her.

David pops his head in. "Rhys. Need you now."

He gives me a crushing hug and groans on the side of my neck. "Duty calls. I'm sorry."

"Go save the world," I say as he jogs away.

He spins, blowing me a kiss. Then he bolts out the door, followed by Moriah and Francois.

"Can I go see the horses?" Lark asks.

"Why don't we go get settled in Ivan's apartment first?" I say.

Lark tugs Mom into the hall.

"Do you really think I can do this, Dad?" I whisper.

He chews his lip. "Work hard. Figure it out. Try to save your husband."

25

In Ivan's bedroom, there's a stack of black Irontrace clothes in my size on his dresser with a note. *Doc's clothes.*

No way, Ivan. I'll keep stealing his.

"Time to tell me the story of your Commander Rhys man." Mom pats the bed for me to come sit with her.

"I'm not sure how many details I can give, because of who he is, and what he does for work, but I'll tell you what I can if you promise to keep it a secret," I say. Mom nods and makes a zipped lips gesture. "He's like a security guard for the whole world, and freakishly good with computers."

I begin with the story of how Ivan got me through the forest, putting himself in danger to personally deliver me to Dad.

"Okay, you can keep talking, but I love him already," she says, smiling.

The recent attack makes her sob for him. She understands why I needed to be here with him to help him recover. His kindness shines through when I tell her that he threw the yard party for Lark.

"*He's* the reason my baby girl can ride horses?" she says, wiping fresh tears.

An equal mix of smiles and happy tears come freely to both of us. She beams, hearing he keeps an eye out, not only for me, but also her and Lark, he believes in me, and he trusted my ideas enough to build my lab.

"Don't worry about the details. It'll work out. He's already shown you who he is. From the moment you walked over to him tonight, the whole group froze. We knew we were watching something special." She laughs. "You should've heard your dad complain. He saw he's got to hand you off to someone else."

I nod. "He does."

"Go to bed. It's late."

"I need a shower to wash the horse hairs off, but then I'm heading to my lab. This is a working trip."

~~~

Back in my lab, I dig through the coolers to see the available tissue samples and surgical simulators. A huge limitation of my lab in Lancaster is that I can't replicate the neural chip portion of the Agora. I take out a sample to examine, and sure enough, the black and silver neural chip components are in there.

I spend a few hours reading manuals, learning commands for INES, and familiarizing myself with my new tools.

Dad joins me in the lab. "Can't sleep. How's it going in here?" He leans close to see what arm I'm replacing on the machine.

"Look at this. It's a miniature cell salvage machine! This micro-suction tip will allow me to catch blood lost in the procedure. It recycles and cleans their blood. They won't lose too much volume because it puts their own blood back in their IV. I don't even have one of these in Lancaster. Genius!"

"Ivan has set you up for success."

"He has. I'm going to start my first sim surgery. Wanna watch?"

He shakes his head. "I know you're excited. But I'd wait. Do your first simulator surgery when you are well-rested with a clear head."

I look at the clock. It's almost 2:30am. "I'll go sleep for six or so hours. I have to get through as many practice procedures this weekend as possible."

"Good plan. Can I stay here for a bit and fiddle around? Mom and Lark are sleeping in Ivan's bed. He must have a lot going on in the control room." He picks up the manual I have been reading on the angiogram machine and flips through it, stopping at a chapter about visualizing blood vessels during procedures.

"No, go for it. I'll sleep on the couch at Ivan's. Later, Dad."
~~~

Opening his door to the *Welcome Home, Story* sign with the flowers, puts a huge smile on my face. I trace my fingers over his handwriting on the sign. He writes with careful block letters, fit for an engineer who frequently creates technical diagrams.

I creep through the apartment getting ready for bed. Putting on a shirt that smells like Ivan is the perfect finale to the day. Surgical plans for Agora removals with INES swirl through my head as I drift off.

My cell phone alarm song wakes me up, disorienting me for a minute. Then everything falls into place.

Mom and Lark are still asleep. I sit at Ivan's desk and open his laptop. Curly hair tangles stick together like reddish-brown vines around my shoulders, my teeth need brushed, and couch pillow lines stamp my cheek, but I don't care, I can't wait another minute to call him.

There you are, beautiful. How was your night? -I

"Hey, handsome! I slept great now that I'm here near you. Where are you? Miss you."

Working, sorry. -I

"It's okay." He must be having a rough night. "Don't worry about me. You need to come sleep."

I will. You going to be busy at lunchtime? -I

"Not if you'll be around," I say, smiling.

Okay, I'll see you then. I love you! -I

"Sorry. What was that, can you say it again?"

The whole computer screen fills up with messages.

I love you. -I

I love you. -I

I love you. -I

I love you. -I

I love you. -I

I love you. -I

I love you. -I

I love you. -I

I love you. -I

I love you. -I

I love you. -I

I love you. -I

I love you. -I

I love you. -I

I love you. -I

I love you. -I

I love you. -I

I love you. -I

I love you. -I

I love you. -I

I love you. -I

I love you. -I

I really, really love you. -I

Tears spring to my eyes. "I love you!"

See you soon. -I

"Later."

Today is the first day I can really tackle the mystery of Agoras. I push my hands off the desk, spinning his office chair and jump up, mid-spin. Buoyed by my purpose to save Lark and Ivan, I walk with light steps to get ready for the day.

In the lab, Dad sleeps crumpled on the couch. I tiptoe to the whiteboard, pull the cap off a marker, and write my surgical plan. This rehearsed all night in my dreams, so the steps flow easily to the board.

1. *Prep & position*
2. *Image/map to confirm Agora boundaries & target vessels*
3. *Incision!*
4. *Control feeding arteries*

5. *Isolate & expose nidus*
6. *Control draining veins*
7. *Resect nidus*
8. *Remove neural chip*
9. *Confirm normal blood flow*
10. *Nerve & muscle function testing*
11. *Apply skin graft patch & closure :)*
12. *PARTY!*

I bounce up the INES platform steps to prep my table and supplies.

"Wait...this is a mess."

The OR table and platform was spotless last night. Wrappers and used instruments on a steel tray catch my eye. A blue surgical towel lays on the table, with irregular outlines under it.

I flip back the towel. A bloody neural chip lays there.

Burnt. The electrical components melted and the plastic hardened into a jagged, drippy block. The silver connections coming out of it have been chopped. Someone panicked and cut them, instead of working them out gently.

I pick the neural chip up with hemostats to examine the other side. It's not as burnt, but its black surface is covered with score marks from someone hacking at it. If these happened while inside the sim? These cuts would have put too much pressure on the chip. A tangle of simulator arteries and veins lay beside it, attached to surgical clips. Those look okay.

My throat goes tight. This surgery did not go well. Did INES malfunction? Or did my dad butcher that sim?

"Dad! You did an Agora removal!" I need to hear what happened. He was a real, true surgeon for a couple of years. If he can't get an Agora out in one piece, it will take me years.

He jerks awake.

"Sorry. I fell asleep here so we could talk. I need a minute. Can you make coffee?"

"Yes. Then I want to hear what caused the burn marks."

"We'll get into that. Caffeine first." He staggers to the whiteboard.

Moments later, the smell of fresh coffee spreads through my lab while I study the whiteboard where Dad writes. He outlines a basic overview of his steps in a list then draws the neural chip, making notes pointing to three parts of it-the power switch, the base of where silver tendrils join it, and the middle section.

"Last night proved to be a more difficult surgery than expected. I was able to mostly follow the plan you made at Ivan's." He trades the tablet with angiogram images for the cup of coffee I offer.

"Look at these clean scans, they are the highlight of my night. I was able to shut down the blood supply to the Agora before removal. No matter what I tried, I couldn't get the Agora out without destroying the neural chip." He holds the chip with hemostats. "These silver filaments are razor sharp. Be so careful. We knew they wrap around blood vessels. But last night I found they also conduct electricity, sending out electric shocks when the neural chip is manipulated."

This is going to be harder than I thought.

"Ivan builds the Agora simulators as close to an actual Agora as possible. He put that on and off switch on the neural chip. If the chip is off, you can hack away at it, and it won't shock them."

"How do we turn off the neural chip in real Agoras?"

"You can't. If the chip is on and you manipulate surrounding structures in any way, the chip releases a fatal burst of electrical current into the brain tissue."

26

"What keeps the neural chips charged or prevents their batteries from dying?"

"I need to talk to Ivan and figure it out. For now, do you want to work through one of the procedures with the chip off and see how it goes?"

"Well, first I want to run through it with the chip on to see what happens for myself. Then I'll shut it off and keep going."

I hoist a surgical simulation model from the fridge. The imitation skin is cold on my arms and chest but will warm once I initiate its startup protocols. The model consists of a set of shoulders, wider and bulkier than mine, continuing up a neck with an Agora in the back to a full head, complete with hair that I'll clip as part of my preparations.

The model's systems boot up. Chilly off-white skin fills with a color resembling pale human flesh when I attach it to the artificial blood supply. The model jumps as its lungs inflate with their first breath, and the vital signs monitor hums to life.

The initial angiogram maps out the area and uploads it to the robot for processing. Another screen flicks on to show me a green path of what the patient's correct blood vessel anatomy should be in the area, overlaid with their abnormal structures from the Agora, softly flashing in yellow.

Connecting the nerve and muscle monitoring probes makes two additional INES screens turn on. Maps of the feeding arteries, draining veins, and surrounding danger zones such as nerves or muscles are ready to go.

Look at me. I'm a real surgeon. My heart is racing, but my hands are steady.

"INES, activate Agora removal surgery protocols."

"Noted, Dr. Ross. Phase one arms ready for you."

I make an incision. INES delicately retracts the skin. The simulator's heartbeat and breaths cause tiny movements in the vessels and tissue I have to account for. My probe touches the first feeder artery. The neural chip flashes, sending a smoking streak of black onto the surface of the blood vessel.

INES yells at me. "Warning! Patient died. Catastrophic electrical injury detected. Resetting the simulator."

"Should I even try again with that? Or shut off the neural chip and proceed like it is turned off?" I ask. "Ivan fixes everything. I could leave that for him to figure out."

"Not even married yet, and already it's 'Ivan fix this, Ivan fix that.' What have I gotten myself into, Alan?" Ivan asks from behind me.

I spin, grinning behind my mask. "You're stuck with me now, Commander Rhys."

Hearing me call him by his title for the first time makes his eyes wide.

"Nice hat, *Dr. Rhys*." He pokes my giant headband magnifier. "What do you need me to fix?"

"You two are quite the pair," Dad says with a laugh. "Ivan, we have an issue we need help with. If you're comfortable watching what happens in the surgery, Story will show you."

I reload the simulator.

"Sure, let me see," Ivan says, stepping closer.

Instead of peeking over my shoulder like a normal person, he leans his chest against my back and rubs his stubbly cheek on mine. His deep voice speaks quietly into my ear, "Good thing you don't need to adhere to sterile technique in simulations."

"You're *never, ever* going to be allowed near me when I'm doing surgery. I can barely remember my name right now."

"Let me remind you. Story *Rhyssss*," he hisses.

I drop my instruments.

My dad clears his throat loudly from just off the operating platform.

"Focus, Commander!" The playfulness in my voice beats out my snappish attitude. He knows he was focusing on exactly the right things. "When the neural chip is turned off, I can push here and do whatever I need to proceed with the surgery. No electric burns. Watch what happens when the surgery starts while the chip is on. This small artery needs work."

I use a pair of forceps to shift it. A smoking black streak shoots down the vessel.

INES yells at me again. "Warning, patient died. Catastrophic electrical injury detected. Reset the simulator."

"That's not what we want. Figured this would happen. Let me do some research," Ivan says. "I'm going to get some sleep first. Be back around lunch."

"Sleep good."

He presses a sleepy, slow kiss against my cheek.

It's hard not to run off the platform with him when he leaves.

A few minutes later, the wall monitor turns on by me to reveal Ivan sitting at his desk.

"Hey, I looked quick. The neural chips are easy to turn off. It's a one-way transaction though. Once they're off, there's no going back."

"Oh, how can I turn them off?" I ask, poised and ready.

"Well, heartbeats don't mess with them, right? So, an energy release, as long as it's no stronger than a heartbeat would be sufficient to shut the chip off so you can operate without frying our brains," Ivan says, grinning broadly.

He can't be serious.

"An explosion, Ivan? Put that smile away. Absolutely not. Why is it always blowing something up with you?"

"A *micro* explosion. Doesn't even count as a real one. I'll show you later. I'm about to fall over. I need sleep. Bye."

"Bye!" The monitor goes black. "Dad, we can't let him do that."

"It may work. I have to say, if a person can figure out the perfect way to create just the right explosion near a spine, it's Ivan. No matter which Helm you ask, they'll say he's the world's top operator for detonations."

"You need sleep too. Head over to Ivan's or crash on the couch here," I tell him, turning back to my surgical table. "I'm going to work my way through with the neural chip off. See you later."

"Have fun in here, Dr. Rhys." He sighs and pauses at the door. "That's a sentence I *NEVER* thought I'd be saying to my precious little girl."

I laugh and turn on my surgery playlist. Music is roaring in the lab. Cameras are recording, Mic is good to go. Taking a deep breath, I turn off the neural chip to get started for real.

"INES, back to stage one of Agora removal."

"Yes, Dr. Rhys." Several tiny retractor arms extend, grasping the edges of my incision and holding it open.

This next step is where the alarm went off last time. I pause, deciding which of the arteries to clamp off first.

The INES tools reach out, silently mapping the vessel paths with precision, guided by Ivan's custom-built visual feeds and touch sensors. Their micro instruments burn tissues shut with cautery as we proceed. Blood loss is minimal, and no alerts have come up for nerve or muscle damage.

I use extra caution disentangling the silver filaments coming off the black neural chip from blood vessels or tissues. They come off easier than I expected, but as I reach in front of me to lay down a two-inch-long section of filament, its dangling tail slices through the glove on the back of my other hand, leaving a sharp, shallow slice across my knuckles.

"Good thing this isn't a real patient," I mutter. Lark has something this sharp in her neck right now. So does Ivan. I roll my shoulders and shake my hands a few times. "INES, did we know the tendrils are this sharp? Make a note that we need to research that."

"I knew they were. The more an external source manipulates the tendrils, the sharper they become. I made a note, Dr. Ross."

I inject glowing dye to see if any vessels still have blood flow. I'm not happy with what I see. I close off some additional vessels, eyes glued to the imaging. "INES, please tell me any additional facts in surgery with details Ivan has taught you about Agoras. I'm still learning.

"Yes, Doc."

"Angiographic confirmation that abnormal blood flows are shut down. Initiate AVM removal steps, INES," I say.

"You got it, Doc."

Now that the Agora doesn't have blood flow, I remove the rest of the AVM.

"Don't tear it," I sing to myself. That could cause a fatal rupture. I get the entire malformation out and lay the tangled mass on a sterile towel.

"Yes! AVM is out. INES, initiate neural chip removal steps."

"Okay, Dr. Ross."

The neural chip itself is mostly in the skin. A block of fibrous tissue surrounds it from years of irritation. INES stabilizes my cuts to remove it before dropping the tissue onto a tray.

I stare at the angiogram. A smile creeps across my face, pushing my mask up. The blood flow looks great. This was a successful surgery. Time to wrap up.

"INES, initiate closure protocols."

The training program we use for this surgery has a variety of arms available for various stages of surgery. A piston arm extends to irrigate the surgical field with saline. The suturing attachments come down like a black metallic spider with slender arms poised over the incision. The robot and I alternate layers of sutures through the muscle, fascia, and subcutaneous tissue. I apply a bioengineered dressing to help the skin heal and stretch.

The fatal mass has been replaced by a neat arc of sutures.

"Congrats, beautiful, you did it," INES says in Ivan's voice as I smooth on the final bandage.

"Successfully completed Agora resection as primary surgeon with robotic assistance. End dictation. INES, initiate self-cleaning protocols." I remove my face shield, gown, and gloves.

The arms extend towards the ceiling into the honeycomb of auto-claves built suspended above the platform. A hissing sound breaks out as the steam builds. I grin. Those dirty surgical tools mean an operation happened. I stand, hands on my hips, making sure all the arms are tucked into their vacuum tubes before a huge smile takes over.

A smattering of applause breaks out behind me.

"Story! You did it! That angiogram looks great!" Dad exclaims.

David, Ivan, and Dad had snuck in to quietly watch the surgery from the viewing area.

Ivan jogs up and kisses my cheek. His smile can't mask the dark circles under his eyes and worry lines on his forehead. "Congratulations. You're brilliant!"

"Thanks!"

"Dr. Ross, Dr. Rhys? Story? I'm not sure what to call you. I really needed some good news today," David says. "Can you get this murder-ous piece of junk out of me next?"

"I'll put you on my schedule," I tell him.

"Same!" Ivan says, squeezing my shoulders.

David shakes my hand, grinning. "Congrats on the engagement. She's a keeper. See you lovebirds later."

"Bye, Delac," Ivan tells him as David turns to leave.

"Magnificent work. Keep it up. Document what you do, make vid-eos, and we'll have research to present to The Bastion. Humans should be primary for this. I need to go check on your mom and Lark. See you later."

"Bye, Dad."

Below the platform steps, there's a large blue button on a metallic rail behind a cover. I reach behind it and press the button with my palm. A fine mist of disinfectant spray shoots over the operating platform. Seconds later, UV light flashes to sterilize the surfaces.

"How are you, my love?" Ivan asks as I dart around to dispose of my trash.

"Happy. Look at this, it's so cool!" I gesture to the platform and smile.

"What can I do to help?"

"Nothing, sit. I'll be over in a minute. You look dead."

"Thanks." He laughs but leans over the arm of the couch, eyes heavy.

I wash my hands then run over and plop beside him. "When do you go back to work?"

"I need to keep going in and out every few hours. For now, I'm happy to be here with you."

"How was your day?"

"Nonstop. I tried going back to the apartment earlier when I called about the neural chips. Moriah called me back after fifteen minutes. The Kernel has so many safeguards in place to keep AI models running smoothly, but they keep malfunctioning because of cyberattacks. Yesterday, some bad stuff went down. People died. Thousands injured."

"What sort of bad stuff?"

"The Helston's hawk drones? There are variations of those all over the world. The counterfeit drones launched attacks everywhere, dropping bombs."

He kisses my hand. "It took David and I 190 seconds to get control of the drones that came over the Lancaster region. We could not have fixed it that fast without you finding those drones at Richelle's. Thank you for warning us."

"Sorry you had an awful night."

"Enough about my night. Have you eaten today?"

"No, you?"

"Yeah. Let's go get you food." He leans forward to stand, but I put my hands on his chest and push him back. He doesn't resist. A bewildered smile creeps across his face.

"You need to go to sleep."

"Aren't you hungry? You've been in here all day."

"Sleeeeep," I say. I'm starving. The high from doing surgery could fuel me in a marathon, but I've never seen him dragging like this. "I'll stay with you. Dad can bring me dinner."

He uses a remote in the arm of the couch to turn off most of the lights in the lab. I pull a table over and prop his feet on it.

"Lean up." I adjust several couch pillows around him, putting a super soft one behind his neck by his Agora. He raises up his left arm and lifts his chin in a silent invitation to sit by him.

Yesterday, his left shoulder was bothering him. I cuddle up beside him and rub his neck, to his shoulder, down his arm and then back up.

"Still hurting?" I ask.

"Eh, sometimes. Good thing I already proposed, I'd do it again just for this shoulder rub." He weaves the fingers of his right hand into my hair and his eyes flutter shut. "How have I ever lived without you?"

My head rests on his chest, and his heart steadily beats in a peaceful rhythm, just for me.

"You don't have to anymore."

He doesn't answer. He's asleep.

How will I ever go outside the boundary and leave my beloved Ivan in here?

27

My eyes open to a soft, whirring sound. The security screen over my windows to the falls is rolling down for the night. I didn't know I had fallen asleep. Ivan has been sleeping for a long time with his head leaning back. I slip my fingers behind his head to feel his Agora.

The thin slice on the back of my hand from the neural chip validates how deadly these are. How do they move, turn their heads, ride horses with the murderous silver slivers coming from the neural chips?

My lab door flings open.

Moriah runs in. "Story, we need him."

I put my palm on his left cheek. "Ivan."

His eyes open slowly. When he sees me lying with my head on his chest he leans up and crushes me in a hug. "It wasn't a dream!" His fingers dig into my sides like he's never letting go.

"Ivan, Moriah's here. They need you."

He sighs into my hair. "Shoot."

With one lightning-fast motion, he flips me flat on my back behind him on the couch. He grins down at my breathless face with a perfect mix of sweet and smug.

"Love you, baby," he murmurs, brushing my hair behind my ear. It's a tender reminder that his strength isn't rough or mean. "Sorry to leave you like this." He takes the rest of my breath away when he gives me a quick, soft kiss then leaps up.

So much for having a normal heart rate...

"Hurry back!" I yell as he runs out the door behind Moriah.

Someone is getting a thank you letter for teaching him to toss people around like that. One second, he was all power. The next he was so careful. That beautiful contrast in him is exactly what I've come to know in the last several weeks. Seeing—feeling—it in person is honestly mind-blowing. And if this is just the beginning?

Breathe.

I lie there, waiting for my head to stop spinning over what's next for us.

Time to get to work so we can have our "what's next."

A plan for tomorrow takes shape on the whiteboard, one bullet point at a time. I make a note that the timer showed today's surgery took nine hours and thirteen minutes. That's way too slow. I'll have to get faster before I touch a real person.

One more lap around my lab to make sure it's ready for tomorrow and I head to Ivan's apartment. Mom, Dad, and Lark sit on his couch talking.

"Hey all, how's it going?" I ask.

"Story! I had the best day! Francois let me take care of the animals with him. Mom watched us. She drank so much coffee." Lark bounces over.

She talks for the next half an hour straight, giving me plenty of time to heat up my food, eat, and make tea.

"I wish I could've hung out with you all. That sounds fun. You look like you're feeling great." Her face is almost glowing.

The sunken areas under her eyes don't look as dark. Is being in The Helm actually good for her? Or is this an emotional boost of summer break fun and living near horses? I'll see what Dad and Ivan think later.

"Lark, Story had a long day working in the clinic, you need to let her heat up dinner and get ready for bed," Mom says. "Are you going to sleep here tonight?"

"No, I'll be in the clinic. Ivan and I took a nap on the couch in the lab. It's time to head back and work."

"Do you have some gross doctor stories to tell me? Blood? Broken bones?" Lark asks behind her twinkling, ice blue eyes.

"Lark! Patient confidentiality!" I gasp, faking shock. Not a chance

I'm telling her what I'm really working on.

"Oh! Right. You're a good doctor, Story." She throws her arms around my neck.

"I'd like to talk to you in the lab," Dad says.

"Great, let's head back."

He's impressed by my rainbow of notes that fill the whiteboard.

"You're right, speed will come. Don't worry about that. Get accuracy down first. I have a simulator program to grow your skills," he says. "Leave the neural chip off."

"I'm ready."

He makes changes to the surgical program while I prepare a fresh sim torso on my operating table.

"Dad, I was thinking, once we get this figured out...can you help me with doing their surgeries? If we divide them between us, we could do Lark and whichever Irontrace want done faster."

"I had a similar thought. We can work opposite shifts in here. Two trained surgeons would get the research we need faster. Let's be honest, there's no way you can do a surgery like this on Ivan."

Dad is a real deal surgeon from back when humans were always primary surgeons. He'll save Ivan. Tears fill my eyes.

"Yes! Please. You do Ivan. I'll assist another surgeon I've trained in Lark's surgery. Keep an extra close eye on them."

"I'm not sure what we'll do with her yet. Her Agora is different than theirs. Ivan needs to review her scans before he builds new, smaller simulators to practice on."

"Do you think she can wait on the surgery? Is she stable enough?"

He doesn't look up from the robot console while typing. "For now. She is. As her dad, I want her to have surgery as soon as possible. From a doctor's viewpoint, it's triage. She has years left. They don't." His eyes bear the weight of all the Irontrace he's lost to Agoras when he meets my gaze. "Sorry, honey. I know that's upsetting because you love Ivan."

I shake my head.

"I did warn you about getting close to him. I'm really scared of what will happen *when* you lose him. David and Ivan are higher priority than Lark. If their Agora ruptures, it would be an absolute emergency. You'd have to do the best you can because they'd be dying anyway. I'm sure The Bastion would understand if it's an emergency. The council members know Ivan can fix anything, anywhere on their Kernel. They've never seen someone like him."

I bite back saying "he's the best."

"Also, the first twenty or so surgeries will be incredibly dangerous. We can't just throw experimental surgery at a nine-year-old. Irontrace are consenting adults. If they want surgery, that's their decision, albeit a risky one. Your mom and I need to see evidence this will work before putting your sister on the OR table."

"That's reasonable," I concede.

"Okay. Time to focus. When operating on real people as primary surgeons, no two surgeries will ever be the same. Some will be flawless. Others will not be. This simulation has some curveballs. You ready?"

"Yes. INES, turn on the music and help me take out this Agora."

"As you wish, Doc," INES says. I laugh.

What will other surgeons think of INES?

I work my way through the first stage of the surgery with no problems. Two hours in, one of the feeding vessels ruptures. Massive bleeding starts.

"INES! Initiate blood loss protocols," I order through clenched teeth.

Multiple new attachments lower into reach. The imaging map flashes red to show the problematic blood vessel. INES swivels a micro cell salvage device into the incision.

Its tiny suction tubes collect the rapidly oozing blood into a filtered container. The blood spins in a centrifuge washing the cells with a saline solution to remove contaminants.

Another arm swivels down to seal off the bleeding vessel. I pause and watch the angiogram. The red warning areas fade away. No other vessels look ready to burst.

Within seconds, the recycled blood from cell salvage is going back into my sim patient in their large IV.

"Angiogram looks good to me, what do you think?" I ask Dad.

"Agreed. Good work so far."

"INES, proceed with the surgical plan."

We keep working, making it through small bleeds. This surgery is a trial by fire. The next few times a bleed happens, INES and I quickly gain control of it. By the fourth one, I'm feeling confident with bleeding complications.

I place my last vessel clip and do a happy dance. Time to remove the AVM. Bood floods my surgical field.

"INES, initiate massive blood loss protocol."

The cell salvage can't keep up. Everything is lost to a deluge of red. I keep glancing from the high-definition imaging to the surgical site but can't find the problem area.

"Where is this coming from!?" I shout.

Dad stays silent.

I grab handfuls of gauze with gel to stop blood loss and stick them on the surgical site.

"Come on! Work!" I hiss at them. Blood seeps through their layers.

Siren-like alarms blare from the vital signs monitor. A loud voice booms from INES.

"Initiating patient revival systems. Step back, Dr. Ross."

I pull out my tools and stand, paralyzed. The gauze I stuck to the surgical site falls to the floor with a sickening splash. Liters of blood pour on the platform around me.

The lab goes silent. INES speaks in a normal volume. "Your patient died, Dr. Ross. Cause of death: catastrophic bleeding emergency."

My once blue shoes, gown, and gloves are stained red with my failure.

"They *died*?" A small silver lip encircles the platform, trapping blood in a pool around my feet. Each step makes a crimson ripple. The squelching sound of my shoes cries out to The Helm that I just murdered my patient.

"My patient died?!" I blurt. Neither Dad nor INES answer me.

Lark's blood.

Ivan's blood.

David's blood.

Who will I kill next? I'm too young for this. I'm too inexperienced to do this. I was wrong. Ivan built INES for nothing.

I drop to my hands and knees and start swishing blood towards the drain on the platform. Clean it up. Get out of here. If no one can see the blood, maybe they won't know I'm a massive failure.

Dad gets up from the desk. "Story. Every surgeon, even ASTRA, loses people. You needed to experience this to understand what patient death feels like. What a death looks like."

I sob while swiping more handfuls of sim blood into the drain. "What did I do wrong? How could I have saved them? This could've been Lark!"

"You did everything right. Sometimes things just go wrong." He walks up on the platform and spreads out sterile blue towels to sop up blood.

We wipe the floor together, our silence only broken by my sobs. My tears drip, swirling into the remnants of the blood.

"How many will die? Should I even be doing this? I'm just butchering them." I stand and tear off my surgical gown, mask, and gloves.

Images flash in my brain like lightning. Lark's blood pouring around me. In one flash she's riding horses, smiling in the sun at Richelle's. In the next she's a blue, cold person on the OR table in front of me. *I cut her open.* I couldn't save her from an Agora rupture.

I see Ivan smiling, laughing. In the next flash, blood pours like a fountain from his neck while I scream. I pull the surgical drapes off and press my ear to his silent chest.

Dad half carries me to the couch. Blood from my knees and hands is getting all over the seat. The same cushion where I sat with Ivan earlier, lulled to sleep by his strong, beating heart.

Living in a world where Ivan's heart has gone still is not an option for me anymore.

Dad presses another surgical towel into my hands.

"Listen. Get it together, Dr. *Rhys*. Agoras will kill them. They're 100% fatal. You're only 50% fatal at this point." He laughs. I glare at him. "They can rupture anytime. If you panic, shut down, and stop your research, Ivan and David *will* die. And honestly, they'll die soon."

My throat is too tight to answer.

He goes on, softer, "We will do more simulations like this. You're a primary surgeon now. In your hands is the power to cause remarkable harm. But in your hands is also the power to give life." He rubs my back like I'm a kid again. "Figure out a way to keep going. Do you think you know Ivan pretty well?"

I nod.

"Would he have built all of this for you if he doesn't think you really have a chance at success?"

Ivan loves me. But he's not an idiot. "No."

Dad smiles. "He and I both believe in you, honey. Believe in yourself. Don't let this one bad surgery get to you."

I bury my head in my hands and take a deep breath. Go back to yesterday. Imagine I'm back in Ivan's arms after he proposed.

Dad's right. They're in danger. And the power to save him, Lark, and the others is in my hands.

"Can you get Mom and tell her to bring me new clothes and shoes?" I ask.

"That's what we do. We move forward," he says.

I'm not sure when he left, but Mom came in a bit later.

"Hey, honey. Here's clean clothes," she says.

"I got simulator blood on the couch. Can you help me clean it please?" I ask her.

"Easy fix, no worries," she says.

"Thanks."

"I talked to your dad. We want you to know that you have options. You're a brilliant, beautiful girl. You have a career that people who have been surgeons for a decade would envy." She opens cabinets until she finds cleaning supplies. "If you can't handle this life, this choice you made to be with Ivan, walk away. No one outside of here knows about him. He may die soon no matter what you do. You're not stuck here to fix these people. Pivot. Do something else. Save yourself the grief and heartbreak."

How dare she?

She doesn't know me at all if she thinks my love for Ivan is a choice.

"You're right. I can do anything. And my choice is to fix Agoras and save people I love." As I yell, a smile spreads across her face. "How dare you throw Lark and Ivan away because they need help? They deserve to be free from Agoras and have choices too."

"Good. You see what I meant. You have choices. They do not. You're their only hope. Every real thing we have was once a hope. Ivan is the real thing. Keep working. Don't get broken by the what ifs."

"I keep seeing blood. It scares me."

"Why is being scared such a bad thing? Use your fear to become excellent. It's just another tool to get better."

She grabs me in a hug, allowing me to catch my breath.

"Can you please go ask Dad to come back?"

28

Seven hours later, I've survived another complicated sim surgery. And more importantly, my patient did too.

"Nailed it! Great job, Dr. Ross," INES says in Ivan's voice.

Where is he?

"Thank you INES. Initiate self-cleaning protocols," I say.

"Head back to Ivan's and get some rest. You've earned it," Dad says, gathering trash from around the surgical table. "I'll be there soon."

On my walk to Ivan's, I nearly crumble against the wall. I don't think I've ever felt this drained in my entire life. I'm not sure what his schedule is today, but mine will involve a nap.

"There she is!" a voice yells from behind me. "Hey, Dr. Ross!"

Someone flings their arms over my shoulders. I twist, trying to get a glimpse of my captor. It's Mai.

"Hey, Mai, how are you?" I ask, laughing from the shock of her friendly greeting.

There's a whole group of young Irontrace with her. All are wearing clinic scrubs.

"I'm great. Meet some of the other girls. We gotta stick together now that you live here," she says. "Ashley, Lucia, Katie, Heather, Dawn, Elisa, Talia, meet Commander Rhys's future wife!"

They take turns grabbing me then flinging me on to the next one to hug.

"Details, we need details!" Katie says, laughing. She hooks her elbow through mine, eyes sparkling. "When is the wedding? You two are famous at all The Helms. Everyone is talking about it."

Talia chimes in, "A wedding? At a Helm? Never thought we'd see the day!"

"Are we all invited?" a girl (I can't remember her name) asks shyly.

I really get to marry Ivan. These people are his friends. They know and respect my "secret" man.

And they're right. This is special. We should include them. "Sorry, we've been too busy to make plans. I'll fill you in on the details when we have some," I say.

"Anything you need, we want to be here for you," Mai says. "Clinic stuff, wedding stuff, a run in the woods with a buddy, we're your girls now. Can we all get your number?"

Well, this has never happened to me. "I'd love that. Running and riding horses have kept me sane for most of my life," I say.

"Same! We're going to have so much fun with you," Talia says.

"And if you need bridesmaids..." Mai bounces and points to the group. I laugh.

Bridesmaids. Richelle! Will she be allowed to come here? We've been planning our weddings since before kindergarten. I have to talk to Ivan about getting her to The Helm.

"Mai, thank you for introducing me to everyone. It was wonderful to meet you ladies. I have to go meet Ivan," I say.

Every one of them gives me a goodbye hug. They're lovely. For people with terminal illness, they're bursting with life. I mentally add them to the list of people I may be able to save someday.

"Story, finally!" Lark throws the fridge open as I walk into Ivan's. "Where have you been? Mom made pancakes. Do you want some? I'll put chocolate chips and strawberries on them."

"Sure, I'd love some, thanks."

The clock shows the time is 10:15. Where is Ivan? I grab my phone to message him.

Hey, come eat strawberry chocolate chip pancakes with me in OUR apartment. - <3

The front door swings open, and Ivan walks in, glancing at his wrist cuff. Smiling brightly, he tips his wrist cuff my way.

"Morning! Alan said I just missed you. How's it going here?"

"We're great! Francois is coming to get me soon and take me to the stables. Is Obsidian your favorite horse?" Lark asks, leaning over the arm of the couch.

"He is. We've been partners for years." He steps close to his office chair where I'm sitting. "I'm having Story withdrawals. I missed you." He lays a hand on my shoulder, towering over me with a smile.

"Missed you. Can we please go to sleep now?" I drop my head on his arm.

His dark eyes are busy assessing me. He leans down to kiss my cheek then whispers, "You have blood smears on your forehead and neck. Get a shower before you scare Lark." My hand instinctively flies up. I wish I had known that before running into Mai and the girls. "Then I'll make sure you get the best nap ever."

I smile. "When do you work again?"

"Tonight. Sleep, baby. Then I have a surprise for you."

"Can't wait."

After my shower, we had a relaxing breakfast with my family. Then Francois came to see if Mom and Lark wanted to go spend the day with him and the horses. Lark drug Mom into the hallway before Francois was done with his question. Dad and Ivan talked about what we've done with INES so far while I tried to stay awake.

Finally, Ivan led me to the big sectional couch and wrapped me in blankets. He was settling beside me when Dad came back out to the kitchen to get a drink.

"Sleep well, you two. I'll be right there. In Ivan's bed. Connected to this living room. With the door open." Dad gestures from his eyes to us in a silent *I'm watching you.*

"Get outta here, Alan. Let us go to sleep." Ivan laughs and waves Dad away.

"How are you?" I lightly run my fingers over his Agora and put a soft pillow behind his head.

"Thanks." He kisses my hand. "I had a long night. I worked on tracking down who took control of the drones. If you look at the Air Titan Division officers in charge of the drones that day, it appears they went rogue and ordered the drones to attack the cities. The AI judiciaries were preparing to arrest those officers. You know how that would end." He frowns, drawing his finger across his throat in a mock execution gesture. "David asked that instead they be taken into custody until I concluded my root cause analysis."

"What did you find?"

"I remotely accessed their computers to sort through the activity logs. Another user logged in to masquerade as the officers and ran malicious commands for the counterfeit drones. I wrote a program to unmask the location where the commands came from. It's running now."

"Does The Bastion normally execute its own officers?"

He snorts and points to his Agora.

"Any pro tips on not getting executed for my research?"

"David and I have proved repeatedly we are looking out for their best interests. We've built a special relationship with most of the council members in Lancaster. Keep working. Let David and I worry about that."

"I will." Saving Lark and Ivan is worth the risk of angering The Bastion. "What happens when they arrest people?"

"They do an interrogation. The person then silently disappears for execution. Or a tragic accident ends their life. Sound familiar?"

"Very."

"Remember the unmanned black trucks that came for you a few weeks ago on the cliffs by Lancaster?" Sadness in his voice snaps me to attention.

My head is resting on his chest, looking up at him. I nod.

"Someone took control of a bunch of those. They drove into crowded areas. Outdoor restaurants, parks, farmers markets, sporting events. They hit so fast and then just powered down. Thousands are injured worldwide, a hundred or so dead. The news footage is horrific. It broke my brain a little to have it playing in the control room all night. I don't know what I'd do if you weren't here."

He leans his head back and twirls several of my curls around his fingers.

"Sorry." I frown.

"People are terrified." His voice is rough. He loves people. I've seen that more than ever these last couple of days. When the world hurts, he does too.

It makes me love him even more.

"I would be if I didn't know about the Irontrace Squadron. People would feel better if they knew someone was looking out for them."

"Yeah, but we're The Bastion's dirty little secret." He tilts his head to look at me, tugging at the curls spiraled around his fingers. "How about you? Did you have a good night?"

I point to his hand. "First of all, never stop doing that." His face lights up and he weaves his hand in my curls even deeper. "You always tell me the whole truth about your days, the good and the bad. I want to do that with you too."

"Please do."

"Dad surprised me with a test simulation that didn't go well. He wants me to be prepared for any surgical scenario, including death. I lost my first patient last night. I know it's just a simulator, but the blood pooling around my feet made me panic. I kept seeing flashes of Lark bleeding out in surgery. Flashes of you dying. I could only see myself as the instrument of your deaths. Dad helped me get it together. I have a whole new viewpoint on the surgery."

"Oh yeah, what's that?"

"Use fear as a tool to fuel my research. A surgical plan exists for normal operations. Fearing complications means switching gears to become an expert in crisis. Dad will be poring over Agora scans today. Any anomalies he finds we're writing into simulations so I can learn to manage tough cases."

He gathers at least half my hair in a soft pull. I let out a happy, contented grumble, I'm already halfway asleep. His strong, steady heartbeat behind his soft black Irontrace shirt thumps in my ear.

"Impressive. Thanks for not giving up on us. Let me know if you need me to change any of the neural chips or INES."

"I'll never give up. Hey. I wanna move here."

"Yes. Stay."

I can't keep my eyes open. "Imagine if we never have to be separated by a boundary."

"Sounds like paradise to me."

I drift to sleep in my favorite place. Ivan's arms.

29

"Wake up!" Lark yells. "It's a beautiful day outside. Let's go explore!"

I yawn and leave my head on Ivan. He's bright-eyed, smiling at Lark and Mom.

"You worked all night, slept for two hours on a couch. How can you wake up so fast?" I mumble at him.

"The Irontrace live to serve," he says with a smile.

"Ugh, so chipper." I stand to stretch.

Ivan said he's got a surprise for me. I've got one too. Instead of throwing on more of his oversized Irontrace clothes and putting my hair in a bun, I take my time putting on makeup then arranging my hair in a half-updo with tendrils. I put on the white dress Mom made for me. From the ruffled tank top straps to the way it falls past my knees, it's the perfect light, summery dress. It's an absolutely terrible choice for horse-back riding, but that's not the reason I threw it in my bag.

Ivan is sprawled on his bed, typing on his laptop. I jump through his doorway, doing a dramatic spin. "Ta-da! No Irontrace clothes today!"

"What!" His jaw drops. He leaps off the bed and barrels at me.

I silently scream with joy when he lifts me onto his right shoulder and runs into his closet, out of view from the rest of the apartment. He leans me against the wall and plants a hand beside my head.

"I've survived explosions, near-drownings, stabbings. But seeing you walk in here almost took me out. Take me to the clinic right now, Doc!" He grasps at his chest, sucking deep breaths like he's dying.

"You're *such* a faker!" In all my life, I've never laughed this hard.

Lark comes running in when she hears the commotion. "You ready for hiking? Let's go!"

Ivan bites his lip and shakes his head sadly.

"No, no, no," he says with a fake sob between each "no."

"Get hiking, Commander Rhys." I wink and drag him after Lark into the kitchen.

We hand walk the horses to explore the top of the falls. Lark and Francois happily chattered about the work he does with the HEAL (Healthy Equine Automated Lifebots) vet units.

Several times on our walk Ivan tugged me close and started to say something but then he'd sigh or smile, thinking better of it. I asked him what was wrong a few times and he just shook his head and motioned at me like I'm the reason he's fallen speechless.

At the top, I follow as he ties Sid to some of the low hemlock branches in the shade.

"This is what we call Overlook. It's one of my favorite places. It makes me feel like a part of the world outside the boundary. Since I came here, I've come out exploring as much as I can. Sid has been my near constant hiking companion for almost sixteen years."

"That's a long time to have a horse! He must be your best friend," Lark says.

"Yeah, he's one of my best friends for sure. He carried something here for us today." Ivan removes a thick blanket from his saddle bag.

He tosses it down and it does the rest. The blanket spreads and puffs into a soft, thick cozy spot to rest.

"That would've come in handy a few weeks ago on my camping trip," I say with a laugh.

"Smart blanket. Does other cool stuff too. I want to show you something." He holds my hand and we walk to the edge of the falls.

The water is deafening as it rolls over the edge, churning hard enough to make the ground under our feet rumble. Goosebumps break out on my shoulders and arms from the chilly mist that clings to me. The wind whips in fierce gusts from below like small tornados.

My steadfast Ivan, unfazed by it all, types into his wrist cuff.

"Look." He points to a small, black drone ascending towards us from the bottom of the falls. It's carrying a box that looks like a cooler. It lands on the blanket. The box pops open to reveal picnic supplies.

"I thought we could have lunch with a view," Ivan says, sitting on the blanket. "Francois! Lark! Come eat."

"This is wonderful, thank you!" I smooth my dress to sit beside him.

We spread everything out while Lark and Francois race to us. Ivan had ordered an assortment of sandwiches, fruits, drinks, and desserts via drone delivery from Atlas Cavern.

"This is how we get supplies delivered if we're out on patrols or work assignments in the forest. Here, these are the best." Ivan feeds me a bite of a chocolate-covered strawberry then pops the rest in his mouth.

Our picnic by the falls was a perfect break from the stress we've been under lately. After lunch, Ivan lazes on the blanket making up outrageous lies of things he sees in the clouds. I lay beside him, sipping lemonade and laughing.

"Story, watch!" Francois yells, running towards his horse and jumping into his saddle without using the stirrups.

"Wow! Great job!" I yell to him.

A hawk screeches, rocketing up from the base of the falls. Ivan jumps up like he's been shot. The hawk flies in a big circle around us before floating down to land on Obsidian's saddle.

"Something is wrong if Helga was sent. We have to go." Ivan hurries over to untie the horses. Francois, Lark, and I gather the picnic leftovers and place them in the drone box.

"Francois. Lark will ride with you. Take your time to get back. Go slow and safe down the hill by the falls. Can you handle that?"

"*Oui!*" Francois says.

"Story, get in the saddle because of your dress." He hops behind me and wraps his arms around my waist. "This will be a quick ride. Head to the side entrance we used the other night please. Go, Sid."

He taps his heels against Sid. We fly down the hill.

In the stable cavern, Ivan slides off Obsidian then helps me down. "You're a fantastic rider, my love."

"You are too."

Moriah jogs over and snatches the reins from me. "Commander Rhys. Delac needs you in the control room right away."

"Thanks, Moriah. Take care of Obsidian please." He guides me away from the stalls. "Come with me. I'll show you the control room."

"Am I allowed to be in there?" I ask. That feels illegal to be in the brains of The Kernel.

"Yes, it'll be fine. Your dad has."

We walk through a long hallway and several doors, far deeper than I have been in The Helm. Around a final corner, we hit a dead end by an elevator. He pushes the down button. The doors slide open to several people in suits and dresses already in the elevator car.

"Commander Rhys, hello!" a woman says cheerily from the front of the group. "How have you been? It's always a privilege to visit the Irontrace."

"Councilwoman, council members, welcome back to The Helm." He lifts our joined hands in a wave to the group, earning several sideways looks. The brief ride down is a nice chance to catch my breath from our fast walk here.

Ivan turns to catch my eye then tips his head with a tiny scowl towards the people riding down with us. I laugh quietly and bump my shoulder into his chest. Not close enough. I need more. I burrow under his arm. He sighs happily.

"This is a long walk if there are emergencies," I whisper.

He leans down and quietly answers, "It's built this way so we can have time to respond if enemies breach us. That's also the reason when there is a problem, I drop everything and run like mad to get here."

We exit the elevator into a hallway with a row of windows overlooking a theater type room. The large, dim room slopes down to a massive wall of monitors at the front. There are at least ten rows of desks with computers. Several dozen Irontrace are scattered throughout the room. David sits at a round table down front with about twenty people in.

Ivan opens the door and ushers the group in, tipping his head to smile at each as they pass. He pushes it shut, leaving us in the hallway alone. "This is a major emergency. The Bastion is here. Sit at my desk and listen in," he says.

"Okay, thanks."

The low light of the computer monitors casts a slight glow on my dress. I must look as out of place as I feel. Several Irontrace keep darting glances at me from their desks.

Ivan's desk consists of three monitors, connected with cables to a laptop. Carved into the desk beside the laptop are the letters $I + S$. I smile, tracing them with my fingers.

"Commander Rhys, thank you for coming." A middle-aged man with hawkish eyes and light blonde hair stands to greet Ivan. "Excellent work on your investigation last night. The information you provided was invaluable."

"Councilman Jordan is right. That was flawless work. The program you wrote to find where the malicious orders came from finished running about an hour ago," David says. "I notified The Bastion, and they called an emergency meeting. The code for the drones to launch the attacks came from a Helm location outside Ottawa, Canada."

"From a *Helm*? Was it compromised?" Ivan asks, disbelief in his voice.

"No. Three Irontrace went rogue. They were found dead inside of their boundary a couple of hours ago. A note on one of their computers says The Bastion has been ignoring their ransom demands," another council member says, turning on a large monitor with a remote.

To the council members of The Bastion,

Your unlimited power has limits. For far too long, you have amassed wealth by oppressing the very people who keep you in power.

Attacks will continue until our repeated demands are finally met. Your citizens seem to be enjoying my antics so far. The tide has begun to turn.

Ivan shakes his head as he walks to the table. The eyes of every council member are trained on him. No one speaks.

I've never heard Ivan raise his voice. My hand flies to my chest when he finally responds, unleashing a tirade towards the group of government officials.

"Did you just admit to having ransom notes that could've prevented these attacks? Acid rain! Extinct viruses! Drone attacks! Trucks crushing people! Those lives can never be replaced, and you didn't take threats seriously." Ivan pounds on the table. "Have you lost your minds? Can you believe this, Senior Commander Delac?"

David steps back and smirks at the other Irontrace. Delac may be the Senior Commander on paper, but Ivan is clearly in charge of whatever this is.

The whole room is quiet. Council members glance between each other. My giant commander with the dark scar down his face crosses his arms and sharply stares at them, waiting.

A rotund man stands up, cleaning his glasses. He steps away from the table and speaks.

"Recently, threatening ransom notes were delivered to a few council members. They thought the demands were fake because the amount of money they asked was outrageous. Each recipient decided not to disclose their note due to the contents revealing sensitive, even embarrassing, information."

"So?" Ivan thunders.

The man continues, "It was promised this information would be released to the public about the council member if the threat was brought to any type of law enforcement. Tragedies began striking not long after each note went unanswered. Now we have no choice but to bring you in on what we know so far."

"Why? Did you get another ransom demand?" Ivan asks.

"Not yet. After the truck attack, we can't sit and wait on another ransom letter," the councilwoman says.

Ivan throws up his hands. His voice is quieter, but firm. "You shouldn't have waited after the first one."

Good point, my love.

"We need names of The Bastion members who have gotten notes. Let them know that henceforth, they do not have any expectation of privacy. Constant surveillance is on every aspect of their lives." David gestures to Ivan.

He strides to sit beside me at his laptop. The council members make themselves busy shuffling papers.

"Councilman Day, Councilwoman Bond, Councilman James, and Councilman Kelley," a man down front says.

Ivan types for about a minute and then locks his computer. "Done. Anything else, Senior Commander Delac?"

"No. We should be good with your surveillance programs," David replies.

"Tell those four no-longer esteemed council members they're responsible for deaths and injuries of citizens they're supposed to protect. Are you removing them and replacing them with new members?" Ivan asks loudly.

He's almost belligerent. I wonder if this is what he meant by having a special relationship with members of The Bastion.

"Yes. We told them they're no longer fit to serve," Councilman Jordan says. He notices me. "Commander Rhys, who's your friend?"

David replies, "She's a clinic staff member I brought on. A brilliant young surgeon. Dr. Ross is here to evaluate Commander Rhys's surgical recovery from the attack a few weeks ago. You know her father, Dr. Alan Ross?"

"Dr. Ross's daughter. Nice to meet you." Jordan nods politely. "You work with Dr. Benedict at Lancaster Medical Hub? You're working on an approach to save your sister from some brain issue?"

I knee Ivan. How does Jordan know so much about me? And how dare he talk like that about Lark having 'some brain issue.'

Ivan shifts forward in his chair, hiding the way he slides his hand on my leg under the desk to steady me.

It helps me find my voice. "Yes. The hospital board has been pleased with my research so far."

"They're incredibly happy with you. I have a particular interest in healthcare issues for The Bastion. I keep an eye on any rising stars in the field. Keep it up. You'll be on a board somewhere yourself soon," Jordan says, smiling at me.

"That would be my dream." *Never in a million years, Jordan.*

David speaks up from the middle of the room, "I need to take a moment to let The Bastion know that the rapid response time of 190 seconds to the drone attack in Lancaster was exclusively due to advanced warning we had from Dr. Story Ross."

The rest of the members of The Bastion look at me as David continues, "Other regions with no warning report an average response time of fourteen minutes. Those regions had a larger loss of life and millions of additional dollars in property damage than Ohio. Dr. Ross saw an unusual gathering of Helston's hawk drones and notified us through proper channels as a high-ranking clinic staff member."

Aiming a spotlight on my face could not have drawn more attention than his words do. A murmuring of thanks breaks out.

"It was nice having you here today. We'll let you know anything else we find," David says, dismissing the council members.

"Great work on this, Irontrace. We have planes to catch," Jordan says. They rise in unison and make their way up the aisle, bidding farewell to various Irontrace.

I sit still like a statue until they are gone. "Jordan seems intense," I whisper to Ivan. "Has he been watching me?"

"You did great. He probably has. They love your dad. Hospitals and most places outside of here are constantly watched."

"Whoa there, Ivan, a nice dress on the lady? You forget to invite us somewhere?" David asks, sitting down on the edge of the desk by Ivan.

"Nah, he hasn't picked a date yet. The sooner, the better. I'd marry him today if I could," I say, giving Ivan a teasing nudge.

Ivan stares at me for a beat, then gets serious. "How does this work, David? I don't technically exist as a person anywhere." Ivan asks.

"Poof. You're married. Congrats." David laughs and waves a hand.

"I am serious." Ivan jabs a finger at the desk. "This has to be legal. She's the sole beneficiary to my Merit Fund."

I have no clue what a Survivor's Fund is, but it must be significant. David drops his smile and nods. "As Senior Commander, I have authority to codify Helm laws. Get married whenever you want. Have your dad officiate. Make a ceremony up yourselves. Or I can do it. It's up to you. Wait here for a minute." He claps Ivan on the shoulder then walks off.

That's news to me that Ivan doesn't exist on paper. It makes sense though. He's on a secret black ops team, in a secure facility, in a guarded cave.

"What are you doing Friday?" Ivan asks, raising an eyebrow. "This investigation will be done by then. I'll be able to take time off."

"Hopefully marrying you?"

His face lights up. "I was hoping you'd say that."

David leans down and hands a thick piece of paper to Ivan.

This certifies that:

Commander Ivan Rhys, of Bozeman, MT, and Dr. Story Ross of Lancaster, OH are lawfully joined in marriage per David R. Delac on this day, June 19, 2050, at the Lancaster, OH Helm.

-Senior Commander David Delac

"Sign it if you're serious," David says, tossing a pen to Ivan.

David is my hero.

Ivan lays a palm on my cheek and exhales. "Are you serious about this, Dr. Ross?" he whispers.

I nod so fast my cheeks get hot. "Sign it."

He grins and signs the marriage certificate. I do too.

"The paperwork is done, congrats. You're married in the eyes of The Helm. Now go plan a real wedding. Make it a big one. I better see Rhys do the chicken dance," David says.

Ivan picks up our marriage certificate like it's a treasure. David walks away laughing heartily like he pulled a trick on his old friend.

"Thanks!" Ivan calls after him. "Well...didn't expect that, definitely not mad though."

I stand and pull him up the ramp. "I'll tell Mai and the others to start planning the actual wedding for Friday. Sound good?"

He bites his lip and nods, caught back up in that adorable, speechless awe from earlier.

"Can Richelle come?" I ask.

"I'll find a way to get her here. Anything for my wife. Wife! I can't believe it."

"Believe it. I have to tell you something. Please don't fight me on it. It's really important to me." I run my fingers through his beard, making sure I've got his full focus. "I'm not going back to Lancaster. But...I want Friday to feel like a real beginning. I won't move in with you until after the wedding. Can I stay here with Mai this week?"

He nods and brushes a tendril of hair behind my ear. "Friday."

We step out of the way of a group coming off the elevator. "I'm sorry. I have to stay here and work for a bit. I'll come to your lab as soon as I can."

"Later husband," I whisper.

"That's way better than sir!" he calls too loudly, making several people turn. We laugh as the elevator doors close.

Figure out how to fix him and Lark! I don't care if The Bastion kills me for it.

Them before me. Always.

30

Mom made a late dinner for us at Ivan's. Lark ate as fast as she could then ran to the stables with Francois.

"Before you guys leave, I have several topics I'd like to discuss," Ivan says in a serious voice, pushing his plate away.

"That doesn't sound good," Dad says.

"Your house and the street you live on are fine. As you know, there was a drone attack on Lancaster on Friday evening. The neighborhood has some damage. There are also areas in the city that were hit. Just use caution and follow any posted detours to stay on stable roads." Ivan looks around the table as he speaks to all of us.

"Is the hospital damaged?" Dad asks.

"No. Over the next couple of weeks, I'll make sure we get the list of improvements to the INES lab knocked out. But first, there's more investigating to do on the recent software malfunctions."

"I thought David said to just let your surveillance program run?" I ask.

"I genuinely don't believe Irontrace would do this. What I am going to say is of critical importance for you to keep top secret, Alan and Amelia." He looks between the two of them before continuing, "Current evidence points to recent software issues being intentionally caused by a group trying to overthrow The Bastion. This evening, I read over what was found at the other Helm. I'm not convinced. David should have called me before he convened that emergency meeting today."

Dad sighs and says, "We won't breathe a word of it to anyone."

Mom nods in agreement.

"Alan, Councilman Jordan has been watching Story. Too close for her comfort. Talk to Jordan and find out why, please."

"I will this week," Dad says.

Ivan pauses and takes my hand. "We think Story's time is best spent here, working on her research. David is wracking his brain for an idea to allow The Bastion to approve us getting our Agoras out someday. She can take mine anytime. She's moving here. Tonight."

My parents gasp.

He rapidly continues, "Not with me. She's staying with Mai. She'll commute to Lancaster for another few weeks to tie up that job. Then she's giving up that role to work here full time."

He didn't mention Friday. Good. Let's see how this goes over first.

"I don't want to be the bad guy. You're both adults. But that's not a good idea," Dad says, crossing his arms. "One of the best ways you can continue your Agora research is flying under the radar. Disappearing from Lancaster Medical Hub? Quitting that job? It would raise red flags. Come back with us to Lancaster, at least for now. Stay on the board's good side. That means you stay on The Bastion's good side too."

"What do you think, Story?" Mom asks quietly.

"I don't care if I stay on The Bastion's good side," I say.

"Well, the last time you were on their bad side, three people died," Dad gently reminds me.

I open my mouth to argue but snap it back shut.

Ivan rescues me. "She and I need to go talk more about it."

"Think about it carefully. My vote is for you to come back to the city for now," Dad says.

"Mine too, if I get a vote," Mom adds.

Ivan forces a small smile. "One final thing. It's too risky to go to Otto's farm. They would know the difference between real hawks and drones. I'm not sure why they are housing drones. Hope that doesn't upset your family."

"Right? Those drones don't look or act like Helga and the other hawks," I say, prompting Ivan to wink at me.

"We can all agree to that," Dad says.

Mom and Dad volunteer to get everything cleaned up from dinner so Ivan and I can have some time together.

We decided to ride back to the Overlook to watch the sunset.

"What do you think about what your dad said?" he asks as we trot along on Obsidian.

"I don't want to leave you." I press my face tighter into his back, trying to memorize the map of him. "Do you think it will make The Bastion mad if I disappear?"

"Jordan and Schrader are watching you already. This is your decision. I won't tell you what to do. The Bastion would love to parade you around for your work with ASTRA."

"As much as I hate to say it, Dad may be right. I'll go back to Lancaster until Friday. Then I'm moving here."

He squeezes my arms. "Can't wait, baby. Give Lancaster a year, then quit. You'll have whipped ASTRA into shape by then."

No! A year? I'm not on board for this plan.

"Whoa, Sid." Ivan stops him at the top of the falls. Our view is an uninterrupted sea of green trees bathed in a deep golden-orange glow, fading into a pink sea of lava near where the sun is going down.

A lonely stump sits a few feet back from the edge. Ivan drapes our picnic blanket from Sid's saddle bag on it and sits, pulling me onto his lap.

He smiles and wraps one arm behind my shoulders. I tuck close against him. He's a warm, solid shelter. Other half. I always thought that was a dumb thing to call someone. But what else would you call someone who makes you ache for them solely by existing? I'm here on Ivan's lap, safe in his arms, and for the first time in my life, I'm *me*. He's forged me into a braver, stronger, version of myself. I want to be this person forever.

Life has always been too loud, too much. Not with him. Things feel quiet. Effortless. This isn't a spark that will wane. He's the spark that will keep me going.

He's the first to speak. "When you leave tonight, do you want me to take you to the exit? Or stay in the control room and make sure you get home safely?"

"I can't do it. I can't go."

He caresses my face, tucking back flyaway curls. "Do you know why I've wanted to marry you, since nearly the first moment we met?" I shake my head. "I want to be tied to you alone for the rest of my life. There's just something about it. Some people don't want that link. I do. I think you do too." I nod. "No matter where we are, I'll know I'm yours. You're mine."

"We don't know how long the rest of your life will be." My voice fails. His eleven months is down to ten. *If he gets ten.*

"Nobody really does though, baby."

I turn towards him, desperately hoping he'll agree. "David said our wedding can be whatever we want—even if we elope. What if we get married right here instead of waiting? I *think* I can walk out of here knowing that we already belong to each other."

"Don't you want to wait and do the whole wedding thing on Friday?"

No. A marriage isn't just about a wedding. It's about the vows you make to each other. I'm ready to promise to love Ivan forever.

Tears sting my eyes.

He frowns. "And the dancing, and cake? There's a bakery in Atlas Caverns with *really* good cake."

I try to keep it together, I do. I never cry around anyone else. But my vision blurs and tears break free.

"What's wrong?" He swipes my tears.

"Marry me tonight. Here. Just us," I whisper.

"You don't want Richelle and Lark there? And to have a huge Helm party with your dad to give you away?"

The wedding, the dances, the party—those are wants. I *need* him. I shake my head.

"Forget it." He grins and slides his hands to my waist, shifting me to my feet. "I'm marrying you here at the falls."

"Wait," I ask. "Are you disappointed about not having a big wedding?"

"Story," he breathes my name in a voice so quiet I almost miss it. He loops his arms to rest his hands on my lower back. "Do I seem disappointed to you?"

I meet his eyes. There's something in them I've never seen. It's a fire flashing, bright and certain. He does *not* look disappointed.

He continues, "I've been on the verge of throwing myself at your feet and asking you to marry me on the spot fifty times today."

I let out a shaky laugh, dropping my eyes to his steady tan arms. These strong arms will hold me when I'm falling apart, scoop me up in his roguish grasp when he's teasing me, and wrap around me every night that the boundary doesn't separate us. They're my home.

No more tears. I'm ready to start my real life with him. I look up.

"I, Story Ross, vow to be your loving wife. I'll laugh with you when life is sweet. Stick close to you on hard days. And love you more every minute. You've taught me more about the world in the last few months than most people will ever know. I promise to keep growing as a person with you by my side. I'll always love you with my whole heart. I'm yours, forever."

He takes a deep breath. "I, Ivan Rhys, vow to be your loving, devoted, husband. I was content knowing what my admittedly bleak future held before you. But you give me hope for a new beginning. You didn't just change my life. You are my life. My world. My dream. My teacher. You've taught me what love really feels like. Thank you. I'll always love you. I'll be faithful and true to you through it all, my perfect darling."

We smile, feeling the weight of our promises settling on us. I slip my arms around his waist, holding him close.

"Time to kiss my bride."

31

We decided that Ivan will stay in the control room and make sure we get home safely. I don't think we could have a more perfect "see you later" than our time together at the Overlook.

Lark is exhausted from the weekend and falls asleep almost immediately in the car.

I lean forward to whisper. "Lark won't be able to keep this a secret. She'd be too excited. But I want to let you guys know. Ivan and I got married at the top of the falls tonight."

"Uhhhhh...congrats!" Dad exclaims. I wondered if he'd be mad, but he's grinning at me in the rearview mirror. "Now you're really Dr. Rhys."

"Honey! That's wonderful. Congratulations." Mom whips around, her face lit up. "There's no way Lark could keep that a secret. I'm still wondering how she'll keep The Helm a secret."

"Thanks." My cheeks ache from smiling, but I can't get the perma-grin off my face. I called Ivan and put him on speakerphone so they could tell him congrats. After their well-wishes died down, Ivan told them I'm moving to The Helm Friday. He was sure to add that "it's not a matter that's up for discussion." Dad hit the rumble strip but didn't argue about it, even after Ivan hung up.

Leaving The Helm as Story Ross felt impossible. Leaving as Story Rhys makes me feel like I can do anything. *I'm Ivan's.* Nothing will ever take this away from us.

"Are we riding to the hospital in the morning together?" Dad asks. "I should be there all day, as far as I know."

"Sure. Does Councilman Jordan work at the hospital?" I wonder if I'll see him there.

"Not every day. The members of The Bastion have different areas of special interest. His is healthcare. He stays up to date with a lot of the hospital board news in our region. If he hears of someone trying to be innovative it makes his ears perk up. He wears it like a badge of honor to latch on to research they're doing and get his name attached to it for credit," he says.

I've been looking out the windows for drone damage now that we've hit the outskirts of the city. But it's almost two in the morning, and I can't see very far in the dark. Dad pulls to the side of the road by some low barricades, and an eerie scene emerges on Baltimore Street. He and Mom whisper about the blocked off side streets in our neighborhood.

The headlights shine on two houses that have been almost leveled. Fire ravaged them. Their remains are charred shells of framing wood and burnt walls. Other houses have portions of the upper floors missing, allowing us to peer into our neighbor's homes.

This is too raw, too personal. No one should see this view into their bedrooms, hallways, bathrooms. I look away, guilt pricking me for invading their privacy, even though I didn't mean to. The ground on the street is littered with burnt items, trash, and stacks of people's possessions. Cleanup will take weeks.

Baltimore Street has one of my favorite houses on it. A sunny yellow color, with navy shutters. The front of the house has two screened decks, bordered by tall ornamental grasses that blow in the wind and thick clusters of purple coneflowers. A couple lives there with their four young kids. Every morning at least one of them waves to us when we leave to take Lark to school.

Their beautiful home is mostly gone.

At the end of their driveway, someone has driven a mini bulldozer to make a pile of their possessions. Many burnt toys peek out of the pile. I hope so badly none of them were among the three Ivan said had died.

Mom cries quietly, Dad reaches out to hold her hand.

"190 seconds," I whisper. I can't imagine what it would look like in our neighborhood if David and Ivan hadn't worked so fast.

Ivan was right. Our house is untouched by the disaster. The

neighborhood is still and silent, making the short walk to our front door spooky.

Dad carried Lark in from the car, and we told each other good night before heading our separate ways. As soon as I get to my room, I put my laptop on my desk and open it.

There's my beautiful WIFE! -I

His wife. I want to scream it to the universe. "Are you working? Can I see you?"

Sorry, I'm in the control room, I can't do a video call. It's boring tonight though. -I

"Good! Hopefully, your night stays that way. I wish you were here."

Me too. -I

"Can I leave this connected tonight?"

You need to sleep. -I

"I promise I'll sleep. But I need to know you're there. I love you, husband," I say, blowing a kiss at the screen.

Ah, you are killing me. Love you, Mrs. Rhys. -I

~~~

The next day at work drags. Leaving him was hard, staying away is impossible.

Tuesday afternoon, my hands hover above my keyboard. Dr. Benedict is not going to like my research report for today. I re-read the first paragraph for the tenth time before deleting it.

I was trying to use the cutting robots to only remove abnormal blood vessels in the AVM. ASTRA struggles with determining healthy, normal vessels from abnormal, diseased vessels. It keeps removing or slicing open the wrong vessels, triggering a hemorrhage, and killing the simulators.

There must be a way to combine cutting and imaging here in Lancaster to increase their decision-making capabilities. Instead of focusing on simulator deaths in the first paragraph, I write out my plans to make the process better. That's my sweet spot. Finding faults with ASTRA
~~~

makes my thoughts flow freely onto the screen.

My last paragraph ends with O*h, and the robots killed 29 simulators this morning, my bad, Dr. B.* I laugh and smash the backspace button again.

Someone knocked hard on my lab door. I opened it to see Schrader. "Hello, Dr. Ross."

"Hi."

He hesitates. I peek around him to the windows.

"Are the plants okay?" I ask.

"Yes. Dr. Benedict asked me to escort you to his office," he says.

That seems worse than if the plants were dead again. I'm glad Dr. Benedict sent someone to escort me for the thirty-foot walk to his office.

"Oh, okay." I tuck my phone in my pocket in case I need Ivan.

Schrader knocks. "Come in," Dr. B. calls from inside.

"Dr. Ross, it's nice to see you. We have some guests here today who are particularly interested in your work. Allow me to introduce you to Councilman Jordan and a few members of the board." He makes rounds of introductions. I need to get comfortable presenting to groups of important people without getting flustered. I plaster a smile on my face and eagerly greet each of them.

"Hello, thank you for coming. It's nice to meet you." I have a suspicion this meeting is a punishment from my mentor.

Ivan's solution to make Dr. Benedict keep his hands to himself was to email several years of photos of Dr. B behaving inappropriately with colleagues to his wife of thirty-nine years. Ivan really did ruin Benedict's life with a few clicks. Oh well, Dr. B. started it.

"Nice to meet you, Dr. Ross," Councilman Jordan says. *Message received. He and I don't know each other from The Helm.*

"Would you like me to talk about how my research is going?" I ask.

"We've reviewed it already. Today was a very different approach. All simulated patients died. How could that be helpful to you?" Dr. Benedict asks, shuffling through some papers, avoiding my gaze.

My list of surgical simulation failures cast from my tablet to the large monitor beside his desk.

"I worked my first few weeks here on seeing what the ASTRA models *can* do. I learned how they handle a case from start to finish with no complications. But real surgeries require them to have expert-level emergency responses. If a patient bleeds out, they must be able to handle that. If a patient has sudden brain swelling, a stroke, or a medication reaction, the ASTRA needs to be able to multitask."

"That is true." he concedes, flicking his eyes to meet mine, then away again.

"Are you pushing the robots to a standard they can't meet? It feels like you're intentionally trying to make them fail, Dr. Ross," Councilman Jordan asks. He squints his icy eyes at me.

Audible murmuring breaks out among the board and council members. Several shift in their seats and stare at me.

Oh no, The Bastion is mad at me again.

I remember Ivan in the control room, yelling at the council members and draw strength from his example. I put my hands in my lap and feel my ring. He knows his field and is an expert. I am too.

"No. I think they can be trained to combine tasks. My surgical stations are for cutting and sawing, controlling bleeding, and taking imaging to show what's happening during surgery. I've shown this current implementation fails. I'm going to find a way to combine the stations. This will allow them to do more tasks per surgery. My models will have training that incorporates advanced decision-making based on their new multifunctional capabilities." As I speak, I visualize myself working as the primary at The Helm and how robotic systems work for me as my assistants. "People place trust in these surgical AI models to save their lives and provide excellent care. I'll help them earn our trust in their capabilities."

Each member of the board is nodding along with me, no doubt counting the dollars I'll bring in.

Jordan speaks again. "I have another concern. Related to your age. Aren't most people still out partying in their early twenties? You're not involved in so many activities and trips on your weekends that you are losing focus on your work at Lancaster Medical Hub?"

This is why my Commander Rhys yells at these people.

"Dedication to my role here fills my working hours. Studies show a part of working at such a high level is having downtime to recharge. I'm following the example of my mentor, Dr. Benedict and spending my off time in a rejuvenating way."

His chair squeaks as he jerks to glare at me. If I'd pulled out a gun and shot him, he couldn't have looked more shocked. "Yes, Councilman Jordan. If The Bastion wants us to be successful, we need to enjoy some recreation."

"Glad to know where your focus lies." Jordan aims a cold, weaponized smile at me.

One of the board members stands up. "This is an innovative approach, Dr. Ross. It's reassuring you have a plan, a path forward. We'll continue to support your research. Thank you for your time." He strides over and shakes my hand in dismissal.

"Thank you all for your time and your trust in me. Have a wonderful weekend!" I cheerily wave goodbye to them and leave Dr. Benedict's office.

The weight of that encounter melts off my shoulders. The board and Councilman Jordan saw it's not easy to intimidate me, and I will stand by my work.

As I walk to the car, I get a message from Ivan.

Concerning things are popping up in our monitoring. I put out a security alert for Lancaster. I'll make sure you get home safely. Love you. -I

That's it. I hate being out here. I'm going home to Ivan tonight. Lark can come stay with us off and on if she wants.

Ugh, no. Not again. Love you. Stay safe! - <3

Lark is on summer break now, and she bounces at me as soon as I open the front door. "Story! You're finally home! What are we going to do tonight?"

"How about a cookout and yard games?" I ask, putting my laptop and work bags on the counter.

"Yes!"

Lark turns on blasting music, and we spend the next hour or so danc-ing while preparing veggies and burgers for the grill. Once Dad gets home, we move our little party outside and have a nice family dinner.

Dad and I are finishing off the last of the homemade strawberry ice cream while Mom uses a huge bubble wand to blow bubbles for Lark. The ones she can't catch float high above our blue house and up over the dark wooden fence into our neighbor's yard.

Dad's phone rings and he groans before answering.

"Hello, Otto." Dad listens for a couple of minutes without saying anything before he scrunches up his face. This call is not a friendly chat. "If the injury is as bad as you're describing, head to the hospital. I'll meet you there to check on her." He listens for a minute, then says, "Okay, we'll see you soon."

He hangs up and shakes his head. "Sorry, girls. Otto is on his way. Richelle was doing fence chores and cut her hand. I told him he should take her to the hospital. He wants to come here first. I'm going to get some bandages and clear a spot to get her cleaned up if needed."

"Aww, no!" Lark exclaims. I can't tell if she's sad about the fun end-ing or Richelle's injury.

"Come on, kiddo," Mom says, carrying the bubble wand up to the porch and putting it in an outdoor toy box. "We can do this more to-morrow."

I gather dinner dishes off the table on the deck. We head inside and as I fill the dishwasher Otto knocks on the door.

"Sorry to see you under these circumstances," Mom says, opening the door for them. Otto rushes in with his arm around Richelle's shoul-ders. Her right hand is tightly wrapped in a blood-soaked towel.

"Don't unwrap that, we don't want the bleeding to get worse," Dad orders.

"What happened?" I ask, sitting on the floor in front of Richelle.

"Hey," Richelle says in a flat voice. She's shaky and pale but not crying. She ignores Dad, silently throwing the bloody towel to the floor and extends her arm onto his lap.

There's a large slice on the palm of her hand, into the base of her thumb. She has multiple deep gashes on her lower arm. Three on the front, and one on the back. This was clearly caused by talons from a large bird.

"Richelle, this looks awful. What happened?" Dad asks, lines furrowing downward around his mouth and eyes. "You need to go to the hospital for stitches and advanced care. Sorry."

"Alan, I would really prefer you handle this for me. Let's keep this between us. A family matter." Otto bites his lip, fighting to keep his voice below a yell.

Dad's voice is firm. "No. Otto. She needs to go to Lancaster Medical Hub."

Otto flushes. "Haven't you been a surgeon forever? Isn't Story a surgeon too? Why are you acting like you two can't help?"

"We train ASTRA models. How did a fence do this to her arm?" Dad asks, shining a flashlight at the gashes on her arm.

"I don't know what happened," Otto snaps.

Richelle finally cries, holding her bloody arm to her chest. "Dad, this really hurts. I'm calling Mom." She pulls out her phone with her left hand, locking and unlocking it. "I don't have cell service."

Otto pulls out his phone. He shakes it multiple times and then turns it off. "Unbelievable, I don't either."

Dad looks at me and silently mouths, "Call Ivan!"

I nod. "Mine's good. Here," I unlock my phone and hand it to Richelle.

"What is up with cell phones in this house?" Otto glares at his phone once it restarts.

"Maybe the drone bombs messed up service," Dad says, covering Richelle's arm with fresh bandages.

"Maybe. Can one of you drive us to the hospital in your car, and one of you bring my truck?" Otto asks, helping Richelle stand. "Tell your mom to meet us there and quit gabbing."

Dad and I glance at each other then glare at Otto. Richelle cries for another minute to her mom before handing me my phone.

I give Richelle a one-sided hug and walk her to the door. "Keep it wrapped. Keep this ice on it. They'll get you fixed up. Message me once you have service again. Love you!"

"Love you," she sniffles into my ear.

"Amelia, can you please follow us in your car?" Dad asks, throwing Mom her keys. "Girls, I don't know when we'll be back. We may stay with them for a while and see how it goes."

"Sure," Mom says, rushing outside with them.

"Bye. Sorry you got hurt, Richelle! See you later!" Lark calls to them as Dad shuts the car door.

"Phew, what an evening! Now it's just you and I."

Lark sits quietly on the couch, staring towards the door. "Poor Richelle. I hope she's okay."

"She will be. The ALICE doctors at Lancaster Medical Hub are great. We should have a movie night. Get your shower and then you can pick one."

Ivan needs to know what happened. And that I'm coming home tonight.

32

I plop at my desk and open my laptop.

"Ivan! Where are you?" I ask loudly as soon as the screen flashes to life.

Geez, miss me much? I've never been so happy to hear a voice scream in my headphones and scare the daylights out of me. -I

"Can you please video call me?"

Let me run to our apartment. -I

"Something happened with Richelle and Otto."

You didn't go there, right? -I

"No, they came here. I listen to my genius husband when he asks me not to do something," I say, smiling at the screen. "It's been a strange night. Otto is mad."

No messages appear for a minute.

Then my screen flashes, and his video appears. I laugh at his heaving chest. He's dramatically sucking in deep breaths to recover.

"There you are! Long run from the control room?"

"Yeah. Everybody looked at me like I'd gone crazy sprinting out the door of the control room. But when my wife needs me, I run." Taking one more deep breath, he leans forward, looking concerned. "What happened?"

He smiles when I lead with, "First of all, hello. I love you so much! I couldn't call you right after work because Lark has been bored. We were trying to have some summer fun with her. So, you know Richelle? She's like my best friend, aside from you. Richelle's had lots of random injuries from farm work through the years. Nothing serious. Just small scratches. She usually comes over for Dad to put band aids on her and tell her she's fine. It's mostly an excuse to get her out of chores for a few days and let her stay with me for girl time. We always have a blast. Anyways, we were chilling in the yard after dinner and Otto called."

Ivan's chin rests on his right hand, patiently taking in my story with a soft smile. His eyes busily search my face, waiting for a significant part.

"Otto told Dad that Richelle's hand was hurt badly this afternoon. Dad told him to go to the hospital. But Otto made a big deal about coming to our house and keeping this in the family or something. When they got here, Richelle unwraps this blood-soaked towel from her arm. She's got huge gashes, I think from talons, like a hawk attacked her. There's a bunch of them. She was mildly in shock from it. Also, Otto was slightly freaking out about he and Richelle not having cell phone service inside our house."

His eyebrows go up. The corners of his mouth twitch down. There it is. Commander Rhys is ready to investigate.

"That's awful. Hopefully she's okay. I'll dig into the Helston Hawk drone activity logs. I can verify if a counterfeit hawk they are rehabbing attacked her. David and I still have your house shielded from any unapproved devices in a certain radius. Phones or any other devices not on my list will be blocked from doing anything sketchy around my wife."

"Thank you."

"How are you? Did your gross old mentor keep his hands to himself this afternoon?"

The way his mouth moves, and the rhythm of his voice captivate my attention. I don't realize he's waiting on a response until he leans closer to look at the screen.

"You alright over there, Story? Your laptop didn't freeze. I built it too well."

"Sorry. I can't focus. Miss you so much. Can I please come home? Tonight? I need to see you. I can't wait until Friday."

"Goodness, Mrs. Rhys. You make me blush." He laughs and fans his face. "I'll make it happen."

"Please do! Get back to work." I smile and wave goodbye.

"Bye." He grins at me before disappearing.

I sort through my closet and the clothes pile on my bed grows. Dresses, shorts, pajamas, all scream Story Ross, med student. Not Story Rhys, wife of Commander Rhys. I should've taken a lunch break to go shopping. My nearly empty bag mocks me. Nothing seems right for this trip.

No Mom. No Dad. No Lark. Just my new little family – Ivan and me. Every time I walk past the mirror on my door, I catch the same giant grin stuck on my face.

"Movie time!" Lark yells, jumping onto my clothes stack like it's an autumn leaf pile. "What happened to your room? Mom will hate this mess!"

"I hate it too. I'll clean up later. What movie are we watching?"

We head downstairs and turn on one of her favorites about a cartoon zoo. We've seen it dozens of times, but she loves it. By the end, she's more asleep than awake.

"Lark, bedtime. You can't keep your eyes open."

She doesn't answer, just nods with her eyes mostly shut.

Once she's tucked in, I head to my desk to wrap up my research for the week. Music fills the room from my laptop speakers.

Without Ivan's help, I want to come up with plans to improve the surgical robots at Lancaster Medical Hub. A basic sketch unfolds on my paper with their current setup. I need to find out who builds these for the hospital. I sit, tapping my pencil on my notebook, reviewing the list of hospital staff I know.

Hey beautiful! What's got you so deep in thought? -I

My face lights up. Usually, Ivan messages me seconds after my laptop opens. This time it took him about five minutes.

"There you are! I'm planning for work in the Lancaster lab. What are you doing?"

I got a notification your laptop came online. It reminded me to talk to David about getting you here. I get off work at 5am. If you want, you can come any time after that and stay. -I

"Permanently?"

I'm all yours. -I

A wave of calm and chaos washes over me. "Be there in three hours."

How am I supposed to keep working? If someone attacks The Kernel, I'm useless for the rest of this shift. -I

The soft sound of the front door shutting drifts up the stairs.

"I'll be right back. My parents just came in. I don't want them to wake Lark." I run out.

My ring buzzes like crazy on my finger. "Chill, baby. I'll call you in a minute." I give it a squeeze. "Hey! How is Ri-" I ask Mom and Dad from the bottom of the stairs.

It's not my parents.

Two figures, entirely in black, stand by the front door. They have masks on, hiding their faces and hair.

My ring! I run from the intruders, squeezing my panic button repeatedly, even though it's already buzzing. They whip towards me, and the closest one comes at me. Ducking around the corner towards the kitchen is my best shot to keep them away from sleeping Lark.

One launches at my waist, pulling me down to the floor off the bottom step, knocking the breath out of me. I'm too stunned to fight back as they drag me in the direction of the kitchen.

Save Lark!

I stretch towards the stair rail to pull myself away from them, but their thick fingers dig in like iron hooks in the flesh under my ribcage, yanking me backwards.

Intruder number one rips me forward and shoves me down on the floor between the couch and the coffee table. My kicks and struggles continue. Even though they're definitely winning whatever this is, I learned something. These two are not fighters. I almost get free a couple of times. Ivan's hold, even when we're just playing, is unrelenting, unbreakable.

The other one sees the mighty struggle I'm putting up and runs to pin my arms and shoulders down hard to the floor. I keep twisting, clawing whatever is in reach, refusing to stay down.

"Story!" Lark screams from the top of the stairs. "People are killing Story!"

The person holding my arms and shoulders leaps up and jogs towards the front door.

Her screams distract my captor just enough for me to wriggle free. I throw myself over the back of the couch and sprint halfway up the stairs towards Lark.

"Go, Lark. Hide!" I yell.

A hand like a vise grips my ankle, yanking me back down. I flail and kick with my free leg and feel my right heel hit their head. They reel backwards, releasing their grip on my ankle.

I jump up and try to make it backwards up the stairs, kicking at them, but I miss every time. The other person sprints up the stairs and fully tackles me. The force slams my spine against the wooden stairs so hard it knocks the breath out of me again.

For a sickening moment, my head swims and I feel like I'm going to pass out from the pain in my back. Unbothered, they drag me down the steps by the ankle. I feel a sickening crack of my ribs as they slam off the edge of every hard stair.

I was mad before. Now I'm furious. I'll do anything to keep them away from Lark. If they bang her Agora around like this, it'll kill her.

"Story, no! Let go of Story!" Lark screams. Something small and bright falls from the top of the stairs. She threw my phone.

It clatters to the floor in the kitchen, several feet away. The screen is lit up, but I can't get to it. I can't tell if it's broken from the fall. Can Ivan hear me?

"Ivan! Blow up my phone!" I scream.

Intruder number two tries to catch my hands. Are they going to tie me up? They can't have my hands. I claw and tear at their face until their mask slides off.

He freezes. The man who just tackled me and fractured my ribs is my uncle.

"Otto!" I scream. "What are you doing?"

"Knock this off, Story!" Otto roars.

He wrenches me down the rest of the stairs. At the bottom, he and the other person pull me away from the stairs towards the open front door.

They're taking me away. Lark will be alone.

I kick off the doorway. I have to do something, anything to stay with Lark. My desperation to protect Lark is reaching a frenzy. Kick, kick, kick. I've got my feet wedged against the doorframe now. They can't get me out.

Otto stumbles two steps backward, then his fingers crush into my biceps, squeezing so hard I scream.

"Otto! Why?" I yell. He seemed okay-ish enough through the years, even though he and I weren't particularly close. I've never liked the way he spoke to Richelle. But he didn't seem like a kidnapper.

"You and Lark have to come with us. You don't understand." He shoves me towards the other person. They readjust, each grabbing one of my arms, intensifying the burning pain.

"Lark! Hide!" It's over. I'm too tired to save us. My toes scrape the floor, then my feet dangle as they haul me upwards, carrying me towards the door.

A blinding light flashes around us. We're thrown forward several feet. They were behind me on either side and absorbed most of the small blast with their backs and shoulders.

Ivan did it! He blew something up. I run, but everything hurts. I can only pant for small breaths. I must have at least a few rib fractures on each side.

Their hands claw at my ankles, trying to sweep my feet and knock me down. This is really my last shot. I fly up the stairs to Lark. She's at the top of the stairs, sobbing. I grab her and run in my room, locking the door.

"Lark, are you okay?" I hug her. "I'm good, are you good? We're fine!"

"Where's Dad? Where's Mom?" she wails.

"Be quiet, I don't know where they are."

"Story's here!" David blurts. My laptop is on my desk with a video feed running to the control room.

Ivan and Moriah run into view.

"Story! Are you safe? Is Lark okay?" Ivan yells. He looks absolutely wrecked. His eyes are wild, tan cheeks are flushed.

"It's Otto! We're in my room," I whisper. I'm sucking shallow breaths and feeling lightheaded.

"Put your laptop on the floor. Aim the screen at your bedroom door. Go in your bathroom. Get in the tub. Lie down. Help will be there soon. I love you so much." The tone of Ivan's voice sends a chill down my spine.

"Love you!" I yell back. Lark is already running for the bathroom. No way she's getting out of my reach again. I rush after her, hurl the door shut, and lock it.

We wait in the tub. Nothing happens.

Do something Ivan, please.

"This is good, Lark. Ivan is helping. We're safe. No one can get us in here," I whisper.

"Can we get up now?" Lark sobs.

"No. Lark, shhshhshh."

Angry banging pummels my bedroom door. I think Otto is beating it down with tools. Maybe an ax? Did he bring one or steal Dad's?

An explosion roars outside the bathroom door. Everything stops. My whole brain rattled. A ringing is raging in my skull. Trying to focus on the door makes the top of my head hurt.

Lark clings to my waist like a koala on a tree. When I push her away to look at her face she's screaming. That's weird, aside from ringing, it's quiet. I twist her frantically, doing a quick check to see if she has injuries. I don't find any. Her Agora feels normal. She's fine.

Something happened to my torso. I think I fell on the stairs? Every time I move it feels like my lungs and chest wall tear a little.

I wonder how Ivan is. I miss him. I love him. He's my husband now. He should be with me. Where is he? Did he just blow up my bedroom?

Faint banging rattles the bathroom door. I can't distinguish if it is my imagination or reality. I try to focus on the door. But I'm tired. So tired. The door flings open. A group of men peer in.

Men. More men I'll have to fight. What is it with men today? Go away!

"Story? Lark?" I hear one of them ask.

They have blue outfits like what Irontrace wears. The man in front has a Helston's hawk logo on his shirt. *Oh no, we're dead.* Some kind of hawk drone soldiers are here for us.

I pull free of Lark's arms and stand, wobbling. These men can't take her. Or me. My shirt from my neck to my shoulder was torn at some point and hangs in tatters on the right. I tuck a part of it under my sports bra strap, preparing to protect Lark.

The one in front is saying something and holding out his hands. Ivan did that when I first met him to show he was harmless.

I don't believe this man, he's not my Ivan. I throw a hairdryer, hitting him in the chest. He doesn't stop. He moves sideways and walks towards us. What can I grab now?

"Story, we are here to help you. Story? Can you hear me?" the man asks.

He takes a step into the bathroom. I jump out of the tub. A shelf hangs on the wall by me, covered with hair products and makeup. I tear the shelf off the wall, scattering small items everywhere. I lurch towards the men, swinging it at them. Lark is in the shower throwing shampoo and body wash bottles at them.

"Story!" Ivan yells. "I sent them. Stop!"

I look around, but can't see him. I drop the shelf, feeling off balance. Ivan sent them?

The man I hit with the hairdryer leads me out of the bathroom. Ivan made a large explosion in my bedroom. My laptop is mostly gone. Black pieces of it have been launched everywhere. Some are stuck in the walls like throwing stars.

"Miss, we're here to transport you and your sister," one of them tells me with a smile.

The wall that held my doorway is gone. Instead of smooth white ceiling, gaping spots of dark night sky are visible. My bedroom window is open. Another man is motioning for us to climb out. That doesn't seem like something I want to do. I glance through the empty window frame. There's a ladder extended up to my window from a huge truck outside.

Lark is still crying. Her little brain is probably overwhelmed by all the action. Mine is. I crouch and wrap her in a hug. "It's okay, Lark. I promise."

"Story, I'm Matthew Sullivan. It's time to go," the man by the window says.

"Ivan?" I haven't heard him since they came into my bathroom.

"I'm here, baby." His voice comes out through their radio. "They have body cameras on, we see you. They're bringing you to me."

Lark gasps, "The Helm!"

"Yes. We'll see you soon. You're okay, Lark. They're good guys. Go with Sully," Ivan says.

Sullivan helps Lark and I climb out the window onto the metal ladder. We descend its narrow staircase to the ground, followed by the rest of the men. Emergency sirens wail in the background. Neighbors are gathered outside, aiming phones at our property.

Sullivan walks over to the crowd and speaks loudly. "Stay back! Gas leak in the area! Evacuate your homes. Please, get out of this area immediately. There is an active gas leak! You could be next."

The neighbors scatter.

"Come here, ladies. We need to set up a perimeter around your house," Sully says, ushering us into the back of a big truck with extra seats.

I watch out the windows as some of the men place caution tape around our house. Uncle Otto's truck is parked in the driveway, close to the house. The passenger door is open, and the interior lights cast a sallow light in his cab.

"Stay here, Lark." I scoot to the door at the back of the truck. Two men are standing (guarding?) us. "Where are my parents?"

"Your parents are on their way to a secure location," he says. "We'll be leaving in a moment to get you there too."

"Can we go now? I want to see Mom." Lark asks.

"I'll ask." He turns and walks to Sullivan.

Several emergency vehicles have flooded the street and yards around ours. A mechanical whirring and clicking gently rattles the top of the truck from the ladder being folded back in place.

An official-looking person in a hat purposefully marches up to the men in blue. They have a short conversation, shake hands, and walk separate ways. Our remaining guard opens the back door of the truck for the official to get in.

For the first time tonight, I almost cry. It's Councilman Jordan.

"Dr. Ross. We meet again. Sorry it's under these circumstances."

"Hi." I don't want him involved in this.

"I'll see you soon to review findings from our initial investigation here."

What does that even mean? Is he investigating my home invasion?

"Okay," I say.

He sits, staring at me. I refuse to speak.

"You've been through a lot. I'll let you go. Goodbye. Sorry about all of this, sweetie," he says to Lark, ruffling her hair.

I open my mouth to yell at him but can't summon the energy.

He shuts the doors and bangs on them twice. The truck pulls away. I watch my childhood home grow smaller from the windows on the back doors. Ivan is my home now. I'm never leaving him again. Goodbye, Lancaster.

33

"My girls!" Mom cries as she and Dad fling open the back doors of our truck. Lark launches into her arms and unleashes a fresh round of tears, recounting her tale of what happened.

Dad reaches out for me. I shake my head and climb past him. I only left The Helm because he thought it was for the best. *Thanks a lot, Dad.*

We're parked at the familiar forest parking area. The men in blue are gathered in the intersecting headlight beams, talking to Jordan and Sullivan. In one final burst of adrenaline, I sprint past them all.

"Story, wait!" Sullivan runs after me.

He chases me towards the tree line, but I'm fast from years of running and make it safely in before he can catch me. He must be unfamiliar with the area because he doesn't pursue me.

"Miss!" Sullivan yells from the darkness. "Come back!"

Ivan, Obsidian, and a few Irontrace are waiting with some extra horses. Ivan leaps down when he sees me. He runs to me, catching me up in his arms as I cross through the boundary.

"I love you. Are you okay? I love you. I love you," he whispers urgently into my neck. My ribs, arms, and back are on fire. His frantic embrace is shattering me.

I squeak a tortured "Ow, ow, ow," onto his cheek. He releases me, looking at me as if he's the monster who caused my injuries.

"Let's go home."

He picks me up with agonizing delicacy, placing me into Obsidian's saddle then jumps up behind me.

"Evans!" he barks loudly.

Obsidian feeds on Ivan's energy, snorting and tossing his head, ready to run.

"Sir?" An Irontrace sits taller, meeting Ivan's eyes.

"Get the others back as fast as you can," he orders, putting his arms like guardrails on either side of me and holding onto the saddle horn in front of me.

I tap Obsidian's sides with my heels before he's finished speaking. In a blink we vanish into the darkness.

He slides his hands over mine on the reins and slows Obsidian to an easy trot, "Whoa, Sid. Baby here, lean as far back against me as you can."

I let my weight slump against his chest.

"Better, thanks. Sid was bouncing me to death."

"I bet. I've been there a few times myself. We're going around to the west side of the falls. We'll take this nice and slow."

The rest of the ride, Ivan focuses all his attention on making sure I'm as comfortable as possible. What will I do when he's not here anymore to put me back together?

Two Irontrace sit on horses guarding the open entrance. They stand in their stirrups and wave to us before Obsidian carries us through.

"Story!" Francois yells. "You are here!"

"Hey, Francois. I am." I smile at my little friend as I pull Obsidian to a stop. Ivan lightly drops to the ground and then turns to help me down.

"Take care of him." Ivan tosses the reins to Francois.

One glance between Ivan and I and he runs away, tugging Sid behind him. Smart kid.

Ivan looks me up and down, assessing me. "What hurts the most?"

"Ribs. Back. Shoulders. Arms." I muster the best smile I can. It's a bad smile. "At least I can walk."

"Are your legs hurting?"

"No."

He squats, tucking his shoulder under my chin. Making me feel like I'm the most precious thing he's ever touched, he locks his arms behind my thighs and lifts me, settling my weight low on his hips.

"Am I hurting you?" he asks.

"No. Don't let go of me." Tears spring to my eyes as I press my forehead to his.

"You're mine, wife. I'm not letting you out of my sight." The possessive squeeze he gives my legs add weight to his words.

Ivan is always in a hurry. But on this walk, he lingers. Several times, he stops to kiss me. It's a soft, certain reminder that I'm really here—I made it back. Every time his beard brushes my cheek or neck, it grounds me to this moment with him. Otto didn't win. My breaths come a little easier.

We run into several Irontrace. Ivan gives them all the same short command. "Keep moving, Operative."

Every one of them makes space for us, wide-eyed that the always smiling Commander Rhys won't spare them a look. I'm sure the sight of the second highest ranked person in their Helm carrying his torn-up wife is going to cause quite a stir. We stop outside the clinic. He adjusts my weight on his hips, leaning me back several inches to look in my eyes.

"I've worked on investigations for years. You need to go to the clinic right now to document these injuries. They'll use them to back up your account of what happened with AJA."

I can't bear the thought of being away from him for a second. "Stay with me. Please?"

"I'm not leaving you, baby."

I bury my face in his neck.

"Need a room, right now, Mai. As private as you can make it," Ivan orders as we walk past the station.

"Yes, Commander! What happened to Story?!" she sputters.

A curtain screeches open and Ivan sits on the bed, still holding me.

An ORION rolls in immediately. "Dr. Ross, I'm here to assess your injuries. Please change into the gown. I'll be back."

"Stop. That's not my name. I'm Story Rhys. Change it on my patient record."

"Done. Dr. Rhys. Let's just get you registered real quick."

"ORION. Get out of here," Ivan orders.

The ORION's screen goes dark and it rolls into the hall.

Ivan throws my hospital gown over his shoulder and stands. "Can I help you change?"

I almost laugh, but it dies in my throat. We forgot to say the "in sickness and health" part at our wedding. Either way, here we are. "Guess we're skipping straight to the hard parts of marriage?" I murmur, stepping close to him. "I'm so sorry."

"Do not apologize." With a deliberate, featherlight touch I didn't expect from a man his size, his hands gently assess the injuries along my ribs and back. "These are broken for sure, baby."

"They feel like it." My voice cracks.

"I can't believe I wasn't there." He sweeps my hair out of the way to tie my gown, then guides me to bed. "I shouldn't have agreed with your dad about you going back to Lancaster. I'm so sorry."

"Don't you apologize either. I agreed with our plan." I wince as I reach for a hug.

"Easy, you'll hurt yourself."

"I'm already hurt. Let me hurt while you hold me."

He carefully lays beside me and puts his arm under my neck like a pillow. "Listen. I'm new at this loving someone thing. I learned from this. You and I are our own family. I've never had one. But I'll do anything for you. What we say goes from now on. No one else gets input on what happens in *our* family."

"I like that. You're doing a wonderful job, husband."

Mai comes in with a shockingly professional demeanor. "Hello, I'm here to take pictures for AJA."

Before I can reply, an ALICE doctor appears on the monitor beside my bed as an ORION nurse wheels in. I hate it, they're taking up our space, making it feel claustrophobic.

The ALICE speaks from the screen. "Mrs. Rhys, we are going to do a quick video and photo documentation of your injuries. Please tell us what happened. Show us any injuries you sustained."

I tell the story while Mai takes photos from many different angles of the dark, handprint-shaped bruises forming up and down my arms, shoulders, and lower legs. While I speak, Ivan leans against the wall, glowering at my devastating map of bruises. His arms speak volumes about how he's feeling. The threat may have passed, but his every muscle is taught, ready to spring into action.

"Story, stay here at The Helm. It's much safer, and your hubs will be happier. He was *such* a grumpy storm cloud the last two days. I don't think he smiled once." Mai laughs as she gives me a careful hug. "Get some rest, I'll be back."

Once they leave, Ivan slides back into the bed beside me. "How are you doing? Really?"

"Happy to be here with you."

"I'm happy you're here too." His left hand trails the bruises that keep darkening. It's like he is trying to memorize each mark.

"This is not how I thought tonight would go," I say with a half-laugh, hoping he'll laugh. He doesn't. He shakes his head sadly, leaning over me in a hug. "Can we stay like this forever? You make the perfect barricade to keep the world away."

"Knock, knock," Dad says from my doorway. "Can I come in?"

Ivan growls. "Ugh. Your dad has garbage timing." The little bed squeaks as Ivan leans back to sit beside me, holding my hand. "Yes, come in, Alan."

Dad rushes in and hugs me. "Honey! I was so worried. Are you okay? Lark is a few rooms down getting checked out. She seems fine. The excitement of coming here has her all spun up."

"Thanks for letting us know," I say.

Leave, Dad. Get out of here.

"I'm proud of your fast thinking and feisty spirit. No doubt that's the reason you both made it until help arrived," Dad says with a sigh.

Ivan shakes his head at my dad. That can't be good.

"We should have more information soon," Ivan says.

"Ivan, you can go help with the investigation. I'll stay here with Story," Dad says.

"No!" Ivan immediately snaps, kissing my hand.

"Thank you," I whisper.

"Understandable," Dad says, sitting in the chair beside me. "What a horrible night. At Lancaster, Richelle got her assessments done. They decided she needed to have emergency surgery to get the talon injuries repaired. After Richelle was taken back into surgery, Otto said he needed to run home to do something at the farm."

"How did Otto fool us for years? When did he turn into someone who would attack his own family?" I ask, adjusting the cooling mat Mai put on my ribs.

Dad pinches the bridge of his nose and shrugs. "I've never seen this side of him."

"I need to know why. Can I come with you to the control room, and you can work on it?" I ask Ivan.

"I'll do whatever you want."

"Help me get some real clothes, please. Then we can go to the control room."

~~~

By the time we reach the control room, every seat is taken. Several extra chairs have been crammed in at odd angles at the table down front. There are many Irontrace, members of The Bastion, Councilman Jordan, Ivan, and David. The wall of monitors has pictures up from inside and outside my house, including Otto's truck. There is also a letter up on one of the huge monitors.

"Come see what we found," Ivan says, leading me to a chair to sit by him at the table down front. He reaches out to hold my hand under the table before speaking to the room.

He reviews the recent reports of Helston's hawks at Otto's farm. As a result, David had placed surveillance on Otto's property. Two people frequently coming on and off the property were identified by AJA models as high interest targets. One of these people, Anthony Moulson, had
~~~

been flagged for buying too much high-end computer equipment and odd financial transactions.

"Moulson helped build the original Kernel. Then became disgruntled and quit about ten years ago. Recently, he built a massive private tech corporation. We found evidence he or someone working with him is the sender of the recent ransom letters sent to council members."

"Good find, Commander Rhys," a council member says.

"Thank you. We also found that the corrupt code for the drone attacks, trucks running into crowds, and acid rain came from IP addresses linked to Moulson's servers. We assume the ChAse-417 virus outbreak code came from Moulson too, but we're working on proving it. It's no secret that for years Otto has been struggling financially. Hundreds of thousands of dollars have been deposited in his accounts in the last few months by Moulson's corporation. Otto and his oldest son were sent to abduct Story and Lark, to take them to this warehouse owned by Moulson." He points to a desolate building on a terrain map. "We found a shocking amount of information Otto has been sending to Moulson about the Ross family for most of this year. We're still digging to see when their relationship began."

David sits beside Ivan. Spine straight, fingers steepled, brows drawn together, he radiates the presence of a Senior Commander today. "Stop saying, 'we' Ivan. You did all this. You kept investigating and refused to give up when the rest of us believed the planted evidence that said the Ottawa Irontrace were guilty of the attacks. *You're* the one who found Moulson."

The council members offer words of appreciation and admiration to Ivan. If only they could see he's firmly holding my hand under the table, tracing fast circles with his thumb.

Ivan continues his report, "Otto's in custody, being interrogated. His truck had zip ties, leg shackles, and injectable sedatives." He gestures to a grim picture showing those items inside of Otto's truck on a monitor.

What fate awaited us if I had listened to Otto? My eyes meet David's, and my mouth falls slightly open.

David jumps up to address the control room, "Thank you, Commander Rhys. Finding Moulson has cleared the names of the dead Irontrace in Ottawa. They did not send out malicious code. Ivan's investigation this week found their login information had been compromised a couple of months ago. Moulson was waiting for a time to act with their access. We're trying to find out how he caused their deaths. We suspect it may be related to him accessing their Agora neural chip remotely. If he can do that, he can take out the Irontrace and leave The Kernel vulnerable."

A scream builds in my throat. How can I keep breathing with Ivan under such a threat?

"Can you set up some sort of computer program to guard the Agoras from remote access?" a council member asks.

"I've already built a program for that," Ivan says.

"Thank goodness. We cannot allow The Kernel to be vulnerable," the council member says.

His demeanor is disgusting. He is completely dismissing the threat the Irontrace are under.

I find my voice, "You cannot allow the guardians of The Kernel, the Irontrace, to be vulnerable. They keep the world, including you, safe. Your Kernel is nothing without them."

"Councilman Barnett, every person here owes a debt of gratitude to these extraordinary people here at The Helm. The safety of the Irontrace must be a top priority or The Kernel *will* fail. Have we sent units to arrest Moulson?" Councilman Jordan asks, bringing the conversation back to safer ground.

"We did. They were unable to locate him," David says. "He's an incredibly skilled engineer with deep pockets. It's easy for people like that to stay in the shadows, even with the AI judiciaries watching for him."

"Good. Keep looking," he says.

"Excuse us." Ivan scoots his chair back. He stands and pulls me up, leading me to the back of the control room. "Hey, we're okay," he says quietly to me when we get into a dim corner.

"I know." I can't turn off the buzzing sensation in my chest. I'd rather be beaten up again than worry about Ivan's Agora like this.

"You can say that, but I know you don't feel it. You have almost broken my hand, my love." He laughs and holds up our intertwined hands. There are four semicircles of bright red blood on his knuckles from my fingernails digging into him. "Just a minute and we'll go home."

"Yes! Get me out of here."

Things seem to have settled down for now. Ivan strides over to David while I tell Dad goodbye. Moriah set up an apartment for him, Mom, and Lark. I walk up to David and Ivan as they are wrapping up their conversation.

"I let David know I have a program to protect Agoras from remote access. He's going to kick it off." He gingerly wraps his arm around my waist and guides me up the ramp. "You ready?"

"Thought you'd never ask."

Ivan swings the door to our apartment open and carefully scoops me up. "I get to carry my bride in."

There are no flowers arranged for my homecoming. No *Welcome Home, Story* sign. Yet somehow, this is far more perfect than my last trip. When I kick the door shut behind us, it feels like I've locked out the whole world—and all its stress.

After a long, hot shower, I need ice packs and pain medicine. Ivan covered all my bruises with deep tissue healing patches. He put a rib repair brace around my torso to support my rib fractures and stimulate rapid bone repair. I asked him to use every Irontrace medical trick he could think of to get me back in the OR as soon as possible. I'm nearly myself again by the time we head to bed.

"I thought I lost you. You said your parents were home, but I saw it wasn't them and buzzed you. I seriously flipped out when you didn't come back to the laptop. I knew you were going straight into a trap." He rolls to face me, draping an arm carefully over my side. "Moriah put thermal imaging on your house. We watched the attack happen in real time. The whole control room went crazy when Lark yelled that people were killing Story. David was ready to launch a whole battalion to your house. I found an Air Titan Division in your area doing surveys from the drone attacks and sent them to you."

I smile softly. "My hero."

"We got to watch you beat the Air Titans with a hairdryer and a shelf. We all knew you were safe by then. I won't lie. There was some laughter." He tucks my hair behind my right ear.

"When do you have to go back to work?"

His dark eyes sparkle as he breaks into a crooked grin. "Not for a week. I told David to lose my phone number. I'm blocking all emails. It's honeymoon time."

Oh, how I love this man.

34

We have our whole lives to catch up on. Ivan told me stories that accompany each of his many scars. He also told me tales that didn't leave scars I could see, but had left him wounded, nonetheless. It left me feeling an unexpected burden of guilt to have led such a peaceful life in comparison.

On our last wonderful morning before he had to go back to work, he made a big breakfast while I decorated the kitchen table with bright flowers from outside our living room window.

Now we sit, studying his treasured atlas.

"When you get my Agora out, I want to take our family all over the world. I'll tell the kids bedtime stories about how I was trapped, but their brilliant mom saved me."

Kids? It never occurred to me he's already dreaming of having kids, even planning out what he wants to tell them, where he wants to go with them.

"How many kids are we having?" I ask, raising my eyebrows.

He actually squirms in his seat. "I'm sorry. Do you want to have kids someday? It's fine if you don't."

"This is my favorite part of getting married after we knew each other for like five minutes. We missed ninety percent of conversations normal couples have."

"You know I'd marry you again after two minutes instead of five. But this exact moment has me sweating."

He's watching me, not trying to influence me.

"I want a whole, huge, life with you. A bunch of kids, pets, a house, everything. We already have Sid and Helga. That's a start. I want to watch every one of your dreams come true and die beside you at a hundred years old."

"I want that too. Every normal, boring thing in life. Let's do it all. But make it into a great adventure." He looks away, clearing his throat. "Keep drinking coffee, beautiful, I'm going to do the dishes."

Making future plans is a heartbreaking game.

They haven't found out why Otto was sent by Moulson to take me, so Ivan told Dad I'm not leaving The Helm. I was thrilled to watch my husband use his powers of intimidation to ensure my dad and everyone else at The Helm understands I'm a full-time resident here now.

Dad and I used our tragic "gas leak" to take a leave of absence from Lancaster Medical Hub. I've got time to practice surgeries in my lab and spend every spare second with Ivan. Routine Agora removal surgeries are easy for me now. My confidence and skills are growing.

Ivan's been busier than ever. He's continued to make improvements to my lab and watching closely for Moulson. He keeps multiple computer programs running to monitor anything that would target Agoras or The Kernel.

Nothing compares with how seriously he takes his new role of being a husband. I've kicked myself many times for not marrying this glorious man the first weekend he joked about it.

It's a beautiful late-July morning in my lab. I'm busy planning a new complicated simulation. The summer sun is shining through the windows, and my favorite surgery playlist is pleasant background noise.

My INES console turns on. Ivan's sitting in our apartment on the couch.

"Hey, handsome! I thought you had to work?"

"Hi." He gives a small wave and a huge smile. "I need a minute with you."

"All my minutes are for you. What do you want for dinner tonight?" I tinker with the surgery simulation program.

"Anything. I don't care. My perfect Story, listen. You're kind, brilliant, funny, and gorgeous." A chill goes down my spine. "I don't think

I would've made it the rest of the day without telling you that."

He's the best and tells me things like that all the time. But his demeanor is off. I drop my hands and scrutinize every pixel. His face looks okay. I don't see any injuries. His jaw twitches.

"I love you, husband." Something is very wrong. I know it. I need to keep talking to him to figure this out. "I'm so glad to see you. I can't make it through a day without you, my love. You know that, right?"

His face crumbles into a sad smile. "I know."

He's dying.

Or his Agora ruptured.

Maybe he's had another stroke.

What is it?

"You know you can't leave me yet, right? We've got plans." He nods but doesn't say anything. "I don't feel well. I'm leaving now to come home."

"Faker." He laughs, but it sounds more like he choked.

"Let me switch to my phone. I really don't feel good. Give me a minute to call you."

"No. Stay there. You don't have a sim patient on the table, right?" I shake my head. "Cool." He takes a deep breath and bites his lip. "Well. I just needed to see you and tell you that you're the best thing in my life. Know that forever, my love."

Where are the jokes? Where is his sarcasm?

He's telling me goodbye. I don't know why, or what is happening. Get home to him. I jump down from the platform and grab my cellphone.

"I love you so much. I'm gonna call you, hang on."

He smiles like his heart has already broken. "I love you, Story Rhys. You're the highlight of my whole existence."

The INES console goes black.

"Ivan, come back!" I yell. "I know you can hear me!"

I squeeze my tracker ring and run for the door.

"Come on, buzz!" I take it off and use both hands to squeeze as hard as I can. "Did I break the button?!"

My phone rings. It's David. "Story, run! Go home to your apartment."

"Are you there? Is he dying?" I run through the lab doors so fast I slam into an Irontrace and almost fall. They spin me around and steady me, staring with giant eyes like I'm a lunatic.

"He detonated the neural chip in his Agora."

"No! WHY?! Why would he do that? I have to call my dad. He's doing Ivan's surgery."

"Ivan called your dad already. He told me you may be buzzing."

"Why, David?" Between sobbing and sprinting, I almost can't get my words out.

Our apartment hallway is serene.

Where is the emergency assistance? Why isn't Dad here helping?

I throw our front door open and toss my phone on the counter.

Ivan is on a stretcher at floor level, hooked up to a heart monitor. His eyes are closed and his head is slumped to the side.

"Ivan!" I run to where David crouches beside him. He's fumbling with a portable electroencephalogram, or EEG, to check electrical activity in Ivan's brain. A grotesque black sunburst of cords is arranged around Ivan's head.

"What happened?" I snatch Ivan's limp hand. He doesn't lace his fingers in mine like he always does. *Don't sit and hold his hand. Move. Help him.* "Wake up, baby! We got you."

His heart looks good on the monitors. I grab stickers for the EEG leads and place them around his head. I silently pray while I wait for the monitor to power on.

"David couldn't stop him, Story," Dad's voice comes from the speaker on Ivan's phone. He's talking to me in his doctor's voice. Not his daughter that needs comfort. *This is bad.* "You know how Ivan is with computers. He can do anything."

David sits on his heels, bright eyes staring at his best friend.

"What did he do?" I'm in emergency mode. I can do this. He's stable. Just keep him that way until Dad gets here.

David speaks softly. "Francois was on patrol today. He ended up on the outside of the boundary. I don't know why. The alarm in his helmet alerted us he was down. Of course, Ivan rode out to get him."

I whip my head. "You should have called me!"

"Ivan made it back over the boundary quickly with him. Ivan was fine. There's something wrong with Francois' Agora. It's not actively bleeding, but there's swelling and increased pressure in the area."

"Ivan was okay though?"

"Yes. This is all before he called you. Your dad logged in from Lancaster and reviewed Francois' scans. Francois is in a coma, but stable. Correct, Alan?" David asks my dad.

"For right now," Dad replies. "Francois will linger. But he won't wake up. The Agora's boundary punishment has started its deadly chain reaction. Taking out his Agora may save him."

I have to do an Agora removal. A real one. The limp weight of Ivan's hand is a reminder that my love isn't here to share this news with. An unconscious person's hand feels heavier than you think it would be. It's warm, making you feel like they're with you. But he's not with me.

"I'm so sorry, Story." David straps Ivan's arms across his chest for transport. "Ivan said if he tried to detonate the Agora for Francois and it killed him; he'd never forgive himself for murdering that little boy."

I know why he did this.

"He blew his neural chip as a test to see what would happen in a living brain?" I choke out.

"He did. I locked him out of the computers in the control room when he suggested it. But he'd already set a timer to detonate it. He got monitors from the clinic and put these heart leads on himself. This brain monitor thing is stuff he put here for me. I flew out of the control room when he called. I was too slow, too late."

"Was he awake when you got here?" I sob, staring at the small green waves on the screens laid out by Ivan.

I keep squeezing Ivan's hand and rubbing his arm. He has to wake up. I have nine more months of him.

"He was like this. I don't...I don't know how to read these screens. Nothing was flashing red. Detonation worked. His neural chip is off. He didn't die," David says. "Your dad has to tell you something you won't like."

"I don't know how long they're okay once the neural chip is off. Something has happened that caused him to lose consciousness. Get him on the table as soon as possible. There was a huge wreck. I'm stuck at the hospital. Go start. I'll take over when I get there."

David turns into Senior Commander Delac. "Story. You'll be fine. You're literally the only person in the world right now that can help Ivan. Your dad will be here soon and then you can assist him and INES."

Dad is a real, true surgeon. He is supposed to do Ivan's surgery. That's what we agreed on. Don't be a panicky wife. Ivan has saved me many times. It's my turn to save him.

"*I* have to do Ivan's surgery?"

"You have to start it." David pushes me closer to Ivan. "Tell Ivan you'll see him soon."

Ivan will be free by this evening if I can do this. My love, best friend, protector, needs me right now. A few weeks ago, I unraveled at the thought of his blood pooling around me. Panic won't win. It can't have me. Ivan has woken me up, transformed me into a better version of myself. I'm ready to cut him, to save him.

I kiss his cheek. "Some part of you can hear me. You will be fine. I'm going to bring you back. I love, love, love you. So much. Come back."

David sucks a sharp breath then locks the side rail in place. "You ready?" He lifts the bed and unlocks the wheels.

I tug Ivan's black rubber wedding ring from his finger. "Let's go."

"I'll make sure someone prepares Francois for surgery. He's stable, but it will be complicated. Bye for now," Dad says.

David pushes Ivan's bed into the hallway.

"It will be complicated." Did Dad mean that for Ivan or Francois?

Crap.

35

We make it almost all the way to the lab before we run into anyone.

"What happened to Commander Rhys?" a short girl with glasses shouts, running up to the bed.

A boy rushes up, reaching out for Ivan's shoulder.

"Agora emergency. He's heading to the clinic. Step back!" David says, stepping between them and the bed. Spreading out both arms like a barrier, he walks towards them, herding them back several steps. He speaks in a sharp voice that makes their eyes go wide. "I trust that you both will show discretion and not speak of this." He points a finger in the girl's face. "That's a direct order. You're the only ones we have seen. I'll know if you disobey and run your mouths about Rhys."

Phew. David is kind of scary. Glad he's on my side.

"Yes, Sir," they both say, standing up straight.

"Thank you," I tell David as we take off in a jog again.

"We have enough Agora's taking people down. Everyone around here is used to it. Ivan was the buzz of the control room this morning for saving Francois like that," David's deep voice cracks. He kicks my lab door open. "What can I do now to help? I'll find a way to keep everyone quiet about this. You just focus."

"We need to get him on the table. Then you can leave."

I have run through dozens of simulators. This is my first time putting a real human on the table. I wish my first surgery could be on anyone except Ivan.

David and I arrange the patient lift webbing under Ivan. INES hoists him from his emergency stretcher to the operating room table. Ivan's hand is at a funny angle by his hip. I dive in front of David and smooth

Ivan's fingers flat so he won't wake up injured.

"See you soon, baby."

The anesthesia system deploys a mask over his face to intubate him. His chest rises and falls. But it's not the Ivan breaths that I listen to every night. Those breaths have a special rhythm that belongs to him. These are a perfectly mechanical rate of twelve breaths per minute.

"You're almost ready. INES, place EEG monitoring." Arms swing down at my order. "I'm going to prep his heart monitor."

It's so real. This is actually happening. Tears sting my eyes.

No! Stay in emergency mode.

"I'm going to listen to your heart one more time." I lay my head in the middle of his chest. His heart beats steady and sure. My Ivan is okay. Keep him this way.

I take a deep breath. "INES, position patient for Agora removal."

"Sure, Doc," INES says in Ivan's voice. Arms reaching from the ceiling. Padded straps cross his legs, chest, and arms. My heart skipped several beats when it rolled him face down into his final position for surgery. The OR lights glare harsh on his tan back. I step close to clip the very bottom of his hair.

"That's disorienting. Hearing his voice." David sits on the steps of the operating platform.

"Keeps it interesting." Done with his hair.

"True Ivan. Entertaining until the e-" David stops. I shoot him a murderous stare. He looks at the floor. "I've never been an Irontrace without him. He's my brother. I *really* need you to be good at this, Story."

I nod. "INES do final prep on the site."

He's ready. I'm ready to fight for him.

Stay calm.

Breathe.

I can do this.

I've been stuffing my feelings down my whole life when stressed. It's like I've been training for this exact moment for two decades.

"Story, you really think he'll wake up?"

Before I can give it any thought, my answer tumbles out straight from my heart, "Yes."

"I'm going to lock your lab door from my laptop so no one can bother you. See you later."

"Bye."

The lab door scrapes shut.

"Here we go, my love. Don't worry, you'll be fine." It's oddly comforting to talk to him, even now.

Mock surgeries did not prepare me for the raw vulnerability of this moment. I hover my scalpel for a second, before gliding it carefully in a shallow incision around the surgical site.

"You're not Ivan. You're a sim. You're just a sim. Go. Cut the sim."

His skin gives way smoothly under my blade, blood welling up slowly. INES vascular control sponges dab it away. Cautery arms reach out, stopping the bleeding. A faint trail of smoke curls up. I catch the briefest scent of something burning. "INES! Turn on the smoke evac filters." Fans whir on softly.

It's not a sim. It's Ivan.

"You're okay, baby." I choke back a panicky breath. "We're both okay."

Layer by layer, INES numerous small retractor hooks pull back the edges of his incision, revealing the pulsating mass of blood vessels and tissue growing out of the neural chip. It taunts me. INES and I settle into a rhythm.

Dad's voice speaks from behind me. "Story. I'm here. I'll take over as primary."

I pause. Dad's here. I don't have to do this. But...his practice time with simulators has been divided between work at Lancaster. I've spent two-hundred and eleven hours working with INES on complex simulator surgeries. Dad has clocked fifty-seven hours.

I look at the open surgical incision. Ivan would never leave me if I were cut open. Bleeding and vulnerable. I won't stop. I'm his best shot of survival.

"We're okay, Dad."

"Story, you don't have to. Go. Sit with David."

"You can watch. Be here if I need you. Help me make any judgement calls." If any complications happen, I can talk to Dad about them. "I won't leave him. Ignore me when I talk to Ivan. It helps me stay calm."

"Do whatever you need," he sighs.

"I need to focus."

I don't talk to Dad anymore, but I talk about each step to Ivan. The mapping hologram identifies where the Agora's bioengineered arteries have reached out and formed connections to the superficial branch of Ivan's transverse cervical arteries. The vessels shimmer like threads of silk under the magnifier.

"INES, get vascular control of the feeding transverse cervical arteries." I watch the arms extend nimbly into Ivan's neck. Small clamps are placed on the targeted blood vessels. It cuts off the connections to the Agora's darker, almost black artificial arteries.

I clip the vessels INES clamped. Are there any leaks? Bleeds? He's okay. I hold my breath, staring at the angiogram. Everything looks great. If this was a sim? I'd be dancing in place while cruising on to the next step.

"It's going well, Ivan." I wiggle my shoulders and hands. "The blood supply to your AVM is cut off. This is great. We're making progress, my love. INES is wonderful. Thank you for building it."

One more confirmation won't hurt.

"INES, magnify the angiogram. Focus on finding hidden feeders under the AVM. Specifically tell me if you notice any involvement with his occipital, subclavian, or vertebral arteries?"

The live angiogram monitor switches views to show only layers of arterial blood flow. I don't see any blood being supplied by feeders lurking under Ivan's muscles or fascia.

"Dr. Rhys, there are no deep, perforating feeders. You are safe to proceed. Pressure within the nidus has been significantly decreased."

"Show me what you see. Zoom in on everything. I want to see it all for myself."

I trust INES, but this is *Ivan*.

New images display in a square on the monitor, INES was right, the AVM is fully isolated from new blood.

"Yes!" Dad exclaims in a loud whisper. "Sorry."

I smile. "See, Ivan, we're doing great." We still have so far to go. I watch his heart monitor. I know what those beats sound like. "You're alive. I'll keep you that way."

"You're doing a wonderful job, honey," Dad whispers.

"Thanks, Dad. INES, move on to nidus resection protocols."

INES and I take turns preparing to dissect the nidus away from surrounding tissues. The tangled mess is thankfully close to the surface of his skin. I smile. Once this heals, I can finally rub the back of his neck.

I stare at the angiogram. We need to shut down the veins that drain the AVM. Which one should I get control of first? I'm getting decision fatigue. I glance between Ivan's incision and the angiogram several times.

"Want to know what I see?" Dad asks.

"Yes."

He points to INES vessel map. "Clip the primary draining veins, number one there on the left, number two on the right. Then address the connections the Agora has built to the occipital veins. You're doing wonderful. Trust yourself. Trust INES. Keep going."

"I'm glad you're in here Dad. INES, place clips on the superficial transverse cervical veins number one and two on the angiogram. Then cauterize Agora connections three and five."

"Yes, Doc," INES says, getting to work.

"INES, how does the angiogram look now? Any swelling or bleeding popping up?" I ask.

"No, beautiful, it looks as good as you do," INES says in Ivan's voice.

I shake my head. It's the perfect break from tension I need to make the final cut and cautery to the draining vein.

No fresh bleeding. No warnings on the angiogram. I've stared at so many of these lately that it feels surreal to be looking at Ivan's angiogram.

"AVM out. No abnormal bleeding. That's really good, Ivan."

"I've wanted Ivan to be free for his whole life," Dad says.

"He's almost free." I can't wait. I'm dragging this fine hunk of a man with me everywhere I go.

I need to get the neural chip out next. The silver tentacles in front of me exactly match up with the imaging map. An almost overwhelming sense of panic hits.

They're so sharp! What if I mess this up? Talk to Ivan. Calm down.

"The tentacles from your neural chip are a bit...weird. Nothing I can't manage. But they are thicker, more embedded than the simulators I'm used to. It's because you've had it for so long. You really are an old man for Irontrace. INES, help remove the neural chip tendrils."

"Yes, Dr. Rhys."

Two arms whir downwards. One holds a small jar full of a polymer hydrogel. The other is a paintbrush attached to a stabilizer platform. Laying my right arm on the stabilizer, I dip the brush tip into the polymer then guide the platform towards the incision. With as much care as I'd use to defuse a bomb, I paint the protective, lubricating polymer onto the neural chip tendrils. Just as Ivan intended, the liquid adheres to the tendrils, creating a low-friction membrane around them.

Slippery and smooth, they slide free.

I suck a deep breath and stare at the angiogram.

"The Agora is out, my love. No new bleeding. Stay with me, please. We're almost done." I exhale and wiggle my fingers.

I won't be okay until Ivan has a full post-op exam. And what if I've missed something and he hemorrhages in recovery? Did I miss anything?

The steps of my Agora removal plan flash through my mind.

"INES, initiate closure protocols."

"You got it, Doc," INES says.

We work in layers.

"You're better than I would have been at this point. Ivan will be so proud," Dad says. His voice is bright with excitement. "Story, you found a way to save Lark. You and Ivan made this happen. I'm...I'm so, so grateful to you and him."

"We can save them all." Tears prick my eyes. "Ivan, we'll be waking you up soon. INES is helping me close."

His final bandage goes on. My smile pushes my mask so high I can barely see. I get to say the words that will guarantee my future with Ivan.

"Successful Agora removal. End dictation."

"Great job, Dr. Rhys!" INES says.

"Thanks. INES, place the patient in the recovery position."

The table repositions him. I take off my gown, mask, and gloves and run my hands through his thick black hair. I put the swoop over to the left the way he likes to wear it. My fingers trace the scar from his forehead to the breathing tube in his mouth.

I rest my head on his chest. The wonderful sound of Ivan's heart thumps in a perfect rhythm. There are no tears for my favorite patient. I'm all smiles.

"We did it, husband. Now wake up."

36

The lab door opens and David bounces in.

"Dr. Rhys! That was incredible! Not to be mean, but I thought he was dead for sure." David sets a water, an electrolyte drink, and a lemonade on my desk. "Sorry, I don't know what you like."

"Thanks. What do we do with him now?"

"I've been thinking about it. The best path forward is honesty. The more details we try to hide, The Bastion will know. They'll arrest all of us. That won't end well. Everyone in the control room knows Ivan went outside the boundary to get Francois. A steady stream of Irontrace have been in the clinic paying last respects to Francois all day."

"They've been through this many times when Agoras take out their friends," Dad chimes in.

David looks around. "A lot of Irontrace helped build this lab. They know Ivan designed INES to be the top surgical robot in the world. INES saved him. INES will save Francois. Your dad and I are going to take Ivan to the ICU for recovery. We'll smooth things out with the ALICE units and staff there. You stay in here for a few minutes."

"I couldn't have done this surgery without INES. It really was invaluable," I say.

Dad rubs his eyes. "Story, I watched you work...I have to say. My skills need more practice. It was best for Ivan that you did it. Do you think you can do Francois' surgery too?"

No! I want to see Ivan. I can't be away from him for one more minute or my heart will burst. The first time he cracks his eyes open I want him to see me. The first words he hears should be that I love him.

"It needs done as soon as you catch your breath. He can't wait either, honey."

"Sure," I say. "Give me thirty minutes."

"Thank you. We'll be back with Francois," Dad says.

I kiss Ivan on the cheek. "Wake up, baby. I'll be there soon."

Prepping for Francois doesn't take long. I throw away my trash and kick off the autoclave process and UV sterilization treatments. The lab fills with the cold, sterile smells of antiseptic and stainless steel. This is my last chance to eat and drink for a while, so I put my feet up and ate a sandwich and fruit from the lab kitchenette.

David wheels Francois in. His tiny frame is dwarfed by his hospital bed. *Lark will be even smaller than him for her Agora removal.*

The thought turns dinner sour in my stomach. I have to get back in emergency surgery mode to get this done with my laser focus.

"Can I stay while you prep him for surgery? Then I'll use Ivan's program to detonate the chip when it's time." David parks Francois near the INES transfer lift.

"Only if you don't get squeamish. I know you've talked about wanting to get your Agora out."

"I'll be fine. I'd like to have an idea of what I'm signing up for." He sits at my desk. "Can I use your laptop to sign into my workstation in the control room?"

"I have no idea how you can do that but go for it."

He's already intubated, so after about forty minutes of imaging, positioning, and preparing the surgical site, it's time for the first incision. David has been silently watching INES and I work.

"David, shut off the neural chip please." I hold my breath. Will the detonation that shut off Ivan's Agora be too much for Francois' small body?

David counts down. "Three, two, one. Done." We pause to watch the monitors. They remain at his baseline.

"Thank you. Patient stable after neural chip detonation. Proceeding with first incision."

There is minimal bleeding. The catastrophic burn alarm doesn't go off. Ivan's detonation program was a success.

Small bleeds spurt from vessels that looked stable seconds ago. *No!*

"Was that supposed to happen?" David blurts.

I ignore David. "INES, bleeding control needed."

Vascular control arms quickly stop the bleeding. The angiogram confirms the bleeding has stabilized.

"Keep going, INES." I say, making my way down to the Agora.

"Yeah...this is, uh, gross. I'm outta here," David says. "Have fun in here."

"Bye."

When I reach the target site for the AVM removal, something I've never seen is waiting. Francois' neural chip is not like any sim.

One long, silver tendril extends up into his skull. Does he have a different Agora model since he is younger than the rest of them? Is this an issue from going outside of the boundary? Imaging didn't catch this, and it's new to me. I pause.

"What in the world is this?" I mutter. "INES, I need a drill."

"Yes, Dr. Rhys." A new arm extends out to me with a specialized drill that has a small bit. INES stabilizes my grip on the drill while I pierce through the bone.

"I do not want to do this. I'm sorry, Francois."

Thank goodness I played with the bone cutting bot in Lancaster.

INES has high-resolution nano-cameras I've never had to use. They'll be able to snake in to see where exactly the tendril is going.

"Turn on the micro-imaging tunnel scopes. We need to do some investigation."

"Anything for you, gorgeous," INES says in Ivan's voice.

Oh, Ivan. I miss you.

The drill rotates away, replaced by an arm with a flexible scope, millimeters thick. The tendril extends at least an inch up into his brain tissue. It looks segmented, not smooth like the rest. I'm going to leave this for the end so I don't rush while working on it.

Dad's voice speaks to me from a monitor by my desk. "Story, that's a tendril of the boundary-induced Agora injury beginning to spread. Sometimes they make their way into the brain instead of around their vertebral arteries. It'll keep growing, sweeping through, destroying his brain tissue over the next few days."

I shudder, tasting bile at the thought. "Gruesome."

Two bleeds start at the same time from different feeding arteries. INES and I stop them. I glance at the clock. I've barely made any progress.

"This surgery is taking too long." I roll my shoulders. "INES, I'm weary. Got any Ivan-isms to help with that?"

"Sorry, Dr. Rhys, I don't know what that is. But if you're tired, wrap it up and go home to your husband. I know he's missing you," INES says.

I continue disconnecting arteries feeding blood to this murderous tangle of vessels. After we work our steps around the nidus, it's time to move onto the veins.

This is better. I'm back in my flow. It's almost time to see Ivan. I smile when I place the final suture on the draining vein. My eyes lock on the angiogram.

The tangle hangs limp, defeated. I stare for a few more seconds. I'm confident the Agora no longer has blood flow. INES and I work to remove it the rest of the way.

"INES. Switch to neural chip protocols."

"Yes, Dr. Rhys." INES swaps arms in a familiar, delicate dance.

Now for the mystery tendril in his skull. I rack my brain for a plan to extract it without causing further damage to brain tissue. *I'm in no way a brain surgeon.* This is so far out of my league. But he has no other option. I can't just leave and call ASTRA. Or Dr. B.

Think, don't touch his brain. Don't open a skull flap. I just need to yank it out.

I puff a sigh. *Yank.* That's the wrong word. I stare at the angiogram. This thing is like a thin noodle of death into his brain. *Gross! I need a nap. My brain is mush.* Noodle. Pasta. Slurp. Wait…*Slurp.* Slide it out?

The polymer!!!!

The hydrogel polymer doesn't adhere to anything except the tendrils. If I can irrigate it up into the skull, it will coat this murder tendril for me. Then it'll just slide out. I think. It's worth a try. It's grown three millimeters in width and length since surgery started. He's literally dying.

Do something. Polymer it is.

"INES, bring down a micro-pulsatile lavage system. Fill its reservoir with 50 ccs of chip removal hydrogen polymer."

"This is a new approach, you must be innovating, Dr. Rhys."

"Sure am, INES."

I reach for the suction fed cannister and put some of the hydrogel polymer in it. I activate the irrigation tip and shoot several drops on the floor by me. Morbid curiosity hits and I swipe my shoe through them.

"Yep. This stuff is slippery. Here we go, Francois." I guide the micro irrigator up into the skull. The polymer adheres to the chip tendril. It slides out, dangling from the rest of the neural chip like a limp piece of angel hair pasta. "It worked! I defeated you, death noodle."

"That was amazing," Dad says.

"Thanks. INES, brain activity report?"

After a pause, INES says, "Electroencephalogram, intracranial pressure, electrical pathways, are at his pre-surgery baseline. You did not cause any additional damage. Patient is stable, Dr. Rhys. Proceed."

I "did not cause any additional damage." That's almost as good as being called a "not nincompoop." I should start writing these gems of praise down.

INES and I removed the rest of the neural chip tendrils from near the vertebral arteries. I drop the neural chip onto a surgical tray. Another full Agora is out.

My eyes linger on the angiogram.

I did it! I grin.

The injected dye trickles out of a blood vessel, making a hazy cloud.

The angiogram flashes red warnings. The bleeding comes from a small branch of the superficial transverse cervical artery.

"INES, initiate blood loss protocols. Stop the bleed."

The cell salvage and vascular control arms swing down into reach. One arm latches onto the bleeding vessel and clamps it. INES rapidly clears the blood from the field. I place a suture around the problem vessel. I'm a bit traumatized that this bled again after my initial closure of it, so I place another suture. I study the angiogram. The warning lights fade away. No active bleeding. INES washes the area with saline. I keep peering back to the imaging.

"INES, initiate closure protocols."

"Yes, Dr. Rhys."

He made it through. Not just through normal, uncomplicated surgery. That was brutal for him and I.

Only time and recovery will tell if he has lasting damage or deficits. After another hour, we're done. Dad and David walk in the lab as I push Francois' bed down the platform ramp.

"You'll be in a medical journal soon if these surgeries go public," Dad says. "You didn't kill anyone. You're 0% fatal in surgeries on humans!"

"Thanks. But I just want to see Ivan. Can you please take Francois to the ICU?"

"I'll stay in here and kick off cleaning. Can you take him to the ICU, Delac?" Dad asks.

"Sure. Fantastic job, Dr. Rhys. Cut me open anytime. I mean it," David says, patting me on the back.

When will The Bastion give me freedom to save Lark, David, and the others?

37

Ivan's recovery room is dimly lit. It's a soft charcoal color that makes his white gown and sheets glow. He lays with the head of his bed elevated. Pillowy cloth ice packs are behind his head and neck. My breath catches at the gentle rise and fall of his chest.

He's alive.

I press the button to collect a fresh set of vital signs. Everything is normal. Brain activity looks great. I need more proof that he's okay. I swipe to the ORION nursing tab. It holds his assessments. He squeezed the volunteer's hands on command. Responded correctly to questions. Has been drinking from a cup. It's hour nine. He should be able to talk to me a little the next time he wakes up.

My weary bones would give anything to lay in his arms. Instead, I scoot a chair close to his bed and rest my forehead beside his shoulder.

"Sorry, baby," he whispers in a scratchy voice.

My head snaps up. His eyes are closed. But he spoke to me.

"Don't be sorry. It worked."

He pats the bed with his hand and moves his arm to make room for me to lay by him.

"How are you feeling?"

"My neck and head are killing me," he says in his scratchy whisper. I jump to adjust his ice pack and pillows. Ivan has a crazy high pain tolerance. If he admitted that, he must be drowning in pain.

"ALICE!" I snap.

"Dr. Rhys. What do you need?" it asks.

"Commander Rhys is having pain. You need to do a better job managing it. Contact Dr. Alan Ross for updated pain management strategies stat."

"A nurse will be in shortly. I'll call Dr. Ross," the ALICE says. The monitor screen goes black.

"How bad does it hurt?"

"Not as bad as calling you yesterday." He squints one eye open. This is a test. Fearsome Commander Rhys lies here, intimidated by the thought of his wife's anger. He sees my smile and decides to take a chance. "Can we go to the beach tomorrow?"

"Go anywhere you want, my love."

He presses a folded paper in my hand. "Read it."

"What is this, I-" It's a printed report of his estimated death date from an hour ago. "Insufficient data? Your estimated death date has insufficient data!"

I fling myself at him, showering him with kisses, making him softly laugh and say "Ow."

"You're so healthy ALICE can't calculate your death date!"

He smiles, catching a handful of curls to halt my barrage of kisses.

"I can save people now! Ivan, you're making my dreams come true."

"This is just the start. Thanks for saving me."

A wave of exhaustion mixed with gratitude hits. I sob. "You only had nine months left. *Nine!*"

He pulls me across his chest. "You married me, knowing I was going to be gone before our first anniversary. Are you some kind of masochist?"

My tears mix with laughs, making me cough unattractively. "Oh please. You...you married me without checking your expiration date!"

Grabbing a handful of his sheets, he wipes my face. "Full faith we'd figure this out. Never checked."

An ORION nurse wheels in, interrupting our moment. It starts doing his hourly assessment.

He ignores its questions and talks to me. "Could you please get me clothes next time you go home? I hate these gowns."

"I want fresh clothes too. I'll go now, be back in twenty minutes." I dart around the ORION, blowing him kisses, as it fires questions his way.

When I get back, some of the volunteers have gotten him up. He stands by his bed, staring at his phone. I think he's attempting to show them he can handle physical activity. He's doing gentle calf raises while he ignores their directions.

"Commander Rhys, we need to do a full assessment," the ORION says.

"I told you five times, I can't stop right now. I'm doing something important," he says. Then he mutters something under his breath at his phone.

"We will be back in thirty minutes, please be ready for your assessment at that time." The ORION rolls out with the closest thing to a bad attitude I've ever seen from a robot. If anyone can frazzle a robot, it's Ivan.

Friends of Mai's, Katie and Talia, are putting fresh blankets on his bed.

Mai carries in new ice packs and lays them in the chair. "He's alive!" She beams at us. "Can't believe he saved Francois then had some new crazy surgery that saved him."

"Yeah, we're thrilled," I say, giving Mai a hug. "How are you?"

"I'm great. That elopement by the falls you two did was the sweetest thing ever. We need to throw your wedding reception. I'll message you later about getting it planned. It'll be the biggest party The Helm has ever seen." She elbows me and does a little dance.

"Yeah, let's plan it. Ivan owes me some dances. Ivan, sweatshirt." I hold up his black sweatshirt behind him. He slides his arms into it.

"Thanks," he says.

"Commander Rhys, you can get in bed," Katie says.

Ivan ignores her.

"We got your bed ready for you, Commander Rhys." Talia, the other volunteer, looks from me back to Ivan. She gives Mai and I a quick, uncertain glance.

"Thank you. We appreciate it. Don't we, Commander Rhys?" I wonder how many times through the years Ivan has subjected them to refusals of care.

"What? Yes. We do, thanks." He doesn't take his eyes off his phone.

I put my hands on his hips and firmly guide him to bed. Once he's settled, I lay fresh ice packs on his neck and shoulders.

"Ah! Cold, but nice." He catches my hand to kiss it. "Thanks, baby."

"You two are just..." Mai presses her fingers to her lips in a chef's kiss. "Perfect."

I grin. "I think so. We'll call you if we need you. Thanks girls."

They smile and duck out behind the curtain.

I can't hold back a laugh. "You're *such* a bad patient. I bet they are all sad when they're assigned to you." He's intimidating enough to approach. When he is refusing to listen to basic directions or engage in friendly conversation? Even worse.

"What? Why?" He raises his eyebrows in shock to be getting chastised but doesn't look at me.

"You don't listen to them, and you're addicted to work. I assume you're working from that tiny screen for a change."

"I could have worse hobbies."

The ALICE screen turns on. "Dr. Rhys. You're needed at the main station for an emergency."

"Gotta go. Love you," I give him a quick kiss and run out.

Moriah is bouncing back and forth between her feet. "Evans is gone!" she yells.

"What?" Evans? Gone?

"Come on." She takes off running through the hallway. I follow.

We make our way to the control room where a large crowd is gathered. Dad and David are in the middle of the group. Josh Evans lays in the middle on his back, head dangling to the side. His shirt has been cut off. Defibrillator pads are stuck to his chest.

"What happened?" I choke out, crouching by Dad.

"Moulson!" David mutters in a voice thick with rage and disbelief.

No one speaks. The sound of wheels rolling towards us is accompanied by running feet. Two Irontrace tear down the control room ramp, pulling a stretcher. Dad, David, and some of the group pick up Evan's slack body and put him on it. They rush back up the ramp and into a waiting elevator.

"Moriah, can you tell me what happened?" I ask as we wait for the next one.

She sucks a deep breath through her nose. "We were in the control room. Councilman Jordan ran in, screaming, waving his phone to show David a ransom email. Turns out, the whole Agora thing was his idea. The letter said they'll tell the Irontrace he put these in our heads and we'd be mad at him. So, he called their bluff and told us himself."

"Is this news to you?" Ivan has never mentioned a particular dislike for Jordan. He seems to dislike them all as a rule.

"Yes! The control room was in an uproar. But the letter also threatened to take out one Irontrace per hour until they get their money. Evans collapsed. We tried everything we could, but he was gone. Your dad ran in. He said something like Evans pupils were blown? I think he said it's a brain injury thing and Evans was *gone* gone?"

"Moriah, I'm sorry."

"Josh was a nice guy. He was always trying to make our work shifts fun. He's been one of Ivan's good friends for like forever. Well, he was a friend of Ivan's. They did dumb stuff like setting our autocorrects to stupid replies and putting office supplies in gelatin." She scrubs a hand through her hair and then makes fists. "Gosh, they were so annoying with that nonsense."

"What about Ivan's program to keep Moulson from getting to the Irontrace?"

"Moulson must've figured out how to get around it. I can't believe Evans is gone. Where is Ivan? We need him."

She and I dash in the clinic as Dad hands Evans off to clinic staff. His eyes meet mine. He gives *that* imperceptible nod. There's no hope.

"I need to go work with Ivan on patching the program," Moriah blurts angrily.

"Moriah. It's okay to take a minute and be upset."

"I'm not like you. I don't do that." *Ouch.* "I just need to fix this. I'm going to the control room. Have Ivan meet me there. This is an all-hands situation."

"Let me talk to David. Ivan hasn't been feeling well."

Ivan will know something is wrong as soon as he sees me. Instead of heading to his room, I take a five-minute detour to check on Francois.

He's propped in his bed in the same position Ivan rests in. The monitors show he is stable.

"ALICE." I prompt the monitor by his bed to turn on. "His next scan is supposed to be in seven hours. I'd like to bump that up to three hours from now instead. His surgery had complications."

"Yes, Dr. Rhys."

"Thanks." The monitor fades to black.

Wandering towards Ivan's room, I run through how to break the news to him. I quietly open the glass door and try to make it through the curtains without any sound, but the hooks at the top make a soft metallic screech, betraying me.

His eyes drift in my direction without moving his head. I break into a huge, forced grin.

His jaw muscles clench. "What's wrong?"

Shoot! "Nothing. I'm tired." I give him a sweet hello kiss. "I went to see Francois. He's good. How are you? How's your pain?"

"It's better. You don't look tired. You're nearly glowing? Like your skin is glowy and vibrant. I don't know. But...something's wrong. Tell me."

If he thinks something is wrong, he'll stop taking pain meds and climb out of this bed to see for himself. Even worse, if he thinks I'm mad at him, he'll try to get up and do something very Ivan-ish to prove he loves me.

I sit on his bed and put my hand on his cheek. "A lot has happened, my love. You should know what's going on out there. But I need you to stay calm. And rest. If you don't promise to be calm, I'll have ALICE sedate you. Your healing must come first."

He steadily evaluates me. Then he closes his eyes and he gives me a thumbs up. "I'm calm. Promise to stay that way."

Maybe his pain meds have dulled him, and he won't remember this conversation. I cling to a small chance if I keep holding his hand and speak in a near whisper my voice will put him to sleep.

"Councilman Jordan got a ransom letter. His secret they were trying to bribe him with is that he's been involved in Project Agora since it began. They didn't realize he's a psycho and is proud of that. He told the Squadron about his role in the whole thing. Moriah said they're all mad." I pause. "Part of the ransom letter is that Moulson will be continuing to attack Agoras until the ransom is paid."

A slight smile touches the corners of his lips. He taps me on the hand to stop. "Oh, we have a program running to keep Moulson out."

He lays, eyes closed, channeling pure peace for himself. I hate that the next updates will take that peace away. He's happy. I'll tell him about Evans later. I lay my head softly on his chest. Maybe if he thinks I'm too tired, he'll leave it alone and rest.

"Nuh-uh, Story Rhys, head up, keep talking. Did you forget who you married?" He twists some of my curls in his hand.

I sit up. My muscles tense, calculating how I can restrain his six-foot, six-inch frame if he tries to leap up. "Moulson found a way around it." I hold both of his hands. "He killed Evans."

His eyes snap open, sharp and wild.

"Evans?"

"Yes. Moriah said he was your friend. I'm so sorry."

He closes his eyes. "Help me stay calm, please. Bring me a laptop."

"Ivan, you can't use a computer. You're barely conscious. Let your body heal."

"Every hour you make me lay here, one more person dies. Bring. Me. A. Computer. I can't live with that on my conscience. You can't either, or you wouldn't have told me. You know I'm the one to fix this."

I give a deflating sigh. He needs more time before he goes back to work. But he may never recover if I don't let him at least try to fix this. "I'll be right back. Promise me you'll rest until I come back."

"Run."

38

David is at the front of the control room, sitting with a group of Irontrace around Jordan. He jogs to me and whispers, "Everything okay?"

"Yes. Ivan sent me to get a computer so he can fix the Agora security program."

"You're kidding. Can he?" David sags with relief.

"If he found out that we didn't let him help, I don't think he'd forgive us or himself." I pile my hair into a messy bun. It's been such a long couple of days. Every time I turn around, more work and stress loom.

Councilman Jordan waves for me to come down front. "Dr. Ross. I'd like to talk to you."

I don't have time for that. I hug Ivan's laptop to my chest. "Sorry. Not a good time. I'll find you later."

"No. Now," he says.

David looks at me, chewing on his lip. He takes Ivan's laptop from me. "Cantone. Please go to the clinic. Page Dr. Alan Ross. Tell him to give this to Ivan. Fast."

My shield against Jordan is gone. I meet his challenging stare with angry eyes as I take a seat across from him.

He takes a sip of coffee before speaking. "When I was a new member of The Bastion, The Irontrace Squadron had just been appointed as guardian of The Kernel. You've seen firsthand how highly trained they are. Tens of millions are invested in each to cultivate their skills."

"They're extraordinary."

"That's because our AI models trained them to constantly excel, be better than others. However, some of the foolish ones started leaving The Helms they were supposed to be guarding."

David steps behind me. His movement draws my attention to a large group of Irontrace who have silently gathered. I'm not sure if they're spectators or trying to protect me.

"You can't take credit for the people they've become. They are extraordinary *despite you,* not because of you." I let my voice drip with venom.

"My point is, they hold too many secrets to stay alive as deserters. Several were shot for leaving. The Bastion demanded a way to control them. A young doctor was doing research on AVMs. He'd discovered a way to manipulate them with implanted devices. I reached out to him. Together we came up with the beautiful beast of the Agora. The Bastion loved our plan. I was appointed chair of Project Agora."

He's a psychopath.

I nod. "That tracks with what I've heard about you. Too unskilled to come up with your own ideas. You latch on to other people's research. A leech on their intellect. You're disgusting to a person like me. I've worked hard for every good thing in my life."

Audible murmuring and low laughs break out around us from the Irontrace.

David takes slow steps until he's behind Jordan. He widens his eyes and mouths, "Wow!"

Jordan laughs. "Do you think I care what some girl from Lancaster thinks?"

"Clearly you do, or else you would not have demanded I sit here and listen to your mea culpa. How many Irontrace have you killed through the years with your murderous Agoras?"

"702."

I shoot from my chair. It's been too long since I slept, I'm not even fully sure what day it is.

"Dr. Ross. We aren't finished. Sit down." He grabs my wrist.

I fling my wrist hard enough that his hand bangs onto the table. "Senior Commander Delac, who's authority am I under?"

"The chief of surgery. When they aren't present, you're the next highest ranking clinic staff member."

"I thought so. And the clinic needs my attention."

Without replying to Jordan's orders to sit, I jog up the ramp.

In the elevator, fatigue hits hard. I fall back against the mirrored wall panel. The dark circles around my eyes are almost the same color as my black clinic scrubs. Ivan had said I looked like I was glowing. Ha, no! I check my phone to figure out what day it is and see a message from Ivan.

SOS. Your dad came in with my laptop. My eyes were closed. Thought the curtain sliding open sound was you. I made some comments to him that were definitely meant for my wife. -I

I send him a quick reply.

Ha! Hopefully, he's not traumatized. Scoot over now. I'm climbing in your bed the minute I get there. Don't wake me up for two days. Love you like mad, see you in a minute. - <3

Moriah is waiting in the hallway when the doors open. "There you are. Come help. Moulson got someone else."

"Do I need supplies from the clinic?"

"No, let's go. We need to ride to help them."

"Who is it?"

I pull on her hand to get her to jog with me, but she yanks it back and continues at a fast walk instead.

"Nathan Cantone. He's been on patrol today alone."

"Oh no! I saw him like five minutes ago."

She sucks in a deep breath. "Well, I heard it was him, maybe it wasn't. Come on. We just need to get out there to help your dad."

My mind swirls. Dad was just with Ivan. I'm too tired. Cantone. Dad. I can't keep straight who is where.

"You ride Obsidian." She hands me his reins.

"Do you know if the patient is conscious?"

"I don't have any details. Your dad told me to find you and hurry."

She spurs her black and white horse on. Obsidian takes off into a fast canter, following her out of the cave front by the falls. I talk to him for most of the ride.

"Good boy, Sid. You wanna go to the beach next week with us? You'll feel so free, no branches whacking at you for once." I pet his wide neck as he runs.

In the last patch of trees before the boundary, Sid plants his hooves and rears up. I almost lose my seat.

"Sid, why?"

Moriah stops. Then she yells. "Now!"

A heavy black net drops onto Obsidian and me. It must weigh hundreds of pounds. I can't even sit up. I'm smashed flat against Sid's neck over the front of the saddle. I kick free of the stirrups in case he falls, clinging to him with my hands and legs.

"Moriah! What is this?" Sid circles, stumbling in the tangles. He won't be able to keep his feet. "Whoa, Sid! Stand! Sid, stand still!"

He lets out a panicked whinny and turns his neck towards my right foot. Then he crashes down on his left side.

"Sid, it's okay, calm down, boy." I squeeze my tracker ring. He fights the net in blind terror, frothing at the mouth.

"Moriah!" I'm scrambling beside him to move the heavy net. He's gonna kick me to death.

Finally, the net lifts. *Oh, no!* Forest wardens are everywhere. My phone rings in my scrub shirt pocket. A warden snatches it.

"No, that's-" I shout. He slams it to the ground and stomps until my phone is silent.

"Why?! I'm a Helm surgeon!" I yell as they yank me between two of them. "Obsidian! You have to get him out!"

Moriah is outside the boundary, unconcerned.

"Come on." Two men drag me away from Sid.

Sid's terrified and angry, the net still clinging around him like a living thing. "Moriah! Help Obsidian! Moriah, tell them who I am!"

She steps back into the boundary toward us unsteadily. She's pale. Her words come out thick, with a hint of a slur. "Wardens! Take off her ring. It's a tracker."

"Moriah! Get back in the boundary!" I yell as they drag me past her. I scream and struggle when a third warden rips off my engagement ring.

"Hello again, trespasser." It's Warden Donegal. He throws my ring beside Obsidian and laughs. "They'll think they found her and it'll be his stupid horse." He wrenches Ivan's wedding ring off my thumb and throws it far into the woods.

No! How will I get back?

Moriah won't help me. Obsidian is stuck. His shrill, ragged whinnies tear at my heart. His hooves and body thud against the ground while he fights.

"Sid! Ivan will help you! Lay down! Stop, buddy, he'll be here soon."

Ivan isn't coming.

I twist to get one last view of him around Donegal. Sid's hopelessly tangled. The fight is all torn out of him. He's on his side, still.

"Sid!"

The wardens ignore my screams. Thrashing is getting me nowhere. Several trucks are lined up where we normally park. Three wardens dump me in the back of a black ambulance and climb in.

Moriah is strapped to a stretcher. "Story, fix me like you fixed Ivan. Don't let Moulson get me."

"How? Where are we going?" The wardens shove me in a seat then place a hobble restraint on my ankles.

Moriah's sweaty skin is a sickening shade of gray. Her lips barely move when she speaks, "Jordan told me to get you out and you could fix my Agora too."

He knows! "Jordan lied to you. I can save you if we go back. Right now, Moriah."

She shakes her head. "He said you'd trick me."

I hop across the cramped aisle to her. I grab a large duffle bag, yank out the blood pressure cuff, and wrap it on her arm. The vital signs monitor flashes on beside her. I hit *START.*

"Moulson…will get me. Like Evans," she slurs.

Oh, Moriah. Her heart rate is 178. The blood pressure reads a shockingly low 58/30. I grab her cold, clammy hands. "Tell them to turn around. He lied. Moriah, you're dying."

Her eyes blink open at me, then widen, taking in the bright white ambulance walls. She looks at me through a fog of pain and exhaustion. "Surgery time?"

I force my voice to stay steady, offering hope in what may be her last minutes. "Yes."

A slow smile spreads across her face. She gives my hand a light squeeze before her hand goes slack. The monitor's shrill alarms get louder.

I rub my knuckles hard on her sternum. No response. "Moriah! Wake up!"

There's no ALICE or ORION to help. I tug her shirt up, putting defibrillator pads on her chest and side.

"Just sit down." A warden grabs my arm, toppling me into the seat by him.

"I have to try." I hop back over to her stretcher. The ambulance takes a quick turn. I lose my balance and almost fall on her. "Sorry," I whisper and grab a bar to steady me. I turn on the automatic defibrillator. "Moriah! Wake up!"

"No shock advised," the machine blares.

She's gone.

"Sit down. Dr. Ross. You know you can't do anything."

I can't lose someone to an Agora today. Not when I just figured out how to fix them. I lean over her and begin chest compressions. Maybe she just needs a bit of help to get into a heart rhythm I can shock. I count under my breath, pressing fast and deep.

"Nine, ten, eleven, twelve, Moriah! Fourteen, fifteen, sixteen, seventeen."

I gasp when the sudden sting of a needle bites into my arm.

39

What is that foul taste? My mouth is dry. An oxygen mask covers my nose and mouth. Every breath has a clean, dry scent.

"Ugh. Plastic," I whisper and grab my throat. It's so scratchy.

Low light filters around thick curtains by my head. When I try to sit up, it feels like the message is delayed to my body.

My heartbeat alternates from too slow to flopping hard. I put two fingers on my left wrist to feel my pulse. There's a wall of bookshelves by my feet. An ornate desk and chair beside me. Expensive-looking stained glass floor lamps are in two corners. A printer whirs, shooting a large stack of papers into a tray.

I'm in an office?

"Good evening, Dr. Ross," a man says. I've never seen him before.

Think. How did I get here?

Ivan. He survived Agora surgery.

Obsidian. Poor, sweet, Sid was trapped.

Moriah. She died.

Where is Ivan? I want Ivan.

"I'm Councilman Box. You were struggling, so we put you here in my office instead of a cell for now. How are you feeling?"

"Bad," I say, gripping my pulse. "My heart is-"

"Yes. On your trip, the overenthusiastic wardens gave you a bit too much." He shrugs. "You wouldn't behave. They did what they had to. We ended up having to revive you more than once. You have a myocardial stun to your heart. I used to train cardiology models, so they threw you in here after you finally got out of the ICU."

"What did they give me too much of? I want a heart monitor."

"No. You're fine," he says.

"Something's wrong," I croak.

Box throws his notebook and pen down on his desk. "Dr. Ross. Your insistence on knowing better than others is why you're here. It doesn't matter if you get better or not anyways." He pushes a button on a phone by his desk. "She's ready."

"What am I ready for?"

"Your interrogation. You're talking, aware, and can sit up. It'll be nice to have my couch back after they disinfect it."

"I thought The Bastion is supposed to help people."

"Don't be surly, girl. That's our sole commitment. To save those who are willing to work with us. But for people like you that try to reclaim a process owned by AI? You're *not* better than ASTRA."

"It was an emergency! I had to save them."

The door opens and two men in olive green enter.

"Let's go for a walk." A man with the name Fields on his shirt tosses my oxygen mask to the floor and pulls me to my feet.

My legs give out. "Use your feet!" the other man barks.

The room swims. My heart races. Whatever they gave me is wreaking havoc on my entire body. They mostly drag me into a wood-paneled hallway. A mercifully short walk takes us to a small office with a few plush brown recliners around a coffee table. Fields shoves me towards the closest recliner.

I suck air, leaned over the arm of the chair, looking around the slightly blurry room.

"Story! How are you?" an unexpected voice rings out.

"Isla? Why are you here?"

"I work on a team to conduct interviews to train the AJA models. It's the perfect role to use my doctorate in anthropology. I've got dinner and coffee for you." She sets a meal tray on my lap and removes the lid with a flourish. "Enjoy!"

The scent turns my stomach. "No thanks."

"I don't blame you. Hospital food is nasty. I'll bring you some good stuff tomorrow. For now, we need to catch up."

Catch up?

She's not fooling me. This is another interrogation. I sit tall and look around. No screens. Ivan can't help me. "Can I call my family?"

"Eventually. For now, I need you to focus." She snaps her fingers. I look at her. "I heard you began working at Lancaster Medical Hub as a vascular surgery model trainer after graduation. Can you please describe your role there to me?"

Last time I was in an interrogation, Ivan told me to keep my answers short. "Why?"

"Just a friendly conversation. You've caused quite a stir."

"I don't know why."

She gives me a sweet smile and hands me a warm cup of coffee from my meal tray. "Part of my job is to find out more about your thought process. There are concerns you're hiding information about your work. You and I go way back, girly. I'm sure you'll be fine. Now, tell me about your role at Lancaster Medical Hub. Then we'll see about calling your family."

I walk her through a typical day and tell her how the board has been happy with me so far.

"That sounds like a wonderful job. Do you have authority to decide what you research each week?"

"Yes. My mentor, Dr. Benedict, trusts me."

"So. What I'm hearing is that you have a lot of freedom in your lab. To do whatever you want?"

My chest hurts. "No. When I interviewed for my role, Dr. Benedict and I discussed my goal to fix my sister's dangerous AVM birthmark. He knows the goal of my research is to fix it for her if I can once she's older."

"Oh, you mean her Agora?" Her words are dangerous. But her demeanor is completely innocent.

Play dumb. "Her what?"

"I've known you since first grade, don't try to lie. You want to fix your sister. She has an Agora." She rubs my arm. "It's a noble goal. You love Lark."

"I didn't know that's what it was for a long time."

"You do now, though?"

I sip my bitter coffee instead of answering.

"When did you begin to question if ASTRA could fix your sister?"

"ASTRA needs trained to fix her."

"I agree. ASTRA can do anything. If you think so too, how did someone influence you to take matters in your own hands? You did not just one, but two Agora removal surgeries."

"I worked with a specialized surgical robot to do those surgeries."

"As the robot's assistant?"

I set my coffee down. "Isla, I'm not feeling well."

"You have been through a lot in the last few days, it's true," she says. "I won't ask you many more questions tonight. But I do have a few. Who made the first incision with a scalpel on the Agora removal patients at the Lancaster, Ohio Helm?"

I refuse to lie. "I did."

"Thank you for your honesty. Who made advanced decision-making in the surgery that far outweighs ASTRA's current capabilities?"

"I did." *And now I'm trapped here for it, instead of laying on a beach somewhere far away with Ivan.*

"Why?"

"There was an emergency."

"For *one* of the patients it was an emergency. Not for the other patient." She waves a hand like *talk, criminal.*

"No. It was an emergency for both."

"Seems to be more of a contrived emergency. You had a senior engineer build a way to turn off Agoras. Don't you feel like coming up with that plan, then hiding it from your mentor and The Bastion is a problem?"

"I saved two irreplaceable lives." I take a deep breath to fight a wave of nausea. "What did the wardens give me? It's wrecking me."

"You know what? You need some rest. Follow me."

She leads me down a short hallway. The dark paneled walls are covered with oil paintings of idyllic scenes. A koi pond with a tree swing and geese. Mountains with a purple and red sunset casting a glow across pine trees. Two farms connected by a meadow of wildflowers. In each scene, The Bastion logo is painted like a corporate smudge on the landscape.

We pass through a doorway at the end into a bright white hallway with a nurse's station. The staff jerk anxiously to attention when they see Isla.

"ORION," she snaps. A monitor comes on. "Story Ross is here. Take over. Make sure she's kept comfortable."

"I've got her, Dr. Varshovski." A middle-aged woman takes my arm, guiding me away from Isla.

"We'll talk more in the morning," Isla calls to my back.

I'd rather not...

Instead of a normal hospital room, I'm put in a transparent glass cell beside the nurse's station. The volunteer points towards the bed.

"Sit down, please. I'll put on your heart monitor, baby. I'm Rosa."

Thank goodness, I'll be able to see what's wrong with my heart. "Can I please have a phone?"

She shakes her head fast. "No! They'd see." She attaches stickers to my chest and arms, then drops a warm white blanket on me. "Sleep well. I promise you're safe now, *Mrs. Rhys.*"

"Wait, don't you need to turn on my monitor screens?"

"Patients aren't allowed to have screens on. I would if I could. But you are safe. You're okay, honey."

"Please," I plead. "I want to see what's wrong with my heart." *And I want Ivan to have a way to contact me!*

The woman tucks blankets around me like I'm a child. I'd fight her on it, but it's actually nice. I feel like death. She gives me a sad smile and slides the glass door shut behind her.

It's okay, Ivan can power monitors on anywhere. He can do anything. He and David must be looking for me. There's a large cup of ice water on a tray. I untuck one arm to sip water, hoping to wash the plastic taste away.

Ivan will find me. Just focus on letting my heart rest and heal tonight. I drift to sleep, watching the screen for a message from my love.

40

The next day was exhausting. Rosa apologized for waking me early and taking me to the interrogation room. Isla asked me questions through breakfast, lunch, and dinner. Every time the door opened, I caught a glimpse of Rosa. She sat in the hallway in a small plastic chair for the whole day.

For over ten hours, Isla's voice stayed in the same low, even tones. She looked comfortable and relaxed while crushing me with anxiety. It feels like she is trying to brainwash me into admitting I'm a criminal every five minutes.

"I better understand the thinking that led you here. But I need to know. If you could go back in time, what would you do differently, Dr. Ross?"

"Not follow Moriah."

"Who?"

I shake my head, "Someone I thought was a friend."

"Have your feelings regarding your actions changed?"

If I can stay alive for another day, that will give Ivan time to save me. "I'm so confused about everything. Can you help me sort things out tomorrow?"

She grins. "Of course! They'll get you in a minute. Good work today. Night for now." She presses a button on the wall and leaves.

I lay back in the recliner with my eyes closed. The door opens. Whoever that is will have to help me walk. I don't recall ever being this tired. What if they're drugging my food and drinks?

This time, there's no guards.

"Hi, honey, let's go," Rosa says.

We make our way to my sad, clear hospital room. Rosa slows to a crawl as we walk past the nurse's station. She nudges my ribs and tips her head to the TV. The news shows most of the area around Bastion offices in Cleveland engulfed in flames. The headline reads: *Protesters breach an eighth Bastion HQ.*

I laugh under my breath.

"I heard that." She giggles. I search her face. She's several inches shorter than me, and very good at avoiding my gaze.

"He says it is going to be okay," she whispers from the side of her mouth. "Story Caroline Rhys."

"Who does?" I whisper. Her smile is small, but definitely there. "Rosa. Who does?"

We turn into my cell, and she gives me an odd, motherly hug, "You know, Doc."

Ivan! She's here to help me.

"Night, baby." She blows me a kiss and walks out.

Once she's gone, I assess myself. My pulse flutters weak and slow. Fatigue overwhelms me. Physically from my heart issue. And emotionally from Isla grilling me. Occasionally, my hands get shaky, but that's anxiety. A sore, unsettling feeling persists across my chest.

I lay in bed, staring at the dark monitor, waiting for Ivan to message me.

"Good morning, Dr. Rhys!" Rosa greets me cheerfully. "You ready to go?"

My head feels much clearer today. "Good morning."

"I put clean clothes in your bathroom. Get a shower. Get ready. To-day is a special day for you," Rosa says, smiling.

"What does that mean?"

"It's a surprise. But don't be scared."

"Can't wait." I smile. *Please let it be a helicopter ride out of here.*

After I'm ready, we make our way to the interrogation room. As we approach the nurse's station, a monitor flashes, showing green letters from a computer terminal.

Help will be there soon, Story.

THE IRONTRACE! I snap my head forward to hide a scream of excitement. Okay, it must be David. No '*-I.*' Wonderful! Ivan is still resting, in recovery. David is sending help.

Isla bounces over to me. I'm so sick of her fake manners. "Story! Nice to see you again. I brought us breakfast sandwiches, fruit, and coffee."

I smile.

"Thanks for letting me ask you so many questions. Great news for you. The data from our conversations has been uploaded to AJA. Today my new AJA is going to have a turn picking your brain." She claps and does an infuriating little cha-cha dance.

"How is that great news?"

"You're helping train future versions of The Kernel. Few people can say that. You'll be famous."

Councilman Jordan pokes his head through the door. "Good morning. We're ready."

"We'll be there after breakfast." Isla unfolds a napkin and lays it on her skirt.

"Perfect," he says and ducks out the door.

David will be here soon. I push away the coffee she offers. It sloshes over the edge. "Isla, how did you get into such an awful job?"

"What do you mean?"

"I know AJA isn't just to interrogate people. If can sentence them to execution. Then they just disappear."

"The guilty ones disappear. You're right. My job is wonderful. I have a hand in training judiciary models to be the best. That's one reason I spent so much time with you. Rebellion like this hasn't come up much, especially from such a high-functioning citizen."

"You think I'm guilty?" I ask. She nods, fast and sure. "How do you define this rebellion you think I'm guilty of?"

"Betrayal. Check! Overthrow of AI. Check! Stepping outside your bounds in the OR. Check! You should never have cut into anyone as primary surgeon. Especially a child and a commander The Bastion considers irreplaceable."

"Think, Isla. Wouldn't Lark feel betrayed if I could fix her, and let her die because ASTRA can't be trained fast enough? How would *you* feel if your mom was dying of an Agora and I could fix her, but I didn't. Betrayed?"

"You've said it yourself. ASTRA can be trained."

"It can. Not fast enough for some of them. Did they tell you who their 'irreplaceable commander' is?"

She glances down. "A Commander Ivan Rhys."

"Any details about his family?"

"Just name, age, and rank. Same for the child you cut into."

"Commander Ivan Rhys is my husband." Her eyes widen, but she doesn't flinch. "His surgery was an emergency. There's no chance he or Francois would have survived. You tell me, should I have let them die?"

She glares at me.

"And if The Bastion views Ivan as so irreplaceable, why did they give him an Agora? They *know* it will rupture and kill him. Agoras are 100% fatal. My husband is the best person in the world. He'll do his job without an Agora."

She finally drops her façade of calm. "Do you know who else was a great person? Seth. I watched Seth die! That storm was sent for you."

"I'm so, so, sorry you lost him. But you and I both know I'm not a criminal." We sit quietly. She's so smart. Maybe an appeal to her logic will help. "Can I ask you something?"

"One question. Then we are going to meet Jordan."

"Do you think *eight* people deserved to have a tornado sent for them because I was curious about humans doing surgery again?"

She shakes her head sadly. "You earned that storm. And now? You've earned much worse."

41

The next room is like a smaller version of the control room at The Helm. Isla, Jordan, Box, and about thirty council members fill rows of seats overlooking the desk.

A large wall of monitors is on my right. Cameras are trained on me from ten angles, making me the unwilling main character of this drama.

"Story Ross. Please be patient. Your interview will begin soon."

This is not my first rodeo waiting for the AI judiciaries. David is sending help. I just have to play along.

"Isla, do they do this every time to intimidate the subjects?"

No one answers me.

The AI judiciary's screen lights up. Instead of a shadowy AI figure, it's an avatar of myself. It mirrors my pale, freckled skin, and dark blue hollows under my brown eyes. If that's how I look right now, I'm not looking the best to head home to my new husband.

I crack up. "Love the software update for interviews."

"Welcome, Story Ross. Please tell us why you're here today."

Story Ross?

"The Bastion hates innovation," I say.

"Please elaborate."

"You all would rather stall surgical innovation that can save countless lives—maybe the whole world—so you can keep geniuses trapped in servitude."

Murmurs erupt from the desks.

"That's a bold statement," the AJA replies.

"I'd rather save lives, instead of taking them. Has Councilman

Jordan told you how he got me here? He manipulated a young woman. His lies directly led to her death. Do you have any issues with one of your council members doing that, AJA? Bastion?"

Gasps fill the seating area.

"Councilman Jordan had authority to get you here by any means necessary," AJA replies. "Why do you think you can bring about something so innovative it can save the world?"

"I'm following the example of our fearless leaders right here in The Bastion." I point to the crowd. "They had an idea to end a war, bring peace and stability to the world, and look how well that's worked out. Why can't I have an idea that could shake things up and save some lives?"

"Do you think it's crucial that humans reclaim processes run by AI models to make their ideas happen?"

"Do you think it's impossible that humans reclaim processes run by AI models to make our ideas happen?" I retort.

"Answer the question."

Stupid computer. "We need more intelligence behind the artificial intelligence. If a human can provide that, why are you so scared to let us?"

Louder conversations break out.

"Thank you for participating in this interview. Your results are being compiled."

The monitors turn off. Bright lights fill the room. Movement catches my eye. Isla stands, waving. She has a grin plastered on her face. An ALICE and an ORION wheel in, parking on either side of me.

A small dome goes up around the arm of my chair, locking me in it from shoulder to hand.

"Oh, this is ridiculous," I sputter. "You know you owe me for saving two Irontrace. You've invested tens of millions in Ivan alone."

I look at Isla. She's clapping.

David is really cutting it close on this one. Maybe he's doing one of those tricks from a movie where they'll pretend to kill me and rescue me that way?

The crowd roars in an excited murmur, pointing at me. Jordan meets my eyes. He plasters a huge grin on his face and waves at me, mouthing the word "Goodbye!"

"Ivan will never forgive you for this!" I yell to him. Ivan may destroy The Kernel himself if they really kill me.

Jordan frowns and pretends to wipe a tear from his cheek.

David is too late. I'll never get to fix Lark and go to the beach with Ivan. I'll never hear if Sid is okay.

I yank and twist my arm, trying to get free. It won't budge. I attempt to stand, but my arm can't move a millimeter. My heart takes off pounding as I fight to get leverage by planting my feet and tipping the chair.

A man walks down from the top row towards me. He's moving slowly, but no one notices him. He gives me a friendly wave. As he walks, a hush falls over the room behind him.

Jordan is looking at the floor now. Isla is staring at her hands.

The man stops beside me. "Dr. Rhys. Remove your arm from that machine."

Dr. Rhys! He's a friend of Ivan's too.

"I'm stuck."

He makes a tsk sound then hovers a small electronic fob around the dome. It opens, releasing my arm. I rub it, forcing blood flow back to my hand. "Thank you."

The council members have gone completely still. It's like they've all gone into a terrifying suspended animation. Vacant, slack faces, with unfocused eyes fill the crowd.

"They look weird," I say, squinting at Isla. She's conscious...but not?

"Come on, let's go," he says.

"But what happened to them?"

He walks toward the door, motioning for me to follow, "I'm broadcasting transcranial magnetic pulses to disrupt their short-term memory and attention. It's a great way to make it in and out of places without drawing attention to oneself."

"Oh."

"Let's go catch our ride."

We walk through the dark, wood-paneled hallway until we enter a lobby. Sunshine spills through a soaring glass atrium. The white marble floor is perfectly punctuated by massive black stone planters holding palm trees and fiddle-leaf figs. Light scents of citrus hang in the air, adding a refreshing note. We round the corner and I freeze.

It's all fake.

The lower windows are smashed in. Broken glass on the floor is mixed with small, burnt items. Caution tape around the area is a flimsy plastic reminder that heaps of money and positions of power do not always result in safety.

"Where are we?" I ask him.

"Lancaster Bastion headquarters. They've been having a bit of a rough go these last few days. It's about time." His eyes sparkle at the broken glass. "We had to take drastic measures to get to you."

They did NOT do this for me. Ivan would never. Right?

The staff at the desk wear the same vacant faces as the council members. No one glances our way as we exit an immense revolving door. There's no glass left to spin. We just walk through empty frames to get outside.

"Ah, bright," I mutter. Sunshine floods my eyes.

Once they adjust, it looks like we've stepped into a war zone. The area around the headquarters is blocked off with metal barriers. A wide concrete stairway outside is littered with layers of abandoned signs. *Down with The Bastion. Abandon AI. Power back to people. Replace the council.*

There are torn banners with similar messages hanging from lampposts and windows of buildings. Some of the signs are burnt black at their edges. They lead in a trail to a charred area on the gray concrete where a bonfire smolders. Peeking out of the ash are warped computers, phones, and tablets, blackened by fire.

My companion walks along, unaffected. He's staring intently into his phone.

"What happened?" I ask.

I step carefully to avoid shoes and torn clothes scattered around. My breath catches when I see a baby's flip flop and toy laying by an overturned stroller. I sprint to peek inside. The blanket is empty.

"Come on, Dr. Rhys. Keep it moving," the man says.

"Aren't you scared? The city was fine two days ago!"

When was our pristine city overtaken by trash and debris? Where are the robotic units to sweep and power wash?

An acrid scent hits. My stomach turns. A shiny trail of chemical residue has created a slick down the steps to the empty seven lane road. Where are the cars? Sidewalks that normally bustle with pedestrians have police tape blocking them off. Where are the people?

"Look around us! What's going on?" I hiss.

I don't understand how he's so unbothered. The bottom few stories of the buildings are marred by angry graffiti. If Lark were here, I would cover her eyes so she couldn't see the words scrawled in large, block letters graphically calling for the removal of AI models.

"Most people are scared to even speak openly against an AI model giving them a parking ticket. Now the city is anti-AI?" My heart takes off in a painful gallop. I press a hand on it and jog after him.

"You'd be surprised what people will do when properly motivated," he replies.

"What does that mean?"

Whoever this man is, he doesn't care that the world has been burnt and trashed. Stress and shock hit me hard. I drop to my knees. "I need a minute." I lean face down on the signs, taking deep breaths.

"Dr. Rhys. We don't have to go much farther. Get up." He pats me on the back.

I sit back on my heels. "I need to go slower. I'm sorry."

His face clouds with anger. "Stupid Bastion hurt you?"

I nod, then rise. He wraps an arm around my ribs.

"Ivan will be very mad," he grumbles.

"You know Ivan!" I could cry. "How is he?"

No response. He's rapidly swiping across his phone screen. We walk down the large concrete stairway. This area is usually where kids come to bike, skateboard, and play in the splash ground when it's hot. It's ugly now. Fences and barriers mar the playground. A mixture of human police and dozens of AJA units stand guard.

Why are all their weapons out? It's like they're prepared for battle to break out any second.

A navy-blue armored truck with black windows parks near the group of officers. "Ah, there's our ride." My rescuer smiles.

As we approach the bottom of the stairs, an expressionless police officer moves the barrier for us.

"Thank you." I smile at him, but his face stays blank. His eyes seem unplugged from any spark of life. I recoil, close to my rescuer, unsure if I'm seeking comfort or protection. "Is he under your magnetic waves too?"

"Anyone I want to be is under their influence. You may be under it right now." He laughs. I don't.

His cold voice makes me recoil. *Who is this man?*

"I didn't catch your name."

We climb into the truck, and the door locks engage.

"Anthony Moulson. Nice to finally meet you, Dr. Rhys."

42

If I wasn't already having palpitations, I sure am now. "Why are you here?"

"You're family, sort of. I had to save you."

A panicked laugh escapes. *There is no way that's possible.* "On my mom's side, or my dad's side?"

"I'm Lark's real dad. So, the Lark side."

"You're lying!" She's so pure and sweet.

"Nine years ago, was the worst night of my life. My wife and I had a beautiful newborn daughter. Our perfect baby girl was fussy. My angel wife asked me to go on a drive, hoping it would calm our little Kate."

He pauses, looking out the window.

"A truck sent by The Bastion hit our car. My wife was killed on impact. I was taken to the hospital, not expected to survive. Kate was in serious condition and was taken to a children's hospital."

"Why do you say the truck was sent by The Bastion?"

He tilts his head meaningfully, "As Ivan has told you in a 'secret' debriefing in the control room, I was an original engineer for The Kernel. After time, The Bastion was using it for horrendous things, so I quit. That was unacceptable. No one leaves The Kernel project without repercussions."

I believe it.

"Once the hospital checked Kate in, she disappeared. I tracked down paperwork saying both of her parents died that night. She became a ward of the state, taken into The Bastion's custody. I have hunted for my baby Kate for the last nine years. Recently, information came to light that your dad saved her from the forest wardens. I know you're trying to remove her Agora. I strongly believe in 'a life for a life.' Your dad saved my daughter. I saved his. My debt is paid. I sent you a message on the monitor at the nurse's station so you wouldn't be too scared on your way to execution earlier."

It wasn't David messaging me or any of my Irontrace friends. Those green letters on the black screen were from Moulson.

"Lark's had a good life. I promise." My tears fall hot and fast. "Please don't take her."

"*Kate* will come back to me eventually. I'm her dad, after all. For now, I'm focused on helping you continue your research so you can save her. What can I do to help you?"

A glance out my window shows the protests have spilled into the Lancaster suburbs as well. Historic homes are damaged. Streets are piled with trash and rubble.

I don't want to work with a murderer.

I don't want the world to fall apart.

I need to talk to Ivan.

"Dr. Rhys. Everyone wants something. What do you want out of life?"

"I want my family to be safe while I continue my research."

"Safety. Done. Do all the Agora research you want. I'll even make you famous for it."

Surely this insane man is lying.

"How do you know what Ivan says in the control room?"

"My dear, nothing, and I mean absolutely nothing is off limits to me. Who was able to get into The Bastion and save you? Your husband and his friends?"

"He had surgery a couple of days ago. He's in recovery."

He smirks and rolls his eyes. "Not true."

This man is speaking nonsense. I won't engage with him.

"I'm your rescuer. *Only me*," he rasps in a near yell, making spit fly out of his mouth.

So gross. I cover my face and lean on the window. On top of whatever heart issues are making me feel faint, the last thing I need is to catch any communicable diseases he may carry. It's dizzying how fast he went from composed conversation to the unhinged person now beside me.

Reaching up to smooth his hair, he speaks in his almost monotone voice again. "I needed to make sure you stayed calm. I sent my old friend, Rosa, to help you. When I sent Otto to bring you and Kate to me once, you greatly disappointed me by the way you treated him. I needed to get you myself this time."

"Ivan will get me as soon as he's out of recovery. He'll find me." I don't believe that Moulson is smarter than Ivan for one second. I've seen Ivan defeat him repeatedly.

"And yet here you are. With me. I'm the one who could waltz into The Bastion's headquarters and free you. I'll be the one who can allow you to do research in complete safety. David and Ivan foolishly allowed you to work with INES, knowing how dangerous it was. I'd never risk your life like that. Your brain is too valuable."

Oh no. He's going to kidnap me and put me in some sort of research prison.

"Listen. You will figure out how to fix Agoras. You'll fix Kate for me when it's time. Since we're family and all, I promise you'll like where I'm taking you today. I'd like to be good friends."

The irony of my situation hits like a tsunami. The world's most evil man has the same life goal that I do.

"Dr. Rhys, you have seen what I can do. My assistance is contingent on absolute secrecy. That includes not telling Ivan who I am. *His* life depends on your obedience. I'll know if you tell him. He'll die. Not quick or clean, like from an Agora. I can assure you I'd make a spectacle of his death. I tried to take him out in the control room, but you'd already removed his Agora, so I settled for one of his best friends, Josh Evans. Ivan has been annoying me for weeks now."

Moulson found my one weakness aside from Lark.

"It's annoying that he's saving the people you're killing?" I ask viciously. "Don't touch Ivan. He's the only person who can help me fix

Lark."

"INES can be rebuilt anywhere in the world. If you become an annoyance, not only will I kill Ivan, but you and Kate will be brought to my headquarters until you're ready to fix her. For now, I'll allow you to go home. It will keep my Kate happy."

The way he keeps saying Lark belongs to him is infuriating. Being around Moulson would wither her spirit. Lark belongs with the hearts and hands that raised her, pouring love and laughter into her days. She needs to be kept far away from this monster whose only link to her is whispered in her genetic code.

"Also, might I remind you. The goal of my attacks is working. The Bastion needs to fall. It will fall. The tide has already turned against it. I'll keep chipping away until a new leader emerges to replace The Bastion. Someone people can believe in. A person who saves them from The Bastion's *murderous* AI models. It's a pity you can't tell Ivan the endgame I'm going for."

His fanatical look is repulsive. Near a large apartment complex, on an empty road, the truck slows. Moulson looks out the window in annoyance. He leans forward and taps on the partition between us and the front. The black screen stays up.

"Our chat is over for now. We'll pick it up again soon. Driver! Are they here?" he asks, smacking the partition again.

No response.

I jump when a guttural sound of frustration barks out of him.

"Driver!" I yell. Maybe he can get me away from Moulson. I lean against my door, and pull the handle, hoping it will unlock. It doesn't, but I keep pulling, testing. It has to unlock at some point. I'll throw myself out of this truck even if it's moving to get away.

The partition comes down an inch. "They're here," the driver says. I don't blame them for wanting to have minimal interaction with Moulson.

He lurches over and angrily whispers hot breath directly into my ear, making me flinch. "Remember what I said. Do not tell Ivan."

My door flies open. "Ah!" I let out a shriek as I fall out of the truck...into the most perfect set of arms. "No way!"

Ivan smiles down at me.

"Wiiiiiiife!" He lifts me into a crushing hug with that familiar iron-like Ivan grip that steals my breath. "We're in the city! I'm free. I love you!"

"I love you!" I repeat it over and over onto his cheek, neck, beard, and lips. He's about to explode from happiness—spinning, holding me like he'll never let go. "Take me home."

He nods but doesn't let go. I peek around his arm. A group of men stand with Moulson, happily chatting.

"Thank you for coming, Air Titans," Moulson says, shaking their hands.

My jaw drops. I jerk back from Ivan.

"You're welcome, Councilman Guthrie," Sullivan replies, laying a hand on Moulson's *(Guthrie's???)* shoulder. "Thank you for helping Dr. Rhys."

I glare up at Ivan. *No!* I wish I could scream it. *He's Moulson, not Guthrie!*

Right? Am I hallucinating?

"What's wrong, baby?" Ivan asks when I dive under his arm.

Moulson waves and grins at us.

I rub my eyes in disbelief and bury my face in Ivan's chest. He shouldn't be up walking and holding me. He's got at least a few days of bed rest left in the clinic.

"You shouldn't be here. You just had surgery three days ago."

Ivan looks like I slapped him. "I did not."

Am I in a dream? Ivan's outside the boundary. In the city. He's alive. How else would he be free if I hadn't done his surgery?

I reach out tentatively and touch his face. It's not a dream. "I did your surgery a couple of days ago. Do you have brain damage?"

"Ha! Goodness, I've missed you. Not that I know of." He turns and crouches to show me his neck. There is no bandage. No fresh incision. This was obviously done weeks ago. The incision I gave him is now a faint pink scar.

"Baby, you were gone for twenty-three days," he says gently. I shake my head as he keeps talking, "I was coming to get you tonight. Then we got a call from Guthrie, the newest member of The Bastion. He's a real good dude. He convinced them to let you go early."

Ivan has been deceived.

"You look like you're not feeling well, my love," Ivan says. "Let's get you home."

"It's my heart."

"What happened?" he asks, worry plastered back on his face.

"They overdosed me or poisoned me. I haven't gotten the full story. Sid! Did Sid survive?"

"Yep! He's still on stall rest from inflammation in his legs." He guides me to sit beside him in an Air Titan helicopter. "This flight will only take about four minutes since Sullivan is the pilot."

"Ivan, stop. What's that man's name?" I point to Moulson.

"That's Mark Guthrie. Brilliant tech guy." He leans out the helicopter and yells. "Mark! C'mere!"

Mark Guthrie (Anthony Moulson???) jogs to us.

Ivan shakes his hand. "Thanks for getting her out. That was quite the surprise."

"I consider it an honor. It's like we're a real family now." His eyes and smile are the same as Lark's. How has he tricked Ivan? "I have to go. Have a wonderful day. I'll be sending you a wedding gift."

He sticks his hand in front of me to shake mine. I refuse, glaring at him.

"Story?" Ivan prompts me quietly.

Moulson's smile twitches down at the corners. He moves his hand closer to me, almost touching my stomach. I lean back, using Ivan as a shield. Moulson's smile gives way to a hard line.

Ivan leans his shoulder in front of me. "Thanks again, Mark. She's been through quite a shock. I need to take her home now." Ivan pushes Moulson's hand away.

Moulson steps away but keeps staring.

Ivan notices and breaks the moment. "Bye!" He slams the helicopter door shut, then kisses my cheek. "We gotta go, your family planned a whole thing. I've missed you so much!"

I can't take my eyes off Moulson. We're locked in some silent battle of wills.

Ivan glances between Moulson and I. "What's that about? You two seem weird," he asks as he buckles the helicopter seat harness over my shoulders.

Moulson holds one finger up to his lips and arches an eyebrow. Though I can't hear him shush me, his pointed look says it all. *He's not Mark Guthrie. He's Anthony Moulson!*

And I can't tell anyone.

There was no talking on that helicopter ride anyway. Ivan and I didn't waste one second on words.

I press my forehead onto his as we land. "I was only gone for two days. I swear."

"No, my love. Three weeks. Look!" He smiles and points out the window.

At the top of the falls there's a group of Irontrace and my family waiting with lots of horses. After a joyful reunion with the group and promises that my mom can come make dinner, Ivan takes me home.

~~~

"I don't want to overwhelm you with questions. I'll tell you what you missed in the last few weeks. You just keep laying there, looking beautiful and listen," Ivan says. "When your tracker ring went off, the control room accessed video feeds around you in the forest and saw you and Sid. Then you were just gone."

He stops, tracing his finger over where my wedding ring should be. "I have our rings, by the way."
~~~

"Leaving Sid almost killed me. I couldn't get that net off. I think it had weights on it."

"It did. Sorry. That would've been so terrifying." He pauses. "David and I had a bit of a falling out. I got up to help find you a few times. He kept ordering ALICE to sedate me. He said it was partly because he needed to let The Bastion's rage at me blow over from the Agora detonations. Partly that he didn't trust me to shut up and not make them angrier. After thirteen days your dad told him to knock it off and let me wake up. Your dad is still ticked that David and the others couldn't find you."

I feel the back of his neck. "David did the right thing. Why couldn't he find me? I wasn't far away."

He sighs. "You were *gone*. Untraceable."

"Even from you?"

"Not once they gave me a computer. The Bastion put me in custody with AJA for a week to interrogate me. I made their life miserable. Then Moulson went off the deep end crazy. Worse than ever. Senior Commanders from everywhere kept demanding my release. That made several council members furious to know I'm indispensable. They let me go. Of course I found you once I got back in the control room a couple days ago. They assured me you were healthy, happy, and conducting surgical seminars. Someone masquerading as you has been emailing me. *A lot*. All lies, obviously. Good thing I sent in a little spy to keep an eye on you."

I wonder if he sent Isla. Or Jordan? "How are you since surgery?"

"Sore sometimes, but mostly great. I carry a badge now to access some areas. Cantone makes fun of me. I think he's just jealous." He rolls over to hug me. "You saved me, my love. I'm eternally grateful. I'm sorry they arrested you for it."

"I love you. It was worth it. I'm so happy you're okay."

"I called an emergency meeting with several council members this morning. I told them I was coming to get you this afternoon or I'd be logging out, and the Squadron was on their own. They really owed Mark and me. We just throttled some plans of Moulson. They got to tout destroying a big chunk of his servers on a news story." He laughs. "People threw a parade and everything. Mark surprised me this morning and said he had a meeting with them and convinced them to let you out as a favor to me."

Hmm. "Mark" throttling Moulson to make The Bastion happy. *What a joke.*

He continues, "Moulson has lit the world on fire, literally in some places. People are traumatized and taking it out on The Bastion. They're protesting all over the world. Council members have been kidnapped. Neighborhood patrols monitor and alert other neighbors about AI malfunctions. People are hosting bonfire parties to burn electronic devices. Not exactly environmentally friendly."

Lark's dad is destroying the world.

"Journalists are hyping up demand for answers from The Bastion. People keep disappearing to AJA custody after speaking out, which is not helpful, and leads to more discontent."

"What's he doing?"

"What hasn't he done? I'll show you our list in the control room tomorrow. Nothing is off limits. He even did something to the UV rays from the sun, intensified them with one of the WARM models. Gave people second and third-degree burns. Who even thinks of doing that? He's a mass murderer."

Ivan's shirt is soaked with my hot tears.

"It's okay. He can't get us in here." He tips my chin up to face him. I won't meet his eyes. "Baby, what's wrong?"

"I'm tired. I'm not feeling well."

He presses his lips together, biting back whatever he wants to say and wraps his hand in my hair. "Your family will be here in a little bit. Try to sleep until they get here."

It will destroy him to know Moulson is his new friend.

It may destroy *us* when he finds out I didn't tell him.

43

"They just let you walk out of an interrogation?" Dad asks.

"Yeah," I say.

Ivan's eyes watch me, sharp as Helga's.

"Wow. They're trying to earn some goodwill with people. I'd like to send that council member a thank you card," Mom says.

I choke on my drink. "No. Don't."

Ivan tilts his head at me. "Excellent idea, Amelia. I would too. What's their name? Guthrie?"

"I'm just glad to be back." I force a grin.

"Story. What's their name?" Ivan asks me in a voice so low I barely hear it.

I squeeze his leg under the table. My eyes lock with his: please stop.

He sighs and stares at me. Commander Rhys is here in full investigation mode tonight.

Mom leans closer, sipping coffee. "Honey, were they nice to you?"

"Isla, the anthropologist, from school was there. She works for AJA as a trainer. She interviewed me for two whole days. It was a weird interrogation. She'd try to pretend she was my friend but ask awful questions. Especially about my work with INES."

Mom smiles. "Oh, how is Isla?"

"She's happy with her new job."

"That's great."

"She's working on training new judiciary models. They talk to you while you're in a chair. The verdict is handed to you right then. The chair just locks you in to administer their punishment."

"Did you get locked into a chair? I'd hate that," Lark asks.

"I did. A big clamp came up and grabbed my arm like this." I dramatically grab her arm. She laughs.

"When was this?" Ivan asks.

"I'm not sure. This morning? Isla and I had breakfast and then they took me there," I say. Ivan's face darkens.

"How did you get out? Did you have to break the murder clamp?" Lark smacks the table with her hand.

"No, I couldn't get out. Someone helped me. They swooped in with a special electronic key to save me from the chair just in time."

Ivan stares at the table, folding and unfolding a napkin repeatedly. He quietly asks, "You mean this rescuer did not tell The Bastion they took you. Instead, they freed you by means of some electronic key?"

"Your guess is as good as mine, husband. I'm just telling you what I saw. I'm a doctor, not a *tech guy.*"

His brows furrow. "Was this hero the same council member who saved you?" Ivan asks.

I nod. Under the table I scratch his palm several times. He shoots me a thoughtful look.

"Were the people mad you got out of their death chair?" Lark asks.

"My hero had a secret invisibility cloak. He can confuse people's minds. To this day, no one knows I left."

"Wow!" Lark gasps.

"They had a what?" Ivan laughs incredulously.

"You heard me. Some kind of invisibility cloak thing? I know it sounds unbelievable."

"Honey...are you saying The Bastion doesn't know you left?" Dad asks.

I nod. "They didn't see me leave. Neither did the AJA guards that were everywhere. One even opened a gate for me. Waved me right through."

Dad and Ivan look at each other for a long, silent moment.

Ivan reaches for my hand. "So, you're sure this *morning* they interrogated you? And decided to execute you?"

"I know I'm having trouble with time. But yes, I believe it was this morning," I tell him. Was it this morning? I don't think Moulson used his brain trick on me.

Ivan jumps up and opens the dishwasher. "Thank you for making dinner, Amelia. It was delicious. I'll clean up."

Mom moves into the chair he abandoned. "Tell me more about how Isla is."

"She's having a rough time. Turns out, she and Seth were in a relationship. His death has left her full of venom. She has a theory that the storm that killed him was sent by The Bastion for someone else but got him instead. From what I saw, she's more than willing to root for the death of whoever that storm was sent for."

I lay my hand on the table over a pen, sliding it off the edge into my lap.

"People do strange things for love," Mom says.

"There was also a nice volunteer there. Her name was Rosa. My rescuer said she's an old friend of his. She kept hugging me. She told me not to be scared. She let me see the news once."

"You didn't just say Rosa, right?" Dad blurts.

"Yes, Rosa. I thought she said she knew Ivan."

Ivan blows a harsh sigh. His back is to us, but his shoulders sit high and squared. Thick muscles strain against his shirt fabric. That name made him mad. *Why?*

Dad looks from Ivan to me, and then back to Ivan. He jumps up, suddenly in a hurry to be helpful.

"I'm going to help, Ivan." Dad noisily stacks plates and cups. "Lark, up. Help us clean."

"She called me Story Rhys. No one else did." I rub my eyes, trying to piece something together. She seems so familiar.

Something shatters behind me. I jump. Mom and I turn to see Ivan had dropped a glass. He and Dad are shooting daggers at each other with their eyes and having a fierce whispered argument.

"You need some rest, honey. Welcome home," Mom says, hugging me tightly.

"I'm going to get ready for bed. Thanks for dinner, Mom. Love you."

"Anytime, sweetie. I'll be back in the morning to make you breakfast once Ivan is at work," Mom says. "Gotta get your strength up."

"That's nice, Amelia. But I'm off in the morning. Maybe in the afternoon?" Ivan says.

They can all chat while I get ready for bed. I'm beat. Dad comes into my room after I lie down.

"Glad you're back. We were all freaking out until Ivan found you." He drops his voice to a whisper, "We told Lark you were on a trip, and not to worry. She knows Ivan and Francois had surgery but hasn't heard why."

"Dad. I was only gone for a couple days."

I don't think Ivan lied to me, but Dad would tell me if Ivan's wrong.

He shakes his head. "No. Weeks. Maybe you were in a coma for a while? Ivan can hack into their EHR system and check."

"It feels like I'm being dishonest, but I'd never lie to Ivan." My shoulders drop. "I really have no clue what happened to me. I remember talking a lot to Isla, Rosa, and a glass hospital room. I think they drugged me. I felt so sluggish. So bad all over."

"You're home. You're safe." Dad hugs me. Over his shoulder Ivan is leaning against our doorway, dish towel on his shoulder. He blows me a kiss, but his eyes are far away in thought.

"Get some rest. I love you," Dad says.

Lark bursts in, throwing herself on my bed. "Good night, Story! Mom said we're leaving. I love you. I'm happy you're back. When can we go ride horses? Francois has not been riding with me. I've been so bored!"

"We'll find a time to ride, I promise. Love you."

"Night, Lark." Ivan steps over towards the bed. Lark catches him off guard by jumping off the bed onto his neck, hugging him. She must have been too enthusiastic and squeezed his scar. His mouth opens in a silent yell as he lowers her to the floor. He composes himself and says, "See you tomorrow."

He walks to me, silently mouthing the word "OUCH!" rubbing the back of his neck. She waves and runs out.

"Aww, sorry, baby." I give an exaggerated frown.

He touches the back of his neck with his fingertips and then inspects them. "Am I bleeding? Lark cannot do that to Francois when she sees him. She'll put him back in a coma!"

I laugh and pull him down by his shirt to peek at the back of his neck. "You're okay. Get ready for bed and get in here, please."

He knows something is wrong. Lying to Ivan will never be an option for me. Pulling the blankets up over my head, I work on my plan.

44

A few minutes later, Ivan pulls the blankets back on his side of the bed and scoots until he's pressed against my back.

"Are you awake?" he whispers softly.

YES! I keep my eyes closed and roll over to face him. "There you are."

I pull the gray sheet up over our heads. Enough light filters through our gray sheet that I can see his smile. I put my left hand over his mouth. His eyes widen. I bring my right index finger up in a silent warning not to say a word.

He nods.

I pull up my sleeve to show him the words I wrote on my forearm.

<u>Do NOT talk!</u> Moulson can hear us. He knows everything!

He's in the <u>control room</u>. He's here.

Rage flashes across his face. He mouths, "How?"

I raise my shoulders in a clueless shrug then pull my sleeve higher to show my upper arm.

Mark Guthrie IS Anthony Moulson!

He hides his identity. You have to believe me.

He will <u>kill you</u> if I tell you. Guthrie/Moulson hates you!

His face and neck flush with anger. I hold up a finger for him to wait. I switch to show him my left forearm.

HE'S LARK'S REAL DAD! He wants to take her back.

He says he'll keep me safe to do my research.

<u>Help</u>. Am I a criminal now?

Several expressions flash across Ivan's face. One of them was definitely "my wife has lost her mind."

What if he doesn't believe me? My heart races at that thought. I can't stop shaking. He wraps me in a hug, holding me tight, kissing and stroking my hair until I relax against him.

After a few minutes, he makes scribble motions, asking for my pen. He pulls up his short shirt sleeve to write on his upper arm.

Before he can write, I push the pen out of the way. He looks at me in confusion.

I squeeze his muscly bicep and pretend to melt.

He laughs and rolls his eyes.

I give his arm a trail of kisses up his neck.

We crack up laughing.

Thank you for telling me. I thought you were mad it took me so long to get you home.

I shake my head no and squeeze him in a wriggly, happy hug. It takes him at least a minute to escape from, leaving us both laughing harder.

He grins. Then writes more.

I'll destroy him.

I smile. Ivan will beat Moulson.

He smiles and writes another note on his arm. *I have at least twenty notebooks you could've used.*

I lose it in a fit of giggles, grabbing the pen. *I panicked! I thought you were mad at me.*

His face breaks into a faux frown. He props on an elbow to smooth static charged curls back from my face. "Never, my beautiful wife," he whispers, folding me against him like only he can.

This is what I've been missing out on for twenty-three days? Unacceptable.

We carefully check our shirts to make sure our ink is covered before he throws the blankets back off our heads. "Ah! It's so hot under there. I'm melting. I need a drink. You thirsty?"

"Sure."

He pins me down in a hug. "You owe me the full story of how you got back, Mrs. Rhys. Tomorrow, David is holding an interview for you in the control room. You ready for that? He'll be asking a lot of questions."

The top of his hair is in shambles from the sheets. I smooth it out and trace my finger over his scar. I can't help laughing at the show he's putting on for anyone eavesdropping. "I guess?"

He jumps up out of bed. When he comes back from the kitchen, he has a big cup of ice water for me, and a small glass of vodka for him with some napkins.

"You want some, baby?" He tips his cup towards me.

"I'll stick with water, thanks."

"More for me."

He shuts off the lights and sips his drink beside me. After a few minutes, he reaches under the blankets. He slides up my shirt sleeves one at a time. A wet napkin smelling of vodka rubs the skin on my arms, the cold alcohol wiping away my written confessions.

I wake up alone in bed. Our bedroom door is open. I hear a faint voice in the living room. Please tell me it wasn't a dream. I really have to be back home.

I wrap the sheets around me and sit up. "Ivan?!" I call out.

He runs in, smiling broadly. "Good morning! David called. He wants us to come to the control room as soon as you're ready. He says he has good news."

"Coffee?" I ask.

"I'll go pour your cup. Wait!" He grabs me and hugs me. "You're home. I love you so much. For the love of all that is good and holy, stop getting abducted and attacked!"

I laugh into his neck. "I'll try."

Ivan stuck to me like a shadow for a speedy run through of my morning routine. I'm ready to face the control room. Ivan's vodka last night had done the trick. There are no ink remnants on my arms. Once I'm dressed in slightly flared dark blue jeans, a white undershirt, and a flowy silk blouse, I'm ready.

"You need two more things to complete your look." Ivan steps to his desk and picks something up. "Your rings, my lady."

He slides my engagement ring on. This time, it's accompanied by a matching gold wedding band with a stunning row of square-cut emeralds around it. Can't believe he remembered me mentioning they're my favorite.

I hold it up to inspect it, smiling at my very heavy finger. "It's perfect! Thank you!"

"Wanted to get those back on you as soon as I could. Let's go see what David wants."

The control room is full of council members. One of them is a murderer.

I yank Ivan's arm to use him as a shield.

"No, Councilman Jordan is down there!" I stand on my tiptoes and whisper. "He was happy when they were going to execute me. He lied to Moriah. He told her if she captured me for him, I'd remove her Agora. I tried to save her, but she died in the ambulance. It was horrible. He's a murderer."

My steadfast protector pulls me under his arm. "I'll take care of it."

We walk into the control room and head to Ivan's desk. He sits at his laptop, fingers flying over the keyboard.

"Everyone is here now," David says from the table in the front.

The monitors are full of pictures and videos of breaking news reports. The Lancaster Bastion Headquarters has been heavily bombarded since I left yesterday. A remnant of its foundation that says *Lancaster Bastion HQ, est 2031* and one wall still standing of the glass atrium are the only recognizable parts.

"Ivan, how? People don't have bombs or any type of weapon that would cause damage like this."

He lifts a hand. "You're right. This is a massive escalation."

Councilman Jordan stands to speak. "Thank you all for coming. I need to make you aware of someone extraordinary in your midst. An innovator is among you, unafraid to stand for what they believe in, willing to risk it all to fulfill their life calling. Dr. Story Ross. We at The Bastion want to honor your dedication. And more importantly, reward it. Please come down here, Dr. Ross."

Um. Jordan says I'm an innovator…And wants to celebrate me?

Ivan joins the crowd in wild applause for me. But his eyes scan, taking in every inch of the room.

I'm not going down there without him. I whisper, "Please come with me."

He nods then follows me down the ramp, carrying his laptop. The video feed switches to some kind of conference call with the other Irontrace on it.

He tucks an arm over my shoulder and whispers, "Whoa. We're in a video summit with all the other Helms."

"Thank you for joining me. Everyone, please meet Dr. Ross. Through her tireless research, she has found a way to remove Agoras. She forged a path with delicate accuracy that ASTRA continually fails at. We're proud to announce she's the first Bastion supported primary human surgeon in twenty-five years."

Ivan is going to say I almost broke his hand again from my grip.

Moulson. He made this happen. He's going to want something in return.

I need to pay attention. Jordan is still droning on, "That's why we've decided she'll begin a surgical schedule to conduct Agora removal surgery on any of you who want it. Starting with Senior Commanders, Commanders, and then working her way through the ranks. Other surgeons will be trained with her method to help. What would you like to tell your new patients, Dr. Ross?"

He makes a fake smile and shoves a tiny microphone in my face. I wrench it free from him and glance to Ivan. He gives me an encouraging nod.

"Hello. Wow, what a surprise. It is news to me that I'm a Bastion-supported primary surgeon. Firstly, Councilman Jordan has his facts wrong." I hold up Ivan's hand in mine. "My name is Dr. Story Rhys."

Ivan grins and kisses the back of my hand, prompting a wave of laughs and whoops.

"Every one of you is a brilliant engineer, and from The Irontrace I've met, a wonderful person. You spend your days working to make the world a safer place. You've sacrificed so much. As soon as I heard about Irontrace, I told my husband that I'd be finding a way to take these awful things out; to give you all a chance at a life with choices. And now here we are. You shouldn't be trapped in a boundary by people who took you from the only home you'd known. I'm so sorry for what you've been through. Don't give up! I'm looking forward to meeting each of you, hearing your stories, and cutting out those murderous Agoras. Free The Irontrace!"

The Helms unmute. A deafening thunder of cheers fill the control room. A flicker of "what just happened" passes between Ivan and me.

"I speak from all of us at The Bastion. Congratulations on your marriage, Dr. Rhys, Commander Rhys," a now shaky Jordan says. "Thank you in advance for saving The Irontrace. Every surgery will be a true gift to the world. Thank you, Dr. Rhys."

"Can I say something really quick?" Ivan asks.

"Please do," Councilman Jordan says. "Commander Rhys needs no introduction."

Ivan steps over to the microphone with his laptop balanced on his arm. "You're all going to love my wife, Story! It means the world to her to be able to save you. She can't wait." He pauses to smile at me.

Then he turns towards Jordan and thunders in his Commander Rhys voice, "Jordan! I have a video here of you lying to Commander Moriah Holden a few weeks ago about Story being able to save her. This lie came at a vulnerable time for Moriah. Her good friend—*my* good friend—Josh Evans had just been killed by Moulson right in front of her. Not only are you a liar, Jordan, you are a vile, opportunistic predator. You're not welcome at this Helm ever again."

Loud gasps break out.

"I won't work with liars or murderers, and my fellow Irontrace, I doubt you want to either. Is he welcome at any of The Helms, Senior

Commanders?" Ivan asks the crowd.

A chorus of "No!" rages around us.

"Bastion, do something about this. Here's the evidence you need." Ivan turns his laptop screen towards the crowd and hits send on an email.

Councilman Jordan runs up the control room ramp.

Ivan waves to the crowd, extends a hand to me, and leads me and my racing heart to his desk. I swear my husband is the coolest person in the world.

Dad is glowing. "Dr. Rhys! Excellent!"

"Thanks," I say, trying to catch my breath.

"Ivan, great job." Dad catches us in a group hug. "That was quite the display. I'm so proud of you both."

David marches over. "Rhys, you scrupulous pain in my butt. You couldn't have waited two minutes for that?"

"He wants Story dead, David. So. No, I could not."

Ivan's jaw is tight. David's mouth is in a hard line.

"I wouldn't have waited either then." David shakes Ivan's hand.

I rush forward, wrapping them both in a tight hug. "Thank you for knocking him out, David. You gave him time to heal."

"I know. He needed it." David smiles. "I'm happy for you, Story. Get these Agoras out of our heads and you'll be the Queen of the Irontrace."

"I'll do my best," I tell him, stepping back to Ivan's side.

"Hate to interrupt but David, I need to talk to you," Dad says, pulling him to the side.

 Ivan tangles his hand up in the curls at the base of my neck, tugging to tip my face up to his. "You're The Bastion's favorite person now *and* the soon-to-be Queen of the Irontrace. Congrats."

Everything is so perfect right now. "As long as I'm your wife, I don't care about the rest of it. You're safe from an Agora. Now I can train a team to save Lark. She'll be safe soon too. We get our happily ever after. Let's get out of here, I'm dying to get back home with you."

"Rhys!" David yells, waving for Ivan to join him down front.

"I'll be right back, my Queen." Ivan gives me a confident wink that makes me unsteady on my feet.

The monitor beside me flicks on. Tiny green letters appear. The room spins.

You're welcome, partner. Do your research and save my Kate. Remember: Ivan is only alive because I'm permitting it.

For today.

*To be continued in **Malice**, book two of The Irontrace Saga...*

The Irontrace Saga

Malformation told how they fell in **love.**
Malice asked how much the heart and mind can **endure.**
Coming Autumn 2026:
Malpractice will dare them to choose **hope.**

Follow T.S. Night on Instagram for more updates:

irontrace_saga_books

Acknowledgments

Before we get into the thank you's, I'd like to say Story's job is *not* that far outside of the realm of current medicine. An expert in the field of surgical robotics was consulted heavily through the writing of The Irontrace Saga. Someone has to program what current robots do. Someone has to train surgeons and scientists to use them. And yes, someone has to fight for patient autonomy and ensure that robots are kept in the proper, ethical place—as a tool, not a primary.

Also, arteriovenous malformations are a type of vascular birthmark that wreak real havoc in lives. If you have an AVM or are a support person for a person with an AVM, know that this series is written by a person who understands that you're truly a warrior. If you have any questions or would like to do your own research on AVM's or other vascular birthmarks, I'd recommend visiting the Cincinnati Children's hospital website.

The Irontrace Saga actually started as an entry for a short story contest to tell two people in my life with chronic illness that the grace and bravery they face every day with have made them into my heroes. As I wrote out the characters and developed what they were facing, I realized that this tale of Agoras and anxiety couldn't be told in one thousand words or less. (Ask my editor, I *struggle* with keeping each book to less than ~115k words.)

Onto the thanks:

First, thank you to my wonderful husband of almost two decades. I'd marry you again, after two minutes instead of five, my love. You believe in me. You've supported my every whim; fully confident I can do anything. Thank you for being my steadfast best friend and an exemplary father to our kids. I love you more!

In age order, because I have no favorite child, and I love you all with a ferocity that's unfathomable:

Thank you, 1, for your expertise in many subjects, scientific and literary, that guided me with fresh perspectives. Never stop in your quest for knowledge. Keep working on your beautiful art, career transition, and traveling.

Thank you, 2, for being genuinely surprised with every plot twist as the series took shape. Every day, you ask how the books are going (even if I haven't touched a laptop). Keep making playlists to inspire and keep my company.

Thank you, 3, for lending me your expansive horse knowledge! You helped make Obsidian who he is. I treasure my stack of beautiful hawk and horse pictures. You're a wonderful designer and a fabulous rider. I can't wait to go back to the barn with you.

Thank you, 4, for the steady supply of logos and bookmarks you created. They have a spot on my desk forever. I appreciate you letting me bring my laptop outside so I could write while you do tricks. Keep coming up with custom brick builds that astound.

My beloved sister, you've taken care of me since I was born and have turned me into the person I am today. You completely supported my first forays into writing from my earliest years. My hero. I love you and your artistic, brilliant husband!

My brothers. One of you treasures my original manuscript from a book I wrote decades ago and has a shocking array of literary recommendations. One of you listened to me plot and obsess over this book by the beach. I can't wait until next year! I love you both and your wonderful families so much!

Mom, when you heard I was writing again, you were all in, begging to help in any way you could. You're wonderful, and I love you. Sorry we lost Dad when he was way too young. I know he'd love being here with us if he could. He was a bright burning light of a person when he was with us.

Thank you, Ramona, my editor. You answered my many, many questions. Your comments made me think deeply about choices I'd made in my writing.

Thanks to the wonderful team of engineers I work with every day. You make the world a better place by sharing knowledge and decades of experience to bring others to your level.

Thank you, readers. This story means a lot to me personally, but it doesn't end here. I'm honored to have shared it with you. There is *much* more to come! If you've made it this far, consider this a little call to action. Reach out to me on social media. I'd love to hear from you, and I'll make sure you get a proper welcome to The Irontrace.

As a family touched by vascular malformations, I'd strongly encourage those who have never heard of these conditions to do some research and bring awareness to them. **To the fighters battling one—may your courage be recognized, may your days be pain free, and may the people around you be filled with understanding to love and support you no matter what.**

<3, T.S.

About the Author

T.S. Night lives with her boisterous family in Ohio. The Hocking Hills region holds a special place in their heart. Having worked in careers from nursing to engineering, she wants to create clean stories that grab hold of you and won't let go. You'll never find cussing in her books. Any elements of romance are written from a place of respect, emotional connection, and humor rooted in her values.

When not building worlds where love is the only thing that can help you beat the odds, she's most likely reading with one of the family's many pets, swimming, hiking while complaining (loudly!) about bugs, cuddled up with her 'Ivan', trying not to break an ankle playing sports with the kids, or testing how many cups of coffee it will take to get the next plot twist typed out. She believes in cliffhangers, characters we can relate to, and that the chaos in fiction will never hold a candle to the chaos we all live through daily.